UNREQUITED

BRENDAN SHANNON

LINCOLNSHIRE PRESS

UNREQUITED

ISBN: 978-0615650579
Copyright © 2012 by Brendan Shannon
Published by Lincolnshire Press

Cover design and interior layout by Indie Author Services

DEDICATION

This book is dedicated to my family, without whose understanding and support it could not have been written.

CHAPTER 1
Tender Is the Night

Now picture this, my point of view
In an ideal world I see the likes of you

—Bryan Ferry

Austin, Texas, October, 2011

I AWOKE TO THE CEILING FAN lazily circling overhead. I had been dreaming about her. Again.

I turned over and saw that Rose was lying on her stomach next to me, deep in sleep. I sat up. Despite the fan's efforts, my neck and face were wet with night sweat. I looked over at the clock on the stand next to our bed; it was only three forty in the morning. I knew that sleep would not return again this night.

After a moment, I quietly lifted the one sheet that had covered me and escaped the bed. I was wearing only white boxers. I slowly crept to our bedroom door, grabbing a burnt orange University of Texas T-shirt that I had left on a chair near the door. I softly closed the bedroom door, put the

T-shirt on, and walked to our office on the other side of the dark house. The office had been our son's room, but we had converted it after he had graduated from Trinity University and moved to Dallas. Entering the office, I first turned on the overhead light and the ceiling fan, then moved to the chair behind the desk facing the window overlooking Barton Creek Preserve to the south and sat down.

Facedown on the desk was a white letter-size envelope. I grimly reached for it and turned it over. My name and address were handwritten and well-centered: John Moran, 2295 Point Bluff Drive, Austin, TX 78746. I stared at the envelope for a few moments. The postmark was from Binghamton, New York. There was no return address. I did not recognize the handwriting.

I opened the envelope, and pulled out the obituary notice from the *Binghamton Press & Sun-Bulletin*. After I tossed the envelope back on the desk, I stared at the obituary notice again. It had been published on the second of October, a week ago. From the photo accompanying the obituary notice, a face stared at me. It had been many years since I had been with her, when we were so young, but it was unmistakably her face. She was standing alone, wearing a light blouse and skirt, with a lake or perhaps the ocean in the background. The photo must have been taken in the last few years, because she had aged.

I read through the notice a second time this night. I had read it first after dinner, when Rose had informed me that a letter had come.

My eyes pinballed off the essential highlights of a life now ended. Born 1954. Died 2011. Married for thirty-four years...Mother of three, with their names...Member of this church, and these organizations...A kind and loving woman...Please send donations to Susan G. Komen for the Cure.

It was just as painful to read the second time. When I first read the obituary notice, the room telescoped; I became flush, and I thought I might pass out. I had to sit back in my chair and take a deep breath. Now I just felt weary and profoundly sad. Not for her or her family but selfishly for me. I leaned back in the chair, closed my eyes, and a flood of images from the past rushed on to the screen behind my eyes. So many memories: her, me, Tip, Binghamton, Catholic Central, Rock Bottom Dam, and the rest. Oh, the rest, indeed.

After a few moments of painful recollection, I dropped the notice on the envelope. I rubbed my eyes, wiping the beginning of a tear away. I stood and walked out of the office, turning the light off.

I walked through the dark house to the kitchen. Without turning a light on, I grabbed a glass (with Bevo the UT mascot on it) from a cabinet above the granite counter next to the refrigerator and then opened the bottom freezer under the refrigerator, grabbed a couple of ice cubes, and dropped them in the glass. After filling the glass with water from the sink faucet, I carried it to the sliding glass door off the family room. With my free hand, I unlocked the sliding glass door, opened it, and stepped out on the back deck.

As I exited, I was hit with a blast of hot, humid air. Although it was early October, there was an abnormal hot spell in central Texas, only adding to the drought the area had experienced in recent years. In the woods behind our house, a pair of katydids sang their rising and falling buzzing song. In central Texas, you get used to the night singing of the katydids. When I first moved here, over thirty years ago, I had trouble sleeping at night with that constant buzzing. Of course, back then I was too poor to rent a place with air-conditioning, and had to sleep with the windows open.

I shuffled to the railing and looked into the darkness beyond. There were no clouds, and the moon was casting a dim light. I sipped the cold water, and, after a moment, set the glass down on the railing.

I heard the sliding door open behind me and turned to it. Rose was standing there, wearing a men's-length T-shirt.

She asked quietly, "What are you doing out here?"

"I couldn't sleep. I reread the notice to make sure I wasn't dreaming."

She shut the door, and glided to my side.

"I'm sorry that she died."

She grabbed the glass and took a sip.

"It is so hot and still out here," she said.

"I'm feeling really old, and it makes me think about what happened back in Binghamton."

"C'mon, fifty-eight is not old," she chuckled and lightly slapped me on my arm.

"That's easy for you to say; you're only fifty-five."

"The double nickel."

"The double nickel indeed."

I put my arm around her shoulder and drew her close. I caught a whiff of an orange scent from her hair.

I said, "How did I get so lucky to find you?" And I truly meant it.

"You haven't said that in a long time."

"I know. I'm sorry."

"That is very sweet. That can get a girl through a lot."

She set the glass down, and, pulling away, said, "I need to get more sleep, or I am going to be in a bad way in the morning. Are you coming?"

"Not right now. I'm not quite ready yet. I'll be back in a few minutes. Get some rest."

She paused for a moment, analyzing me.

"OK, John, don't stay too long out here. You need more sleep too."

"I won't be too long."

She turned and I watched her head back to the house. She opened the sliding glass door, entered the house, and closed the door.

I picked up the glass of water and moved to one of the white canvas lounge chairs on the deck. I sat down and tilted the chair back so I could lie flat. I looked up at the black central Texas night. Living in West Lake Hills, we are far enough from the lights and hazy air of Austin to still see a million stars twinkling on a clear night like this. I could make out the Big Dipper and the Little Dipper. I remembered a time in Boy Scouts when Tip and I had camped out at a park high in the hills above Cayuga Lake, and we stayed up for hours observing stars for an astronomy merit badge. At one point during the evening, a shooting star had blazed across the horizon to our amazement.

Lying there thinking about Tip in the good times

inevitably brought me once again to the fall of 1975 when my life changed forever, and I became a broken man, until Rose saved me years later. I shivered in the warm night as I mentally checked off the highlights of that bitter period. "Divorced" my mother. Check. Lost the love of my life. Check. Killed my best friend. Check. I shivered again on this warm night as I thought about the black swirling Susquehanna on a New Year's Eve so many years ago. Check. And then, as I thought about Tip, I heard him screaming those words that have haunted me for so many years, *"You're responsible!"* Double check.

The katydids kept buzzing. It would be a long time until I slept again.

CHAPTER 2
Chance Meeting

I never thought I'd see you again
Where have you been until now?
Well how are you? How have you been?
It's a long time since we last met.

—Bryan Ferry

Binghamton, New York, August, 1975

IN THE SUMMER OF 1975, it was nearly impossible to find a good summer job in Binghamton or the other Triple Cities near Binghamton if you were a college student. What a change one year could make. In the summer of 1974, despite Richard Nixon's travails, the economy was chugging nicely along and college students seeking summer employment were hired by the hundreds at IBM, GE, or Singer Link, at wages above minimum. But by the time summer rolled around in 1975, the economy was weak and college students were fighting to get fast-food, delivery, or other low-level jobs.

I had been hired early in June by Chenango Valley Warehouse. I think the owner took pity on me because he had gone to high school with my dad. My job was to move boxes of stuff stored in a decaying three-story brick building in North Binghamton, not far from the Chenango River to the west and the railroad yards to the south. Near the intersection of Route 17 and Route 8. The warehouse had been constructed in the 1920s as a manufacturing plant for shoes, but had been used as a warehouse for almost twenty years in 1975. There was no air-conditioning in the dark dreary warehouse; we were forced to open windows to receive airflow, if only a hint. On those hot, humid summer days, we could smell the foul odor of the Chenango, and the drying mud on its banks, and the dead carp as the river dried up in the summer.

Even with my prodigious consumption of beer (preferably Rolling Rock) that summer, I still lost ten pounds due to the manual labor and the oppressive heat in the warehouse. From eight to five, except for a blessed one-hour lunch break, I was lifting heavy boxes from pallets that we hauled from the warehouse out to the decrepit receiving dock and then carried onto waiting trucks, or the reverse. It was mind-numbingly boring, and all for minimum wage. My T-shirt would be drenched with sweat by ten o'clock in the morning every day, and I would have to immediately shower when I came home so that my mother would permit me to eat dinner with her and my stepfather.

There were ten other employees in the warehouse when I joined. All but one was an ex-con. This was the only work they could get that year too, as construction work had dried up. A couple of the ex-cons were in their fifties. I couldn't believe they could do it all day. After eight hours, I was exhausted and famished. When they received their paycheck each week, they would cash it and get drunk as skunks, so drunk that I could smell the booze in their sweat all the next day. Then they would have little money left to last until the next paycheck. They would invite "the college kid" to go out with them, but I demurred. I knew those nights would be trouble. Before the summer ended, two of them got into a brawl at a local dive bar over an overweight bleached-blond waitress, and then continued the fight the next day on the third floor of the warehouse. They both were fired.

As I was often too tired to go out with my friends during the week, I would make up for lost time on the weekend. I would usually hang out with my old high school buddies at The Pine Lounge on the Westside of Binghamton, a solid driver shot from my high school, Catholic Central. We would drink Rolling Rock beer, flirt endlessly (to little effect) with girls we knew at CC or from the surrounding neighborhood, and pump quarters in the jukebox to listen to music we liked. I guess the main reason I hung out at The Pine Lounge was that my best friend from childhood, Tip O'Neill, was a regular there.

His name wasn't really Tip, of course. It was Tommy. His dad started calling him Tip because his dad grew up in North Cambridge, Massachusetts, and Tip O'Neill represented that district in the House of Representatives when young Tommy was born in 1954. In 1975, Tip O'Neill, the congressman, was the Majority Whip for the Democrats, on his way to becoming Speaker of the House in 1977. Tommy's dad always believed that his son Tip was going to make a fine politician someday because Tip was a fierce debater around the O'Neill house. No O'Neill house rule, which generally was put in place due to Tip, would be imposed without vigorous dissent. Tip may have indeed been a politician if life hadn't broken him.

On Saturday, August 16, 1975, Tip and I were seated at The Pine Lounge bar. My summer job in the warehouse was over in one week, and my senior year at nearby SUNY-Binghamton was about to begin. I was in a good, mellow mood. The Pine Lounge was packed that sultry hot summer night. Tip and I were draining Rolling Rocks and watching the Yankees blow out the California Angels on the small black-and-white TV that sat high above the bar. "Wish You Were Here" by Pink Floyd was playing on the jukebox. Cigarette smoke hung over the bar like a fog.

I heard the husky voice of Ann Dunn before I felt the tap on my shoulder. "Look who's here — it's Moron and Tip. What a surprise." *Moron?* Nobody had called me Moron since high school except for Ann (and Tip when he was drunk). I indifferently turned to her, but was shocked to see Mary Lou Mooney with her. Ann and ML, as Mary Lou was known to us, had graduated from Catholic Central High School with Tip and me. They were smiling with a tipsy glow.

Tip turned as well, as I said, "Ann, ML! This is a surprise."

Ann said, "Surprised? Aren't you two happy to see two beautiful women?"

She was right about one of them. ML was a stunner. Five foot six inches, long straight blond hair, perfect cheekbones, laughing eyes, thin, with breasts that seemed to hug every top she wore. In middle school, I had developed a schoolboy crush on Julie Christie after seeing her in the movie

Fahrenheit 451, and ML strikingly resembled her, but with white-blond hair (and better teeth). Always the contrarian, Tip was a Diana Rigg fan. Those catsuits that Dame Diana wore in *The Avengers* were too enticing for him.

Ann Dunn was shorter than Mary Lou by two inches, with stringy dirty-blond hair. She wasn't heavy, but she was carrying a few pounds too many. She had a most impressive rack, perhaps the largest in our high school class. She and I had gone out for a while in the second half of our junior year and first half of our senior year; her breasts were the first I had ever fondled. But it did not end well.

Tip asked: "Can I order you girls a drink?"

Ann replied, "Hell yeah. A Rock. Are you buying?"

Tip said, "Yeah, I'll buy. I'm rich."

ML said, "I'll have a screwdriver, Tip."

"Shit, a screwdriver? What the hell kinda drink is that?" Tip asked.

"I like screwdrivers. They're better for you. You don't get a hangover."

Tip sighed, turned back to the bar, and motioned to Mack, the charming, rotund, bespectacled bartender working the bar at The Pine Lounge.

I asked ML, "How's it going at BC?" She was at Boston College.

"Like, senior year, baby! Are you still at SUNY-Binghamton?"

"Unfortunately. One more year, and my sentence is up!"

Ann said, "You're the one who wanted to go there. I tried to tell you. You should have gone to a real college—like Columbia." Of course, Ann was attending Columbia.

Tip shook his head, "At least you guys are going to college."

Ann sniffed, "You should be going to college, you knucklehead. Talk some sense into him, Moron." God, how I hated to be called "Moron" and she loved to needle me with that name.

I slapped Tip on the shoulder and said, "Talking sense to Tip is like me trying to dunk over Kareem. It ain't gonna happen."

Tip said, "Some friend you are, JM." He turned back to the bar, "Hey, Mack, my money's getting cold out here!"

Ann touched my arm, "ML broke up with her boyfriend."

ML shook her head, "C'mon Ann. You said you wouldn't get into it."

My heart raced. *There's still a chance.*

In her freshman year at Boston College, Mary Lou had met Dino. Dino was from Rome, Italy. They had been a couple ever since, and rarely apart. I had only seen her handful of times since college began, and we had spoken little. On all of those occasions she had been with Dino. I had both envied and hated him.

I asked, "What happened?"

Tip turned back to us holding out a Rolling Rock bottle and the screwdriver. "Here you go, ladies. Courtesy of ol' Tip. How about a toast?"

They grabbed their drinks from Tip. Grabbing my Rolling Rock from the bar behind me, I said, "Tip, ML broke up with her main squeeze."

Tip jerked his Rolling Rock from the bar, and turned back, "Well, well, well…Let's drink to old times and new adventures."

Her eyes glazed, ML cried out, "And new boyfriends!"

We clinked the glass and the bottles, and I took a healthy swig. Ann finished a quarter of her beer. Wiping her mouth, she said, "Here's to Saturday night and getting wasted!"

Tip said, "Word!"

We clinked again. And drank deeply.

Tip leaned further into our little foursome, and looking at Ann suddenly serious, asked her, "Hey, Ann, did you hear I got a new job?"

Ann quizzically looked at Tip.

Tip patted my shoulder, "Look, JM, Ann is giving me the hairy eyeball."

Ann asked, "New job? What is it?"

"Planting Tulips."

"Planting Tulips where?"

He reached out with his index finger and stroked her lips, while saying. "Planting two lips right there." And then he laughed loudly.

I groaned with the girls, and Ann said, "You gotta come up with a better line than that, asshole."

Tip laughed and said, "Stick around. I will."

And so it began.

After another round, and more toasts, Ann stroked Tip's arm, and said, "C'mon, Tip, let's play foosball." There was a foosball table in the back of The Pine Lounge after the juke-box, but before the narrow hallway that led to the restrooms. Tip and I had spent a lot of quarters on that table. Tip was much better than I, even with his bad leg. He had great control of his front line, and could fire some angle shots that would baffle me and my goaltender.

"Ah, I don't want to play, Ann. Dig?"

"C'mon, Tip. Are you afraid I might beat you?"

"I'm not ashamed, I'm just afraid."

Ann looked at him quizzically, "What?"

I interjected, "*Catch-22*, Ann."

She shook her head, "I don't know what you guys are talking about. Are you playing or not?"

Tip laughed and said, "OK, I'm down with it. Let's go. ML, have my seat. I'm going to go kick Ann's ass."

I said, "I'm sure you'd like to do that."

Tip frowned at me, and gingerly got off his bar stool. ML brushed intoxicatingly close, and sat down. Ann grabbed Tip's arm, and led him to the back.

She looked at me with those blue eyes. *Those eyes.*

"So, how have you been, John Moran?"

"Fine, I guess. I'm sorry about your boyfriend."

"Thanks. It makes me sad to talk about it. So, let's not. Let's talk about old times."

And so we did. We talked about Catholic Central High School where we first met. In freshman English class. Students in every class at CC were seated alphabetically, at least to start the year. Moran was right after Mooney. I remember that first day when she entered Room 102 in her blue uniform jumper with CCHS stenciled on it, and every guy in that room watched her glide effortlessly to her desk right in front of me. She grabbed her name card, and glanced at my name card. She sat down, turned to me, and smiled.

"Hi."

She had me at that "Hi."

I spent four years in high school sitting behind her,

staring at that long blond hair reaching almost to her rear. If I sat at the right angle, I could see those shapely legs, revealed by a rising short skirt, usually one crossed over the other, and bouncing to some mysterious tune in her head. I would watch her play with hair with her thin fingers, with the fingernails shellacked in some bright color, changing every week, if not sooner.

She had impossibly pure skin. I had acne throughout high school, and envied, if not hated her when my skin was at its worst. How could God be so cruel to allow me to have acne and someone already blessed like her to have none? When you were fourteen in a Catholic high school in 1968 in Binghamton, New York, you still blamed a nameless, faceless God.

To address my acne, my mother took me to an old dermatologist, Dr. Langger. She would always schedule an appointment for early in the morning, so I would miss a couple of periods of school. He was a stooped old man, with a shock of white hair, and an Eastern Europe accent to his English. I called him "The Butcher"; he would have me lie under a sunlamp for fifteen minutes, then he would come in the room and with a handkerchief he would squeeze the most egregious zits on my face, and then wipe away the pus and blood. It was sheer agony. Each time, I left Dr. Langger's, I was angry at him, but even angrier with my mother for believing that this abuse would help with acne, and that I would have to show up late to a class, looking like I had just returned from Miami, with red blotches lighting up my face. Not good in high school, not good at all.

But then, after delivering my absence note to whatever class I would enter late, Biology, Ancient History, Spanish, I would hurry to my desk, and ML would be there, smiling at me, seeming not to care about my repulsiveness.

For improbably we had become friends. We sat near each other all those many hours in all those classes and she grew to like me, apparently because I wasn't crude like most of my male classmates, but I was kind of funny. I found out later that the girls in my class considered me to be the "nice guy," and not exciting enough to merit any real interest. Before a class would begin, she would turn to me, and ask if I had watched Laugh-In the night before, or if I liked the latest Bread song. If there were class projects, she would inevitably include me in her team. The best class projects were two person projects where I could bask in her beauty alone.

She didn't have a close girlfriend for a while at CC, until she and Ann became besties late in our sophomore year. She was friendly with the other girls, and would get invited to sleepovers and parties, but there was a distance nonetheless. Perhaps it was jealously; perhaps it was her lack of pretense.

However, she was great friends with her three sisters, two older, one younger. Her oldest sister, Beth, was a senior at CC in our freshman year of 1968, while her second oldest sister, Marcy, was a sophomore at CC that year. The youngest sister, Cathy, was the "surprise," only seven years old in our freshman year. Each sister was more beautiful than the one before. The guys at CC joked that her father, Dr. Mooney, a leading orthopedic surgeon at Lourdes Hospital in Binghamton, was a man with a magic dick.

Her family lived in a stately colonial house at 200 Riverside Drive in Binghamton, the street where the wealthiest residents of Binghamton lived at the time. Behind their house, a field of an acre in length ran downhill to the slow-moving brown Susquehanna River that divided the Westside of Binghamton from the Southside of the city.

From her first day in high school, it didn't take long for the upper class vultures to take notice of ML. Within three months after beginning her freshman year, she was dating a junior at CC who was a starting guard on the varsity basketball team. They went out for two years, until he went to college, and discovered an even greater affection for pot. She was unattached for six weeks, and then became the girlfriend of the senior quarterback for Binghamton Central High School, our public school archrival. They dated for the rest of high school, and into her freshman year at BC, before she met her "Italian Stallion" at BC.

She was a cheerleader for the CC varsity basketball team all four years, ending up as captain in our senior year. She also was a very good tennis player, having taken years of lessons at the elite Binghamton Country Club. But in those days, CC had limited girls' sports, and tennis was not one of them. During the time that I was dating Ann, ML, her jock Binghamton Central boyfriend, Ann, and I would play mixed doubles. ML and the jock would toy with us for a while, before crushing us. It was humiliating to lose to that jerk, and worse to see the two of them together. I could never understand what a sweet girl was doing with an asshole like that.

In the fall of our senior year at CC, Ann and I broke up; we had run our course, and Ann had gotten bored with me I think. Somehow, after the initial disappointment of her telling me after school one day that she didn't want to be together any more, we still remained friends, although it stung badly at the time. Maybe it was because she was my first girlfriend and I retained a sweet spot for her.

"Remember that oral project in Spanish we had in Mrs. Matthews's class?" ML asked, drawing me back to the present.

"You mean the one about Dali?"

"That's it. I did his biography, and then you spoke about his paintings."

"And then that bitch asked me questions about his life, and I didn't know anything, cuz I hadn't looked at any of that. She just grilled me and I didn't know shit. She hated me. I ended up getting a B in that class and you got an A. You were her pet."

"I was not!"

"Yeah, sure."

"Remember when you left the Weight Watchers flyer on Sister Martha's chair in Geometry?"

"I didn't do that! It was Tip. But she blamed me for it! That fat cow deliberately kept me from getting a hundred on the final, even though I got everything right."

"C'mon, John, she did not."

"She did! I am serious."

She finished her screwdriver.

I asked, "You want another one?"

"Sure. Why not?"

She *was* tipsy. I yelled down the bar to Mack, who was arguing with an older guy.

"Mack, another screwdriver, and a Rock!"

"We had a lot of fun in high school," she said wistfully.

"I think you had way more fun than I did."

"You going out with anyone now?"

"No. I'm still waiting for the perfect girl."

"Good luck with that."

Mack crashed a screwdriver and a Rolling Rock on the bar behind use. "Two bucks, Moron."

I gave him a five. "Bring me the change, and change your attitude."

He grabbed the empty Rolling Rock and glass on the bar. "Change my fucking attitude for a CC boy. Ha!" He stormed off.

I handed her the screwdriver, and she said, "Thanks, John."

I grabbed the new Rolling Rock. I tapped it against her glass. "To old times."

We both drank. She was staring at me while she drank with those piercing blue eyes. *Those eyes.* It was almost too painful, and I broke eye contact.

I glanced to the back of The Pine Lounge. The foosball table was empty. I did not see Ann or Tip. I pointed.

"Tip and Ann seem to have disappeared."

"Really?" She looked around the room. "She's my ride."

"Don't worry, I can take you home."

Suddenly, we heard shouting near the front door. As The Pine Lounge was packed with bodies, we couldn't see the source of the commotion. But after a moment, I could see the crowd separating, like the parting of the Red Sea in DeMille's *Ten Commandments*. And then I saw Ann; she was jogging through the crowd, and she was completely naked, those pendulous breasts were jumping up and down with each step.

I yelled to ML, "Oh my God, Ann is streaking."

Ann ran near us, shook her ass at us, and then raced on, disappearing in the hallway in the back.

The shouting at the front of the bar got even louder. Turning to the front, I now saw Tip, with a goofy smile, limping naked through the crowd. As he neared us, I was drawn to the ugly scar down the right side of his leg. I had only seen the scar below his knee, when he wore shorts. I had never seen the long scar on his thigh. It was not pretty.

He moved to us. "How about some applause!"

Both ML and I started clapping; she was laughing, and pretending to cover her eyes.

Mack leaned over the bar, "Hey, asshole, don't be a jerk, put your fucking clothes on, or I'm gonna toss your sorry ass."

Tip gave him the finger, twirled in a circle, and shouted, "Yeah, streaking, baby!" He triumphantly limped to the back and disappeared.

"What in the hell just happened?" I asked.

ML sipped from her screwdriver, and then burst out laughing. After a moment, I laughed uproariously too, and said to her, "I can't believe those two."

Streaking was a fad in 1975, but usually on college campuses, or in large public gatherings, not in a small bar on the Westside of Binghamton. It was one of those moments. You had to be there.

After a few minutes, Ann and Tip, now dressed, reappeared by our side, arm in arm.

Tip barked at me, "How about that, JM?"

I said, "You are a piece of work, Tip. I wasn't expecting that. You got me on that one."

Ann blurted to ML: "Tip and I were playing foosball,

and I was kicking his ass. It just came to me. I told him if I won, he had to streak through the bar with me."

Tip said, "She won."

Mack was behind me now. He yelled at Tip, "Nice job, douche bag. Don't do that again. We ain't losing our license over your schlong."

Tip, "Yeah, yeah, yeah. You'll keep taking my money. Get a load of him."

Ann leaned forward, "Let's blow this place. Let's go dancing."

ML started rocking in her chair, "Hoo-Hoo. Let's do it. C'mon, John."

I looked at Tip, "If he's going, I'm going." Luckily, Tip shook his head yes.

First, we debated where to go. Tip and I suggested a bar in Vestal that played a mix of music, mostly rock; the girls wanted to go to The Bank in downtown Binghamton for disco. Tip resisted for several minutes; he hated disco with a passion. But Ann and ML wore us down and won the debate. Then we decided that Tip would ride with Ann, and ML would ride with me.

We quickly left The Pine Lounge, squeezing our way past the crowd. A few patrons patted Tip on the back, congratulating him on his streaking achievement.

As we neared my baby blue 1965 Galaxie 500 convertible, ML erupted, "Oh my God, you still have this car! You have to put the top down. You absolutely have to put the top down!"

With the top down, on that hot humid late summer night, we cruised to downtown Binghamton, only ten minutes away. She turned on WENE radio; the song "Lying Eyes" by the Eagles burst forth, *"Honey, you can't hide your lying eyes."*

I looked over at her, her white-blond hair was blowing in the wind, her fists were pumping in the air, and she was singing to the words. She was magnificent.

The Bank was a dance club located under the old Binghamton Savings Bank across the street from the aging Courthouse in downtown Binghamton. ML and I descended the stone stairs. I paid our cover fee to her mild protests, and we entered the gloomy interior. Barry White's "What Am I Gonna Do to You" boomed from the speakers over the dance floor lit by a circling ball sending showers of reflected white light around the room.

I looked around the large dimly-lit crowded club, searching for Tip and Ann. I spotted them in the rear of the club sitting at a table. They were kissing, or, at least I thought I saw them kissing. I pointed in their direction to ML, and we headed that way.

Ann and Tip were not kissing when we sat down at the table. We ordered a round, another screwdriver for ML, Michelobs for the rest of us (The Bank was too refined to carry Rolling Rock).

The shimmering keyboards of KC and the Sunshine Band's "Get Down Tonight" filled the room. ML grabbed my hand, "C'mon, let's dance. I LOVE this song."

We hurried to the packed dance floor. She led to me a small empty space. Turning to me, she leaned in, "You know how to bump?" I lied, and said yes.

The now forgotten bump was a dance that began in the 70s

where dance partners would "bump" hips on every other beat of the music. I had seen couples perform the bump in a local club, and on TV, and thought it couldn't have been too hard.

And so we began. The music pounded above our heads
Baby, babe, let's get together.
We lightly tapped our hips to the beat.
Honey, hon, me and you.
We dropped lower, hips tapped.
And do the things, ah, do the things.
We dropped even lower still, continuing to tap our hips.
That we like to do.
We dropped even lower still, continuing to tap our hips.
Do a little dance, make a little love,
We raised halfway up, not missing a hip tap.
Get down tonight.
Back to standing, hands in the air.
Get down tonight.
When that song was done, we kept dancing. To Chic, Barry White, Earth, Wind & Fire, more KC and the Sunshine Band. Sitting down. Another round of drinks. At one point, Ann finally dragged Tip to the dance floor, but I knew it was a struggle for him. He rocked about the floor; I knew he couldn't do the bump. Not with his leg.

At one point, "My Eyes Adored You" by Frankie Valli was played. ML and I raced to the dance floor. We moved together, arms around each other, and she placed her head on my breast. I could smell the scent of a cut lemon on her hair. We moved as one around the floor. I saw Tip nearby, slow dancing with Ann. He looked over to me and gave me a twisted smile and thumbs up.

After a moment, ML tightened her grasp, squeezing me tight. I had never been held any tighter. I dropped my hands from her back to just above her hips. We continued to sway, barely moving. With the alcohol, the sick sweet smell of her hair, the music surrounding me, the fact that I was holding the girl I had desired for years, I closed my eyes, and I thought I was in paradise. My hands dropped even lower, ending on her hips.

When the song ended, we didn't break apart immediately. She finally looked up at me. I should have tried to kiss her, but I didn't. I held back. She leaned up and kissed me on my cheek, and we left the dance floor, as another Barry White song burst from the speakers overhead.

When we returned to our seats, Tip and Ann were not there.

"Are Tip and Ann still out there?" I asked.

"They left."

"What do you mean they left?"

"She's taking him home, which means you're taking me home." She was slurring her words now. She threw back the last drops of her screwdriver.

"Tip and Ann. Wow. Who could see that coming?"

"Life is funny, John."

"You ready to go?"

"Yes…I am freakin' blasted." She was too.

Arm in arm, I guided her out of The Bank up the stairs, and to the Galaxie 500. She was singing a medley of songs we had heard that night and leaning on me. Upon reaching the car, I opened the passenger door, and eased her in. She fell in, and then rose, crying out, "What the hell?" She reached underneath and held up two empty Budweiser cans. She flung them out, "Binghamton Assholes."

"That's why I don't leave the top down, ML." I walked around the car, and vaulted over the driver's door into the car. There was another empty can of Bud on my seat, I dropped it over the side, and got behind the wheel.

She blurted out, "Can you believe the assholes in this town?"

I didn't answer her, but started the car, and headed south on Collier Street, past the old stately courthouse, and took a right on Hawley Street, followed by a quick left on State Street, driving past the large rust-brown rectangular Broome County Veterans Memorial Arena. ML, Tip, Ann, and I, along with several high school classmates had gone to the very first concert at the Arena two years before. Chicago was the main act; Bruce Springsteen was the opening act. We had never heard of him, and he was poorly received.

As I was driving, ML became more subdued, and we drove in silence. I didn't know what to say. I turned right onto North Shore Drive, and started heading to her house. Even though it was two fifteen in the morning, it was still a hot humid night. My shirt was damp with sweat, but the night air was refreshingly cool as it flowed over the wind-shield. We crossed the Veteran's Memorial Bridge that sat over the Chenango River shortly before it merged into and became a part of the Susquehanna River. After we crossed the Chenango, North Shore Drive became Riverside Drive.

"Don't take me home yet."

I looked over; she was staring at me, with those sky blue, and now glazed, eyes. "OK, ML. Where do you want to go?"

She pointed off to our left, "Turn down Oak Street."

Oak Street was twenty yards away. I hit the brakes and slowed down and turned. Oak Street had a gentle slope from Riverside Drive down to the Susquehanna. We slowly passed homes on both sides of Oak Street; there were no lights on at this hour. At the bottom of Oak Street, there was a flat dirt patch before the Susquehanna, where a couple of cars could park, but it was empty that night. I stopped the car, and turned the lights off, but left the engine idling. My nerves were aflame with anticipation.

She leaned back against the door and sighed.

"I can't believe he broke up with me, John."

"What?"

"Dino. My boyfriend. We were together for almost three years."

No wind in the sails now.

"Um, we came here to talk about him?"

She closed her eyes. A tear dropped down the right side of her face.

"I need to talk about him…I really loved him, John. I really did."

I turned the car off.

"He had to go back to Italy for law school. His family wants him to live there. He didn't want me to be his girl-friend if he was going to be in Italy. Rome, Italy, actually."

"I'm sorry, ML."

"I told him I would come and visit him, that we could make it work, but he just wanted to break it off clean."

She opened her eyes, "I am so trashed." She looked up, "The stars are spinning."

"C'mon, ML, let me take you home." I lied, "It'll be

better in the morning."

She moved closer to me, and ran her fingers through my hair. He face was flushed, and her eyes were red.

"You are so good to me, John. You were always good to me. We've been good friends for a long time. How come we've never kissed?"

"Because we never—" She suddenly threw her arms around me, and planted her lips onto mine. Our tongues quickly met and danced together. It was overwhelmingly intense.

After a minute, she pulled away. "Let's just screw."

"What?"

"I don't care anymore. Let's just screw our brains out."

I could not believe I heard that offer. After all those years of frustrating obsession, I was presented with the opportunity I had long fantasized about. But there was a voice in my head that was my conscience, or Catholic guilt, that acted next.

"ML, you don't know how much I want to do exactly that, but I can't do it tonight."

She vacantly stared at me. "Why not? What's wrong?"

Against her resistance, I removed her arms from around my neck. "Look, you're really drunk, and you just broke up with your boyfriend. I can't do it this way. I just cannot do it this way."

"It doesn't matter, babe. Who cares what happens?"

"We'll both care—"

She yelled, "I DON'T CARE!"

"Shhh! You're going to wake up people."

She moved back across the seat, away from me.

"You've really hurt me, John."

She started to cry.

"ML, I'm sorry. I know when I wake up in the morning, I am going to hate myself, and regret this moment, but I think I need to take you home now. You have no idea how I am going to regret this."

She didn't say anything, but looked away, her sniffling continuing.

I gave up on conversation. I started the car, backed it up, turned to the left, and drove up Oak Street. When we reached Riverside Drive, I turned left, and headed to her house. Nothing more was said, but she was quietly crying. She finally stopped crying as we neared her house in less than five minutes.

I turned into the driveway off Riverside Drive, and pulled forward on the long driveway, stopping near the stone path leading to the front door.

"ML, I have never wanted to hurt you. I have never wanted a girl more than you."

"You have a funny way of proving it." She opened the door, and staggered to her feet.

"Do you need some help?"

She turned to me and shut the door, "Oh, hell no. I'm OK." I watched her stumble to the front door, struggle with opening the front door with her key, and then tumble in. After a moment, I backed out and drove home.

When I crawled into bed, I lay awake for hours. The smell of cigarette smoke reeked from my clothes, but I could still smell her perfume lingering. My mind replayed the evening, considering over and over what I should have said and done. At some point I finally drifted off to a fitful sleep.

CHAPTER 3
All I Want Is You

Don't want to hear what's going on
I don't care What's new
Don't want to know about anything
'Cause all I want Is you

—Bryan Ferry

Binghamton, New York, August, 1975

AT ELEVEN FIFTEEN THE NEXT MORNING, my mother woke me up by shaking my shoulder. "John, John, get up."

"What? What's up?" I turned over to look at her, standing over me. She was wearing a blue summer dress. She continued, "C'mon, get up, John. We have to leave for church in thirty minutes."

I put my hands over my eyes. "Mom, you've got to be kidding me. You woke me up for that?"

"I'd like you to go with me."

"Mom, please. I'm not going. But say a prayer for me."

"You smell like a brewery. Where were you last night?"

"At The Pine Lounge. With Tip."

"That figures. He's some smoky friend to hang around with. You can do better." She had never been a fan of Tip; he was not made welcome at our home since high school, and had not visited it for some time.

"So, you're not coming?" she asked.

"No, Mom, I am not coming."

"Oh, this makes me so angry." She stormed out.

I pulled the sheet over my head, and tried to go back to sleep, but it was not to be. I lay in bed just long enough to hear my mother finally leave. I rose and walked downstairs to the kitchen. The house was thankfully silent. Owen Williams, my stepfather, was gone as well. Sunday was his fishing day. He was not a church going man either, and worse yet, was not even a Catholic.

After breakfast and a shower, I stayed in my room, still bathing in the memories of the night before. And contemplating what I should have done the night before. I listened to the *Dark Side of the Moon*.

At a quarter to three, I heard the phone ring downstairs. After a few moments, I heard my mother yell from downstairs. "John, phone!"

I got off my bed, opened my door, and yelled back, "Who is it?"

"Some girl."

I raced downstairs, passing my mother by, as she said, "Where was all that energy this morning?"

I ran to the phone lying on the kitchen table, and said, "Hello," into the phone.

"Hi, John." It was ML. "How are you?"

"Fine. Great. How are you?"

"I didn't feel too good this morning. I got out of going to church, but the parents weren't too happy."

"I know what you mean."

"Can you meet me tonight, John?"

"Tonight? Yeah, sure. Where and when?"

"How about at seven o'clock at Number 5?"

"OK, that's good."

"Check you later, John."

"Yeah, I'll see you tonight." My heart was in my throat, and pounding away. I put the phone back in its receiver.

"Who was that?" asked my mother, as she stood in the kitchen entrance.

"Um, Mary Lou Mooney. From high school, remember?"

"Yeah, I remember her. Her father's a doctor?"

"He's a surgeon at Lourdes Hospital."

"What did she want?"

"Oh nothing, I bumped into her last night. She just wants to get together to talk about school tonight. She goes to Boston College."

"You've gotta work tomorrow. Don't be out too late."

"Mom, what am I, five years old? I know my schedule. Thanks." I turned and walked (or did I skip?) back to my upstairs bedroom.

The Number Five was in a converted fire station on Vestal Avenue near the Washington Street Bridge. The walls of the interior were red brick, with the fire slide still in the middle. A classy restaurant was on the second floor, and a lively bar was on the first floor. On Friday and Saturday nights, pop bands would often play, and there was a small dance floor in front of the equally small stage.

At seven o'clock, I walked through the swinging glass doors into the dimly lit bar. I spotted ML sitting at the end of the bar on a stool facing me; she waved to me. I felt my face flush. I waved back and smiled; goofily, I am sure. As I walked to her, I could feel the eyes of the two male bartenders watching me. No doubt they could not believe that I was with her. She already had a tall full mug sitting in front of her.

"Hi, John, have a seat. Quick." She patted the stool next to her.

"Why quick?"

"I've been here like five minutes and some creepy guy tried to chat me up."

I sat on the stool she had patted. "Where is the guy?" I turned to look around the bar.

She lightly grabbed my arm. "Don't be so obvious. Look over your left shoulder at the table with the three guys. Check the guy with the open shirt."

I casually peered over my shoulder. The guy looked like Joe Pepitone in his prime: blow-dried black hair, gold chain, an open shirt to the middle of his chest, with a mohair sweater of chest hairs escaping. I shook my head, and turned back.

"You know how to pick 'em, ML."

"What can I get for you?" a tall bartender in his forties asked me.

"Rolling Rock, please. No glass."

He moved away. Over his shoulder, he said, "A buck and a quarter."

I asked ML, "You want another?"

"No, thanks." She held up the mug. "It's a Coke. No

booze for me tonight. I was just hammered last night."

Throwing two dollars on the bar in front of me, I said, "Yeah, you were."

The bartender returned, set the Rolling Rock bottle down, scooped up the two dollars, and walked away.

"That's what happens when I go out with Ann. She can drink me under the table."

"ML, she could probably drink you, me, and Tip under the table."

"Before we met you guys at The Pine, we had gone to The Other Place and had a couple of drinks there, and then a shot of peppermint schnapps. Aw, it was bad this morning. Bad, bad, bad. My parents were ticked off."

I tapped the Rock bottle to her mug. "Here's to pissed off parents." She laughed and drank with me. The Rock was icy cold and tasted wonderful.

She set the Coke down, and said, "I had the spins last night before I fell asleep. The ceiling was just flying. I hate that. I couldn't even take my clothes off."

"I've never seen you that drunk."

She sipped from her Coke again, and stared off for a second. I drank from the Rock. There was an awkward silence. She turned and looked at me again.

"So, what happened last night?"

"What do you mean?"

"C'mon, John, what happened? I have this vague memory of you taking me home. I mean—I remember being at The Pine Lounge. And then at The Bank, but it gets foggy after that. I kinda remember you dropping me at home. Did anything else happen?"

"You really don't remember, ML? C'mon!"

She patted me on the arm. "John, I really don't. And that's what bothers me. I hate to be that drunk. I do…stupid things."

"Uh-huh."

"Did I do anything stupid?"

"How do you define stupid?"

"John?"

"ML, we had a few drinks at The Pine Lounge, we went to The Bank and danced for a couple of hours. We had a few more drinks. Then I poured you into my car—"

"The blue convertible?"

"That's the one. It's sitting outside right now. I took you home from The Bank." I decided to take the high road. I didn't want to embarrass her. I could never cause her pain. I suppose she knew that all along. And in the end nothing happened due to my absurd chivalry. "But you were pretty drunk."

She stroked my arm. "Thanks, John, for taking me home, and for putting up with me. That will teach me to go out drinking with Ann."

"Can you believe that she and Tip got together?"

"Did you talk to him today?"

"No. Did you talk to Ann?"

She frowned, "Yeah, I did. They went back to his place and messed around."

"She went to that dump? It is a complete pigsty."

"That's what Ann said. Ann's worried about Tip, John."

"She didn't seem too worried last night."

"She was worried this morning. He's really down about

things. He just puts on a show like he's not. He was in a bad
way by the time she left. He told her he felt very down about
the rest of us going to college and making plans for the future.
He was telling her all about his leg and how it bothers him.
And then he told her how much he missed his mother."

"Oh, man."

"And, he's just working delivering furniture. It sounded
so depressing."

"He just seems that way when he's been drinking."

"Honestly, John, have you been with him recently when
he hasn't ended up drunk?"

I pondered that for a moment. "Not really. But he's only
twenty-one. C'mon, that's what everybody is doing. Getting
blasted. Like you last night, for example."

"I don't know, John, but the CC people I run into say
he's a mess. I wish we could do something for him."

"He'll get his life in order, and go back to school. You
wait."

"You're his closest friend, John, will he listen to you?"

"Listen to me?" I snorted. "He doesn't listen to anybody…I try to talk to him, but he just blows me off."

"Well, keep trying, he probably needs you more than
ever as a friend right now." She flipped her hair, and leaned
onto the bar. "John, we were such good friends in high
school. How did we drift apart?"

"I don't know, ML; I wish all of us at CC had stayed
closer, but it's hard when you start leading separate lives,
hundreds of miles apart."

"John, tell me more about you now. Do you have a
girlfriend?"

The same bartender appeared in front of her. "Freshen up the Coke?"

ML peered into the glass, and pushed it to him. "Yeah, thanks."

He pointed at me. "Another Rock?"

"Sure."

He said, "That'll be two-fifty," and walked away.

She reached for her small black purse on the bar. I said, "ML, I've got it." I pulled three dollars out of my pocket and put them on the bar.

"Thanks, John. Must be nice to have money."

"I wouldn't know, ML, but I have enough pocket money for a Coke and a Rock."

"So, what about the girlfriend question?"

"You know you asked me that last night."

"I did?"

"Yeah, and it's still the same answer. No, I don't have a girlfriend. It's pretty impossible to meet anybody at SUNY-B because I'm living at home, and I'm from Binghamton, and those people from the Big Apple and Long Island at SUNY-B are not interested in us natives. Since high school, I think I've had two girlfriends. Neither lasted long. Last year I dated a girl from Endicott for a few months. She was going to Broome Community College. But that fizzled out. Nothing anywhere as serious as you are."

She frowned. "As I was. Not anymore."

"I'm sorry, ML. It's his loss."

"Thanks, John, that is sweet. I am going to miss him a lot this year. We have been so close the last couple of years. It's going to be hard going to school without him there. But I'm just going to have to move on."

"You won't have any problem finding companionship, ML."

"I'm not looking for companionship. Dino and I were soul mates. Or, at least I thought we were. That's what I'm looking for." God, I wanted to hold her right then.

The bartender set the glass of Coke and the Rock bottle before us, "Here you go."

I said to the bartender, "Keep the change."

He said thanks and walked away.

She sipped from the new Coke. Then, holding her glass up, she said, "I'm finally starting to feel better."

I said, "Here's to feeling better," and we toasted again.

"Let's change the subject. So, John, what are you gonna do after you graduate?"

"I'm kinda thinking I would get a master's degree in English. Did you know I'm majoring in English?"

"No. What do you want to do after that?"

"I'd like to teach English, especially English literature."

"You always got good grades in English class at CC."

"That's because I was copying off your test in front of me."

She snorted, "Right. That never happened. Where are you thinking that you would go to grad school?"

I sipped from the Rock. "Cornell. Syracuse. Maybe NYU like my sister. That would be a trip."

"Why don't you come to Boston? BC and BU have great graduate programs."

"I hadn't thought about Boston."

"You should. It is such a fun town. I love it."

"So, ML, what are you going to do after school?"

"I'm going to go law school."

I sat up. That was new news. "Law school? I thought you were going to be a teacher."

"I was, and then I changed my major. Actually, Dino was the one who convinced me to go for law school. He's studying to be a lawyer in Rome."

"When do you take the LSAT exam?"

"In the fall. October. Not looking forward to that. I'm not really looking forward to much at the moment."

"It will get better. I know it."

"Aw, that's sweet too. You are on a roll tonight…You know you should come visit me. In Boston. You know—over a weekend."

My heart started beating so fast, I thought it would burst from my chest cavity. "Really? Do you mean that?"

"Of course I do. I'll have time to show you around Boston now. You can figure out whether you like it or not for grad school. We can even catch a Patriots game. I've got an apartment with another girl; we've got plenty of room. It would be so much fun. Really!"

"Wow. You're pretty convincing."

"John, when I get back, I'll check my schedule, and the Patriots schedule, and I'll write and let you know when to come."

"When do you go back?"

"Actually, tomorrow. I only came home for the weekend because we were breaking up, and he was leaving. I thought it was better to be gone."

Tomorrow? My heart sank on that news.

"ML, now you've given me something to look forward to. Other than leaving Binghamton in a year."

She picked up her glass. "Let's toast to a weekend in Boston." We clinked her glass and my Rock again.

We spent another hour in Number 5, mostly reliving events and memories from high school. And I fell hard. She set the trap with those blue penetrating eyes, that ironic smile, the flip of her hair, the light touch on my arm, the licking of her lips, her to-die-for figure. And I walked right into it. By the end of that hour, I was putty, and she could have molded me any way she wanted to.

Eventually she said she had to leave. We walked out of Number 5 into another humid summer evening. Over the distant west hills, I saw lightning flash. A summer storm was not far away, bringing relief, if only briefly, from the heat and humidity. I walked ML to her car (a 1974 white Bonneville) that was in the parking lot behind the Number 5. When we neared her car, she reached into her purse, and pulled a set of car keys out. "Thanks for meeting me tonight, John."

"This was great, ML." And it truly was.

She unlocked the car. "I wish I was sticking around some more, but I have to get back." She turned to me, with a quizzical smile, "Please tell me you're going to come visit me in Boston."

"I am there. Just let me know what a good weekend to come is."

"It will be worth it. I swear to you." She moved to me, and I thought she was going to reach up and kiss me, but instead she reached out and hugged me. And, I reciprocated. She did not release me. "Oh, John, I have missed you. I've got to get you out of Binghamton."

"Only one more year."

She finally moved away, releasing me. "That's right, John." Was that a tear I saw in her left eye? She opened her car door, and slid in. "Good night, John, say hi to Tip, and take care of him. I'll be in touch." With that, she shut her door, started the car, backed out of the parking spot, waved (which I returned), and slowly drove away. I watched the white Bonneville until it turned out of the parking lot and out of view.

I slowly walked to my car and got in. I heard the distant rumble of thunder from the approaching storm. I inserted the car key into the ignition, but didn't turn it. I closed my eyes, and concentrated as hard as I could on remembering how she looked, and how she spoke, and the pleasing scent of her perfume. My stomach was in knots. I was both exultant yet bitterly disappointed that I had not kissed her, or really tried to. I thought about how a kiss would have changed the dynamic between us, a line crossed that could never be in place again. I thought to myself: "You putz! How could you blow that opportunity?" I pondered the mystery of the last twenty-four hours, when the girl of my teenage dreams had not only reentered my life, but had suddenly become the focus of it. Maybe there was a God, as virtue had been rewarded finally.

After a few moments, I recovered and left the parking lot. I headed up the hill towards home. While basking in the afterglow of the evening, I reflected on our conversation. Suddenly, I thought about her remarks regarding Tip. I felt uncomfortable, perhaps because Ann had reported what I had perceived (but ignored) for some time. I looked at the clock in the car. It was only nine fifteen. At the next cross street, I checked traffic and did a U-turn. I thought I would stop by Tip's apartment and check on him.

Tip lived in a small one-bedroom apartment that sat on top of a garage behind his uncle's house off Beethoven Avenue, not far from both CC and The Pine Lounge. Having The Pine Lounge within walking distance was a major reason why Tip lived there. It took me ten minutes to drive there. I parked on the street and walked to the driveway that led to the garage. I could hear a television set from his uncle's house. There was a light on in Tip's apartment. I climbed the steps to his apartment, and knocked on the door. No answer. I knocked again, a little louder. "Tip," I called. Again, no answer. I waited a moment, and retraced my steps.

I drove to The Pine Lounge, parked, and entered it. It was fairly crowded for a Sunday night, but not as jammed as it had been the night before. I walked around the small interior, past the bar itself, but Tip was not there. I asked Mack if he had seen Tip that night. He had not. I didn't even stick around to order a Rolling Rock. I knew I would have to check up on Tip soon.

CHAPTER 4
Remember a Day

Remember a day before today
A day when you were young.
Free to play alone with time
Evening never come.

—Rick Wright

Binghamton, New York, September, 1975

MY HOMETOWN, BINGHAMTON, NEW YORK, sits in upstate New York near the border with Pennsylvania, four hours from New York City by car, in a valley surrounded by hills, bisected by both the Chenango River flowing from the north, and the Susquehanna River rushing from the northeast. For centuries, the Oneidas had farmed the land that now constitutes Binghamton and surrounding cities, growing mostly corn, but also tobacco, beans, and squash. They had also hunted the ample game in the heavily forested hills. The Oneidas were members of The League of the Iroquois, along with the other tribes in upstate New York: the Senecas, the Cayugas, the Onondogas, the Mohawks, and later, in the early 1700s, after being driven out of North Carolina, the Tuscaroras. It is believed by some scholars that the Founding Fathers of the United States were familiar with The League and its governing laws, and that the United States Constitution incorporates some of the League's ideas. Other scholars dispute this belief, but, regardless, in 1988, the United States Congress passed a resolution to recognize the influence of the Iroquois League upon the Constitution and Bill of Rights.

The majority of the Iroquois supported and fought with the British in the American Revolution, but that support led to the decimation of The League. In 1779, Major General John Sullivan and Brigadier General James Clinton led an expedition into upstate New York that established a scorched earth policy to be emulated by General Sherman many years later in the South during the Civil War. As General Sullivan duly reported to Congress, "With one exception, there is not a single town left in the country of the Five Nations ... We have not left a single settlement or field of corn." One hundred sixty thousand bushels of Iroquois corn were purportedly destroyed, and in one Cayuga town, 1,500 peach trees were destroyed. The Iroquois fled to Niagara, where many died over a bitter winter, and the Iroquois eventually settled in Canada.

On June 27, 1786, the fledgling New York State granted title of 30,000 acres near the Pennsylvania border to three men, including a William Bingham, politician and land owner from Philadelphia. The three co-owners partitioned the land in 1790, and Bingham ended up with 13,000 acres, including what is modern day Binghamton. Ironically, there is no record that Bingham ever set foot in the city bearing his name.

In 1800, Bingham began to sell or lease his vast holdings, and a settlement soon grew up at the confluence of the

Chenango and Susquehanna Rivers, first called Chenango Point, and then later, Binghamton.

The city began a steady and prosperous growth. The land was rich and many crops could be grown, despite the severe winters. Pioneers established sawmills on the Chenango and Susquehanna enabling small scale manufacturing.

Its central upstate location was advantageous for transportation from the east, for the city soon became a major stagecoach stop for travelers heading west. In 1837, the Chenango Canal was completed, connecting the city to the Erie Canal; the population was 2,000 in that year. In 1848, the New York and Erie Railroad opened in Binghamton, and by 1850, Binghamton's population had more than doubled from 1837 to about 5,000.

On April 9, 1867, Binghamton was incorporated as a city by an act of the New York State Legislature, and in 1870, the first pavement was laid in the city, and the population was about 13,000, again more than double from 1850.

During this period, the residents of the area coined the title "Valley of Opportunity" as it seemed that any entrepreneur with a vision and determination could succeed. In addition to the blessings from agriculture and transportation, Binghamton soon had successful companies manufacturing shoes and boots, tobacco products, scales, carriage hardware and trimmings. In 1889, a manufacturer of time pieces, the Bundy Manufacturing Company, was established near Binghamton. Over a century later, this company still is thriving and is better known as IBM. Ironically, IBM closed its last manufacturing operation in Endicott, one of the so-called "Triple Cities" that is downriver from Binghamton, in 2002, shortly after a large underground chemical plume, mostly composed of a trichloroethylene (a liquid cleaning agent linked to cancer and other illnesses) was discovered in Endicott, which was releasing (and continues to release) toxic gases into homes and offices in a 350-acre swath south of the former IBM facility.

With this surging economic growth in the area, the population exploded further, fueled by waves of immigrants from Italy, Poland, and Ireland, reaching about 40,000 in 1900, and continuing to expand in the first part of the 20th century to nearly 80,000 persons in 1930.

After World War Two, Binghamton's population continued to grow briefly, reaching its peak of slightly more than 80,000 persons in 1950. However, the economic engines that had powered the city for a hundred years were disappearing. Tobacco products, scales, agriculture, shoes. All mostly gone by 1960, and not replaced to any degree in the city.

However, the population of nearby communities, which either housed high tech companies, such as Endicott with IBM, or housed the high tech employees in new housing tracts, like Vestal, grew at the expense of aging Binghamton. By 1970, Binghamton's population had dropped to about 65,000, and the city's once flourishing retail stores began to close. The population decline has continued to this day as Binghamton in the 2010 Census reported about 47,000 residents. The city has lost almost half its population in sixty years, and its population is not much larger than in 1900.

So, that is why in 1975 with the city's businesses imploding and in an economy suffering a deep recession, I was sweating all summer long at the Chenango Valley

Warehouse with the ex-cons and the drunks. I finished working on Friday, August 22, 1975. The crew took me out for pizza and beer after work, and we all got drunk as skunks.

On Saturday, August 23, 1975, I wrote a letter to Boston College requesting an application for its graduate school.

On the following Monday, August 25, 1975, I began my final year of undergraduate education at SUNY-Binghamton. I was taking four courses: Survey of Math, American Poetry, Medieval History, and the class I looked forward to the most, Postwar British Literature. It was hardly a ballbuster schedule, but I had taken much more difficult course schedules earlier, so that I could coast a little in senior year and spend more time prepping for the upcoming GRE test in October. I only signed up for the math class because I had to; I needed a math class in order to graduate. Somehow I had done well in math in high school, but it was not my strongest subject matter.

After Labor Day, I began to get anxious about ML. I had not received the promised letter. Rationally, I knew that it would take several days for a letter to come from Boston, and that she had just returned, and needed time to check her schedule and the Boston Patriots schedule. Emotionally, I wanted that letter immediately, as it would provide confirmation that there was an interest on her part. I was on edge.

I was also on edge that September as it had become tense at home. Mary Kate and Owen were having problems; they were frequently arguing, mostly regarding his drinking, or his absences from home. Actually, it was Mary Kate arguing; Owen would just sit there with a vacant smile and suck on his scotch on the rocks. And, if Mary Kate was mad at anyone, she always ended up mad at me. I was an unfailing disappointment to her.

Mary Katherine O'Neill was born in Binghamton in 1923. She was one of three children: two girls, one boy, each born two years after the other. Mary Kate was the oldest, and therefore had the bitterest memories. Her father was a salesman for a shoe company, and his territory was upstate New York. He was an alcoholic, and when the Great Depression hit, her father increased his drinking as times got worse. Eventually, his liver failed, and he died a miserable, prolonged death in 1938.

Mary Kate's mother took care of the children and her husband as best she could. But being Irish, she also had an affinity for whiskey, and even when her husband died, she did not stop drinking. She lasted until 1941, when she also died from liver failure. When her mother passed, Mary Kate was a senior in high school. She had planned to attend a nursing college in Scranton, Pennsylvania, an hour south of Binghamton, but with the death of her mother, she was faced with the unenviable task of raising her two siblings and managing and paying for the rented house in West Binghamton. She found a job at IBM in nearby Endicott and rode the bus to and from Endicott every day for several years.

With her salary as a secretary, it seemed that Mary Kate was going to be able to pay the bills. But she wasn't. The parishioners at St. Patrick's Catholic Church would often bring food and clothing, at least for the first few years. To help pay for the house, and to afford a car, she took in some boarders: young, single, working women. Her brother joined the Army as soon as he could, and died in the Battle of the Bulge in late 1945. Her sister, Moira, was the baby; she graduated from high school in 1944, and moved to New York City with friends, later was married, and moved to Florida where she died in a head-on crash in 1965.

After her siblings graduated from high school, for the first time, Mary Kate started going out with her girlfriends to dances and clubs. She dated a few men, but nothing serious. She was promoted twice at IBM, and became a senior secretary, supporting a project manager of engineering.

In 1948, a girlfriend arranged a double date. My father, Jack Moran, was Mary Kate's date. They had seen each other around town, but had never actually met. They went to a movie on that first night, and then dinner. Apparently, there was an immediate attraction. From what I have been told, it was hard not to like my father.

Jack Moran was born in 1922, also in Binghamton, the first son of Patrick and Elizabeth Moran. He was followed by his brother Michael in 1924, and his sister Margaret in 1927. Jack was a big man: six feet one, and over two hundred pounds. He was the life of every party: a lovable, laughing Irishman, with a twinkle in his eye, a whiskey in his hand, and a joke to be told. He had been quite a football player at Binghamton North High School (one of two public high schools at the time in Binghamton). There had been some talk locally that he might get a football scholarship, but in the end, it did not happen. A crushing knee injury in his senior year ended that dream. He was devastated. After graduating from Binghamton North in 1939, he attended a local community college for a year, but didn't do well. He wasn't really interested in school.

So, Jack followed in the footsteps of his father, and joined the Binghamton Police Department in the fall of 1940. When World War Two began, due to his knee injury, he was unable to serve in World War Two. His younger brother Michael did join the Army, but perished at the Normandy landing in 1944.

Jack's combination of Irish charm and physical enforcement served him well as a cop, and he was well liked by his superiors. It didn't hurt that his father was a then-lieutenant of the BPD. When he and Mary Kate met, Jack was on the verge of becoming a sergeant, after only eight years on the force.

Jack and Mary Kate married in 1949 at St. Patrick's Church on a sunny June day. After a wedding reception in his parents' backyard at 20 Oliver Street on Binghamton's Irish Eastside, surrounded by relatives, neighbors, and friends, the happy couple honeymooned at Niagara Falls for a week, returned to Binghamton in the afterglow, and settled into their new life together. As my mother told me more than once, this period was the happiest time of her life. After the loss of her parents and her brother in the war, she longed to be a part of a family, and Jack's parents accepted her openly and treated her well.

In August of 1950, Mary Kate discovered that she was pregnant, and on April 1, 1951, she and Jack welcomed my sister Elizabeth (but soon known only as Lizzie) to the world. And the curtain came down on their bliss. A few months after she became pregnant, Mary Kate had left employment at IBM, as it was the company's policy to not employ pregnant women, and certainly not married women with children. With no work to interfere, she could devote her attention to Lizzie, and, it turned out, she needed to.

Shortly after she came home from Lourdes Hospital, Lizzie suffered from colic, crying uncontrollably and without cessation, mostly at night. Needing his sleep, Jack would try to sleep away from Lizzie, but in the small apartment they rented on the Westside of Binghamton, there was really no escape. He would often sleep at his parents' house just to get enough rest. Mary Kate suffered through Lizzie's torture as best she could, while sleep-walking through life. She later told me that she thought she would go insane on many a late night alone with the screaming child.

Lizzie's colic lasted for the better part of a year, and the once-happy parents were never quite as close again, as their love had been stretched too far, and never snapped back to full strength.

But life went on. Despite the loss of Mary Kate's income, the couple were living within their means, and saving money. In May of 1953, his father gave $2,000 to Jack, and my parents bought the house on 59 Vine Street on Binghamton's Southside.

On March 21, 1954, I was born. By all accounts, unlike my sister, I was a happy infant, and slept well. My sister welcomed me, and was proud of her baby brother.

In 1955, Jack was made a lieutenant, and his father had become a captain in 1950 (I always knew my grandfather as "The Captain" more than "Grampa"). Jack was on the fast track to become chief someday. I still have a black and white photo that was taken that night at our house where there was a celebration of his achievement. One of his parents must have been the photographer. In the aging photo, Mary Kate holds me, and a smiling Lizzie sits on Jack's lap. Jack holds a false smile, and his eyes are perceptibly glazed. He holds a glass of beer in his left hand away from Lizzie. His round face looks heavy, and his face has at an extra chin underneath. His hair is cut short, and the hairline is receding. I don't see any grey hair in the picture, but it's hard to tell. Mary Kate doesn't even have a pretense of a smile, she stares vacantly into the camera. While seated next to Jack, she slumps away from him, so that there is a distance between them. I never saw this photo growing up. Lizzie found it in a shoebox of photo's under Mary Kate's bed after she died.

There was no Christmas in 1958. Jack died on December 23, 1958. He was driving home from the BPD station late on December 22, and wrapped his 1953 Oldsmobile around a telephone pole on Court Street. Mary Kate later told me it had been sleeting that night, and he must have hit an icy patch, and perhaps was going too fast given the weather. After he was pried from his car, he was rushed to Lourdes Hospital. He received last rites at three o'clock in the afternoon on the twenty-third, and left us at five forty-five in the afternoon on that same day.

I have no memory of Jack—none. That saddens me now. Lizzie has a few memories, but those images have faded for her over time. I often wonder if she is the only person now alive that has any memory of Jack. That thought saddens me too.

My earliest memory is of Mary Kate and The Captain at our home, crying and holding each other after the funeral. It's odd how that is my first memory instead of a happier time. I suppose it must have been that as a child I was deeply moved, or frightened, by the sight of these two towering figures in my life so utterly distraught. The Captain was always an imperial, imposing figure in my young life, and I must have been shocked to see any display of emotion from him.

After Jack's death, Mary Kate soldiered on, just as she had done so before when her own parents had died. The Captain and Elizabeth tried to help her as much as they could, as did her friends. But it seems that she made a decision to build a wall in her life to keep emotion both from entering or escaping from her private prison. I know I cannot recall a single hug or kiss that I received as a child. After Mary Kate's death, I was surprised to find out from Lizzie that she also received no such sign of affection, but she was convinced this coldness had only started upon Jack's death.

While Mary Kate did receive a monthly pension from the City of Binghamton for Jack's service, she struggled to make ends meet with two small children. We were not Dickensian poor, but we led a simple life. Later, when I started elementary school, Mary Kate returned to work as a Kelly Girl—a temporary secretary, again at the now sprawling IBM plant in Endicott.

In June of 1965, Mary met Owen Williams at a picnic. Owen was a World War Two navy vet from Columbia, South Carolina. After the war, he had attended Georgia Tech and received a degree at electrical engineering. After graduating from Georgia Tech, he was hired by GE in its defense aircraft division, and ended up at GE's plant in nearby Johnson City, the other "Triple City" in the area. Owen designed wiring for fighter aircraft, and led a simple life. He had never been married when he met Mary Kate at that picnic. He was forty years old.

Neither Lizzie nor I were happy to see Owen enter our lives. To us, he was a redneck Baptist with a hick accent.

He also liked to drink scotch, and would frequently visit our house carrying a scotch bottle with him. Since Mary Kate did not drink, we were unfamiliar with alcohol in our house, and were surprised by Mary Kate's tolerance of Owen's drinking, as she had always made negative comments about alcohol and drunks to us (The Captain's taste for Jameson's whisky was excepted from her rants).

I was very uncomfortable watching Owen cuddle Mary Kate, and her laughing at his banal jokes. One late night, I slipped out of bed, crept down the stairs from my second floor bedroom upstairs until I could peek around the corner to see our living room, and in disbelief watched them passionately kissing on the couch. I could only bear to watch for a brief moment, and then stealthily crawled back to my room. It took a long time that night to fall asleep, as I was traumatized by the horror of what I had just seen.

"I don't want to know!" Lizzie screamed at me the next day in her room when I tried to tell her what I had seen the night before. "It's gross!"

We shouldn't have been too surprised when Mary Kate sat us down at the kitchen table in October and told us that she and Owen were going to marry in six weeks. Lizzie and I both ended up crying. Mary Kate tried to console us at first, but, as we continued to resist, her anger kicked. "What are you two crying about? This is going to be better for us all. Mr. Williams has a nice job, and can take care of us. And try to think about your poor mother. You think it's been easy trying to raise you two on a secretary's salary and that crummy city pension? Well, do you?"

"No," we stiffly replied.

"It hasn't been, believe you me. You should be thankful for what you have. You're mighty lucky to have a parent looking out for you two. You know I had nobody when I was nearly your age, Lizzie. I expect you two to treat Mr. Williams as well as you treat me."

Through her sniffling, Lizzie asked, "Do we have to move to his house, Mom?"

"No, Mister Williams has agreed to move here because he knew it would be very hard on you and John to leave your friends and schools. That shows you the kind of man Mr. Williams is. You should thank him for that."

So, six weeks later on November 29, 1965, Mary Kate and Owen married in a small wedding at St. John the Evangelist Catholic Church just off Vestal Avenue on the Southside of Binghamton. Since Owen was Baptist, he had to agree in writing to raise us, and any other children resulting from the marriage, as Catholics, in order for the marriage to be consecrated in a Catholic church.

I uncomfortably walked Mary Kate down the aisle, at her insistence. I had told her I didn't think it was such a good idea, but she persisted, and her threats ended my resistance effectively. It was a sparsely attended wedding, a few friends and relatives for both bride and groom, and mercifully short. There was a wedding reception at a local restaurant. Owen was in a good mood, fortified by scotch, Mary Kate was proper and composed, accepting the congratulations of the few attendees with detached grace. For their honeymoon, they flew to Miami, and stayed at the Fontainebleau Hotel.

While they did not attend the wedding, The Captain and

Elizabeth agreed to house Lizzie and me while the happy couple was honeymooning. Lizzie and I received one post card each from Mary Kate written in obvious haste, saying little more than they were having fun and would see us soon.

After the sunburned couple returned from Miami, our house at 59 Vine Street was a home filled with buried anger. Lizzie and I were angry with Mary Kate for disrupting the civil harmony that had existed before; we were also hostile to Owen for colonizing our mother. Mary Kate grew increasingly angry with the two of us for not supporting her marriage and for our barely disguised contempt for Owen.

Lizzie had begun her freshman year at CC that September of 1965, and, after the wedding, she directed all of her energy into being out of the house as much as possible. She joined clubs at school, acted in plays, ran for student government. When she turned sixteen, she started working at the Woolworths Store in downtown Binghamton. She had an active social life and a boyfriend her last two years of high school. Her grades, which had been good in grade school, improved greatly in high school. She ended up earning a Regent's Scholarship, and chose Saint John's University in New York City as her college. She and Mary Kate were never close again, and rarely spoke, and when she did visit on her rare forays home, the conversations were brittle and forced. Lizzie did not believe in forgiveness.

I also tried to spend as much time out of the house as possible. When not at school, I would be with Tip, either at his house, or riding our bicycles around Binghamton, in search of new adventures. When I was at home, I would usually close the door to my room and read. I watched much less

TV at home. If I wanted to watch one of my favorite television shows, like *Star Trek*, I would watch it at Tip's house in
the furnished basement with its color TV.

Owen seemed content for the first few years, and I believe
he actually did not know of our quiet revolt. He floated
through life with the same goofy, vacant smile. During the
week, he would have one or two scotches after getting home
from work, and after dinner, he would retreat to the family
room, and stare at the TV, while nodding off, before finally
stumbling to bed. On the weekends, the one or two would
triple, and his face would turn crimson, the southern accent
more pronounced, and his already loud laugh would rever-
berate around the house.

To his credit, Owen never tried to be our dad. Oh, he
would invite me to go fishing with him (and I sometimes did),
but he did not force himself upon us. He never yelled at either
Lizzie or me. He never interfered in an argument between
Mary Kate and either of us. He never demanded respect. Over
time, I grew to appreciate him, and even to pity him. He was a
good man who was dealt a hand that could not be won.

As we retreated from Mary Kate, she responded by walling
herself off from us. With her free time from not being forced
to work, she reached out to her friends, and joined a bridge
club and a garden club. She signed up to take classes at the
local junior college, Broome Community College, to obtain
an associate degree in business administration. She became
more active at St. John the Evangelist Church, and became
a Red Cross volunteer. She read our report cards diffidently.
She refused to pour Owen a drink, and noticeably frowned
on his scotch habit, but over time, she was resigned to it.

Lizzie graduated with honors from CC in 1969, and left for St. Johns in late August. Fifty-nine Vine Street became even chillier: we acted our parts, and no more.

I started my freshman year at CC in the fall of 1968, beginning my mad crush on ML. Four years later, in late May of 1972, on a hot and humid night, I graduated from CC, barely making the top ten percent of the class. Despite my fear of being drafted that had worried me in high school, the draft ended in my senior year, and I could focus on college without worrying about being conscripted and sent to Vietnam. Cornell University was my first choice to go to college, but I was not accepted there. I was accepted at Syracuse, Lemoyne University (also in Syracuse), Colgate University, and SUNY-Binghamton (now Binghamton University). After being rejected by Cornell, I decided to attend Colgate. I had been deeply impressed by the beauty of the campus and the small college town of Hamilton. It also seemed to have a very fine English program, my major of choice.

Mary Kate did not push any school or plan for me. She would ask me what my plan was, or where I was thinking about going, but she took no active role in the decision process. I was on my own. She did tell me that if I went to Colgate, loans would be needed, as the money she had set aside for college would not last four years. Like Lizzie, I had also earned a Regent's Scholarship, which forced me to look at colleges in New York to receive the scholarship money.

After graduating from CC, I worked in the summer of 1972 for the Binghamton Parks and Recreation department, helping the maintenance crews with mowing the grass, picking weeds, trimming bushes, etcetera, at City properties. It was boring and mindless, but it permitted me the freedom to be out of the house all day, and then hang out with my friends at night. The drinking age was eighteen in New York then, so after graduation, I discovered the many bars in Binghamton. I also discovered Rolling Rock beer, and we soon became close friends.

Two months before I was to leave for Colgate, I stumbled home from a Parks and Recreation happy hour, and I fell onto the bed. I turned onto my back, and contemplated my future. I heard Mary Kate's footsteps climb the creaking stairs to the second floor. After a moment, she entered my room.

"I heard you come in."

"I went to dinner with the crew from work."

"You smell like a brewery," she snorted.

"C'mon, Mom."

"John, you know I don't approve you drinking at all. I am not happy about it."

"You don't seem to mind Owen's scotch."

"He is an adult and can choose how he wants to live. You are still a child living in my house. And I don't like it."

"Mom, I'm legal. If I can go to Vietnam and die over there, I am old enough to have a goddamn beer."

"Don't swear at me, young man."

I said, "Aw, jeez," and put a pillow over my face.

She stormed to my side, and ripped the pillow off, "You think I like to see you come home drunk?"

"Mom, I'm not drunk."

"You look like something the cat dragged in. If you keep going down this path, bad things are going to happen."

"Mom, just be thankful I'm not smoking pot."

"Who's smoking pot? Do you know anybody smoking pot? Is that Tip smoking pot?"

He was, but I wasn't going to tell her that.

She kept going. "How you can hang out with that bum is beyond me. He's never going to amount to anything."

I'd heard this speech before, but was too tired (intoxicated?) to fight.

"Mom, please, I gotta go to sleep. I have to work tomorrow. Can you give it a rest?"

She silently fumed for a moment, almost quivering in her disgust. She turned and walked out of my room, leaving with a final blast, "I just wish your father was here!"

Yeah, me too. I got up and walked to my door, and closed it, hearing the sounds of her angry footsteps going back down the stairs.

One week later on a Saturday morning in late June of 1972, I woke up about eleven and stumbled downstairs to the kitchen. Mary Kate was seated at the kitchen table, pensively drinking coffee.

"Morning," I said, as I walked to a cabinet to retrieve a box of Cheerios.

"Good Morning, John," she said without emotion.

I set the Cheerios on the table, then grabbed a bowl and spoon from another cabinet, and brought them back to the table. I headed to the refrigerator to get milk.

"What time did you get in last night?"

I opened the refrigerator door. "It was late."

"It was actually four ten. I heard you come in."

I yanked the milk out of the refrigerator and closed the door.

She continued. "I don't know how you can stay out that late. The bars close at three."

Sitting down, I said, "We went to the Park Diner for a snack afterwards." I filled the bowl with Cheerios.

She sipped her coffee, set the cup down, and shook her head. "John, you have to change. It's just not healthy what you are doing. Getting up at the crack of dawn to work, and then staying out all night. It's just not healthy."

I took a large helping of Cheerios and forced them into my mouth. I crunched them as loudly as I could.

"You're eighteen now, and you think that you know a lot. But you don't, John. You really don't. I know how it is. I was eighteen once. Of course, I had to actually work and take care of a family when I was eighteen. You and your sister have it so much easier. You have no idea. Really."

I ate in silence, staring at the Cheerios box.

She sighed, "Cat got your tongue?"

I stammered, "I'm eating."

"Look, John, you're not a bad kid, and you've done well in school. You're more mature than your friends. I know that. I just think you are capable of achieving a lot in your life. I want to see you succeed. I don't want to see you fall into the traps that are out there. Can you look at me? Is that so bad?"

I looked up at her. "No, it's not bad, Mom."

"I've been doing some thinking, John, about college. You want to go to graduate school after college, right?"

"Yea, if I can."

"I've been looking at our finances, John, and for you to go to graduate school, you're absolutely going to have to take on a loan. Probably a big loan. And you'll have to pay that back for years after you get out."

"I know. A lot of people do that."

"If you went to SUNY-Binghamton instead of Colgate, we could save a lot of money, and that money could be used towards your grad school costs."

"I don't wanna go to SUNY-B, Mom. It's like a high school with ashtrays."

"It's a good school. Everybody I talk to says it is a real good school."

"I just don't wanna go there. I want to go someplace different. Someplace fun."

"I would like you to go to SUNY-Binghamton, John. It's in your best interest."

I was getting agitated, "Why should I go there? Lizzie didn't have to go to SUNY-B. She got to go St. Johns where she wanted to go to."

"Yes, and she's gonna have to pay off the loans she took out to do it, and she's not going to grad school."

"I'm going to Colgate."

She sipped from her coffee, set the cup down, and rubbed her forehead, then said, "John, if you go to SUNY-Binghamton, then I will give you my car. Please change your mind."

I was dumbstruck. Her car? I loved THAT car: a baby-blue 1965 Ford Galaxie 500 convertible. She rarely let me drive it. But it was beautiful, a work of art, especially with the top down. "You'd give me the Galaxie 500? It would be mine completely? That's what you're promising?"

She sighed, "Yes, John, the Galaxie 500 would be yours."

With that, she had me. She had played the game well; she identified my weak spot and took advantage of it. Over that weekend I typed up a letter to Colgate, informing the school that I was declining admission, and then the next week I contacted SUNY-Binghamton, and told them that I was indeed coming as a freshman.

And, so that is how I ended up at SUNY-B. In my first semester, I quickly realized the mistake I had made. It didn't take long to hate SUNY-B, mostly because I was a "townie" in a school predominated by students from New York City or Long Island who lived on campus, and were not particularly friendly to the rubes from upstate New York. I felt like an alien. Only a handful of CC graduates went to SUNY-B, and none of them were my close friends.

The only positive to my first year at SUNY-B was that my acne gradually improved over the course of that first year (and was almost completely gone by the fall of '75).

Lizzie graduated from St. John's in May of 1973, and did not return to Binghamton, staying in New York City. She lived with girlfriends in Manhattan and got a job at Macy's as a clerk. She rarely came home after graduating, usually for a holiday, and didn't stay long. She would call Mary Kate occasionally, but the calls were short and perfunctory.

Freshman year dragged into sophomore year and then junior year. The length of my hair got longer each year despite Mary Kate's biting remarks. Each day at SUNY-B seemed the same during the school year: wake up about eight, drive to school on another grey cold morning, attend classes until three or so, either hit the library afterwards for a few hours or play pick-up basketball in the SUNY-B gym, drive home, eat a silent dinner with Mary Kate and Owen, retreat to my room to study, or lose myself in my rock music, emerge about ten o'clock for a snack and then TV (a movie on WOR in New York City, or The Tonight Show with Johnny Carson on NBC, or the Dick Cavett Show on ABC), climb upstairs to bed and read some more, and then doze off to begin again.

On the weekends, I would hit the Binghamton bars on Friday, study at the SUNY-B Library on Saturday, hit the bars again on Saturday night, and lounge around the house on Sunday, watching sports on TV with Owen. My mother had no interest in sports, not even the sports I played in high school. I recall her attending our sectional basketball championship game in my senior year, but that is it.

It was a depressing existence, and the generally dreary Binghamton weather only added to my dour spirits.

I lived for the holidays and the summer. I worked at the Parks and Recreation department in the summer in 1973 and 1974 as well, saving a nice chunk of funds. I partied with classmates returning from school, played a lot of basketball, and stayed away from 59 Vine Street as much as possible. The Galaxie 500's top was down every day it wasn't raining, and I felt like a BMOC (big man on city). Carefree, young, and cool; what a great combination.

And then came August of 1975, and my chance encounter with ML in The Pine Lounge, and my world was turned upside down.

On Saturday of the Labor Day weekend of 1975, I met Tip at The Pine Lounge. I had not seen him since our evening with ML and Ann. I called him during the week, and he agreed to meet me. He was seated on his usual stool at the bar. He had a half-empty Rolling Rock in front of him, and was smoking a cigarette. A pack of Lucky Strikes sat next to the Rolling Rock. I had never seen him smoke before, except for pot.

"What the hell is this?" I said, grabbing the Lucky Strike pack as I sat on the empty stool next to him.

"Hey, JM, how's it hanging? Where you been? I'm ahead of you by two."

"I'll catch up, wise guy. What's with the cigarette?"

"I've decided to pick up another bad habit. I don't have enough of them. Can you dig it?" He tapped his Rock on the bar, and yelled, "Hey, Mack, bring JM here a Rolling Rock!"

"C'mon, Tip, cigarettes?" I threw the Lucky Strike pack on the bar. "Man, that's for losers."

"Well, I'm a loser, aren't I?"

"Tip, don't be ridiculous. I don't think Ann thought you were a loser last weekend. Huh, c'mon, fess up to that action."

"Hey, get bent. We just messed around, man."

"Yeah, sure. That's not what I heard. You didn't take her back to your place, did you?"

"Yeah, but first we did it in her car."

"Oh, man, that is so high school."

"Listen to you busting my balls." He tapped his Rock on the bar again. "Hey, Mack, can we get a beer down here? In fact, make it two beers."

Mack was talking to a couple of guys at the other end of the beer. He looked our way, and gave the finger to Tip.

"Hey, look, JM, I'm still number one with Mack!" He

stubbed out his cigarette in an ashtray on the bar, and then chugged down the remainder of the Rolling Rock, finishing with a loud, "Ah! Man, that's good shit!"

"So, you gonna get together with Ann again, lover boy?" I asked.

"What the fuck, JM? What do you think? It was a one shot deal. She's back at Columbia now."

Mack set two Rolling Rocks in front of us. "Two bucks, assholes."

I reached to pull my wallet out of my back pocket. "Lemme get this one, Tip."

Tip pushed my arm away. "I got this one. I'm the working man, and I got paid today. You're just a poor college kid." He pulled a wad of money from his shirt pocket, extracted a five, and threw it on the bar towards Mack. "There you go, don't keep the change."

Mack snorted, "Fuck you, O'Neill, and the horse you rode in on." He reached into his pocket and pulled out three dollars and dropped them on the bar in front of us, and walked away.

Tip laughed, "That is one beautiful human being."

We grabbed our Rocks and tapped them. I said, "Here's to you and Ann."

"Fuck you," Tip said.

We drank heartily.

Tip then tapped my Rock again. "And here's to you and ML."

He drank. I didn't. "There's nothing there, Tip."

"Yeah, sure, I saw how she was crawling all over you. She was more horny than Ann. C'mon, tell me you scored that action. With the best looking fox in Binghamton. Please tell me you scored."

"She was drunk, Tip. I couldn't do it."

"You have got to be fuckin' joshing me. Major bummer. That was your big chance, man. You been after that trim your whole life. How often is she in town? You are such a dumb ass."

"Tip, I couldn't take advantage of her like that. It wouldn't have been right."

"Jeez, listen to you. What am I, a fuckin' confessional? You are such a loser." He tapped my Rock again. "So, let's drink to two losers." He drank, and this time so did I.

So, we two losers proceeded to tie one on, first at The Pine Lounge, and then later I drove him to Thirsty's Tavern on Vestal Avenue on the Southside, another old stomping ground. Things got weird there. We drank a shot of Jameson's in honor of Eamon de Valera, the first President of the Republic of Ireland, who had died the day before. The shots tasted so smooth, we had another. Then, followed the two shots with plenty of Rocks too. Sometime after midnight, I went to the restroom, weaving my way past the pool table and then the Pong machine.

When I returned to the bar, Tip and an older drunk guy were yelling at each other, and being restrained by a couple of bouncers. Tip was ferociously trying to break free from the bouncer, and was cursing him. I tried to calm Tip down, but he was all worked up. The older drunk guy kept pointing at Tip, and repeatedly yelling, "Asswipe." Each time, he yelled, Tip got more enraged. Finally, the bouncer had enough, and forcibly pushed Tip to the door, past tables. Tip resisted, and yelled every swear word he knew (and he knew them all) at the older drunk guy, and then the bouncer.

The bouncer pushed Tip out the door, nearly striking a couple of girls who were about to enter. "Now chill, man!"

"You fuckin' asshole! Come on outta there, and I'll kick your ass! You big pansy!"

The bouncer was staring Tip down, he was about six three and two forty. He had been a lineman for Binghamton North a few years before. He would have torn Tip to shreds.

"C'mon, Tip, let's go," I pulled him away. "He ain't worth it."

"Listen to your friend, buddy-boy," the bouncer barked.

"I ain't afraid of you!" Tip screamed at the bouncer. I jerked him away from the angry glare of the bouncer.

I directed Tip to the Galaxie 500 with him resisting, and convinced him to get in, and then I walked to the driver's side, and got in as well. "What the hell happened?" I asked.

"That old drunk pushed me, and didn't say sorry. What the hell kind of a world is it where a fuckin' drunk can't say he's sorry? You know, I could kill that bouncer."

"Sure you could. You and what army?"

"I could blow his fuckin' brains out. That'd show that fucker."

"Yeah, sure, let's go get your bazooka and blow Thirsty's up."

"Let's go!" he barked.

I started the car, and pulled out of Thirsty's parking lot. As I turned onto Washington Street, heading for the Washington Street Bridge back across the Susquehanna, I asked the silent, fuming Tip, "Where to? The Park Diner? The Pine Lounge for a nightcap?"

He said, "Nobody pushes me around like that. Take me home. I'm gonna get my shotgun and come back and blow that fucker away."

I laughed, "Oh, yeah, your little BB gun is going to scare him."

"I'm not talking about my BB gun. I've got a double barreled shotgun at my apartment, and I'm ready to use it."

I realized he was serious. "Where did you get a shotgun?"

He smiled. "I took it from The Big Asshole's house. He doesn't even know."

"The Big Asshole" was his nickname for his dad. Things had gone awry between them after Tip's accident and his father's later remarriage.

"Tip, what do you need a shotgun for?"

"Protection. I live in a dangerous neighborhood."

"Don't be ridiculous. You live in Binghamton, not the Bronx."

"Just get me home. Then we'll pick up the shotgun, and head back. Maybe I'll blow the windows out. Now that would be funny."

Even in my alcohol haze, I could muster enough brain cells to know I had to dump Tip.

When we neared Tip's garage apartment, he ordered, "Pull up by the staircase, and turn the lights off."

I turned the car into his uncle's driveway, killed the car lights, and inched near the stairs leading to his garage apartment.

He barked, "Don't turn the car off. I'll go get it, you wait here."

"Tip, give it a rest. Thirsty's isn't worth it. It makes no

sense."

He punched me on the shoulder. "Does anything make sense? Does my life make any sense? I'm a fuckin' loser and I have no chance with my fuckin' leg. But I WILL NOT be treated like a chump by that prick! I'm gonna show him! Now are you my friend, or are you just another asshole? Huh?" He punched me again, a little harder this time, and spewed: "Huh, are you? Are you with me, Moron, or not?"

To placate him, I said, "OK, let's do it. Stop hitting me."

He got out. "I'll be right back."

I watched him limp to the base of the stairs, and struggle up them, dragging that right leg. I waited until he opened the door to the apartment. Then I slammed the car into drive and floored it out of the driveway, hitting the curb on the back of the Galaxie 500 near the muffler. Without looking for traffic I emerged on Beethoven Avenue. Luckily there was no traffic at that hour. Turning the car lights on, I raced away. I actually hunched over as if expecting the blast of a shotgun through my back window. My heart was pounding as I drove away. I kept looking in the rearview mirror, but didn't see Tip.

In a few minutes, I reached the intersection of Beethoven Avenue and Riverside Drive, across from the Lourdes Hospital complex. Instead of turning left and heading home, I turned right onto Riverside Drive.

I slowed down as I neared ML's house at 200 Riverside Drive, finally stopping in front of her house. There was no traffic in either direction at that late hour. I stared at the dark house and remembered what had happened two weeks ago. Could it only have been two weeks? I was overcome by profound longing. As I sat there looking at her front door, I had a sudden memory pop in my head that I had repressed for years, and I shivered. A car's headlights popped in my rearview mirror, and I slowly drove away and headed home. But I was accompanied by an awful memory of my senior year at CC.

Earlier in our senior year, ML and I were inducted into the newly formed National Honor Society at CC, and after a short election period, she was voted president and I was voted vice-president. Both titles carried little weight. Our meetings were infrequent, and there was little fund-raising considered. However, early in our last semester of senior year, ML decided that the NHS had to conduct an event that would be unlike anything that the other organizations at CC had ever done. Her idea was to organize a bus trip to New York City to see Fiddler on the Roof in early April of 1972. And that is what NHS did. We sold tickets at lunch time, we put up poster board announcements in the hallways, we had information about the trip included in the morning announcements. Despite the cost, we somehow filled up a bus, and got a couple of teachers to chaperone.

Of course, none of my jock friends would be caught dead going on a bus trip with the NHS, or see some stupid Broadway play. Tip was off in his own world then, and just laughed when I asked him to come. Ann had a family commitment and could not make the trip either.

I sat next to ML on the way to New York City and in the Broadway Theater. I actually enjoyed the musical more than I thought I would, but it was probably because I was seated next to ML, drinking in the joy of just being in her universe.

I remembered ML singing "Sunrise, Sunset" on the way back to our bus. On the four- hour trip home, she fell asleep, and after a while, her head rested against my shoulder. I looked down and saw that beautiful long white-blond hair, smelling faintly of lemons, nuzzled against my shoulder. I could see her chest moving rhythmically as she breathed, and my desire for her was overwhelming. When she awoke as we neared CC, she yawned and apologized for using me as a pillow. I assured her it was OK.

After that trip my teenage crush developed into an obsession. She was all I could think about or fantasize over. When I saw her, my heart would race, and my face would flush. I couldn't help myself. It was intoxicating, but incredibly frustrating.

I had heard through the teenage grapevine that ML and her jock boyfriend had broken up, again. Hearing that news, I knew that I had to ask ML to our senior prom scheduled for late May, just before graduation. Normally, guys at CC would ask girls to the prom about two to three weeks before the big date. But I didn't want to wait to be aced out by someone else. I decided to strike first.

But then self-doubt would envelop me; she had NEVER expressed any interest in me. When I looked in the mirror, and saw those whiteheads on my face, it was a blow to my ML fantasy. I wavered in my plan. Each day at CC was more torture as I sat behind her, and thought about going to the prom with her, and being the envy of every guy at school, but unable to see how I actually could ask her.

I never told anyone, including Tip, of my plans. At that

point, he was just going through the motions of graduating, and becoming more withdrawn as graduation neared.

Finally, I couldn't stand my fear anymore, and decided that if I didn't make my move, someone else would ask her. Early in the evening on Friday, May 1, 1972, I left our house, and walked down hilly Vine Street until I reached Vestal Avenue, and walked to the enclosed pay phone next to the Rexall drugstore on the other side of Vestal Avenue. I closed the door, and sat there for a few minutes, gathering courage and rehearsing the phone call. I put a quarter in the phone, and dialed her number that I had written on a piece of notebook paper.

After two rings, a female voice answered. It was her younger sister, Cathy. I was dripping with sweat in that enclosed box.

I asked, "Is Mary Lou there?"

"Yes, she is. Who's calling?"

"John Moran."

"Oh, hi. Let me get her. She's upstairs."

My heart was pounding. It was like a drumbeat in my ears.

Then ML picked up the phone. "Hello?"

"Hi, ML, this is John."

"Oh, hi, John, How ya doing?"

"Good. Really good. What are you up to?"

"Ann and I are going to the movies in about a half hour. You wanna come?"

"Oh, thanks, no. I kinda have something to ask you."

"What?"

"I heard at school that you and Tony broke up, and I

was just wondering if you would like to go the prom with me this year."

I was now drenched with sweat. There was a pause that seemed forever.

"Wow. This is a surprise, John."

"I know it's a little early, but just thought I would ask."

"Gosh, that is so nice of you. But I am going to the prom with Tony. I'm sorry."

"Oh. OK. I guess I had bad info."

"Yeah. I don't know who you heard that from but you can let them know."

"I will. OK, well, this is kind of uncomfortable. I'd better let you go."

"Yeah, I do have to get ready still."

"Have a good weekend. I'll see you next week at school."

"Yeah. I'm sorry, John. Thanks for asking."

"Yeah. OK. Good-bye."

"Bye."

I slammed the phone into the receiver in frustration. My skin was soaked in sweat. I flung open the phone booth door, and felt a rush of cool air flow into the booth. I numbly sat there for a few minutes as I beat myself up for being such a putz. After the appropriate period of self-punishment, I slowly walked home.

As I walked into CC on the following Monday, I dreaded seeing ML. I didn't have to wait long as she was in my Advanced Biology class. I got to the class early, and pretended to intently study the notes from the last class, keeping my head down, although I was actually watching the classroom door out of the corner of my eye. So I only saw her lithe legs enter the classroom, and walk towards me. I heard her say, "Hi, John," and I looked up, but she had already passed me by, as I blurted out a feeble "Hi." She sat in the back of the classroom a few rows away. I was miserable, and thought everybody in the class must have known and was having a good laugh.

After that, I avoided her every chance I could, and she wasn't seeking me out either. Our relationship had changed; my stupid move had led to misery and despair.

On Friday of that week, I drove Tip and myself in my mother's Galaxie 500 to a gathering of key senior boys at "Tiny" Wheeler's house. His real name was Mark but everybody at CC called him Tiny because he was biggest lineman on CC's football team. Tiny was built like a fireplug with a bowling ball for a head, standing six feet and weighing two forty. His parents were out of town for the weekend. The stated purpose of the gathering was to plan the "senior skip day" that had been the talk of the locker room for months. But it turned out that there was another purpose, much to my humiliation.

There were a couple of kegs in the garage, and the beer was flowing. When Tip and I arrived, most of the guys were pretty well in the bag. We poured a couple of beers and made our way to the family room, where guys were spread out. For a while it was fun, as insults were traded and ridiculous stories about our teachers were told. At some point I ended up on the couch with my back to the wall, and the room entrance in front of me. After an hour or so, and after I had drunk two beers, things changed.

Tiny stood up, holding a full cup of beer. He was lit, and addressed the room. "Wait a minute. Wait a minute. I got news for you."

Someone yelled out, "What the fuck you talking about?"

Tiny looked around the crowded family room, and then pointed at me. "You. Moron." He shook his finger at me. "Who heard about what Moron did?"

The room exploded in shouts. Tiny continued, "This fucking douchebag asked Mary Lou Mooney to the prom!"

The shouts were directed at me: "Are you fucking kidding me?", "Asshole," "You are a moron."

Tip was sitting across the room from me. He stood up, shook his head, and said, "Tell me that isn't true, JM?"

Tiny spilled some beer from his cup, and moved to me. "Tell him, Moron. Tell us all."

I was surrounded and had no choice, "Yeah, I asked her. She said no. End of story."

The room erupted in laughter, and more insults directed my way: "Asshole," "Moron," "Douche bag."

Tiny moved menacingly closer to me, "I think Moron has got a big crush on the best-looking girl in Binghamton. Isn't that right, Moron?"

I should have been smart enough to laugh it off, or agree with him, but the two beers and being cornered caused me to lash out. "Your mother. Fuck you, Tiny, and the horse you rode in on."

I could see right away that was the opening that the small brain of Tiny was seeking. He smirked, and looked around the room, and said, "Did you hear that, guys, Moron told me to go fuck myself. What do we do with a wussy that has a big crush on a girl? Why, we help them out. Get the ropes!"

Realizing that something ugly was happening, I quickly stood, but, before I could move, Tiny threw me back on the couch. "Hold him!"

The football jocks on either side of me grabbed a hold of my arms, and despite my struggles, I could not move.

Tip stood up, and said, "Let him go, Tiny. He's a chump."

Tiny turned to Tip, "Go smoke some pot, Tip. That's what you do best anyway."

Tip looked at Tiny for a moment, hesitated, looked back at me and then walked out of the room, saying, "I want nothing to do with this."

As he left, a couple of other guys walked into the room, carrying ropes. Then I was thrown to the floor, fighting to break free, but unable to do so, as there were too many of them. I pleaded with them to let me go, but the pack was looking for a victim and I was it.

Soon, they had me hog tied, and carried me out to Tiny's car, and they forced me into the backseat. I kept yelling obscenities at them, and that only fired them up more, as they were laughing, pointing at me.

A few moments later, Tiny got into his car, along with his best buddy, Butch Skeen, another lineman. Tiny started up the car, and drove away from the house. Butch rode shotgun. Led Zeppelin's "Stairway To Heaven" burst forth from the radio.

"Where you taking me?" I yelled.

"You'll see, Moron. We're just going to help your love life. Aren't we, Butch?" He and Butch laughed as they drank their beers in the front seat.

At that point, I began to get scared, as I thought about what these jerks might be up to. Dropping me off a bridge into the Susquehanna? Dumping me in the woods somewhere? Burying me alive?

But within a few minutes, the car stopped, and Tiny and Butch got out. I heard them speaking quietly to other guys. Then, a door to the backseat was opened, and I was rudely jerked from the car, with my tightly bound legs landing on a street. I could see that Tiny's car and another car were parked on a street, and there were about ten CC football players around me, most of them intoxicated. Butch was holding my shoulders.

I cried out, "Help, Help me."

Butch put his hand over my mouth, and said, "Shut up, Moron. Who's got the washcloth?"

One of the guys handed him a washcloth, and he forced it into my mouth, despite me shaking my head violently.

I was picked up by most of the group and they started to hurry to our destination. I couldn't tell where we were for a few moments. After a minute, someone yelled out to stop. They stood holding me, panting, and laughing. I hated them all. I silently cursed each one of them, and planned to extract my revenge on them.

We started forward again, with more urgency. From my point of view, I could really only see the sky and trees, but I could tell we were crossing a busier street, with more street-lights, and then I could see the outline of the second story of a house as we got near. My heart sank as I realized that it was ML's house.

They hurried as they neared the front door, and then suddenly I was lowered down on the top step right by the front door. As I landed roughly on the concrete step, I started to struggle with the ropes that held me. My kidnappers dashed away, laughing as they disappeared from view. I saw them run across Riverside Drive onto a side street and then disappear from view.

Despite my struggles, I could not loosen the tight bonds. I started to wiggle like a snake shedding its skin, at least trying to get away from that front door. I could see a light shining out of the front room nearest the door. I dreaded discovery and the resulting humiliation. As I slowly inched my way to the edge of the top step, I saw a figure limp across Riverside Drive and make its way to me. It was Tip, of course.

As he reached me, he held his finger to his mouth, telling me to be quiet. He gingerly removed the washcloth from my mouth. Then he pulled a pocket knife from his pants, opened it, and quickly cut the ropes that were binding my feet, and then my legs.

He whispered, "Let's go." He hurried away from the house, and I followed him, my arms and hands still bound. We crossed Riverside Drive, and made our way to the side street where Tiny had parked his car. But the cars and the jocks were gone.

We stopped running; I was winded. Tip cut the rest of the rope, and we tossed the rope and the washcloth into some bushes near us.

"Oh, man, thanks, Tip. You saved my ass."

"You're fucking welcome."

"How did you know where I was?"

"I figured out what these pea brains were up to. They're football players; they ain't very smart."

"I am going to get each one of them, Tip. I'm going to get them back for this."

"No, you're not, JM. You're going to take this and forget about it."

"That's easy for you to say. You weren't just kidnapped and dropped on ML's porch."

"Forgot about these assholes. In a month, we'll never see them again. Besides, the joke's on them. They're going to go prank call her house and tell her to look on the porch, and you won't be there."

He threw his thumb out, "C'mon, let's go."

"Where we going?"

"To go pick up your car, dummy."

We started to walk back to Tiny's place but we walked cautiously, looking out for the jocks to return.

As we walked in the shadows, Tip asked, "Why didn't you tell me that you asked ML to the prom?"

"Because she shot me down. Besides, you haven't exactly been around much lately."

"Why would you even think about asking her? She's so far out of your league it isn't funny."

"We're good friends. I thought she might want to go."

"You were thinking with your dick and not with your head. You got a Regent's scholarship for God's sake, you should be smarter than that. Man, when tonight gets out at CC, it's going to be tough. I hope you're up for it."

"Thanks for your support."

"Hey, who rescued you just now? Me!"

"Yeah. Thanks, Tip. You saved my ass on that one."

"Damn right, I did."

We walked in silence for a few minutes. A car's headlights came around a corner towards us, and we dashed off the sidewalk and hid behind some maple trees. After the car passed harmlessly by, we moved back to the sidewalk, and continued our march to Tiny's house.

When we reached Tiny's street, we surveyed it from the corner, looking to see if any of the jocks were lurking outside. We didn't see any, so we cautiously hurried to the Galaxie 500. Reaching the Galaxie 500, I unlocked the car, we jumped in, and peeled out.

I dreaded going to CC on Monday, and thought about having Mary Kate call in sick, but I decided I had to face the school eventually, so I went. As I walked to my locker on that morning, I could feel eyes watching me, and hear snickers, even if they never happened.

Whenever I would bump into one of the jocks as I made my way to class, they would yell out, "Hey, it's lover-boy Moron," or, "Hey, Moron, got a date for the prom yet?" Even the lowly freshmen would chuckle at these outbursts. I was humiliated.

I didn't see ML until third period. She was waiting outside of our World History classroom, and stopped me. She shook her head, "I heard you were on my porch Friday night."

"Not by choice."

"So I heard. Everybody thinks I helped you out."

"I had other help."

"John, how could you let those guys do that to you?"

"There were more of them than me. Tiny can be pretty persuasive at two hundred forty pounds."

She sighed, "Assholes." She held her books tighter and said, "We should go to class." She turned and walked into the classroom. After a moment's pause, I followed her. I could feel all eyes in the room watching ML and me as we walked to open seats and sat down.

For the rest of the school year, ML and I were cordial, but there was a distance between us. She didn't seek me out any longer, or share a joke or story, or smile when I approached her. I was crushed and heartbroken. I didn't go the senior prom; I couldn't overcome my fear and humiliation to ask another girl. ML went with her boyfriend; Ann went with Butchie (and was I mad at her for that!); and Tip went with the easiest girl in the sophomore class. And I spent a long lonely night in my room listening to Who's Next:

No one knows what it's like
To feel these feelings like I do and I blame you!
No one bites back as hard on their anger
None of my pain and woe can show through

I shivered as that memory came to an end as I eased the Galaxie 500 in front of 59 Vine Street and turned it off. I quietly let myself into the house, and lightly climbed the steps to my room. I found my Who's Next album, and put it on my record player at a low volume. I lay down on the bed and listened to the synthesizers of "Baba O'Riley" kick in. I was soon out.

The next morning, I awoke with a start to Mary Kate shouting downstairs. I sat up, and looked at the clock on the table next to my bed. It was only ten o'clock. Then I realized I didn't feel too chipper, a result of the Jameson's shots from the night before, and lay back down. She was shouting at Owen. He was apparently going fishing, although I could not hear his voice. Mary Kate had made plans for them to go to a picnic at Chenango Valley State Park with some of her friends, and was thoroughly pissed that he would leave her to go alone.

After a few minutes of her fevered yelling, I heard the back door slam, and then heard his car backing down the driveway.

A couple of minutes passed in silence, and then Mary Kate's angry steps came up the stairs.

"Oh, God, I don't need this," I thought. I threw a blanket over my face, hoping that might throw her off.

She threw my door open and stormed in. "Wake up! John, wake up!"

Without moving, I said, "Mom, I'm sleeping."

She stepped to the bed, and ripped the blanket away that was covering my face, screaming, "Get out of bed, mister lazy. It's ten fifteen in the morning."

"Mom, I'm tired."

"Well, if you didn't stay out all night carousing with your smoky friends, you wouldn't be so tired. Now get ready to go to church with me, and then you're going to a picnic with me at State Park."

"I'm not going to church, and why should I have to go to your stupid picnic?"

"Because I'm telling you that you're going. This is still my house, and you live here with my rules."

"Oh, please."

"Oh, please, yourself, mister smarty pants. You've got it pretty easy around here. You don't lift a finger to help out ever. I have to clean up after you, cook for you, clean your clothes. You've got it made. And you don't appreciate any of it. The thanks I get is a lot of lip. Don't you have any conscience at all? Well, you got anything to say for yourself?"

"I'm sorry if you and Owen aren't getting along, but that's no reason to take it out on me."

"He's another baby I have to take care of. You should help me with him, and take my side. He would listen to you."

"I didn't want you to marry him in the first place."

She glared at me in silence, shaking and her fists closed. I thought she was going to hit me. She slowly spit out through clenched teeth, "I married him to make your and your sister's life better. And this is the thanks I get. You be ready at ten forty-five to go to church with me, or you will… be…sorry." She turned and walked out, slamming the door behind her, shaking the room.

"What am I doing in this nuthouse?" I asked myself. "I have got to get out of here." I could only think to escape.

I hopped out of bed, collected some textbooks that I needed to read, and stuffed them into my backpack. After that, I took a short shower, washing the smoke off from the night before. I didn't shave, but got dressed quickly.

Grabbing my backpack, I cautiously opened the door to my room, and inched down the stairs, squeezing on the side, as there was less noise than in the middle of the stairs. When I neared the first floor, I peeked around the corner. I could not see Mary Kate in the living room or dining room, and could not hear her in the kitchen. I set foot in the living room, and tiptoed to the front door. Reaching the front door, I threw it open and ran across the porch, jumped over the stairs to the sidewalk, and then ran to my car. I flung the driver's door open, threw the backpack in, and dove into the front seat. I started the Galaxie 500 and sped away. I didn't look back.

August 31, 1975, was a sunny, but breezy late summer Sunday. I drove to SUNY-B (after first stopping at a

McDonald's for breakfast) and planted myself in the library.
I found a deserted corner on the second floor, and pulled
out my massive Medieval History textbook. Despite opening
the book to the assigned chapter, I couldn't concentrate. I
fumed over Mary Kate and how ridiculous she was, with my
angry thoughts consuming me. "I am not an infant; I'm
twenty-one years old. Who is she to treat me like a child?
She's impossible to live with; I don't see how Owen does it.
I can't wait to graduate, and get the hell out of there. And
I will never come back. I'll show her; I'll never come back.
I should have gone to Colgate, I knew I should have gone
to Colgate. What a dumb ass! My life would have been so
different. What a dumb ass!" I made a vow that I would no
longer put up with her shit, no matter what.

I bathed in such anger and self-pity for a few hours,
then stuffed the barely read Medieval History textbook into
my backpack, strolled to the Student Union building, and
headed to the Pub downstairs. The booths were full, but there
were a few empty tables. After setting my backpack on one of
the tables, I ordered a couple of pieces of oily pizza and a
beer at the bar from a girl with long frizzy hair wearing a tie-
dyed shirt underneath white painter pants. I was delighted to
hear Pink Floyd's "Welcome to the Machine" playing on the
sound system. I ate alone, pretending I was reading the latest
issue of Pipe Dream, the SUNY-B student newspaper.

After lunch, I headed back to the library. Clouds had
started to roll in to the area. I spotted a lightning flash to the
west. Rain was coming our way. My desk was still open on
the second floor, and nobody was seated at the desks nearby.
I pulled the Medieval History textbook out, and began to

force myself to read my assignment for the next day, and to not think about Mary Kate.

Within a half hour, a fierce thunderstorm enveloped SUNY-B. Even inside the library, I could hear booming thunder blasts, and the lights flickered a couple of times. It was tough to concentrate, but I managed to keep my focus.

Late in the afternoon, I nodded off. I awoke at six thirty and felt tired. I went to the bathroom on the second floor, walking by some large windows. Sheets of rain were blowing across the campus in waves. A chill hit me, and goose bumps grew on my exposed arms. I felt quite alone in the world, bereft of attachment.

When I returned to my desk, I was re-energized, and put the Medieval History textbook back in my backpack, and removed "The End of The Affair" by Graham Greene and started reading it. Unlike the dry Medieval History textbook, I soon became absorbed in the story; it flowed so beautifully, and the text was so wonderfully written, that time passed quickly. After reading a hundred pages, I looked at my watch. It was ten thirty. It was time to go. When I stepped out of the library, it was noticeably cooler and a gusty west wind made it even colder. I put my head down, and tramped across the empty plaza to a distant parking lot.

I stopped at McDonald's for the second time that day, ordered two cheeseburgers and a large Coke from a scrawny, thin male teenager with bad acne. I empathized with him because I knew that had been me only a couple of years before. I found a copy of the Sunday Binghamton *Press* on one of the tables and grabbed it. I ate the burgers slowly as I read the paper; I was in no hurry to go home. The

McDonald's was not busy, not at that time of night.

A half hour later, I finished and finally drove home. Vine Street was quiet. Few lights were on in the houses on either side of the street. As I neared my house, my insides began to churn with the prospect of what awaited me.

But the lights were out there too. I parked the Galaxie 500 out front and, carrying the backpack over one shoulder, glided to the front of the porch, and quietly climbed the steps onto the porch and then moved to the front door. I tried it; it was locked. I got my key out, suddenly fearing that the lock may have been changed. But it wasn't; I unlocked the front door, entered into the dark living room, closed the door, and listened for a voice or movement. There was nothing.

I climbed the stairs to my bedroom, shut the door, and turned on the light. I set my backpack down. There was a piece of paper on my pillow. I walked to the head of the bed, and grabbed it. It read, "I AM VERY ANGRY WITH YOU! THIS IS THE LAST STRAW! I WILL NOT BE TREATED THIS WAY!" Underneath the writing, was written simply "MOM."

Inexplicably, when I saw that piece of paper on the pillow, I had expected an apology. But as Mary Kate had proved time and time again, she subscribed to the philosophy of the character Captain Nathan Brittles in the classic John Ford western *She Wore a Yellow Ribbon*, "Never apologize, it's a sign of a weakness."

I stared at the paper for a moment, shook my head, and set the paper down on my dresser. I knew she was not kidding and that we had reached a new stage, but I could not conceive her twisted plan.

CHAPTER 5
One of These Days

One of these days I'm going to cut you into little pieces

—Pink Floyd

Binghamton, New York, September, 1975

AFTER I AWOKE THE NEXT MORNING, I got ready for school and again sneaked out of the house. I did not see or hear Mary Kate or Owen, but he was generally gone by the time I left for school every day anyway.

I stayed away until late in the evening. When I returned to the dark quiet house, I sneaked up the stairs into my room. There was no note on the pillow this time.

And so the week followed that pattern: sneak out without contact, come home too late for contact. On that Wednesday evening, there was a letter laid on my bed. Excitement briefly filled me as I thought it must be from ML, but instead it was from my buddy Mark Nolan at SUNY-Buffalo. Disappointment is an understatement; I was miserable.

On Friday September 5, 1975, I went to The Pine Lounge hoping to run into Tip, but he never appeared. I was leery of showing up on his door, given his last volatile outburst and the alleged presence of a shotgun. But because I didn't want to go home, I just sat at the bar and sucked down Rolling Rock after Rolling Rock, feeling progressively more sorry for myself.

I got home late, probably after two o'clock. No note, no mail. I was feeling low that ML had not sent me a letter as she had promised. When I turned out the lights, I could only see her face lustily staring at me as she had that night in the Galaxie 500 a few weeks back, and fantasies were born and raised.

I awoke the next morning and lay in bed for a while, thinking about ML, and Mary Kate, and then about my future. I knew that if I was going for a master's degree, I needed to get serious about graduate school applications and the upcoming GRE.

After my contemplation time, I arose, threw on a T-shirt and sweatpants and stumbled downstairs. I was prepared for verbal abuse from Mary Kate. The house was quiet: no TV, no radio, no sound of enterprise. I walked into the kitchen; it was spotless, it looked new and as if it was for sale. No coffee brewing, no meat thawing in the sink, no bread by the toaster. It was antiseptic and cold.

I sneaked down the hallway from the kitchen and observed that the door to Owen and Mary Kate's room was closed, and I heard no noise. I retreated back to the kitchen, and as quietly as I could, got out a bowl and spoon and a box of Cheerios, and set them on the kitchen table. When I opened the refrigerator door, I noticed that it too was exceptionally clean, and quite empty. There was no milk. That was annoying. So, I ate the Cheerios from the box, and drank a glass of water.

After cleaning up, I dressed, grabbed my backpack, and headed back to the SUNY-B Library. I studied, took some practice GRE tests, worked on a couple of graduate school applications, and read periodicals for the rest of the day. That evening, I attended a showing by the Film Society of two Nick Ray movies: *In a Lonely Place* starring Humphrey Bogart and *Rebel Without a Cause* starring James Dean. Nick Ray had been a visiting professor at SUNY-B from 1971–73, and had filmed a movie with students there, titled *We Can't Go Home Again*. As a freshman fascinated with the cinema, I had volunteered to work on the movie, and even had a small part. It had been a truly bizarre and fascinating experience.

I didn't see anyone I knew in the half-filled lecture hall where the films were shown, so I sat by myself. Nobody sat near me.

While driving home afterwards, I considered heading to The Pine Lounge, but decided to just go to my house. It was the same: quiet and dark, if not forbidding. I read for a while, and then fell asleep.

I woke late on Sunday, September, September 7, 1975; it was after ten o'clock. When I came downstairs, the house was deathly still. I walked into the kitchen; there was no sign of life. I opened the refrigerator, and checked on the milk status. No milk.

I eased down the adjoining hallway. The door to Mary Kate's room was closed. I could not see a light.

I pondered for a moment as to what to do. There was enough of a guilty conscience that I thought I should be the first one to apologize and return matters to at least a semi-harmonious détente. So, I moved to her door, and knocked.

"Mom?" No answer. I knocked again. "Mom, are you in there?"

I waited a moment, but there still was no answer, no sound of a person moving in the room. I started to get anxious, and left the hallway, walked through the kitchen, out the back porch and to the unattached two car garage at the end of the driveway. I lifted the wooden garage door and peered inside. Mary Kate's car was there, but Owen's car was gone. Now troubled, I closed the garage door, and returned to the house.

"Mom," I said louder as I knocked on her door with more force. "Mom, open up. I'm not going away until you open up."

Suddenly a sheet of paper flew out the bottom of the bedroom door. I bent down, and picked it up. She had written: "I AM NOT SPEAKING TO YOU. PLEASE TAKE CARE OF YOURSELF."

"Mom, c'mon. Will you come out of there please?"

No answer.

"This is ridiculous, Mom. I'm sorry."

No answer.

I pounded on the door, while crying out: "Open up!" After a few moments of pounding on the door, I stopped, and angrily yelled to the door, "The hell with you then!" and stormed off.

The next two weeks were no different. I did not see her (or Owen). I would leave for school in the morning, and come back late. My mail was no longer dumped on my bed; it was left at the bottom of the stairs. One day a legal-sized envelope from Boston College arrived; a graduate school application and other materials about BC were enclosed within.

In between classes at SUNY-B, I either went to Campus Pub for food and a beer, or went to the library and studied for the GRE or worked on graduate school applications (or just mused about my unpleasant circumstances). I spent a lot of time thinking about ML. She was my one beacon of hope in an unpleasant world, but inevitably it would make me miss her more, and then to wonder why she had not written. I feared desperately that she had found another guy upon returning to school, and that I had lost my one chance to be with her. That prospect was too terrible to consider for long.

On Friday, September 19, 1975, I left the SUNY-B Library at eight thirty at night, stopped at a sub shop in Binghamton, and ate a turkey sub. While eating alone in the sub shop, it hit me that I had not spoken with anyone for two weeks, other than when ordering food. I needed to see Tip and tell him what was going on at my house now. I decided to go The Pine Lounge, and hoped he would show up this time. Plus, it would be nice to be in a crowd having fun.

I parked my car on Seminary Avenue, across the street from The Pine Lounge, and walked to it. Upon entering the bar, I was hit with the smell of beer and cigarettes, and the sound of Led Zeppelin's "Kashmir" from the speakers. Looking for Tip, I walked past the booths that were half occupied and made my way to the bar. There were two stools available. I sat down on the end, leaving an empty stool next to me.

Mack saw me and sauntered over. "Hey, look, it's half an asshole," he said loudly. "Where's your other cheek?"

"Funny man. Just get me a Rock."

He walked off, saying over his shoulder, "Got a Rock rolling your way. A buck."

That first Rolling Rock after two weeks tasted so sweet, like liquid gold going down my throat. After a few sips, I started to feel better. There was a Yankee game on the TV over the bar. It felt really good to be in a clean, well-lit place with a Rolling Rock in front of me, surrounded by others seeking alcoholic absolution.

Two Rocks later, I heard Tip at my side. "Hey, JM, where you been?"

"I saved you a stool, Tip, sit down. The Rocks are tasting great."

He sat on the stool. "Thanks for being a chicken shit two weeks ago. I thought you were my friend. You just ran away."

"Tip, it was a dumb idea. I was helping you."

Mack appeared. "Here's the other cheek. One Rock or two?"

"Make it two," Tip said, "I need to catch up to JM here." Mack walked back.

"So, how is work?" I asked.

He reached into his jacket pocket, and pulled out a pack of Lucky Strikes and a lighter. "I'm still not over you dumping me at home and running away." He extracted a cigarette, lit it, inhaled, and then blew smoke at me. "You owe me one."

I waved the smoke away.

He continued, "And work sucks the big one. You should try it, see how you like it."

"What do you think I've done the last four summers, ass-wipe?"

He snorted, "That ain't fuckin work, that's acting at work. Fuckin' Parks and Recreation department? Biggest bunch of slackers."

"Yeah, right, delivering furniture is so much higher on the work pyramid."

With a flourish, Mack plopped two Rocks in front of Tip. "Two bucks, Tippy."

Tip pulled three dollars from his pocket and threw them on the bar. "There you go, fuckwad. Keep the change."

Mack picked up the dollars. "I will. And nice mouth." He turned and started to walk away, stopped, and looked at us, and asked, "Wanna hear a joke? How do you make a hormone?"

Tip blurted out, "You don't pay her! C'mon, Mack, that joke is as old as your underwear."

Mack peered at Tip, "Oh, you got a better one?"

Tip sat up, "Yeah, I do." He took a drag of his Lucky, blew smoke in Mack's direction, and said, "Can I borrow your ass while my face is on vacation?"

Mack laughed derisively, "A real funny guy." He turned and walked away.

Tip crushed his cigarette in an ashtray on the bar, and drank from his Rock, while watching Mack walk away. Setting the bottle down, he said, "I'm sure I could kick his fat ass."

I chuckled, "You couldn't kick his ass."

He turned to me. "I can still kick your ass, JM. Just like the old days."

"I can run faster now."

"Oh, so now you make fun of me cuz I got a bad wheel. You're some pal."

"Hey, Tip, I'm just joshing. C'mon." I reached out and tapped my Rock on his. "What's eating you, tonight?"

He tapped his Rock to mine, drank a long gulp, and then said, "I'm fuckin pissed off at everything. My life sucks, JM. I live in a dumpy apartment. I don't have a car. I don't have a girlfriend. I got friends like you who are assholes. And my fuckin' job. I make no bread at all, and oh man, you wouldn't believe the shitheads I have to deal with. Take this afternoon, I gotta make a run to Pennsylvania to deliver a couch. This guy Matt, another fuckin' loser, is with me. We spend an hour trying to find this place out in the middle of nowhere. We get there, and the house is on a hill. Picture this, the gravel driveway is like fifty feet below the house. To get to the house you have to climb like a hundred steps. We knock on the door and this old battleaxe lets us in, and she starts shitting on us because we're late. Matt is about to go off on this witch, but I hold him back. I'm trying to do the right thing. So, then she shows us where the stuff is supposed to go in a rec room in the back of the house. So, Matt and I wrestle this beast of a couch off the truck, and we stumble up the steps; he's swearing at me the whole time. Finally we get to the door, and we're beat, and my leg is killing me. She holds the door open, but the couch is so damn big, it barely fits through the door. Then, we somehow get it to the rec room and set the mother down. I've got gloves on, but my hands are sore, and I have a couple of scratches, my leg is sore, and my arms feel like they're going to fall off. Matt and I are standing there and she doesn't offer us a drink of water or say thanks. She's just staring at the couch. So, I go back to the truck and get the paperwork for the witch to sign. When I get back in there, she wants us to move the couch to a different spot in the room. So, we put our gloves back on, and move the fuckin' couch around to where she now wants it. Then I grab the paperwork, and ask her to sign. The bitch says she won't sign until she looks at the couch. Get this—she gets on like her hands and knees and has her nose up the couch checking every inch of it. After about five minutes, she calls us over, and says, 'Look at that! There's a scratch." I look to where she's pointing, and sure enough there's a small scratch on the back of the couch. You almost need a magnifying glass to see this thing. Then she starts going off on me about how much she paid for this couch and was promised top quality. She's getting all worked up, her face is as red as a beet. And I'm like, 'what the fuck?' I'm getting paid peanuts and this shrew is using me like a punching bag. And then she starts yelling at me to take it out and put it back on the truck. And that's it, JM, I ain't taking that monster out of that house. I just yell at her, 'Lady, I don't build the furniture, I just install it! Take it up with the company." I motion to Matt, and we practically run out of there. She's cursing us all the way out of the house, down the steps, into the truck, and out of the driveway. She was fuckin' nuts. We're so pissed off after that, we stop at a bar just north of the border and have a beer."

He pulled a Lucky out, lit it, took a drag, blew smoke in the direction of the ceiling, and continued, "Dig this, when I get back to the store, my boss, the prick man, he calls me in to his office, and lays into me, chewing me a new asshole. That bitch gave him an earful, so he lets me have both barrels, about customer service and my piss poor attitude. Of course, I do have a piss poor attitude, and with him chewing on my ass, I gotta really piss poor attitude. So, how was your fuckin' day?"

"Better than that. But not much. Mary Kate is not speaking to me anymore."

Tip snorted, "Something wrong with that?"

"Not really, but it's kind of weird. She never comes out of her room, at least while I'm there."

"Sounds perfect to me. Cool beans." He tapped my Rock with his Rock. "If The Big Asshole acted like that, I'd still be living at home."

"And I haven't seen Owen in two weeks either."

"This gets better and better. Can I move in now?"

"Absolutely not."

"Asshole."

He took a drag on his Lucky, and I took a good pour of my Rock. After placing the Lucky in the ashtray, he said, "Did I tell you I got a cat?"

"No."

"I came home from work last week, and there was this small tabby cat, you know, the orange ones with the stripes, meowing outside my uncle's house. The thing was starving. So, I took him upstairs with me, gave him some milk. He inhaled the first saucer, so I gave him like three more. He lapped them up, then jumped up on my lap while I was lying on the couch, and starts purring like a lawnmower, and then falls asleep. So, he's been with me ever since. We're roommates."

"That's pretty damn funny. You and a cat."

"Yeah. I'm really a dog man, but what can I say. His name is Pussy."

"Pussy? I thought he was a male cat?"

"He is. I think it's kind of funny, you know … Pussy … a cat?

"Yeah, Tip, real knee slapper. Well, at least you're getting some pussy every night."

"Eh, fuck you, JM. You don't appreciate shit."

"Well, just be careful with your alleged shotgun so you don't blow your Pussy away."

"Keep rolling, you're a regular Rodney Dangerfield. And whatdya mean, alleged? I told you I took the old man's shotgun. It's sitting in my place carefully hidden. If anybody gives me shit, from now on, KABOOM. Including you, douche bag."

"What if your dad finds out?"

"The Big Asshole? Fuck him. He's so stupid he'll think he's been robbed, and won't even call the police cuz he's so fuckin' lazy. Lemme tell you, once turkey season rolls around, I'm going hunting near Walton. A guy I work with says that you get up in those hills around Walton, and it's crawling with turkeys. You should go with me. It will be like the old days. Remember hunting squirrels on Ross Mountain with our BB guns?"

"Yeah, I remember, Tip." And I did remember those good times with Tip before the accident; I remembered them all too well. Over the next hour, we reminisced about our hunting and fishing expeditions when we were young, and Tip came alive again, with a spark in his eyes and excitement in his voice. He didn't even smoke for that period of time. Of course, we kept on drinking. A few more Rocks. Then, we celebrated God knows what with a shot of Jack

Daniels, then later a second shot. After that second shot, I was flying.

Later, a tall skinny guy named Rick that Tip knew joined us at the bar. Tip had met him at a party recently, and they had become friends. Rick told us about a party he was going to that night, in nearby Conklin. I wasn't interested, but Tip convinced me to go, and after the two shots and the Rocks, I was amenable to almost any suggestion. So, after tossing a few more deeply original insults at Mack, we left The Pine Lounge, and climbed into Rick's Volkswagen bus parked around the corner from The Pine Lounge. I knew I should have driven, but I still was in enough possession of my faculties to know that I was over the inebriation line to drive to an unfamiliar place.

Rick had a twelve-pack of Genesee beer in cans in his car, and we quickly opened one each and started to drink. Tip lit a Lucky, and alternated between sipping from the Genny can and taking a drag off his Lucky. Rick had a tape player in the car, and we drove to the music of Lynyrd Skynyrd. Twenty minutes later we turned off NY7 in Conklin, an eastern suburb of Binghamton on the Southside of the Susquehanna River. We pulled into a long gravel driveway, and drove up to a decaying two-story colonial farmhouse hiding among huge maple trees. The lights on the first floor were on. Rick parked the VW Bus, and we hopped out, and walked to the wooden steps. They were cracked and even in that dim light, you could see the paint was blistered and peeling.

Rick said, "Watch out for these steps. They're loose."

We gingerly climbed the steps onto the wooden porch.

Rick walked to the front door, knocked twice and entered, followed by Tip and me. We walked into the sparsely furnished living room: there was an aging couch, sinking into itself, and a couple of chairs, sitting on a slick wooden floor with a few warped boards. "Dark Side of the Moon" by Pink Floyd was playing on a record player against a wall, and wires from the back of the receiver next to the turntable led to a couple of stacked Advent speakers sitting on the floor in two corners of the room. The room was very warm, and infused with the sickly sweet smell of pot. I was immediately uncomfortable. Laughing voices from a room nearby could be heard.

As he entered the room, Rick called out, "Hey, the party is here." Two girls who looked like they were in high school and a guy appeared from the kitchen around the corner. One of the girls had jet black long straight hair, was short and a little stocky. She was wearing blue bell-bottom jeans and a very loose top. The other girl had dirty blond hair, was rail-thin, and had acne scars. She was smoking a cigarette and wearing white painter's pants with a T-shirt underneath. The guy had long stringy hair tied into a ponytail, and looked older than the girls. He was wearing a tie-dyed shirt over brown dirty corduroy pants.

The girls rushed to Rick cooing, "Ricky, you're here." They hugged him at the same time, a little too demonstrably. Then they looked at Tip and I, "Who are these two?"

Rick turned to us, pointed at Tip, and said, "That's Tip; he's cool. And that's his friend, John." He put his left arm around the stocky girl, "This is Becky," and then he put his right arm around the other girl with the dirty blond hair,

"This is Shelly." He pointed to the unsmiling guy, "That's Dennis." We both said "Hi" at the same time. Becky and Shelly moved away from Rick, walked to Tip and me, and studied us. As they neared me, I could see their eyes were glazed.

Dennis walked to Rick, and said, "Gimme some skin," and they slapped their palms together.

"Whatdya think, Beck, are they cool?" Shelly asked.

"Yeah, I think so." Becky said, and then looked over to Dennis, "Whatdya think, hon?"

Dennis slowly glided to us, studying us. He stopped near Becky and put his arm around her. "You guys cool?"

Tip laughed, and said, "I'm way fuckin cool, man."

I said, "I'm with him."

Still looking at us, Dennis held his cheek next to Becky's cheek, and said, "Yeah, I think these guys are cool. We'll let 'em play. Rick, did you bring the stuff?"

Rick tapped his jacket, "Right here, my man."

Dennis let Becky go, and waved us to the couch. "Far out. Have a seat, boys. I need to visit with Rick for a minute. Girls, take care of these boys."

As Rick and I sank down into the couch, Dennis and Rick walked away, and headed down a hallway out of view. Becky stood over us and asked, "What can we get you, beer, vodka, tequila, or grass?"

"What kind of beer you got?" Tip asked.

"Molson in bottles, you know. Is that OK?"

"Dynomite."

Becky and Shelly giggled, and left the living room.

I looked at Tip. "What the fuck are we doing here, Tip?"

He slapped me on the shoulder. "We're here to get wasted and that is what we're going to do. You got a problem with that, JM?"

"I thought we were going to a party. There's nobody here."

"Well, we're here."

"Yeah, but so are those girls. C'mon, they're jailbait."

"Don't fuck 'em."

"Don't worry about that."

The two girls reappeared in the living room, and carried two opened Molson bottles to us. "Here you go," Shelly said as she handed a Molson to me. She sat down on the floor in front of me, and sipped on her Molson. After handing the other Molson to Tip, Becky also sat down on the floor in front of Tip.

I drank from the Molson, and then asked, "So, is anybody else coming tonight?"

Tip laughed, "My buddy here doesn't really think this is a party without a big crowd."

"Tip!"

Becky and Shelly looked at one another and laughed.

Tip went on, "He also thinks you girls are too young to party with."

Becky frowned and pointed her Molson at me, "Hey, don't be an asshole. We're legal, you know. Or, at least my ID says I am." She and Shelly laughed again and tapped their Molsons together.

"Who's worried about your ID, doll?" Dennis asked as he and Rick entered the living room, their business apparently over.

Becky pointed at me again with her Molson bottle. "That one?"

Rick sat down in a chair facing the couch, and as Dennis walked behind Becky, he said to me, "Is there a problem, man?" He started to massage Becky's shoulders.

Tip sat up and said, "There's no fuckin' problem. He's cool. Many thanks for the Molson, man, this is hitting the spot."

Dennis said, "No problem, man, happy to share with people that are cool. That's what I'm about: sharing." He was way too creepy for me. I suddenly saw Charles Manson in my mind, and Dennis was a little too similar to Manson. He continued, "I've got some excellent Mexican tequila straight from Mexico that I'm going to pop. It's even got the fucking worm in it. We're going to do a few shots to get this thing rolling."

He pointed at me, "You ready to do some tequila, toilet?" The girls laughed at that.

I said, "Toilet?"

Dennis snorted and said, "Yeah, you know, John. Toilet. Get it?" The girls laughed anew.

"I got it. That's a good one."

"So, you gonna do tequila shots with me, Toilet?"

I had never drunk tequila in my life, but I wasn't going to let this asshole embarrass me.

"Sure, bring it on."

"Good. You're drinking the worm."

An evening of over-consumption began. The five of us did several shots of tequila in a row, and Dennis was right, I drank the shot with the white limpid worm in it, although

I didn't taste anything going down. After the tequila shots, the girls, who were pretty hammered by then, went and got some plastic cups, and we played caps, guys against girls. The guys lost more, so we ended up drinking more beer than they did. By the end of our caps game, the room was losing focus for me.

Dennis then appeared with a couple of joints. He said the grass was from Mexico; his buddy had brought it back along with the tequila. We passed the Js around, and everybody took a toke. I had smoked pot before, but it did not interest me. Except on a night like that, when I was hammered. This pot had powerful buds; as I expelled the smoke, my brain turned to mush. The girls brought out brownies that they had made. I ate one, spilling much of it on me. The room was closing in; smoke lingered in the air overhead like a slow moving fog.

Then Dennis appeared with a bong, and set it up. The others took hits off it. I declined; even though I was in the stratosphere, I had enough brain cells to see the bong was a bad idea. They accused me of being a lightweight. They were right. Somebody got me another Molson, and I sipped on it while sitting back in the couch, in my own world. The others were laughing loudly and singing along to Pink Floyd,

> *Us and Them,*
> *and in the end, we're only ordinary men.*

At some point, I stumbled to my feet, and asked where the bathroom was. Dennis pointed toward the hallway off the living room, "First door on your left." I walked a tightrope in that direction. I heard Becky yell out from behind me, "If you shake it more than once, you're playing with yourself!" The others burst into renewed laughter. Upon reaching the hallway, I held onto the wall and guided myself down the hallway. I finally reached the bathroom, turned the light on, and shut the door. The bathroom was a mess, facial hairs were in the sink, mold sat in the corners of the bathtub, a wet towel lay on the floor next to the bathtub.

I took care of business, bobbing and weaving over the toilet. I suddenly felt very tired. I opened the bathroom door, turned the light off with my third attempt, and turned left towards rooms at the end of the hallway. I could hear the others back in the living room singing. I staggered into the first room on my left, and, in the darkness, saw a mattress lying on the floor. I fell on to the mattress, and rolled on my back. The ceiling was spinning; I closed my eyes, and the insides of my eyelids were spinning.

At some point, I must have passed out, because I awoke to Rick shaking me violently and yelling. "Get up, we're leaving."

I sat up. "Huh? What?"

"You passed out. Get your ass up."

My head was buzzing, and my stomach was angry. I lurched to my feet.

"Oh, man, I was out."

"Yeah, no shit, lightweight."

He left the bedroom, and called back, "Let's go." I followed him out and stumbled to the living room; it was empty. No music was playing.

I looked around, "Where is everybody?"

Rick grabbed his jacket off a chair and put it on. "Dennis is with Becky, and your buddy Tip is with Shelly upstairs." He didn't seem happy about that. "C'mon, grab your coat, let's go." He walked to the front door.

I grabbed my jacket off the floor, and put it on. Rick flung the front door open, and a cold wind blew into the room. I tottered after him as if I was on six inch heels, closing the door behind me.

We got into his car, and Rick started the VW Bus and jerked it into reverse, and screeched out the gravel driveway onto NY7. He slammed on the brakes, and then gassed the car forward, at an ever accelerating pace. He drove wildly, weaving around the road; luckily, we didn't encounter any oncoming cars.

My stomach was roiling. I blurted out, "Man, I think I'm gonna be sick."

He slugged me with his right hand. "Don't you fuckin' barf in my car, asshole! Don't you fuckin' do it! Roll the goddamn window down."

I rolled the window down, and laid my head out the window. I was assaulted with images of bare trees, wet pavement, street lights, mailboxes by the side of the road. It was too much to process. I closed my eyes, and silently prayed for relief.

Sometime later, I felt the car come to a stop. "Get out, man," Rick barked at me.

I opened my eyes. We were stopped in front of 59 Vine Street. I closed my eyes, and leaned back in the passenger seat. "What are we doing here?"

"Your buddy told me to take you here."

"Gotta get my car."

"No way, get out."

"I'm not getting out. Take me to The Pine Lounge."

"You fuckin' asshole." I heard his car door open. A moment later, the passenger door opened, and I was rudely grabbed and pulled from the car, landing on the street. "I said get out!" I landed on my side, and felt a shot of pain. I heard the car door slam shut. I rolled over onto my back and put my arm over my eyes. I heard the driver's side door open and close, followed by Rick's car racing away.

I lay in the street for a few minutes as the world spun around me. I slowly rose to my feet and wobbled to the front porch. I reached out with my hands and grabbed the porch steps and crab-walked up them to the porch. Upon reaching the porch, I was on my knees, and, feeling worse with every movement, I inched my way to the front door on my knees. I reached into my pocket and extracted my keys. After a few unsuccessful attempts, I inserted the house key into the lock and managed to open the door. As the door opened, I tried to rise to my feet, and I could feel bile rising in my throat. I grabbed the door for support, but fell forward, and threw up in heaving gasps on the entryway floor and rug. Within seconds, the living room overhead light came on, and Mary Kate stood over me, wearing a bathrobe, and yellow rollers in her hair, her face as red as a fire truck, and her eyes wide open and angry. She bent down, her first slap on my face was a surprise; I didn't see it coming. The second slap I did see coming, but I took it anyway. Then she grabbed a hold of me, and roughly pulled me toward the open front door, screaming, "How dare you do this to my house. Get out! Get out!" In my weakened condition, I was unable to respond or resist. She pulled me out the door, and as I lay on the porch, she kicked me away, "Don't you even think about coming in here."

As I lay on my back on the porch, I mumbled, "I'm sorry, Mom." I heard her take the keys out of the door, and then a moment later, I heard the keys land on the sidewalk where she threw them. I heard the front door slam. I rolled over onto my back, breathing heavily. My stomach was still in revolt. The porch overhead was spinning like a top. I closed my eyes and lay there. The cool night air felt good against my hot cheeks.

Later, I heard the front door open and Mary Kate throw something on the porch. I opened my eyes. She was a whirling dervish, reaching into the house, and throwing my stuff onto the porch: clothes, pillows, books, records, blanket, a suitcase.

"Mom, what are you doing?" I weakly asked.

"Stay out and stay away," she coldly replied. She threw my basketball at me. It hit me in the leg, bounced away, and then dribbled down the porch steps onto the front lawn. She went inside and slammed the door shut.

After a few minutes, I rose to a sitting position, still feeling like shit. I looked at my possessions lying all over the porch, found a pillow and my comforter, crawled to them, and wrapped myself up. At some point, I blessedly passed out.

CHAPTER 6
Childhood's End

You shout in your sleep.
Perhaps the price is just too steep.
Is your conscience at rest if once put to the test?
You awake with a start to just the beating of your heart.
Just one man beneath the sky,
Just two ears, just two eyes.
You set sail across the sea of long past thoughts and memories.
Childhood's end

—Roger Waters

Binghamton, New York, September, 1975

WHEN I AWOKE ON SATURDAY, September 20, 1975, it was an overcast grey morning, and I was still wrapped in a blanket burrito on the porch. I had a splitting headache, and my body ached. After a moment, I reflected on the previous evening, thinking that it must have been a bad nightmare, but the evidence of Mary Kate's wild anger surrounded me. I thought about what I was going to have to do to make it up to her. I knew it was not going to be pleasant. I thought to myself, "Goddamn Tip! It was his stupid idea to go that party."

I checked my watch. It was eight thirty. I decided to face the wrath of Mary Kate. I recalled Mary Kate throwing my keys; I found them on the sidewalk. I picked them up, and moved to the front door, but then noticed that the house key was gone. I tried the door but it was locked. I rang the doorbell, and waited, rehearsing my apology. But she did not come. I rang the doorbell again, this time holding it down with my finger. I knocked on the door. But still she did not come.

Then I got angry. I pounded on the front door, swearing at her to open the door. After a few minutes, I gave up in disgust, walked down the driveway, and climbed the back stairs to the back door to see if she had somehow left that door open. It was locked too. I pounded on that door for a few minutes to no avail. A drizzle began to fall. I thought for a moment about what my next step was. I retreated down the driveway, but stopped at the windows to her bedroom. There was no light in the room, but I knew she was in there, probably watching me behind the curtain. I walked over to the windows which sat above my head, and pounded on the window frame. "OK, I'm leaving, Mom, are you now happy? Good-bye and good riddance. Don't look for me."

I stepped back, angrily staring at the silent windows. The drizzle had become rain, bouncing off the driveway pavement. I turned away and walked back to the front porch.

I sat on the porch for a few minutes, and watched the grim rain fall in waves. After a half hour, the rain began to let up, and then it stopped. I realized I needed to get the Galaxie 500; it was the only shelter I seemingly had. I left the porch and started walking on the wet, puddle-filled sidewalk away from the house, past Tip's old house, down Vine Street, until I reached Vestal Avenue. I turned left, and walked past empty storefronts and then the Art Theatre, showing XXX rated films, until I reached Washington Street. I turned right onto Washington Street, and kept walking, crossing the Washington Street Bridge over the angry Susquehanna River below. Fifty minutes later, I reached the Galaxie 500.

I drove the Galaxie 500 back to 59 Vine Street, and parked in front, driver's side nearest the porch. The rain started coming down again. I opened the trunk, and walked to the porch.

It took me a few trips to stuff my scattered possessions into the trunk of the Galaxie 500 through a now driving rain. While grabbing items, I found my brown teddy bear that I had been given as an infant. It had been in my closet for years, gathering dust. An eye was missing and his fur was patchy. I set him aside, and when I had finished packing the car, I came back to the porch. I held the teddy bear up, wished him well, and set him by the front door. I turned and left. I trotted through sheets of rain to the car.

Flinging open the driver's door, I leaped onto the seat. I was soaked. I shook off the rain like a dog. I blew air on my fingers to dry and warm them, then reached inside my jacket and wiped them on my shirt. I started the car. I looked out my window through the rain drops sliding down the window at the lonely shell of 59 Vine Street. My old teddy bear sat at the door staring lifelessly at me. I turned and drove away. I never set foot inside 59 Vine Street again.

I had no plan. I first drove to SUNY-B, continued west to Vestal, then across the George F. Johnson Bridge over the Susquehanna to Endicott, past the IBM complex, then turned east, and headed back to Binghamton. I thought about driving to Tip's and staying with him. But I was pissed at him, and didn't really want to deal with his issues. Then, it hit me that I should just drive to Boston and be with ML. Oh, God, how that was an enticing thought! Man, I hungered to be with her. To hold her again, to kiss her without a care. She was only six hours away.

Of course, at some point, I knew that fantasy was just that, a fantasy. Christ, she hadn't even written me like she said she would. I knew that showing up on her doorstep would more likely turn her off. I also wanted to finish up at SUNY-B, get that degree that I had worked so hard for, and just move on.

As I was cruising on Highway 17 east to Binghamton, it hit me that my only option was to try and stay with The Captain, until I figured out my next steps. After I exited Highway 17, I drove through Binghamton to The Captain's house on the Eastside.

The Captain lived in the two-story home on 20 Oliver Street that he had bought in the 20s right after he joined the Binghamton Police Department. At one time, all of his neighbors on the street had been Irish cops in the BPD. But over time, with deaths and retirements to Florida, the neighborhood had changed, and new blood occupied the neighborhood. He was disappointed in his later years that neither of his immediate neighbors was even Irish.

As I child I had loved his house; it was filled with happy memories of birthday parties, holiday dinners, and Christmas presents under the tree that The Captain would set up in his living room. I parked the Galaxie 500 in front of The Captain's house underneath the giant maple tree that guarded the house. The rain had slowed again.

I climbed the stairs to his porch and rang the doorbell. A few moments later, The Captain opened the front door, and I could see he was surprised to see me standing there. I had not seen him since we had Easter dinner together. Although he was seventy-six that year, he was still a large, burly man with broad shoulders, a shock of white hair, and bushy white eye-brows to match. He always wore a pressed white dress shirt, blue tie, and a sport coat during the week, and on the week-end he would replace the sport coat with a sweater. Since it was a Saturday, he was wearing a sweater, red in color.

"Hey, Johnny, boy! This is a surprise. C'mon in." He opened the door wide.

I entered, "Hi, Grampa."

He closed the door behind me. "I was just having a sand-wich in the kitchen. Come on out." I followed him from the entry room, dominated by a bookcase filled with his beloved *Reader's Digests* and his recliner chair. Next to the recliner was a table on which sat his favorite pipe and tobacco in a pouch.

The kitchen was starkly white, with white paint on the walls, white appliances, and a white linoleum table in the middle of the room. "How is school going, young man?" he asked as he sat down at the table. A sandwich sat on a green plate next to an open can of Genesee beer.

"School is going good. I'm in my last year you know." I sat across from him.

"Is that right? How time flies. You want a sandwich? Beer?"

"I'd really like a soda."

"Help yourself. I've got a couple of Cokes. Grab one from the fridge."

I walked to old white GE refrigerator. He said, "So, what brings you up here on a rainy Saturday?"

I opened the refrigerator, reached in, and grabbed one of the two Coke bottles sitting in the sparsely filled refrigerator. I closed the door, and walked back to the table, "Grampa,

I've got a big favor to ask you." I sat down.

His smile thinned, and he arched his eyebrows. "What's up? You in trouble?"

I opened the Coke bottle and took a pull. "Not really, Grampa. But I kinda need a place to stay for a little bit."

"A place to stay? Where's your mother? What's going on?"

"I think she's thrown me out."

"What the heck? What happened?"

I told him the story, beginning with the freeze-out at home in the prior weeks, although I left out the details of the previous evening's party. I told him I had a few too many drinks at The Pine Lounge, and that led to my vomiting. He didn't ask any questions, but listened in silence, without a trace of expression on his face. After I finished, I drank deeply from the Coke. My recovering stomach welcomed the Coke with open arms.

He pushed his chair back from the table, and put his hands behind his head. "Johnny, that was really dumb on your part. I'm not too happy about hearing that you were so drunk. You know your mother has had a difficult life really. I'm not sure she has been the same since Jack died. You're too young to appreciate how difficult life can be when a spouse dies. I had a rough couple of years myself after Elizabeth died. I've only recently felt that I was emerging from a dark fog. So, I can see how your mom has had a big struggle. What do you want me to do?"

"Well, I was hoping you could let me stay here for a little while, until things get sorted out."

He chuckled, "Stay here, eh? You're not gonna throw up

in my house next, are you?"

"Absolutely not, Grampa, I've learned my lesson. It was a mistake."

"If you throw up in my house from being plastered, I'd probably throw you out too."

He ate his sandwich, while I sat awaiting his decision. He wiped his mouth after finishing his sandwich, and then said, "Here's what I'm gonna do. I'm gonna call your mother, and see if we can patch things up. I'm gonna call upstairs, you wait down here."

He stood and carried his plate to the sink, setting it down underneath the tap. He turned and strode out of the room. I heard his footsteps on the steps leading upstairs, followed a few moments later by the sound of a door closing.

I sat at the table and played with the Coke bottle, making it dance to some unheard song.

After a few minutes, I heard him coming down the stairs, and then he reappeared in the kitchen. "She didn't answer." He leaned against the refrigerator. "I think I might take a drive over there. It might be better to see her and plead your case anyway. You OK with that?"

"Sure."

"OK then. You make yourself comfortable in the living room. I think Notre Dame is playing Purdue in football. Should be a good game. Meanwhile, I'll run over to your house and see what I can do."

He grabbed his keys and left. I turned on the television in The Captain's living room and found the station with the Notre Dame game. I planted myself in his plush easy chair and impassively watched. After a few minutes, I fell asleep.

I dreamt about ML. We were at a school dance in the dark CC gym, and had been dancing a fast dance amongst a large crowd. As the music intensified, she had disappeared into the crowd that was feverishly pressing and surrounding me, preventing me from moving. I was frantically trying to fight through the crowd to find her when I awoke to The Captain shaking me with a grim smile. "Hey, Johnny, wake up, boy."

I sat up, blurting out, "What's up?"

He tapped me on the back, "For starters, how about you getting out of my chair and sitting on the couch?"

In the background I heard Keith Jackson, yell "Whoa Nelly!" from the television.

Still groggy, I rose out of the chair. "Sure, Grampa, have a seat."

He walked over to the TV and turned the sound down, then returned to his recliner and dropped into it. He looked at me and said, "Johnny, if you're going to be staying here, you're gonna have to follow the rules, and one big one is, this is my chair. If I'm here, my chair is my chair."

I walked over to the couch and sat down, rubbing my eyes.

Grampa sat back in his chair. "I spoke to your mother. She was home."

I leaned forward, "What happened?"

"I rang the doorbell, and I heard someone move to the door, but I didn't actually see her. She wouldn't open the door for me, but at least she spoke to me. You were right, she's thrown you out. She says you're an adult, and should be responsible for your decisions just like she was at your age."

"So, she's abandoning her own son."

"For the time being, it appears so. I told her you were going to stay with me. She was OK with that. She wished me well. It was a very strange conversation. I'm actually a little worried about her. You should be too."

"I don't care anymore, Grampa. She's been mean to me my whole life; I could never do anything to please her. What have I done that's so wrong? I've always got good grades. I couldn't have gotten into SUNY-B if I didn't have good grades. Right? I work hard. I've never been arrested. I've never humiliated her. She doesn't know how lucky she is. My God, some of the punks I went to school with! She doesn't know how lucky she has had it. It's just ridiculous."

He paused for a moment, as if thinking what to say next, and then continued, "Owen's gone too."

That news hit me. "What do you mean, he's gone? When?"

"She didn't say. I didn't ask too much. It wasn't the best time to engage in a long conversation."

"Imagine that. Wow. Things have really fallen apart."

"Yeah, Johnny, they have. I didn't know any of this. Your mother's always been kind of a private woman. After Jack's death, Elizabeth and I would try to include her in things, and she would bring you guys occasionally, but she resisted a lot. I always thought it was because we reminded her of Jack, and she couldn't bear it. She really loved Jack. He might have been her only love. Maybe that's why she's having issues with you too; you remind her of Jack. I don't know."

"Maybe we're just black Irish, Grampa."

He snorted, "I don't believe in that bullcrap! I used to hear that on the force, and I didn't believe it then and I don't believe it now. And you shouldn't either."

I looked out the window. It was starting to get dark outside.

I asked, "So, can I move my stuff in?"

He exhaled, "First, you have to agree to my rules. Rule one: don't come here drunk. I don't want to see that. There won't be any upchucking in my house, boy. Rule two: if you live here, you go to church with me every Sunday, starting tomorrow. Rule three: my chair—you heard that one. Rule four: it's my TV, we watch what I want to watch. Rule five: I don't want to hear any of that loud rock music. I know you young guys like it. I don't. Rule six: your hair can't get any longer than it is right now, and it's plenty long. That's it. Got it? Agree?"

What choice did I have? "I agree."

"OK, c'mon, let's go look at your new room."

He climbed out of his easy chair and headed to the stairs, and I was right behind him. On the second floor of The Captain's house, there were three bedrooms and a bathroom. The Captain ushered me into the room closest to the stairs. "You'll go in here."

I walked into a small bedroom sparsely furnished with two single beds, a bookcase filled with Reader's Digest issues from the 60s, and a dark wooden dresser sitting in front of each bed. I walked to the closest dresser, trailed by The Captain. Sitting on the top of the dresser in a fading frame was a photo of my father in his youth. I grabbed the frame.

"That's your dad. His high school yearbook photograph. This was his room. And his brother Michael's."

"I don't think I've ever seen this picture. Doesn't look much like me, does he?"

"No, he kept his hair decently short." He flipped my hair, "What is all this?"

"It's the style now, Grampa."

"I know but you guys look like girls. I never have gotten it."

I gingerly set the frame back.

Grampa pointed to a larger frame hanging above the dresser. "That's his high school diploma."

"That's cool." I studied it for a moment, then turned away, and walked to the bed. I sat down on it, testing the mattress. Finding it satisfactory, I lay down, with my head on the soft pillow. It felt good to lie down on a comfortable bed after the last twenty-four hours.

The Captain walked to the other dresser and lifted up another photo frame. "That's Michael, right before he went into the service." He stared for a moment at the photo and then gingerly returned it to its location on that dresser. He shuffled over to two windows that overlooked Oliver Street below. He pulled the curtain back, "This gonna work for you?"

"Yeah. Thanks a lot, Grampa." I looked over at him studying the outside. "This is kind of weird. I mean, I'm gonna live in the room my dad grew up in. Especially since I didn't really know him."

The Captain turned to me, and tried to discreetly wipe a tear away. "Yes, this is strange for me too. Nobody has lived in this room since he left us to be married. God, I'm feeling old right now. Who would have thought my two sons would be dead so long ago?"

He composed himself again and walked to the doorway, "C'mon, let me show you the bathroom."

I got off the bed and followed him across the hall until

he stopped by a closed door to the second bedroom on the right. "That's Margaret's room. We don't use it much anymore."

His daughter, Margaret, now lived in Detroit; she was a married to an engineer at General Motors, and had two daughters and two sons. She rarely visited. I had met my four cousins only a handful of times over the years.

When he turned the light on in the bathroom, I could see that it was quite large, and the walls were painted white, with a black and white checkerboard tile floor, and it was dominated by a large white porcelain claw tooth tub sitting imposingly in the middle of the room. "If we're gonna share this, you need to be neat, and pick up in here." He moved to a cabinet, and opened one of the doors showing its contents to me, "Towels and toilet paper in here." He shut the door and walked to the tub. "You'll find this out, but the hot water does come out HOT, so I recommend you pour in a half foot of cold water first."

I asked, "You don't have a shower?"

"No shower. You want a shower, you need to get one somewhere else. This has been good enough for my family for nearly fifty years, so it'll be good enough for you too."

He walked out of the bathroom, turning the light out on me. I followed him out. He pointed to the third bedroom just outside the bathroom, "This is my bedroom. I close my door at night, but I've been told that I snore, so if I were you, I would also close your door too. Any questions?"

"No. Thanks again, Grampa."

"OK, you better bring your stuff in now. While you're doing that, I'll order a pizza from Cortese's. I can't eat that spicy stuff, so just cheese and mushrooms. OK?"

"That's good with me."

"OK, but you have to pick it up when you're done unloading."

So began my life with The Captain at 20 Oliver Street. For the most part, my schedule stayed the same: up around eight in the morning on the weekdays, then off to classes at SUNY-B, followed by pick-up basketball games in the gym, then studying in the library. Later, when I came home to The Captain's house, he was usually in his easy chair in front of the TV in the darkened living room. Sometimes, he would be out cold, and I would wake him up. He would ask me about my day, and I would give monosyllabic answers, until he got tired of asking. Then I would saunter into the kitchen, look for food in the nearly-empty refrigerator, and make a sandwich, or make something in a can, either soup or Beefaroni. Occasionally, he would bring home takeout for two, and I would wolf that down.

On Saturdays, I would sleep late, to his dismay. After I awoke and pounded bowls of cereal down, he would enlist my aid in various work projects around the house. One Saturday it was raking the leaves from his front and back-yards to the street gutter. Another Saturday, it was helping to take the screen windows down and putting the storm windows up. On a third Saturday, I painted the trim on his front porch. I guess in his mind I was earning my stay.

After I finished my assigned task on Saturday, we would watch a game on TV, and then later he would reward me by taking me out to dinner, usually to the Little Venice on 111 Chenango Street north of downtown Binghamton, his favorite restaurant (and mine too). Inevitably at the Little

Venice bar heading into the restaurant, we would run into an ex-cop that he worked with on the BPD, and they would trade war stories from the "old days."

Dinner at the Little Venice was a fine plate of home-made pasta and meatballs, and a glass or two of the house Chianti, and our mood always improved after the Chianti. We didn't talk all that much, except about sports or current events. Mary Kate was never spoken about.

The Captain kept calling her without success, and he stopped by 59 Vine Street a couple of times, but after the first time, she wouldn't even answer the door. I was so pissed at her that I didn't bother stopping by or calling. I accepted that she was out of my life for good.

Of course, despite the turmoil, I had not forgotten about ML. I would often think about her during classes when my mind would thankfully wander about. I would especially think about her in my bed late at night before I fell asleep in the quiet of The Captain's house. Sadly, I was more bitter that I had not heard from ML as she had promised me than I was at Mary Kate for expelling me. Every couple of days, I would drive by ML's home on Riverside Drive, and my heart would sink. By the end of September, I realized that I had blown whatever chance I had with ML, and that one evening together had been it for me, and I had let her slip through my fingers.

That realization only increased my burning desire to graduate and escape from the misery and bad memories of Binghamton. At that time, there was an old joke among the young people of Binghamton that the best place to see Binghamton was in your rearview mirror. And I couldn't wait to see my hometown in my rearview mirror.

CHAPTER 7
Swept Away

You say it's nothing
But a game to play
Oh I'm feeling swept away

—Bryan Ferry

Binghamton, New York, October, 1975

BY EARLY OCTOBER, fall had sprung forth in Broome County. The hills were a Monet painting, awash with color: the deep green of pine trees, mixed with the burnt orange and red leaves of the maple and oak trees. The fall was always the best season in upstate New York; the days were temperate, the nights cool, and the mosquitos and gnats that were so annoying in the summer had disappeared.

Lizzie called The Captain's house on Wednesday, October 1, 1975. She had just found out from Mary Kate that I had been thrown out. After I told her what happened, she told me that I was way better off with The Captain than with Mary Kate, and I agreed with her. We promised to keep in touch, but, of course, we didn't.

I had not seen Tip since that fateful weekend two weeks before. But after leading the quiet life for two weeks, I was incredibly restless and bored. So, on Friday, October 3, 1975, after studying at the SUNY-B Library following my classes that day, I drove to The Pine Lounge. About eight o'clock I entered the bar, and scanned the room for Tip; he was not there. Although it was busy, I was able to take possession of a barstool. *Sanford and Son* was silently showing on the small TV that hung over the bar. Mack came over to me, and I ordered a Rock, my first in a few weeks. It tasted sublime, a golden bouquet of hops. I sat there by myself for two hours, sucking on Rocks, listlessly watching whatever was on the TV, and observing others in the bar laughing and partying, and progressively feeling more sorry for myself.

It was a little after ten o'clock when she appeared. "There you are! I thought you had disappeared!" I heard ML say from behind me. My heart leaped into my throat, as I turned. ML was by herself, dressed in impossibly tight jeans, a white turtleneck, and a sharp brown leather jacket cut at the waist. Her long blond hair glistened as if a bright light were shining behind her. She was smiling at me.

"What are you doing here?" I blurted out in shocked surprise.

"I'm home for the weekend. My cousin is getting married tomorrow. Where have you been? I've been trying to get into touch with you for weeks."

"What? What do you mean?"

"I sent you a couple of letters. Then, when I didn't hear from you, I called your house. I spoke with your mother. Didn't she tell you?"

"No. This is the first I've heard about it."

"Well, you guys are close, aren't you? Can you order me a drink?"

"Uh, yea, sure, what can I get you?"

She pointed at the Rock. "I'll have one of those. It's been a long time."

I got Mack's attention, and he lumbered down to me. I ordered ML a Rock, and after Mack ogled ML, he stepped away to grab a Rock from the cooler. I hopped off the stool, and pointed to it, "C'mon, sit down."

"OK. So, are you really telling me that you didn't receive my two letters?"

"No, I swear, this is the first I've heard about it. And I didn't know anything about your phone calls. When did you call?"

"I called Tuesday of last week, and then Wednesday, as in two days ago."

"And you spoke to my mother?" Oh, I was pissed at Mary Kate now.

"Yeah. Well, I assume it was your mother. A woman answered the phone at your listed number. I got the number from my mother. Your mother, or the person, took my message. I asked her to have you call me. She said, OK. Your family hasn't moved, right?"

Mack dropped a Rock in front of ML, I threw a dollar on the bar. He vacuumed it up, and left. She grabbed the bottle and drank.

I said, "Actually, I have moved in with my grandfather."

She set the bottle on the bar, "Really, when did that happen?"

"A couple of weeks ago." So, I told her the whole story. Well, most of it. I left out the party and the barfing. I just told her Mary Kate threw me out, and I had not spoken to her in a long time. She was shocked, and listened wide-eyed, sipping her beer.

When I finished, I drank from my Rock. She said, "Wow. That's a drag. I'm sorry, John. That's terrible. It's hard for me to believe that a family could have such bitterness. I'm so close to my mom and dad, and my sisters. I'm really lucky, I guess."

My thoughts flashed to Mary Kate, and Tip's father. "You are lucky, ML, I envy you."

She tapped her Rock against mine. "Here's to better days ahead."

I said, "I'll drink to that." So we did.

She set her empty bottle on the bar. "You wanna get out of here? It's kinda loud and smoky in here tonight."

"OK, sure, where should we go?"

"Let's go get a pizza. I'm starving. Pancho's Pit on Riverside Drive?"

"Pancho's Pit? Haven't been there in a long time. Sounds good. I didn't have all that much for dinner either."

I finished my Rock and set it on the bar. Then I escorted her out of the bar, watching all the guys in the bar undress her with their eyes as she glided through it, and feeling empowered that I was with her and not any of those assholes. I walked ML to her car around the corner, and said I would see her at Pancho's. I stayed there until she pulled out and headed away. Then, I sprinted for the Galaxie 500 parked a hundred yards away.

As I jumped in my car and pulled away from the curb, my joy and excitement was foremost, but as I continued to drive I began to focus pure rage at Mary Kate for coming between me and ML. I could give no mercy, contemplating what kind of a parent, or even a human being, treats a family member that way. Oh man was I pissed. My anger continued and burned like a blowtorch as I drove into the Pancho's Pit parking lot a few minutes later. I parked my car next to hers.

I sat for a moment and forced myself to calm down, and to forget Mary Kate. I would deal with that anger later. I got out of the Galaxie 500, locked it, and hurriedly walked into the restaurant.

Pancho's Pit was a small aging restaurant in a strip mall off Riverside Drive in adjoining Johnson City, blocks away from the large homes on Riverside Drive. It specialized in subs and pizza. She was waiting for me inside, near the entrance. The high school aged hostess led us to a table for two in the back. We ordered a small cheese pizza and two Cokes from a middle-aged, heavy, unsmiling waitress.

After the waitress left, ML turned to me and asked, "John, what are you really going to do?"

"I don't know. I guess stay with my grandfather until I graduate, and then get the hell out of here."

She put her left hand on my right hand. "I'm so sorry. I feel bad for you. I mean, that is just horrible."

"Thanks. Believe me, I am bitter, but I'm fighting it. I don't want to let it, you know, consume me. Let's focus on school, fun, the future, anything other than my screwed up family."

She removed her hand, and grabbed her Coke, and sipped it. Then, she said, "That's a good attitude, I think. Things can only get better, right?"

"Right. Nice pun too."

"What?"

"You know, things go better with Coke?"

"Oh, I get it. You've always been one step ahead of me with the cultural references. Let's focus on your trip to Boston. You still want to come, right?"

"You bet."

"In my letters that I had sent you, I found out there's really no good Patriot home games until December, when both the Bills and Jets come to play. Sorry about that."

I thought for a moment. "Nothing before that?"

"Not really. There's a home game the week before Halloween, but I'm swamped the following week with big papers due, and a couple of mid-terms. And earlier in October, I'm going to New York City with my roommate to stay with her folks. The weekend of November 9th works best for me."

That was disheartening. "I can come next weekend, ML."

"I do want you to visit, John, but next weekend is just not good for me. November is much better for me."

"OK. I'll plan on that November weekend. But it seems like a long time away."

She reached into her purse that was hung over her chair. "It's only a month, it'll fly by." She pulled out a sheet of paper and a pen. "I'm going to write my address, and my phone number, so we can keep in touch." She wrote on the paper, ripped it in half and handed both halves to me, "OK, write your grandfather's address and your new phone number for me." I took the half with her information, studied it for a moment, then stuffed it in my pocket. I wrote The Captain's information on the paper, and then handed her half back to her. "Here you go."

She studied it. "Where's Oliver Street?"

"It's on the Eastside, not far from Cortese's."

She folded her half again, and then stuck it and the pen into her purse. I sipped from my glass of Coke.

Turning back to me, she said, "You know, there was another reason that I wanted to get a hold of you."

My heart flared again, and I asked, "And that would be?"

"It's kind of late notice now, but in my letters I was asking if you would go with me to my cousin's wedding tomorrow. I had responded to the invitation a couple of months ago that I would attend and bring a guest. That's when I still with Dino of course. I know this is really last minute, but are you busy tomorrow?"

"Tomorrow? What time?"

"The wedding is at eleven thirty. Then there's a reception from one thirty to five thirty at the Holiday Inn Arena in Binghamton. It'll be fun."

"I can't believe you're asking me to go now. This is kind of surreal."

"You're going to have to wear a suit and tie, of course. Do you have one at your grandfather's house that you can wear?"

"Yeah, I've got a suit. I haven't worn it in a long time. But I can clean it up. I even have a pair of black shoes I can polish."

"It won't really matter."

"I'm not going to know anybody there. Is it going to be kind of weird for me to show up? Is your extended family going to think that I'm Dino?"

"Don't worry, it'll be fine. I'll take care of it."

The waitress then delivered our pizza. We attacked it vigorously. While we were eating, we turned our conversation to school. She told me about her political science and history classes she was taking at BC, her roommate, and BC's football team. I told her about how much I was enjoying my English class, and my current interest in the rock band Roxy Music (she had never heard of the band).

After we ate, we made plans for the next day. I was to pick her up at ten thirty at her house. Her parents and her two younger sisters were going to go separately, and we would meet them there. Over her stiff protests, I paid the bill. She convinced me that she would leave the tip, and she did. We left the restaurant and walked to her car. Before I could make a move, she gave me a hug, and thanked me again for the pizza and going to the wedding. As we parted, she unlocked her car, and got in. I walked around her car, and got in the Galaxie 500. I followed her out of the parking lot, and onto Riverside Drive. I was right behind her all the way to the driveway to her house. As she turned the car into that driveway, I flashed my high beams at her and waved as I passed by.

I drove back to The Captain's house, or maybe I floated all the way home. My heart was soaring as it could not have contemplated only a few hours before, and how I had been raised from the depths of youthful despair to the heights of desire. All I could see was her beautiful face smiling at me. Perhaps this was God's way of balancing out things, to reward me for how Mary Kate had behaved. While my anger at Mary Kate was vigorously renewed with what I had heard that night, I did not dwell on that anger too long, focusing on ML.

The Captain's house was dark and silent when I entered. I crept up the stairs, but they still creaked. Outside my room, I paused, and could hear The Captain snoring, even though his door was closed.

I got ready for bed. I tried to read some more Graham Greene, but it was a losing effort. I could only think of ML, replaying our moments together, and thinking about the next day, anticipating what might happen with her. I remembered our time in the car only a few weeks ago, and hoped that I would have another chance like that, hopefully tomorrow. I fantasized what it would be like to kiss her, and lie with her. It was a long time before I fell asleep.

I awoke with a start. I had not set my alarm clock. I looked at it now. It was nine thirty. I jumped out of bed, raced to the bathroom, and started the water in the tub going. Then I ran back to my room and flung open the closet door. I found a white button down shirt and my one blue suit that fortunately Mary Kate had thrown on to the Vine Street porch, and tossed them on the bed. I then stripped and jogged naked to the bathroom, and jumped in the tub, still filling with water.

Twenty minutes later I was clean, shaven, and dressed. I headed downstairs. The Captain was in his recliner, smoking his pipe, and reading the Sun-Bulletin. He said, "Whoa, look at you." He sniffed the air. "Man, how much of my Old Spice did you bathe in?"

"Is it that noticeable?"

"Nah. I'm just having a little fun with you, young man. And where are you off to?"

I walked to the kitchen, and yelled back, "Going to a wedding. I've got to split in five minutes."

As I entered the kitchen, trailed by the sickly sweet smell of The Captain's pipe, he called out, "Who's getting married?"

"A cousin of a friend of mine." I looked around the kitchen, and grabbed a banana from a bunch sitting on the bar next to the refrigerator. I poured a glass of water into a glass, and set it on the bar. I wolfed down the banana and then drained the water. I set the glass in the sink, and walked out of the kitchen into the front room.

As I headed for the front door, The Captain eyed me with a smile on his face. "Have fun, young man. Make sure you don't catch the garter, you're too young to get married."

"Don't worry about that, Grampa," I opened the front door. "See you later."

"I certainly hope so."

I closed the door, and moved quickly to the Galaxie 500. I pulled out abruptly and sped away. I raced to ML's house, but with Saturday in-town traffic and lights, I didn't get there until ten forty-five.

I parked in the empty driveway, and walked to the front door, and rang the doorbell. She opened the door a few moments later. She was smiling, "I thought you might have overslept."

She stepped out of the house, wearing a powder-blue full-length dress, and her hair was up in beehive. She was carrying a wrap and a small off-white clutch purse. In her black high heels, she was almost as tall as me.

"I did over sleep a little. I'm not used to getting up this early on Saturday."

She locked the front door. "Neither am I. Let's go."

As we walked to the Galaxie 500, she said, "My folks already left. We'll meet them there." I opened the door, and she got in.

After getting in, I put the car in reverse, backed out onto Riverside Drive, and then headed to the church. I announced, "You look great today, ML."

"Thanks, John. Nice threads yourself. We look like we're going to a prom at CC."

"Geez, I hope I look better than that."

"I wish I had gone to senior prom with you instead of Tony. What a mistake that was. He got drunk and was obnoxious, and then passed out after the prom. At times, it all seems like a long time ago. At other times, it seems like it was yesterday."

We arrived at St. Patrick's Church at eleven. St. Patrick's was a large red pressed brick Roman Catholic church built in 1873 and it sits on Leroy Street on the Westside of Binghamton. The small parking lot at the church was filled with cars, so we had to park on Leroy Street a block away. As we climbed the stone steps to the church, ML greeted distant relatives who arrived at the same time, and introduced me to them.

We slowly made our way into the old church. One of

the tuxedoed groomsmen met us at the back of the church, and asked us if we were groom or bride. ML told him bride, and we strode down the aisle, past rows of seated attendees. She pointed to her family about two thirds up. She entered that row and I followed, seated on the outside. Her father, mother, and two sisters scooted down the pew as we moved into it. ML introduced me to her sisters, Beth, her oldest sister, and Cathy, the youngest sister, her mother, and her father, and I gave them a small wave. She had told me earlier in the car that her older sister Marcy was in Europe on a semester abroad.

What a striking family they were! Beth and Cathy (even at fourteen) were a little taller than ML, but equally blond and beautiful. Her mother wore a stylish dress, her dyed golden hair was teased out, and she wore a large pearl necklace. Her father wore a blue pinstripe suit, crisp white cotton shirt, and red foulard tie; his salt and pepper hair was short, and his skin tone was ruddy. They looked like they could have stepped out of the pages of *Vanity Fair*. It was intoxicating to feel a part of this family.

Within a few minutes, the wedding began, starting with the priest and the groom, followed by his groomsmen, walking to the front of the altar from the sacristy at the front of the church. Then, the invisible organist in the organ loft at the back of the church began playing "Here Comes the Bride." We stood and stared at the back of the church. First, a wide-eyed small boy and girl, carrying rings on little pillows, slowly and stiffly walked towards the altar. One by one, the bridesmaids in their pink dresses slowly walked down the aisle, then the bride, dressed in a white gown with a long train, holding her father's arm, and jubilantly smiling as she looked around the church. As she passed our pew, I looked over at ML; she was broadly smiling, as her eyes followed the bride. At that moment I wanted ML to be my bride; I could see the two of us meeting on that altar and committing to each other for a lifetime. For the rest of the wedding service, I only saw the two of us on that altar, holding hands as we faced each other reciting the wedding vows, exchanging wedding rings, and then kissing each other in deep bliss.

After the service, the priest introduced the happy smiling couple to the attendees for the first time as a married couple, and the church exploded with applause. The happy couple walked off the altar, down the aisle, to the back of the church, to the music of "The Wedding March" played loudly on the church's organ. Groomsmen and bridesmaids arm in arm followed quickly. As they reached the back of the church, the back rows of attendees began to file out. I led our pew out to the aisle, waited for ML to stand next to me, she grabbed onto my arm, and we moved slowly with the crowd to the rear of the church, eventually walking out to the steps, into a bright, fall sunlight.

As we reached the steps, ML said to me, "Wasn't that a beautiful wedding?"

"Yeah, it was."

Beth and Cathy arrived next to us. As I stood by and listened, the three of them spoke excitedly about the bride's dress, her flowers, the groom's tuxedo, the ceremony. In a few minutes, ML's mother and father joined us on the steps. Her father moved to me, and stuck his hand out, "Hello, John, Mark Mooney. Nice to see you again."

I sheepishly extended my hand and we shook hands, his grasp tighter than mine, and said, "Hello, Dr. Mooney."

"John Moran, you remember Mary Lou's mother?" Mrs. Mooney stiffly moved to me and extended a gloved hand to me. "Hello, John." I limply shook her hand. She continued, "Nice of you to come on last minute notice."

"Hi, Mrs. Mooney. It was a bit of a surprise."

Dr. Mooney said, "Mary Lou says you're going to SUNY-B. How do you like it over there with all those radicals?"

"I am looking forward to getting out of there."

He snorted, "I'll bet. What are you studying?"

"My major is English."

"And what do you want to do with that degree?"

"I'd really like to be a teacher. In college, actually."

ML stepped to my side and said, "C'mon, Dad, no need for an interrogation yet. John, my dad has an undying curiosity about any of my dates."

Dr. Mooney laughed, "You bet I do!"

Shaking her head, ML said, "Oh, Dad. Mom, did you bring the rice?"

"Oh, I left it in the car, honey. Why don't you and John go get it for us? Mark, give her the keys."

Dr. Mooney reached into his pocket, and pulled out his car keys. Handing them to ML, he said, "There should be a bag in the backseat."

"OK, we'll be right back. Save our spots." She put her arm though mine, "C'mon, John," and pulled me down the steps. I gave a small wave as we left.

As we walked away from the crowded steps, she said, "God, my dad can be a pain sometimes. Try not to sit next to him at the reception or he'll interrogate you the whole time."

"Your parents are cool. Keeping it real, you're lucky."

She grabbed me a little tighter, "Aw, that's sweet of you to say. I do love my family, and I miss them." She must have realized how that might have stung. "I'm sorry about what happened with your mother, John. I couldn't imagine fighting with my mom or dad that way. Maybe she'll change some day."

"I'm not going to hold my breath."

We retrieved the Ziploc bag full of white rice from the backseat of her father's white Cadillac, and then walked back to the steps, where the crowd was milling around. As we neared the steps, a woman came out of the church door, and proclaimed, "They're coming out."

We rushed through the crowd to stand next to ML's family, and we distributed the rice in equal measures to the group. A few moments later, the bride and groom came out of St. Patrick's Church to loud applause, and then the crowd began throwing the white rice at them, and they dashed down the steps and into the waiting limousine in front of the church. During the barrage, we were also pelted with errant rice, and after it ended we were laughing and brushing rice off us. ML had some rice in her hair, and I gingerly removed the pieces from her golden tresses.

As the crowd began to break up and move to their cars, we said good-bye to ML's family, and walked to the Galaxie 500. ML was holding my arm close. I could catch traces of her perfume as the wind lightly danced around us. The sun was still shining brightly; it was a beautiful fall day. Red and gold leaves were falling from the maple trees lining Leroy Street. I kicked some of them out of the way as we walked. ML said, "This is the kind of day I picture for my wedding. And that was the wedding that I would like to have. She looked so beautiful. And he looked handsome. They are a great-looking couple."

"Like us."

She looked up at me, and smiled. "Of course. Like us."

We got in the Galaxie 500 and drove away.

ML sat facing me as I drove. "Do you ever think you'll get married, John?"

I laughed. She said, "Why is that funny?"

"I was just thinking of an old joke that I heard: Marriage is an institution, and who wants to be in an institution."

"Geez, that is lame."

"I know, I'm sorry. But to answer your question, I'm sure I will get married someday. I hope I do anyway." With you!

"I really thought Dino and I were going to get married. I had this whole plan in mind that I would graduate from BC, go to work for a year, maybe two, and then we would get married. We talked about it many times. We even talked about where we would have it, and where we would like to go for a honeymoon. Maybe that's why it was such a shock when he broke it off. If he wasn't serious, why would he even talk about those things? That's what hurts."

"It's his loss, ML. He made a huge mistake. He'll regret that the rest of his life."

In the corner of my eye, I saw her wipe a tear away. She said, "Christ, I am ridiculous. Thinking about him. Let's just have fun. Whatdya say, John?"

"Sounds good to me. First one to finish their first drink wins."

The wedding reception was held at the Holiday Inn Arena which was a short distance from St. Patrick's Church; it's an eight-story hotel that sits above the east shore of the Chenango River near its confluence with the Susquehanna River. It was the newest hotel in Binghamton at the time, and was the preferred location for a wedding reception.

We sat at a table with ML's family and an older couple, whose names and affiliations I forgot right after I was introduced. I was seated between ML and her father, as I expected I would be, despite her earlier warning. Maybe it was the drinks, or the live band playing the hits, or the constant banter at the table, but I laughed more in those hours than I had in months. Dr. Mooney told outrageously funny stories about his practice and patients that had the table guffawing. ML kept me busy hopping on and off the dance floor. And when she wasn't demanding my dancing services, her sisters made me dance with them. But when I was dancing with them, I kept an eye on ML at our table, admiring her, but also fearing that someone would ask her to dance.

Dr. Mooney and ML's mom were a striking couple on the dance floor, and they floated in each other's arms, while I stumbled around with ML patiently holding on. To my dismay, the three girls pushed me out to the floor to try and catch the garter that the groom tossed with great drama, accentuating every move, from slowly removing the garter from his bride, to flinging it over his shoulder blindly. I didn't jump for it, and the prize went to the groom's brother. The girls loudly berated me when I slunk back to the table, but Dr. Mooney clapped me on the back and congratulated me saying, "You're too young, believe me!"

Later, the girls practically ran to the floor to compete for the bride's bouquet. When the bride threw the bouquet into the air, there was a surge of single ladies to get it, but Beth as the tallest on the floor was able to out jump the rest, and she plucked the bouquet out of the air. When ML came back and sat down, she impulsively leaned over and gave me a kiss on my cheek. Red-faced, I looked over at her father and mother, but they were engaged in conversation with the bouquet-winning Beth.

I turned back to her; she was sipping her champagne. "What was that for?"

She set her glass down. "For coming with me today. For having fun and being my friend again after all these years."

"I'll drink to that." I picked up my champagne glass and held it to her. We tapped glasses and sipped from our glasses. When I set my glass down, she grabbed my hand, "C'mon, let's slow dance." She led me to dance floor.

The band had started playing the Chicago song "Color My World." We found an open space on the crowded dance floor, and merged together. She quickly put her arms around me and laid her head on my shoulder. I pressed my hands into her back, and, in looking down, I could see a sheen of sweat on her neck. As we swayed around in a tight little circle, I recalled our last slow dance at The Bank a little over a month ago, and how tightly she had held me then. She only lightly held me, and her hands never moved. As the song came to an end, she broke away, and looked up at me with a slight smile, grabbed my hand, and led me off the dance floor back to our seats.

The reception broke up shortly after the bride and groom left to loud applause and cheering. ML and I walked to the parking lot with her family. It was now dark, and a chilly wind was blowing from the northwest. At Dr. Mooney's Cadillac, I shook his hand, and hugged her mother, Beth, and Cathy. Then ML and I walked to the Galaxie 500 nearby.

As I started up the car, I said, "What should we do now?"

"I need to go home. We're going to my grandparents' house tonight."

"Well, that sounds like fun."

"Yeah, I know, boring. But I have to do it."

"Can we get together later?"

"I'd really like to, John, but we're going to be there a while, and then I have to get ready to fly back to Boston early tomorrow morning. I think my flight is like nine o'clock."

"Well, I just will have to go home and be bored."

"Oh, c'mon, John, didn't we have a lot of fun today?"

"It was a blast, ML. You are lucky, your parents are great. Your dad is so funny. I never realized that before; he always looked so ... so stern to me when we were in high school."

"Yeah, he's pretty silly. But he's a really good surgeon. I'm proud of him."

When I turned the Galaxie 500 into her parents' driveway, the house was ablaze with lights. I got out, opened the door for her, and accompanied her to the front door. On our way, she said, "So, please let me know about coming to Boston. I really want you to come."

"I'm definitely coming."

"Great, that gives me something to look forward to."

Then, stopping at the front door, she continued, "Thanks

again for going with me today. It made it so much more fun. I had a blast."

"Me too. It was way more fun than I thought it would be."

She leaned back against the front door, "Remember the last night you were on this porch?"

I shook my head. "Did you have to bring that up? I've been trying to forget that night for years."

She stared at me for an uncomfortable few seconds, and then said, "I have to go in. But I want you to know that you made me smile on the inside today." She moved to me and kissed me lightly. Overcome with pent up desire, I put my arms around her and pressed against her. She pulled back, "Not here, John." She removed my arms. "I'll see you in a couple of weeks."

She opened the front door, "Good night. Thanks again."

I waved and said, "Good night. I'll see you in Boston."

She smiled, "You better!" She stepped into her house, and firmly closed the door.

I stood there a moment, then turned and slowly walked back to the Galaxie 500.

I got in, started the car, and backed out. As I drove away from her house, I shouted as loudly as I could, "YOU FUCKIN' DUMB ASS!!! DUMB ASS!!!!"

I drove back to The Captain's frustrated: frustrated that the kiss had gone so wrong, frustrated that she could not spend more time with me, frustrated that she had to leave so soon, frustrated that I was living with my grandfather in dumpy east Binghamton and not on Riverside Drive, frustrated that I was going to SUNY-B and not Colgate, or better yet, Boston College.

When I got to The Captain's house, he was sitting in his easy chair in the living room watching TV in the otherwise dark house. "Hey, How'd it go, young man?"

Dropping onto the couch in the living room, I replied, "It was fun."

"Who did you go with?"

"Mary Lou Mooney. I went to high school with her."

"Is her dad a surgeon at Lourdes?"

"Yeah."

"He operated on several of the guys on the force. He's got some bucks."

"I know. They live on Riverside Drive."

"That figures. Well, just remember, John, it's just as easy to love a rich woman as a poor one."

"Oh, man."

"You liked that one, didn't you? You wait, you'll use that line again."

I slowly rose to my feet, "With that, I'm going upstairs. I've got to get out of this monkey suit, and my feet are killing me."

"You going to eat?"

"No, I had so much food at the wedding. It was ridiculous."

"OK, well, if I don't see you later, sleep well. I'll see you in the morning. Don't forget Mass tomorrow."

I sighed, and walked to the stairs. "I can hardly wait."

After I removed my dress clothes, I put on a T-shirt and a pair of sweats, and closed my door. I sat on my bed. My feet were aching from dancing in my rarely worn dress shoes. I grabbed *The End of the Affair*, and opened it. I had a paper due on the book in two weeks, and I had made little prog-ress in reading it. After the first few paragraphs my mind started to wander back to the wedding and the reception, in a kaleidoscopic swirl of images. I set the book down on the bed. I closed my eyes and tried to recall in as much detail as I could of every word ML had uttered that day, every look she gave me, each light kiss. And right before I fell asleep, I pondered over and over her last words, "Not here, John." What the hell did that mean?

About ten the next morning, I woke up. It was drizzling outside, and my room seemed ten degrees cooler. I got up, walked to the bathroom, and relieved myself. When I came back to my room, I put a sweater on, and started working on the Boston College graduate school application. The Captain stopped in at ten thirty, and advised me that we would leave for St. Paul's Church at eleven fifteen, and I better be ready.

After we returned from the service and ate lunch, I returned to my reading and kept going until two o'clock in the morning, when I finally fell asleep.

Over the next few days, I agonized over whether I should write ML or call her. By calling her, I feared appearing too desperate, too hungry. But to hear her voice, her laugh…that would lift me. But she might not be there, and I dreaded speaking with a roommate who would have no idea who I was; that would be extremely uncomfortable. Plus, a call to Boston would be an expensive long distance call that would show up on The Captain's bill. I definitely couldn't do that.

A letter would be less threatening, less urgent. And I

could craft my words so that I wouldn't say something awkward or stupid, or at least less so. I could be in touch for only the price of a sheet of paper and a stamp. So, I decided to write her a letter.

I wrote a first draft in the SUNY-B Library on the following Tuesday afternoon, after classes were done. Later that night on my bed at The Captain's house, I revised my first draft; it had been too honest and direct—"I think I am falling head over heels for you." I changed that line to "We have had so much fun recently that I miss being together. How about you?" On Wednesday afternoon back in the library after class, I revised the letter again, and changed that key line to "I am really looking forward to visiting you in Boston. I hope you are too." On Wednesday night, back on the bed, I rewrote most of the letter again, and went for a light tone, joking with her. I just couldn't bring myself to share honest emotion with her. Not yet. I feared rejection in the worst way. So, the line changed to "Boston better be ready for me, as I am ready to do it up right!"

On Thursday, I mailed the letter at the SUNY-B campus post office. I was happy.

CHAPTER 8

Shine On You Crazy Diamond

Remember when you were young, you shone like the sun.
Shine on you crazy diamond.
Now there's a look in your eyes, like black holes in the sky.
Shine on you crazy diamond.

—Roger Waters

Binghamton, New York, October, 1975

ON FRIDAY, OCTOBER 10, 1975, after I was done studying at the SUNY-B Library, instead of going home, I drove to The Pine Lounge. I was in a good mood; it had been a good week. I thought I might run into Tip there; I was almost ready to forgive him for setting in motion the events that led to my eviction from Mary Kate's house. I sat alone at the bar for two hours, and downed a couple of Rocks, but Tip never showed up. I asked Mack if he had seen Tip there lately, and after giving me some shit ("What am I, a fuckin' babysitter?"), he said he had not seen Tip.

Following a late breakfast the next day (I slept until eleven in the morning), I drove to Tip's apartment. I parked the Galaxie 500 next to the creaky stairs that led up to his garage apartment.

I climbed the stairs and knocked on his door. I knocked again a few moments later after no response, and called out, "Hey, Tip. It's John, open up, man." I didn't hear anything. I tried the doorknob; the door was unlocked. I cautiously pushed the door open, and stepped in. The room I stepped into was dark and smelled of cigarettes, alcohol, and a hint of pot.

I called out, "Hey, Tip, you here buddy?" A small tabby cat raced by me, and dashed out the door.

I cried, "Shit," and leaped back out the door, and chased the small cat down the stairs. I caught it before it got to the bottom.

"Where you going, little fella?" As I picked it up, the cat meowed and struggled in my arms to escape. I climbed the stairs, entered Tip's apartment again, shut the door, and set the angry cat on the floor. The cat ran away.

I searched the wall near the door, found a light switch, and flicked it on. I was standing in a small living room connected to a tiny kitchen. The room was a shambles. There was junk everywhere: clothes scattered around the room, old newspapers, empty boxes, dishes, ashtrays filled with dead cigarettes, glasses holding mysterious substances. I moved carefully through the piles to the kitchen area. On the small stove sat a pot filled with the remains of what looked like chili. An open bottle of vodka stood next to the stove on the tiny counter next to the sink. The porcelain sink was filled with dirty plates, silverware, glasses, and another pot, containing a black gelatinous substance. On the floor there was a dish half full of cat food, and an empty saucer.

I opened the old refrigerator that was emitting a low hum. A lone bottle of Budweiser sat on the middle shelf next to an open package of American cheese slices and a carton of milk. I picked up the cheese, and could see the beginning of a green mold on one edge. I opened the freezer door on top and sitting inside was a solitary metal ice tray. The cat came into the kitchen and rubbed against my leg, meowing loudly. I shut the freezer door, grabbed the milk from the refrigerator, and smelled it to make sure it was not sour.

I announced to the cat, "Here you go, little fella," and poured some milk into the saucer, as the cat voraciously lapped up the pouring milk. After filling the saucer, I returned the milk to the refrigerator.

I closed the refrigerator, and gingerly stepped to the bedroom in the back. I turned the light on. A mattress lay on the floor. Clothes were tossed everywhere around the room. You couldn't walk anywhere in that room without stepping on a pile. I couldn't tell whether they were dirty or clean. Two stacks of books almost reaching the ceiling stood at the foot of the bed against the wall. A small cheap brown alarm clock sat next to the bed on an old table that also held a bong, a plastic bag half full of weed, and an ashtray overflowing with cigarette remains. Several *Playboy* and *Penthouse* magazines were lying on the bed. I shook my head in disbelief.

The cat ran by me, and jumped on the bed. It was purring, and kneading a thick blanket that lay on the bed. I knelt down and stretched my right hand to the cat, which smelled it, and then after approving my scent, started rubbing its head against my hand. I petted it for a few moments. "You like that huh, little fella?"

I then stood, backed out of the bedroom, and flicked the light switch off. I took another look around the living room and kitchen. I could not see any loose paper or writing utensil. I headed to the door, checked to make sure that the cat wasn't nearby, turned off the light, and walked out, closing the door behind me. I walked down the stairs that angrily creaked at me, and walked to the Galaxie 500. From the back seat, I retrieved a pen and sheet of white paper from my backpack, and wrote a note to Tip, asking him to meet me at The Pine Lounge that night. I carried the paper back up the stairs, and wedged it in the door, near the doorknob.

I left and drove to SUNY-B to work in the library. My earlier bright mood was gone; I was profoundly dispirited. How had Tip ended up in such squalor? He had been blessed with so much ability and personality that I could not believe the way he was living now. Growing up I had always thought that Tip was going to make it big. No, I knew he was going to make it big, and that he would pull me along with him on his road to fame and fortune. And now he was living in a pigsty, working at a dead-end job, and I was a boarder in The Captain's house, just trying to survive a final year of SUNY-B.

My first memory of Tip is when I was five years old. I was playing with my sister on the front porch of our house at 59 Vine Street on a sunny warm day in late August, when a green Mayflower moving truck stopped in front of the empty house three doors down. I ran inside and told Mary Kate, and she hustled out to the porch, and stood with us as we watched the moving men in their green uniforms open up the truck in the back. A large Buick pulled into the driveway, and a couple got out of the car with their three young sons. Mary Kate said, "Looks like those are our new neighbors. One of those boys looks like he might be your age, Johnny."

Later that day, Mary Kate cleaned us up and took us with her as she brought over some brownies to welcome the new neighbors. Tip's mother greeted us at the front door, and invited us in. Tip and his brothers ran downstairs and followed us into their kitchen. His dad entered the house from the backyard. Introductions were made and brief histories were recited. Brownies were dispensed to hungry children along with sweet lemonade in paper cups. While the parents visited in the kitchen, Tip asked if I wanted to play, and I said yes, so he led me to the top of the stairs in his house, and then showed me how he slid down the steep stairs on his bottom. He laughed all the way down, and I followed his lead. We kept playing until Mary Kate left and dragged me unwillingly home. I was thrilled to have my first friend on my block.

Soon we were inseparable. We started kindergarten at St. John the Evangelist Catholic School a few days later. After school each day, we would get together and play until dinner. On the weekends we would play all day together.

As the years went on, our childhood play turned into older games of kickball, hide and go seek, or kick the can, usually played in the street in the summer. In the fall, we would play football in our small backyards. In the winter, we would play basketball, shooting baskets at the hoops attached to our detached garages. Tip was a much better athlete than I, smooth and fluid. He could beat me handily in every sport, although sometimes he would let me narrowly beat him, because I was a sore loser. If I lost a game, I would stomp and sulk, and occasionally even cry in frustration.

When we weren't playing sports, we would be playing games of Stratego, Battleship, checkers, and later, chess.

We competed fiercely in these games as we did in sports. I would beat him in the games much more than in athletics. He was a better loser than I; he would smile and always want to play again. He never got tired of competing.

In the long cold grey winters of our youth, after school or on weekends, we would often drag our toboggans and snow saucers up Vine Street above our houses. We would be bundled up in our parkas, boots, gloves, and hats as we trudged up that hill. We would spend hours zooming down upper Vine Street, avoiding any stray cars that appeared. As the day would go on, the snow would get so worn down that you could race quickly down the hill, shouting in delight, and always trying to make it farther on your current run than any prior run.

As we got older and sledding seemed so childish, we would bring our ice skates to the ice rink at McArthur School next to McArthur Park on the Southside that the City of Binghamton would create each winter by flooding a field adjacent to the school, and we would speed around the ice rink with total abandon. You could even skate there at night because the school's floodlights would shine far enough that you could see well enough on the rink to skate. We would meet our friends there, and often a game of "Blackie" would be called; Blackie being a game of "Red Rover" but played on ice. We would skate for hours, and come home weary and cold, and frequently Mary Kate would make hot chocolate for us. Drinking hot chocolate and sitting in our kitchen soon warmed our hands and noses.

But we loved the summers best, and looked forward to its return anxiously every year. During the summer, Tip and I would frequently go fishing, mostly to the nearby south bank of the Susquehanna River. On any weekend day during the school year when fishing season was open, or on any day during summer, we would rise early and leave for the day, carrying our fishing poles, our paper bag lunches we had made the night before, and a small bucket of worms. We would find the worms at night with flashlights in our backyards, or on the baseball field at MacArthur Park. We would carefully hunt for a worm by being careful to sneak up on it, after spotting it in the dim light of our flashlights, then reaching down and pinching it against the ground, and plucking it from its hole. Over time, we discovered that the best time to hunt for worms was during a rainstorm, as the worms would emerge from the ground as if escaping drowning. There were many nights we would go out into a fierce rainstorm to the amazement of our parents, and reenter our houses later, soaked to the skin, and covered from head to toe with mud.

Over the years we found a few places on the Susquehanna riverbank where we liked to fish. One of our favorite spots was west of Rock Bottom Dam, where a large maple tree had fallen partially into the river after a violent winter storm, creating a slow backwater pool that housed bass, perch, and bluegills. We would sit on the fallen tree and cast our lines into the water, and anxiously await a bite, sometimes with our legs in the river to cool us off. If it was a particularly hot day, and the fish weren't biting, we would jump off the log into the pool, swim to shore, and then do it over and over again. We never kept any of the fish we caught as our parents had no interest in eating fish caught from the muddy Susquehanna.

We hated carp and suckers. If we caught one of those bottom feeding fish, we were merciless; death would be swift.

Usually we would bang their heads on the dead log or on a rock on the shore, and then throw them back in the river, to drift away. If one of the neighbors had been to South Carolina in the past year, Tip would have a supply of firecrackers and cherry bombs purchased at Pedro's South of the Border. He would hand me the garbage fish, and I would hold its mouth open, and then he would light a firecracker, or preferably, a cherry bomb, force it down the fish's throat, and then we would toss the poor fish to its watery grave. Within a few seconds, there would be a muffled explosion, water would shoot into the air, containing pieces of the fish. We would stomp our feet and wildly cheer the hated fish's demise.

When not at the tree spot, we would make our way east along the muddy banks of the Susquehanna to Rock Bottom Dam, a gravity dam nine feet high and stretching 460 feet north and south across the Susquehanna, supplying drinking water to Binghamton. Walleye, pickerel, and pike would sit in swirling pools below the dam, looking for smaller prey. There were usually older fishermen at Rock Bottom, who were casting for these bigger fish.

In springtime, the Susquehanna was a dangerous, swift river, swollen with snow melt and we had to be very careful around the dam. Falling into the Susquehanna at that time of year would most likely mean death due to the fast current, or the inescapable undertow right below the dam, or the frigid temperature of the Susquehanna. But in the summertime, we could walk into the river on the surface of the dam, and on a hot day, the river would cool us off as it flowed over our legs. We were rarely successful at catching the bigger fish, as we were fishing with worms. The older fishermen who fished with lures that flashed and danced through the river like a small fish had more luck than we did. When one of these grizzled anglers would catch one on our side of the river, we would rush to his side to excitedly watch him fight the lunker and finally reel it in. Unlike us, those older fishermen, if they caught anything, would put it in a creel they carried, or throw it in a bucket of water on the shore.

Around dinnertime, we would trudge up the bank, across Conklin Avenue, continuing south to Vestal Avenue, through the surrounding neighborhood, and up Vine Street to our houses. On our way, we would make after-dinner plans, usually playing a game in the street, to be followed by sleeping outside in our sleeping bags. Our porch was preferred, as we could sleep near the action of the street; Tip's house only had a back porch. Mary Kate was surprisingly amenable to Tip and I sleeping outside.

When I would get home after a day like that, I would climb the stairs to my room and jump on my bed, tired but happy. Soon I would be absorbed in a Hardy Boys adventure, or a Tom Swift fantasy, or a Chip Hilton sports story. I would often fall asleep within minutes, until Mary Kate woke me for dinner. In those languid summer days, she would cook burgers or hot dogs, with sweet yellow corn and baked potatoes. Lizzie and I would race down the stairs to the kitchen, and as we hurried to see who could eat the most food in the least amount of time, we would discuss our adventures that day. Between the three of us, we would inhale a gallon of fresh lemonade that Mary Kate would make from scratch each morning.

After dinner, my sister and I would clean up, trading off each night who would wash the dishes, and who would dry them. As a reward for prompt and thorough cleaning, Mary Kate would give us ice cream in bowl. Sometimes, she would pour chocolate or caramel syrup over the ice cream. If she did pour a syrup, I would quickly stir the ice cream and the sauce together, admiring my masterpiece for a split second before stuffing huge spoonfuls of the mixture into my mouth, leaving an ice cream half-moon above my lips.

Later, we would run out onto Vine Street where we would meet our friends in the neighborhood, and play kick the can or hide and go seek until dark. Then, either Tip or I would ask if the other could sleep over. Tip and I would get our sleeping bags and pillows and drop them on the porch. We would watch TV for a few hours, and about eleven o'clock, Mary Kate would force us to brush our teeth, and then usher us to the porch, and we would crawl into our sleeping bags. She would say good night, and close the front door, leaving a light on in the living room.

Tip and I would stay awake for a while reliving the day and the fish we had caught, or the fortunes of our beloved Yankees. We would excitedly make our plans for the next day. Sometimes we would see fireflies flitting about the shrubs around the porch, and we had glass jars with us that we used to trap them in. If we trapped a firefly, we would carefully cover the glass opening with our hand and set the glass jar, with its opening down, on the porch near our pillows. We would marvel at the dim light that the imprisoned fireflies emitted. Tip would usually fall asleep first. I would be awake watching the fireflies, and then lying back on my pillow, content and thinking that lying in your sleeping bag next to your best friend on a warm summer's night was the best thing in the world.

Mary Kate would occasionally take Lizzie, a girlfriend, Tip, and I to nearby Chenango Valley State Park for the day. Mary Kate and the girls would head to the sandy beach the state had deposited at Chenango Lake in the park to swim and sunbathe at the pine tree lined lake. Tip and I would grab our fishing poles and worm bucket, walk to the lake's outlet, and fish. If we didn't have any bites, we would keep moving around the lake and try different spots. After a few hours we would head back to the beach. Mary Kate would go with us to drop our fishing gear in the car, and then we would return to the beach, pick up my sister and her friend and head to the park's grill. We would buy hamburgers, fries, and a big glass of root beer, and head to the nearby picnic tables (under a wooden cover), where we would eat the food quickly, with Mary Kate telling us, "Don't eat so fast, you'll get an upset stomach!" We didn't care; we ate like lions attacking a fallen gazelle.

After lunch, we would walk back to the beach, and lay on towels. Mary Kate said we had to wait a half hour before we could go swimming, otherwise we might drown. So, we would sit on our towels, watching other kids running into the lake and swimming with abandon. Every five minutes, we would ask how much time was left, and Mary Kate would wrinkle her nose, look at her watch, and tell us how much time was left. When our time was finally up, we would sprint to the lake and run into it, until it was so deep you had to fall forward into the cold water. The water in Chenango Lake was always cold, even on the hottest day of summer, so that when you first dove under the water, your head suddenly felt as if it was in an ice pack. Then, you jumped out of the water into the hot sun, and cried out, almost in relief.

Tip and I would race each other to the floating pontoons that were the edge of the swimming area on the lake, and then race back to the beach. We would do handstands on the bottom of the lake near shore, our fingers inserted into the muddy bottom, holding us up as long as possible, before we fell over, or one of us would push the other over. We would have "chicken fights" with my sister and her friend of the day. Although they were older, we would often win as Tip was fierce in a chicken fight.

When our summers ended, we would reluctantly begin school at St. John's Catholic School. I was a much better student than Tip, even in our early years. He was not dumb, but he was not sharp. He could pick up concepts but it would take him repeated effort and concentration to grasp math problems that I thought were easy.

Our teachers were nuns, of course, and they were mostly fierce educators, not willing to permit non-conformity or dissent. This did not sit well with Tip, who, even as a boy, was not one to repress his opinions, even when faced with the wrath of an angry adult. At St. John's, there was a narrow "cloak" room next to each classroom, where we children hung up our coats on metal hooks, placing our lunch boxes underneath. Often, if corporal punishment was to be handed out, it would be administered in the cloak room, where the blood curdling cries of the offender would traumatize the rest of the children, achieving the desired effect of maintaining discipline.

Tip was familiar with the punishments of the cloak room. Beginning in third grade, he seemed to end up in the cloak room at least once a semester for various offenses, usually mouthing back to a sister. However, in sixth grade, we had the dreaded Sister Helen for a teacher; she was an older woman, with no patience or sense of humor, who enforced discipline ruthlessly. Tip seemed to visit the cloak room once a month in that year. However, unlike the other offenders, Tip never cried out; he had a high tolerance for pain. When he was in the cloak room, we could only hear Sister Helen grunting as she smacked him on the bottom, or her more favorite punishment, hitting the offender's open palm with a ruler.

Unlike Tip, I was mostly a model student, or at least I was smart enough not to get caught. However, it was in sixth grade that I endured punishment for the only time in elementary school. Sister Helen demanded neat desks. Being neat was never my strong suit, particularly as a boy. Periodically, she would inspect our desks. One day in January, 1966, she was walking around the classroom, quizzing the class on math problems, carrying her chalkboard pointer, and waving her rosary beads around her aging fingers, when she stopped at my desk, and tapped the top with the pointer, "Open it."

In abject fear, I opened up the desk, knowing I was dead. The desk was filled with books and papers thrown about. I also had a decaying apple that had been in my lunch a few days before and some Bazooka Joe bubble gum which was not permitted in the classroom. Sister Helen looked at the contents of the desk for a moment, then cuffed me in the back of the head, "Boy! I will not put up with that in my classroom! You come with me!"

She yanked me out of my chair, and, pinching me on the ear, dragged me to her desk in the front of the classroom. The room was silent, and I could see my classmates looking at me with wide open eyes, as if they were watching an automobile crash in slow motion. When she had dragged me to her desk, she thrust me towards the metal garbage can, and yelled, "Pick that can up, mister! You're going to clean that desk out NOW!" I grabbed the garbage can, even as her hold on my ear did not let up, and then she dragged me back to my desk, as tears started to come into my eyes, more probably from the embarrassment than from the actual pain I was enduring. When we reached my desk, she released her death grip on my ear, and roared, "Mister, that desk better be spic and span in the next five minutes, or you will be even more sorry than you already are!" My desk was indeed spotless in record time. Even though she returned to teaching while I cleaned out the desk, I could sense the eyes of my classmates on me, although I refused to look at any of them as I was ashamed and fearful of crying. After I brought the garbage can to the front of the classroom, and returned to my seat, I looked at Tip, who was two rows away in the front of the room. He looked back at me, smiled and shook his shoulders in commiseration. My punishment was a good lesson to all in the class, however. During the rest of that year, there were no other students caught with an untidy desk.

When I reported this treatment to Mary Kate that night, she exploded in anger, slapping my face, and yelling, "What is wrong with you? How could you be so stupid? I don't want to hear any bad reports from those blessed nuns. You are incorrigible. After all I do for you, you behave like some heathen. You don't know how lucky you are to go to St. John's. Go to your room and think about it, and when you come back you better apologize for your disgrace!"

I went to my bedroom upstairs, shut the door and then did cry, feeling sorry for myself. For the first time, I considered running away, imagining that life on the road could not be any worse than sixth grade with Sister Helen and life on 59 Vine Street with Mary Kate. But it was January; it was snowing outside, and the temperature was ten degrees above zero and falling. If it had been summer, I might have actually made a break for it. Well, at least to Tip's basement.

Unfortunately, that wasn't my last incident in sixth grade. In late May of 1966 (almost made it!), I was caught by Sister Helen passing a note to Kathy Stallworth, my crush in sixth grade. I had made the mistake of saying in the note that I hated sixth grade and Sister Helen. She forced me to accompany her to the cloak room. As she pushed me away from her in the cloak room, she barked, "You hate sixth grade now, Mister Moran, wait until I am done with you." Her face was beet-red, and she was carrying the dreaded ruler.

"Hold your left hand out." She always inflicted punishment on the hand that you didn't write with, so you could still do work in class.

I limply extended my left hand.

"All the way out!"

I stretched my left hand an inch further.

She grabbed my left arm and forced it out, parallel to the floor, "Don't play with me, boy. Hold that hand steady, and keep that palm facing up!"

She put the ruler in her right hand, and then whacked the hell out of my left hand.

"Keep that hand up, boy!"

She whacked a second and then a third time. My hand

was screaming in pain, and I was biting my lip, fighting back tears. But I was determined to not give her the satisfaction of seeing my cry.

"Now get out! And I better not see any more funny stuff, or next time it will be worse. Believe you me!"

I walked out of the cloak room, and walked quickly past my classmates to my desk. I walked by Tip's desk on my return route, and he whispered, "Dumb Ass!" as I walked by. I didn't bother reporting this assault to Mary Kate after the last incident. I knew there would be no sympathy.

But somehow we survived sixth grade, and moved on to seventh grade, and we never had another sadist like Sister Helen again.

But school was not just classes, homework, tests, church, etcetera. Before school and during lunch, Tip and I found ways along with our friends to entertain ourselves. When we were younger, we would often play marbles in the school parking lot, hoping to win the marbles of others, particularly valuable ones like cats-eyes or bumble bees. Or, we would play games with baseball cards, such as throwing them against a wall, and the boy that could get closest to the wall would win the other cards in the game, with the best play to have the card end up leaning against the wall, standing up. If only we had known how valuable those baseball cards would be years later!

If we weren't playing with marbles or baseball cards, we would play tag or hide and seek, running with abandon on the school yard or parking lot.

As we got older, we would play whatever sport was in season before school and at lunch.

Beginning in middle school, we could try out for the school basketball team that played in the Catholic Youth Organization league. Tip and I made the team in seventh grade, and Tip started, the only seventh grader to start on the team. He was fierce defender on the court, and had a great crossover move that got him to the basket repeatedly, often leading to foul shots. I played sparingly; I was not as quick as Tip, but I had a decent outside shot. When I was on the court, Tip would often drive to the basket, near me, drawing my defender away, and then he would hit me with a pass, as I stood open. If I had a chance to set myself I could reliably knock a fifteen footer down.

In eighth grade, we both started, and Tip was the star, along with our big man, Mark Nolan, who had grown to six feet. I was the third option. Our basic play was for Tip to beat his man to the basket. If Nolan's man moved to defend, Tip would feed Nolan for a short shot. If Nolan's man did not move, Tip would take it hard to the rack. If another defender moved to defend, Tip would whip a pass to the suddenly open man, and often that would be me. I ended up averaging about eleven points a game over that year. We only lost to the team from St. James; they were loaded with talent that year (and some of them would be our teammates later in high school at CC).

Beginning at the end of sixth grade, Tip became a morning delivery boy for the Binghamton *Sun-Bulletin*, delivering the morning paper to homes on our street and in the surrounding area. I would sometimes join him. We would meet on Tip's porch at four thirty in the morning and wait for the *Sun-Bulletin* truck to pull up, and the driver to drop the bundled papers on the street, and then speed away. We would carry the papers into his kitchen, and then fold them tightly together into a flingable brick, and put the newspaper bricks into canvas newspaper bags. Then we would carry the bags outside, mount our bicycles, with the paper bag over our shoulders, and take off. Then we would speed around his paper route, throwing the tightly wound papers onto the porches or steps of the subscribers. If you could throw the paper such that it landed standing up against the front door, it was a source of great satisfaction.

Near the end of Tip's route, he had a few businesses on Vestal Avenue that he delivered to, one of which was the Binghamton Bakery. The bakery opened very early in the morning; we would enter the back door of the bakery, carrying the two papers that the bakery had delivered to it. On most days, the rotund unshaven baker sweating near the ovens in the back would give each of us a freshly cooked glazed donut, and we would attack our donuts as we left the bakery.

After climbing back aboard our bikes, we would continue to the last stop on his route which was a gas station on Vestal Avenue, near the intersection with Vine Street. We would wedge the paper into the handle of the locked door of the station, and then buy a bottle of Tahitian Treat soda from the soda machine that sat next to the front door. With the route now over, we would slowly drink the Tahitian Treat with one hand as we slowly rode our bikes home, with the first light of the summer sun rising over the hills to the east.

It was in middle school that we became Anglophiles. Our favorite programs were imports from England: *The Avengers*, *Secret Agent*, and especially, *The Prisoner*, which we watched religiously, and argued about its meaning incessantly. Our favorite bands were British; Tip preferred The Rolling Stones, while my band was the Beatles. Lizzie and her friends were obsessed with the Beatles, and she had every album and forty-five, which I later inherited when she left to go to St. John's. Unfortunately, they were left behind when Mary Kate tossed me on my ass, and I don't know what happened to them.

As we got older and entered high school, we left the Beatles and the Stones behind, and became fans of The Who and Led Zeppelin. And then in our senior year, Tip began listening to Pink Floyd and one day he brought over his Meddle album, and played "Echoes" on my record player, and I was hooked as well. When *Dark Side of the Moon* was released, I was enthralled, and I listened to DSOM so many times, that my album's grooves were worn away by 1975.

Later, during my freshman year at SUNY-Binghamton, one day at lunch in the SUNY-B Pub, I heard an odd British band over the speakers. When I asked at the cash register, I was told it was Roxy Music. I soon bought Roxy's first album, *For Your Pleasure*, and I was astonished; its lead singer with his doomed romanticism and sly wit was singing "*my song.*" Tip didn't care for Roxy Music at all. "It's not angry enough; it's not rock and roll," he told me after one listen. With each album in the early 70s, I thought Roxy Music was blazing a new trail. Tip ignored my entreaties to give the band another listen. He only listened to his big three of The Who, Led Zeppelin, and Pink Floyd. Of course, since he was liberally doing drugs, his choice of music was no surprise.

Beginning in sixth grade, we started to get more interested in the girls in our class, and they were even more interested in the guys, despite Sister Helen's best efforts. For the first time, we were invited to a birthday party with girls from our class. It was awkward; the guys would stand on one side of the room, and the girls on the other. We would only meet over food, although the host family would force the boys and girls to interact during a game or singing "Happy Birthday."

In seventh grade, we had our first dance at St. John's in the basement of the church. The school provided an old record player with tiny speakers and it was set up on a table in the back, with the volume turned as high as it would go. To the music of the Beatles, the Rolling Stones, The Beach Boys, Paul Revere and the Raiders, etcetera, the girls in our class would dance together with abandon. We guys would hang together in our group, dressed in uncomfortable sport coats and ties, watching the girls out of the corner of our eyes. Occasionally, one of the girls would break from the pack, walk over and drag one of the guys out to dance. Tip was popular with the girls; he looked like a young James Dean with black hair, and he had an easy banter with them. I was far too shy to be as popular.

In seventh grade, a girl named Debbie Fenwick had a crush on Tip, and he was not opposed to her attention. She pursued him by sending him notes, calling him at night, and sitting with us at lunch. Tip had his first date, arranged by Debbie, and I was invited to go along as accompaniment to Debbie's best friend, Sharon Scott. I had barely spoken to Sharon in school, so I was not anxious to go. But she was kinda cute, and Tip worked me until I said yes.

Tip's dad dropped us off on a cold Saturday afternoon in January, 1966, in front of the Ritz Theater in Binghamton to see *The Sound of Music*. The girls were already in the lobby when we arrived. Polite gentlemen that we were (having been warned by our parents), Tip and I bought the movie tickets, and then we got two big buckets of butter drenched popcorn, and walked with Debbie and Sharon into the theater. Debbie forced us to the middle of the theater, and then she had Tip go in first, followed by Debbie, Sharon, and then me.

I was uncomfortable to begin with, but having to sit next to Sharon made me extremely uncomfortable. Tip was too far away to talk to. Before the movie began, the girls laughed and chattered unceasingly, while I sat there, consuming most of the second popcorn. While Debbie would try to include Tip in the conversation, Sharon practically had her back to me, and would turn in my direction only to grab a handful of popcorn.

Finally, the movie started, and I was soon lost in the story. At the intermission, the girls got up and went to the bathroom, leaving us behind. After they left, Tip smiled at me, and whispered, "I felt her up."

"What?"

"You know, tits?"

"I know what tits are. What did they feel like?"

"Soft. Like a squishy peach."

"You're something, Tip."

"Hey, make a move on Sharon. She likes you."

"You think so?"

"No, not really."

No. Not really. I sure didn't try anything and we endured the rest of the movie together, although I was more interested in trying to slyly look over at Tip and Debbie to see what was going on there.

At the end of the movie, the girls insisted that we go to the Carvel ice cream across the street from the Ritz. We bought a large banana split and shared it, laughing as the chocolate ended up on our faces. Sharon even smiled at me, as I dropped a piece of banana on the table, and scooped it, yelling, "Five-second rule!"

Later, Sharon's father pulled up alongside the curb outside Carvel, and the girls got ready to go. Sharon said goodbye to us, and smiled at me, as my face flushed. Debbie waited behind as Sharon left, and then she kissed Tip on the lips as he stood there, surprised. Then, she danced out of the Carvel to the waiting car.

Tip hit me on the shoulder, "Did you see that? Did you fucking see that?"

"Yeah. I sure did. Is she going to be your girlfriend?'

"I dunno. We'll see. But what about that kiss? That was something."

For the rest of the year, Debbie and Tip circled each other, sometimes coming together for a brief periods, but often apart, as Debbie would find some perceived fault with Tip. Sharon would mostly ignore me.

In eighth grade, the school dances continued, but we also started having parties at our houses. In October of 1967, my basketball buddy Mark Nolan had a party, where only the "cool" kids were invited. Mark had spent much time before the party invitations were extended to figure out whom to invite. He consulted with Tip and I to verify what girls to invite. After much negotiation, a list was reached that consisted of ten guys and ten girls. Mark's parents were either extremely dumb or the most trusting parents in Binghamton, because they allowed us to have the party in a retrofitted two room apartment above their unattached garage.

Mark had moved his record player to the apartment, and for the first hour, we just played music, ate from sheets of pizza, and drank soda. At some point, a "Twister" game was opened, and we contorted ourselves around each other, leading to close contact with the opposite sex. After an hour of Twister, Mark grabbed an empty Coke bottle, and announced we were going to play "spin the bottle." I had heard about this game from Mark who had played it at another party he had gone to, and was uncomfortable with the idea, as I had not kissed a girl before, and was afraid of ridicule and the resulting embarrassment.

We got on the floor in a circle, with Mark orchestrating us so that it was boy, girl, boy, girl, etcetera. After the players were suitably arranged, Mark spun the Coke bottle on the carpet. It spun a few times and then pointed at me. Everybody laughed, and Mark sheepishly announced that it would only work if a boy could kiss a girl or a girl could kiss a boy, and he wouldn't kiss me if he his life depended on it. So, he respun, and this time when the Coke bottle stopped spinning, it was pointing at one of the girls. Both Mark and the girl leaned forward, and quickly kissed, to the approving cries of the group. The bottle was then passed to the girl on Mark's left, and continued in a clockwise direction.

When the bottle reached Tip, he spun the bottle, but then reached with his hand so that it stopped pointing at Debbie. Some of us cried foul, but he and Debbie kissed, and didn't separate for a few seconds, the longest of any pair.

Other than Mark's first attempt, I was not the target of any further spins. I was the last guy before the bottle would return to Mark. When the girl next to me handed me the bottle, I set it carefully on the carpet, and gave it the hardest spin I could. As it spun, my excitement was keen. The bottle finally slowed, and stopped, pointing at Sharon Scott. I hesitated for a moment, but she moved forward and I met her lips over the Coke bottle for a brief moment, and then she pulled away, and I pulled back to spot. I passed the bottle to Debbie who was seated on my left. As she was spinning, I looked over at Sharon, she was laughing, and avoiding my stare.

We played spin the bottle for an hour. I had two more chances to spin, and my victims were Debbie and another girl in our class. Those kisses were even shorter than one with Sharon. On Debbie's final spin, she did what Tip had done, and forced the bottle to point at Tip. This time, when the met over the Coke bottle, they locked lips for a long time, and clearly were French kissing, to the raucous applause of our group.

It was about this time that Mark's mother entered the apartment, to announce that it was time to go home, and Mary Kate was out front waiting for Tip and I. It had been quite an evening, and the highlight of eighth grade for me. Although I had been aware of some red spots on my face around that time, within a couple of weeks, my skin turned blotchy, as my hormones kicked in. I completely lost confidence in myself, and as the girls looked askance at me, due to my acne, I retreated into a shell, focused on sports first and academics second.

Tip and Debbie were a couple throughout eighth grade, and went out a couple of times. Tip invited me to go with them and Sharon, but I just couldn't face her with how I was looking, covered with red spots or worse, ugly white infected heads on bright red pimples. When

I looked in the mirror, I could not believe the face that stared back at me. My bitterness grew over the rest of the school year, and into high school, and I became quiet at school and sullen at home. I blamed Mary Kate for her DNA that had been passed to me.

I graduated from St. John's in June of 1967 with academic honors, and even won a prize for the best grade in English in eighth grade. Tip won an award for best athlete in the class, and he deserved it.

I looked forward to high school at Catholic Central in the fall; I needed a new beginning, and thought that my situation could only get better there. I also looked forward to playing sports at CC; the school always had good athletic teams, and I wanted to be a part of them.

Over the years, Tip and I fished less and less, and after graduating from eighth grade, we never went to fish at the Susquehanna again. Our time that summer was spent playing sports; Tip and I would walk to MacArthur Park and throw a football to each other in the morning, and in the afternoon, we would play basketball, either one on one, or with our former classmates at St. John's. In the evenings of that summer of 1967, we would often listen to music, mostly in my room since I didn't share it with a younger brother like Tip. Or, we would make phone calls from the rotary telephone in Tip's basement to girls from our class. Or sometimes, we would make prank calls, like the one to any drugstore in Binghamton: "Hi, do you have Sir Walter Scott in a can? Well, you better let him out!" At the end of that summer, Tip quit his paper route, as his dad wanted him to focus on school and athletics at CC.

Starting freshman year at CC was disorienting, as we were now thrown together with kids from other Catholic schools in the area, even kids living in nearby Johnson City and Vestal. Due to my insecurity and my acne, I retreated further into my shell. Since I had excelled at academics at St. John's, I was made part of the freshman Honors program, which is where I first sat behind ML. I had little in common with the other Honors program students. I was far more interested in the Knicks, Giants, or Yankees than any of the other boys in the Honors program, and so I felt like an outsider. Given the stiff competition, I also struggled academically in that first year of high school. I hated CC and wished I was back at St. John's.

When my first report card came home, I had a 79 in Biology, and Algebra was in the low 80s. Mary Kate made me sit down at the kitchen table and show her the report card. I could see her disappointment, and then anger, as she studied the report card for far too long.

"These grades are not good."

"Mom, I'm in the Honors program. The classes are tougher than grade school."

"You're smarter than this. You should be doing better."

"I'm trying, Mom."

"You must not be trying hard enough, or you would have better grades. There's not going to be any more TV on school nights until these grades get better. A lot better."

Of course, I protested this inequity. But to no avail. She was intransigent. As she was on most matters.

Unlike me, Tip blossomed at CC, at least socially. He became popular almost instantly. He was friendly and outgoing, and kids liked his smile and his unflappable insouciance. He was elected as freshman class vice-president. He became second-string quarterback on the JV team, and when the starter was hurt, two games in, Tip finished out the year, throwing a few touchdown passes. He was one of only three freshmen to start for the JV football team. I had made the team as wide receiver, but played little. I caught one pass from Tip in our last game, for fifteen yards.

At our first high school dance in the CC gym, Tip and I arrived together, but our evening was markedly different. I had not wanted to attend as my face had broken out, making me look like a facial pizza, but Tip had cajoled me to go. While I milled around with the other geeks from my classes, Tip was soon dancing with one girl after another, as I jealously watched him jump around to the fast songs, and meld together with his partner on the slow songs. I didn't dance once the entire evening, and I silently vowed to never go to another school dance again, and I didn't, until senior year when Ann and I were an item.

Once football season ended that first year, basketball began. CC had a reputation for producing well-coached, disciplined basketball teams, and the CYO teams were a good feeder program. Tip was one of three freshmen to make the junior varsity team that year, and he was the only one that started, at point guard. He had a solid year, averaging almost double figures, and the team finished second in league, losing only a handful of games. You could tell the varsity coach was keen on Tip, and it was a certainty that Tip would be on varsity as a sophomore.

I started on the freshmen team at off guard, and had a respectable year, averaging a little over ten points a game.

Most teams threw a zone at us because of our quickness, and that left me open for my long jump shots. As teams would change their defenses to guard me more closely, I would have more freedom to throw passes to my teammates cutting to the basket for easy shots. We went undefeated and were league champions for freshmen.

Beginning with the second half of my freshman year, I grew more comfortable with CC and my classes, and my grades improved over time, until by the end of the year, all of my grades were in the 90s, and I also had a score of 93 on the New York State Regents Biology exam, a score that I was immensely happy with. Perhaps my improved grades corresponded with my growing friendship with ML over the school year. At first, I was too shy to do more than respond with short, curt answers to her inquiries. I thought at first she was just having fun with me in a cruel teenage way; I could not believe that a girl that attractive could be that friendly to me. But over the course of the year, as she commiserated with me over grades, or asked me what I thought about some issue, I could see that she was really genuine, and there was no hidden agenda.

I think part of that may have been that she was a sports fan, surprisingly. Her father, lacking any sons, had tried to instill a love of all teams New York in his girls. ML seemed to be the daughter that absorbed her father's love of sports the most. When I realized that she was almost as big a fan as I was of the Knicks, I was shocked. After that we would often talk before class about the current state of whatever New York sports team that was currently playing.

Summer of 1969 finally came, and we had survived freshmen year. Over the next few months, Tip and I would play hours of basketball at our homes or MacArthur Park, or we would go to CC when the school had an open gym. When we weren't playing basketball, we were throwing the football in the street, or we would ride our bicycles to Recreation Park near CC and play touch football with classmates. It was during that summer that Tip began to be absent when I would stop by his house; he was hanging out with older basketball players on his JV team, and while good athletes, they were also known as "bad boys." They would get together at one of their houses when their parents were gone and carouse. Tip began drinking beer with them, and he was drunk for the first time. As a promising athlete, he found himself welcomed in the upper class macho fraternity at CC, and reveled in that acceptance.

His new friends bothered me because I knew they were knuckleheads and I feared their influence on Tip. And I didn't like them taking Tip time away from me. As the summer wore on, Tip was absent more frequently, and so I spent more time reading and watching reruns on TV, or shooting hoops alone in my driveway.

For perhaps the first time, I looked forward to school starting. I thought that with the start of school, Tip and I might return to our old pattern of hanging out, and I looked forward to another year with ML.

But Tip had entered another country, and had been changed by his stay there. While we were still good friends, and did things together in those first few months of sophomore year, Tip was also recruited by his new pals to accompany them at lunch, or on weekends.

My first period of sophomore year was Geometry, and my heart soared when ML glided into the classroom, wearing her mandatory uniform of white blouse, blue sweater, and plaid skirt, a skirt that was a couple of inches higher than as a freshman. She said hello to other students, looked around the room, spotted me, smiled, and came over to me.

She put her books down near the placard that rested on the desk, "John, John, John. Here we are again. How could summer go by that fast?"

She sat down, and her perfume surrounded and enveloped me. All was right with the world. In the few minutes before that first class, we caught each other up on our summer. Her family had gone to Cape Cod for three weeks in July, and she had played a lot of tennis and gone swimming at the Binghamton Country Club every day. Her skin was brown and her hair was near white from her days in the sun.

And a moment later our geometry class began, and with it, sophomore year. Very quickly I was absorbed in my classes, with projects, quizzes, homework: the homework that never seemed to end. I was also on the junior varsity football team and earned a starting position as a wide receiver. Tip was now the starting quarterback, and he was an impassioned leader on the field. While he was prone to pranks and fun off the field, even in practice, on the field he was controlled and compelling. He had a good arm and could throw a tight spiral thirty yards on a rope. We had a good line, and a swift running back named Mikey Caldwell, who was one of the few blacks in our school. With that talent, we had a good team. Until our final game of the season, we had only lost one game and that was a three point loss to Johnson City on a last minute field goal.

Although I was not the fastest player on the team, I had decent moves and a good set of hands, and the practice that

Tip and I had in the summer paid off. I caught twenty passes from him that year, and four were for touchdowns.

Our last game was against our public school archrival in Binghamton, Binghamton Central High School. The JV game was on Saturday, November 8, 1969, at one in the afternoon. We had a rally at CC on that Friday as the varsity team was playing Binghamton Central for the league championship on Friday night, November 7, 1969. The CC cheerleaders led by ML performed a few dance routines, and then led the assembled school in cheers, followed by the varsity coach, introducing the star players for the team, who charged up the assembled students with short impassioned speeches and repeated requests for fan support that night. Then we sang the CC alma mater. We were fired up as we headed out of school.

Tip and I had made plans to go to the game together earlier in the week, but when I stopped by his house at six that Friday night to walk over to North Stadium, his stepmom said he was gone, and that he had left an hour before. I was pissed.

So, I walked to North Stadium in north Binghamton alone wearing my CC green jacket on a cold November evening, as a bitter wind blew fallen leaves through the streets. I could see the bright field lights of the stadium towering in the distance. As I neared the stadium, the streets were full of cars streaming to the nearby parking lots. I joined the throng heading into the stadium. It was quickly filling to capacity on both sides. I headed to the CC side, passing by a few intoxicated Central kids, one of whom yelled over to me that "Central is going to fucking kill CC." I hurried away.

On the CC side, I walked by the packed stands looking for Tip or a familiar face. I looked out onto the field where the teams were warming up. The CC cheerleaders were also on the field. I spotted ML quickly; she was wearing her green top emblazoned with "CC" on it, a green hairband holding back that blond mane, green gloves, and a white pleated skirt, exposing those oh-so long legs to the cold November air.

I turned and walked on the track by the stands. At the opposite thirty yard line, I heard my name called. Mark Nolan was standing and waving at me about halfway up. Since he was now six three, he was hard to miss. I heard him yell, "Moron, get up here, we got room!" Feigning no embarrassment as I heard people in the stands laugh, I climbed the stairs, and forced my way down the row, saying "Excuse me" as I squeezed past. As I reached Mark, he punched me on the shoulder, "About time you got here." He was with three of my teammates from the JV football team, and we exchanged greetings as well. They all squeezed together and made room for me. When I sat down, Mark asked, "Where's your brother?"

"I don't know where Tip is. He wasn't home when I went to get him."

Mark snorted, "Ah, pussy. He's probably afraid of getting beat up by some Central fag."

At seven, we stood for the National Anthem, and at five after seven, the game began. It was a hard hitting, well-played game, but CC dominated in the first half with a crisp passing attack, and our stands were rocking throughout the first half, yelling at every big play. Going into the halftime we were leading 16–0 (we missed an extra point after our last touchdown).

At halftime, I left the others in the stands, and headed down to the restroom behind the stadium. There was a huge line into the men's restroom, and an even longer one into the women's restroom. As I was standing in line, I saw Tip emerge from the men's restroom and weave away. I got out of the line and jogged to him, tapping him on the shoulder, "Hey, asshole, where you been?"

He turned to me, with a broad smile. He was drunk as a skunk. "JM, you fucker. We are going to beat these assholes but good." He was rocking on his heels.

"Tip, you're blasted. Are you crazy? The coaches are going to see you; they won't let you play tomorrow."

"You think I give a fuck, Moron? You really think I give a fuck?"

"C'mon, Tip, let's get out of here. You're gonna get caught, you dumb shit."

He scoffed. "No fucking way. I want to see us win. C'mon, let's go meet the guys, we'll have a beer together. C'mon, douchy." He staggered off, bumping into people as he melted into the crowd. I didn't follow him. I was both angry at Tip for being such an idiot, and sad that he had chosen his CC friends and their self-destructive ways over me and our years of friendship. I turned away and returned to the back of the line to the men's restroom.

The second half of the game started ominously, as on the second play, the Central halfback ran sixty-five yards for a touchdown. After the successful conversion, the score was now 16–7.

Following the kickoff, a short run, and two incomplete passes, CC punted to Central. Central then powered its way down the field on an eighty-five-yard drive, running fifteen straight times leading to a one yard plunge by their fullback.

On our side of the stadium, it was now quiet, while the Central side was going crazy. After the successful PAT, the score was now 16–14.

After Central kicked off, CC again struggled, getting just one first down, and punted to Central. You could feel the momentum change in the stadium. On the second play after the punt, Central's speedy halfback went seventy-two yards for a touchdown. After another successful PAT, the score was now 21–16, Central. We thought the game was over.

Central kicked off, and after a short return to the twenty-eight yard line, CC then began its own long drive, which consumed the rest of the third quarter, and into the fourth quarter, finally having a first and goal at Central's two yard line. After four straight off tackle runs, finally CC scored. In the stands we went nuts, screaming at each other. With the successful conversion, the score was now CC 23, Central 21, with about six minutes to go on the clock.

Central got a good kickoff return to their forty-five yard line, and then proceeded to churn out the yardage against the exhausted CC defense. With a minute and a half left, the Central halfback went on a sweep, avoided two tackles, and danced into the end zone. With the successful extra point kicked, the score was 28–23.

CC returned the kickoff to the thirty-five yard line. After one incomplete pass, a CC receiver made a great catch, moving the ball to the Central thirty-five yard line. After a couple of successful out passes, CC made it to the fifteen yard line, with only forty seconds left.

The first play was a slant pass to a CC receiver, who had the ball in his hands, but he was popped by the Central safety, jarring the ball loose. On the next play, the CC quarterback scrambled around trying to find a receiver and then was dragged down at the twelve yard line, as the clock ran. CC quickly lined up, and spiked the ball, leaving eighteen seconds to go, but a fourth down. The stadium was literally rocking at this point, as on both sides, fans were jumping up and down, and screaming at their teams. When CC snapped the ball, the quarterback dropped back, looked to his right, and then fired a bullet to the tight end near the two yard line, but the Central safety just got his fingers on the pass enough to deflect it out of the reach of the CC tight end. CC lost possession on downs, and Central snapped the ball once, with the quarterback taking a knee, and the game was over. Final score: Central 28, CC 23.

The Central stands were now rocking, and their band played the music to the Central alma mater over and over, while their players and coaches celebrated on the field. On our side, our fans gloomily filed out of the stands, while some of us cursed the refs, the Central players, or our coaches. It took a few minutes to file out of the stands, and as my JV teammates and I inter-mingled with the jubilant Central fans, they taunted us, with "We're Number One, We're Number One!", "CC sucks! CC sucks! CC sucks!", or "Public School Rules!" I saw a few shoving matches, but we avoided that action, and headed out of the stadium.

We quickly walked away, at first part of a large throng of fans, and then thinning out the further we got from the stadium. We walked through a residential neighborhood around the stadium, and as we hustled on the dark streets with a cool wind at our backs, little was said in our group. We were too pissed. We were passed by many cars packed with Central fans, their horns beeping, and blue Central Bulldog pennants stuck out the windows at us. We reached Robinson Street, and turned left and headed west towards Binghamton's downtown.

At the intersection of Alice Street and Robinson Street, Mark and I said good-bye to our three JV teammates, who were headed to the Westside of Binghamton. Mark and I walked down Alice Street heading to the Tompkins Street Bridge to cross the Susquehanna to get to the Southside and home. We were about halfway to Court Street, when Mark and I heard someone yelling behind us. We turned to see who was yelling, and saw Tip, about fifty yards behind us, sprinting as fast as he could run and yelling, "Hey, JM! JM!" About one hundred yards behind him, there were three guys wearing Central jackets, racing after Tip. They didn't look too happy.

Mark sighed, "Oh, shit. Goddamn Tip."

We waited for Tip to reach us, my adrenaline rising. As Tip neared us, he yelled out to us, slurring the words, "You see those assholes? They're after me! Go! Go! Go!"

We stood there until he reached us, and then we stopped him. He reeked of beer and his eyes were bloodshot; he was clearly still hammered. "Lemme go, those fuckers are gonna beat the shit out of me." He tried to pull away, but Mark held him with large hands.

Mark snorted, "Tip, I ain't afraid of those guys. I'll beat the shit out of them."

At six foot three and weighing about two-twenty, Mark was surprisingly quick for a big man. He also had a nasty temper when he got mad, which fortunately was not much.

The three Central guys were yelling and cursing us, as they neared us.

Tip struggled to free himself, "You fuckers are nuts; they're gonna kill me. Lemme go, Nolan. JM, tell him to let me go."

Mark pulled Tip closer and yelled into his face, "When did you become a chicken shit?"

Then Mark tossed him away, and Tip stumbled and went to one knee, as Mark roared at him, "Run if you want to, you drunk pussy! I'm not afraid of those guys."

Tip weaved to his feet, and said, "You don't understand, they're gonna fuckin' kill me! C'mon, JM." He turned and jogged away, running towards the intersection of Alice Street and Court Street.

Mark and I watched him for a moment, and then turned back to three Central guys nearing us. Mark said, "OK, let's back up slowly. You get behind me. Those guys aren't gonna want to mess with me." So, I started walking backwards, behind Mark, and we retreated. He retreated with his fists raised.

As the three Central guys got close, they slowed down, as they finally noticed Mark and his imposing figure. One of them yelled, "Hey, man, we don't have a beef with you. Our beef is with the guy behind you. So, just let us go, and no harm."

Mark barked back, "He's with us. It's over, man."

"But that fucker pissed on me, man. You can't let a guy piss on you, man. He needs to learn a lesson."

"Get over it, asshole, or get what's coming!"

It was at that point that I turned to look behind me. Tip was jogging to the intersection of Alice Street and Court

Street. Without pausing, or looking for on-coming traffic, he kept going. In what seemed like slow motion, I saw him make it halfway across the street and then a large white car raced into view, headed at Tip. He didn't seem to hear the approaching car. I heard the awful sound of brakes yelling as they were applied with force, but it was too late, and I saw the front of the car drill Tip and throw him in the air and to the left and out of my view.

"SHIT!" I yelled and sprinted to the intersection. The white car sat where it had stopped. As I reached the intersection, I looked to my left and could see Tip. He had been thrown about fifty feet in front of the car. He lay still and his right leg was at a ninety degree angle. I looked over at the white car; it was a Cadillac, and its driver and only occupant was an old man sitting behind the wheel, staring straight ahead as if in a daze.

I ran to Tip, crying out to him, "Tip! Tip!" When I reached him, I kneeled down next to him. He was lying on his side, his face was littered with small cuts, and a large gash on his forehead was bleeding into his left eye. "Fuck, NO!" I cried. I ran back to the car. As I neared the driver's door, I could see the old man watch me. He reached over and locked the door. Reaching the door and out of breath, I started yelling, "Call an ambulance! Go call an ambulance! My friend is hurt badly!" He just looked at me as if not understanding. Then he looked away from me over my shoulder, as I heard footsteps nearing me. I turned to see Mark running to me; I didn't see the three Central guys behind him. Taking in the scene, he cried out, "Holy shit, what the hell happened?"

"Tip got hit!"

I heard the white Cadillac start moving, and I turned

back in time to see it pull away from us, around Tip lying in the road, and speed away, as I yelled, "You son of a bitch! Come back you son of a bitch!"

Mark spat out, "Fucker!"

I ran back to Tip, with Mark running behind me. I stood over Tip, as tears started to well in my eyes. "Jesus, Mark, what are we gonna do?"

Mark looked down at Tip, "He looks bad. Real bad. That dumb ass!" He grabbed my jacket, and shook me, "You stay here. I'll go get some help."

"What?"

"Stay with him. I'll go get help. You got it?"

"Yeah. Yeah, I got it. Hurry, Mark. Please hurry."

He turned and ran towards downtown, while I kneeled next to Tip. As I first kneeled there, I saw him suffer a spastic fit briefly and then he became still again. I saw headlights of a car coming at me in the distance, so I stood up, and waved my arms frantically, and moved into the lane of traffic. The car slowed down as it approached me, and then just kept going as I yelled in frustration at it.

After cursing the car, I went back to Tip, and sat back down. He was motionless. I spoke to my friend who could not hear me, "You've done it this time, Tip, you've really done it this time. Don't die on me, Tip, please don't die on me. Just hang on, buddy. If you go, I don't think I can make it."

Looking up into the cold black night sky, I spoke to the God that I had stopped believing existed, despite the constant indoctrination at CC, "Can you hear me? Please let him live. He'll do good in his life, he will be something. Just don't let him die. He's my friend."

Moments later, I heard the sound of a siren in the distance. I turned to look back down Court Street and saw a black and white Binghamton Police Department squad car racing towards me, its red and white lights flashing. Within moments, the police car came to a screeching stop near me, its flashing lights bathing the fallen Tip in a red and white glow. The siren was turned off, and a burly older police officer jumped out of the car and trotted to me. I could hear another siren approaching.

The cop knelt down looking at Tip, and said "What happened, kid?"

"My friend got hit by a car."

"Did you see it?"

"Yeah. Is he going to be OK?"

"I don't know. The ambulance is on its way and should be here in a few minutes. Were there any other witnesses?"

"I don't know."

"Are you OK?"

"What?"

"Are you hurt at all?"

"No. I'm OK, nothing happened to me."

The cop stood up and pulled out a small pad of paper and a pen.

"What's your friend's name?"

"Tip O'Neill … Tom is his first name. Everybody calls him Tip."

"Where does Tip live?"

"On my street. Vine Street."

"What's your name?"

"John Moran."

The cop stopped writing. "John Moran? Was your dad Jack Moran?"

"Yeah."

"I worked with your dad. He was a good man and a great cop." I didn't respond, and there was a short uncomfortable silence.

After the short pause, he went on, "You got a phone number for Tip's house?" I gave him the phone number.

The second siren became louder, and then we saw an ambulance speeding to us. The ambulance pulled over a few feet away from Tip, and two ambulance techs, dressed in white, jumped out of the ambulance, quickly removed a gurney from the back and wheeled it over to Tip. The tech looked at the cop, "What happened?"

"Looks like a hit and run."

The tech knelt down and looked Tip over with a flashlight. He looked over at the cop again. "You get the alcohol?"

"Yeah, I smelt it," the cop replied.

The tech motioned to me, "He should probably go."

"Yeah, we'll be at the car," the cop said. He tapped me on the shoulder, "C'mon, your friend is in good hands. Let's walk over to my car, I've got to call this in and then we'll sort this out."

The rest of the night was a blur. Tip was loaded into the ambulance, and it sped away to Binghamton General Hospital. I sat in the back of the police car, and gave a report to the cop, and then later gave a report to a detective who showed up twenty minutes later. When Mark Nolan returned to the scene, the detective took a report from him too. Neither of us mentioned the three Central guys. We were asked if we had been drinking and we said no. The detective asked if we knew if Tip had been drinking, and we both said we didn't know, but he had not been drinking with us. The detective was suspicious but he didn't press the matter.

Mary Kate showed up on the scene at some point. I was still in the back seat of the cop car. I watched her speaking with the cop, and then coldly look over at me, not a trace of warmth on her face. The cop finished up with her, and walked to the police car where I sat, opened the door to the backseat, and said, "OK, John, your mother's here, time to go home."

I climbed out of the BPD car, and walked to Mary Kate. I awkwardly stopped near her. The interviewing detective approached us.

Mary Kate said to the detective, "So, that's it for tonight?"

"Mrs. Moran, if we need anything else from John, we'll let you know, but you're free to go."

She looked at me, "Well, John, let's go." She turned away and started walking to her car, parked down the block. I started to follow. The cop reached out and grabbed my shoulder and stopped me. Startled, I looked over at him.

"John, stay out of trouble. Your poor mother doesn't need any more problems in her life. Make your father proud. Remember, if you lie with the dogs, you can't soar with the eagles. OK?"

I mumbled, "OK."

He released me and slapped me on the back. "Get out of here."

I slowly walked to our car, trailing Mary Kate. She opened the driver's door, and got in. I followed her, and went around the car and got in the passenger's front door.

We sat in silence for a minute. Mary Kate was gripping the steering wheel tightly and I could see the veins popping on her wrists from the tense grasp. Her face was as red as a beet.

Finally, she relaxed her grip, and staring straight ahead, she angrily said, "I wish your father was alive now so he could take a belt to your backside, mister, because you need it."

"I didn't do anything wrong, Mom."

"SHUT UP!" she yelled, "I don't want to hear it."

She started the car up, and pulled away from the curb. "Just be quiet. I need to think."

We drove home in silence. I was angry but fearful, as I had never seen her so mad. We crossed the Tompkins Street Bridge, west on Conklin Avenue, south on Mill Street, then right and west on Vestal Avenue, finally left on to Vine street, up the hill, and then into our dark driveway. She parked the car, opened her door, got out, and marched to the back door. I followed her. She stood inside at the open back door waiting for me. I looked down and tried to go by her at the door. She reached out with her hand, cuffed me on the back of the neck, and propelled me into the house. "Get in there!"

As I was pulled into the house, I stumbled, and then kept on walking to the kitchen, in the next room. As I quickly marched through the kitchen, trying to get away from her, she barked at me, "Come back here, you. Sit down at the table."

I stopped, turned, and walked back to the kitchen table that she was standing next to. She pulled out a chair, "Plant your bottom right there, mister!" Never looking at her, I sat down. She sat across from me, her eyes red with anger and disgust, her hair askew, and her hands firmly on the table.

"All right, now tell me the whole story and don't lie to me, or you're going to be in big trouble with me, mister."

So, I told her what happened that evening. As I had done with the Detective, I left out the three Central guys. She didn't buy it.

"That is bullcrap. Now tell me what really happened."

"I told you, Mom. That's exactly what happened."

"Where did you guys get the booze?"

"We didn't have any booze."

"Sergeant Walsh said you guys reeked. How much did you have?"

"I didn't have any, Mom! Smell my breath! Smell my clothes!"

"Don't you yell at me, young man, or I'll tan your hide! I'll ask you one last time, where did you get the booze?"

"I didn't have any alcohol. I just went to the game, tried to come home, and there was the accident. That's all that happened."

She slammed her hand on the table forcefully. "Liar! You better go to confession this week, young man, and pray to God for forgiveness. And starting tonight, you are grounded until December!"

"What? Are you kidding me? That is not fair. I didn't do anything wrong."

"You were drinking alcohol even though you are a minor, and you lied to me about it."

At that moment, a sleepy-eyed Owen appeared in the doorway leading to their bedroom, and asked in an irritated voice, "What's all the yelling about?"

Mary Kate flashed icy eyes at him, and said, "This doesn't concern you, Owen, go back to bed."

He asked, "This doesn't concern me?"

She said quickly, raising her voice, "Go to bed."

He stood there for a moment, deciding his next course of action. It seemed as if he were going to respond, but then he turned and shuffled away.

She turned back to me. "You woke him up. Are you happy now?"

"If we weren't having this stupid conversation here in the kitchen, he wouldn't be awake."

"You think this is stupid, do you? Who told you that Tommy O'Neill would never amount to anything? He's a bad kid. Anyone could see that he was bound to get in trouble and drag anyone around him down. But you were oh so smart. Well, mister smarty pants, how does it feel now? Who was right?"

"I didn't do anything wrong. I didn't drink anything and I didn't lie. Call Mark Nolan, he'll tell you."

"Oh, he'll lie just like you. I know how you teenagers are. You lie like rugs. A parent can't trust a one of you."

"You're ridiculous, Mom, and pathetic."

"Ridiculous? Pathetic? You're now grounded until Christmas. You want to keep going?"

I was so angry I sat there, fighting the powerful urge to tell her to go fuck herself. My hands were clenched so tight, my knuckles turned white. Oh, how I wanted to haul off and cold cock her evil smiling face.

But I fought that temptation, and exercising incredible restraint, I rose from my chair, turned away, and walked out of the kitchen, through the living room, up the creaking stairs to my bedroom. I slammed the door shut and lay down on the bed. I had a headache that was building. I rubbed my temples vigorously as I tried to rub the pain away.

I began to think of a plan to run away from home. If I stayed up a couple of hours, the bitch would fall asleep, and I could sneak out. I could fit some clothes into my book bag. I had about one hundred twenty dollars in my room. That would get me through a few days. I thought about the note I would write to the bitch and how I would finally tell her how much I despised her and her stupid rules, and that I would never see her again. I had a great time thinking what words of hate I could include in such letter. Oh, it would be beautiful!

And then the next thing I remembered was waking up on Saturday morning, November 8, 1969, to another cold grey November morning. The lights were on in my room, and I was still dressed in the clothes from the night before. I remembered that I needed to be at CC by eleven for the JV game that day at one at North Stadium.

The house was quiet when I came downstairs; Mary Kate and Owen were gone. I quickly dressed and left. I walked to CC. It took me fifty minutes to get there, but I made it in time to get dressed with the team.

In the locker room, our coach announced what had happened to Tip, and most players were shocked by the news. We said a team prayer and loaded on to the school bus taking us to the game.

The game was a disaster. Our backup quarterback was a freshman, and he was nervous. He fumbled the first snap, but recovered it. We got one yard on a halfback sweep, and then he overthrew a pass to me by ten feet. On our first punt, the Binghamton punt returner made some nifty moves, and raced seventy-five yards to score. It was all downhill after that. Binghamton just grinded us, running methodically down the field. It was 23–0 at half time. We finally scored a touchdown, and a two point conversion, with a couple of minutes left but the final score was 36–8. It was a quiet bus ride back to CC, and we showered in disappointed silence.

It was a slow walk back home later that Saturday afternoon. As I neared our block, I saw lights on at Tip's home, walked to the front door, and rang the doorbell. His mother opened the door; she looked at me with blood-shot questioning eyes. "John?"

"Uh, hi, Mrs. O'Neill. I was wondering how Tip is doing."

She didn't make any move to let me in, so I stood at the door, feeling the heat of the house slip by me.

"He's hurt really badly, John. He has a broken pelvis, a broken leg, his elbow is fractured, contusions, abrasions. He's not good, John. He's in a coma. He's not good."

"Oh man. I feel so bad for him, Mrs. O'Neill. What hospital is he at?"

"He's at Binghamton General, John. He's in the emergency room."

"Can I go see him?"

"No. They won't let you in the emergency room. His father has been there all night and today."

"OK. Will you let me know when I can go visit?"

"His father will let you know, John."

"OK. Well, I'll get going."

"John, what really happened?"

"He was trying to cross Chenango Street, and a car plowed right into him."

"Weren't you with him?"

"I was behind him quite a bit."

"The cops told his father that Tip smelled like a brewery. He's going to want to talk to you about that."

"Yeah. OK. Good-bye, Mrs. O'Neill."

"Good-bye, John."

I turned and walked down the steps, heard the front door close and lock behind me.

I continued to my house, opened the front door, and walked to the steps leading to my bedroom upstairs. Mary Kate flew out of the kitchen, and spat out, "Where have you been?"

"I had a football game today."

She rushed to me, "You are grounded, young man. Don't you remember me specifically telling you that last night? Don't you?"

"I remember, but I didn't think it meant I couldn't do school stuff."

"Grounded means everything. Until January. You are not free to go anywhere except to school, or with me. Do you understand me now? Do you?"

I barked out an answer, "Yes."

"Good. Go to your room. Dinner will be ready in thirty minutes."

I turned and marched up the stairs and into my room, again slamming the door shut as loud as I could slam it.

Little was said over dinner, even between Owen and Mary Kate. I ate quickly, washed my dishes and retreated to my room. Blissful fantasies of running away again filled my head as I tried to read that night. But I knew I didn't really have the guts to pull that off. Maybe if Tip had been around and gone with me, I might have been strong enough to do it, but not alone.

On Sunday evening, November 9, 1969, I was laying on my bed studying for a US History exam the next day when I heard the doorbell ring, followed by the door opening and the sound of muffled voices. After a moment, Mary Kate yelled from the bottom of the stairs, "John, come down here! Right now!"

As I reached the bottom of the stairs, I saw Tip's dad sitting on the couch behind the front window. He looked at me with exhausted eyes, his skin the color of cement. I had never seen him so lifeless. He wearily said, "Johnny, I need to talk to you."

Mary Kate was seated across from him in one of two chairs that faced the couch, separated by a small table. She motioned me to sit in the other chair. I saw that he was tightly gripping his fedora with both hands as he watched me sit down.

"How is he, Mister O'Neill?"

"He is in very bad shape. He had a lot of injuries, but he's making progress."

"Mrs. O'Neill said he was in a coma."

A stray tear escape his right eye and slalomed down his face. "Yes. He's still in a coma."

Mary Kate blurted out, "Dear God."

"I can't tell you how difficult it is to see him that way, Mary Kate. It rips my heart out."

She replied, "I am so sorry for you. What can we do to help?"

Looking at Mary Kate, he said, "I need information that Johnny can give me." Then, he turned to me, pulled a small pad of paper from his jacket and a pen from his pants, and said: "I need to know what happened with Tip on Friday night, Johnny. I'm not here to cause any trouble, but I need to know."

"I wasn't really with him that much, Mr. O'Neill. We were supposed to go to the game together, but he wasn't home when I stopped by. You can ask your wife."

"But you were with him when he got hit by the car."

"I wasn't really with him. I was behind him by about fifty yards."

"So, you were with him part of the time?"

"Yeah, only for a few minutes on the way home."

"He had been drinking, hadn't he?"

"Yeah."

Disgusted, Mary Kate exhaled, "I knew it."

As he wrote a note on the pad of paper, he asked, "Where did he get the booze?"

"I don't know, Mr. O'Neill. I really don't. I didn't see him except for a few minutes at halftime. And then after the game."

"Where do you think he got the booze?"

"From some older guys at school." Then, I then told him the whole story of that fateful evening. He asked few questions, and took notes. When I finished there was an awkward silence as he reviewed his notes.

After a minute, he looked at me, "Thanks, Johnny. I won't let anyone know that you told me all of this." He then stood up, and addressed Mary Kate, "I'm sorry to burst into your home like this. I'm not myself; I hope you understand. I'll leave you two now. I know Johnny has school tomorrow, and should be getting ready for bed soon. "

Standing, Mary Kate said, "Don't you worry about us, Mister O'Neill, you just take care of your family."

Tip's dad moved to me and put his right hand on my shoulder, "Thank you again, Johnny. Please be there for Tip; he's going to need you." He then shuffled toward the front door, with Mary Kate trailing him saying, "Please let me know if there's anything I can do for you to help out. If you need someone to watch the other boys, or cook them a meal, you just let me know."

Reaching the front door, Tip's dad opened it, and looked back at us. "I appreciate your offer; it means a lot to me. The one thing both of you can do is keep Tip in your prayers. He needs the grace of God to get through this. Good night." He hesitated, as if he wanted to say something more, but then stepped out, and pulled the door shut behind him. Mary Kate moved to the picture window, pulled the curtain back, and watched him leave. I heard his heavy steps across the porch and then down the steps.

After she turned the outside light above the front door off, Mary Kate moved away from the door, and looked at me. "That poor man. The troubles he has had. The Lord has set a path of obstacles for him. I will pray for that boy, but only out of compassion for his father." Her gaze hardened, "And you should pray for Thomas and yourself. Pray that the Lord will forgive your lying."

"I didn't lie."

"You were drinking too. I know you were. I'm not stupid. You think I fell off the vegetable truck?"

Exasperated, I stood up. "You're wrong, Mom." I walked to the stairs. "But you believe what you want."

"If you won't admit it to me, you better go to confession this week, and admit your sin to God, and get absolved."

I said "OK" as I headed up the stairs.

Tip's injury was the talk of the school that following week. During every morning announcement, there was a moment of silent prayer for Tip's recovery. The CC campus was rife with wild rumors regarding his injury. One troubling rumor that some students had heard was that Binghamton Central students had jumped Tip after the game and beat him into a coma, and there was talk about marching over to Binghamton Central and calling them out for a rumble. I patiently explained to anyone who would listen that rumor was unfounded and what had really happened. Teachers I didn't even know stopped me to inquire about Tip's injury and his status. To have such a severe injury to a CC student was unknown.

Tip remained in a coma for five days, finally emerging in a daze to a new world on the following Thursday, November 13, 1969. After leaving the hospital, Tip's father stopped by our house briefly to report the good news and he advised me that Tip didn't remember anything about the night that he was hurt.

A few days later, on Sunday, November 16, 1969, I was

permitted to visit Tip for a few minutes. Mary Kate drove me to Binghamton General Hospital, not far from our house. We went to the gift shop and I bought him the current issue of *Sports Illustrated* and a get well card. I wrote a short message in the card, and headed to the elevator. At the elevator door, Mary Kate said that she didn't want to see him; it would be too difficult for her, so she stayed in the waiting room. That was more than OK with me, so I rode the elevator to the sixth floor alone.

Tip was on the far side of a double room that he shared with an old man having difficulty breathing, who was surrounded by his family, and a curtain that separated the two patients. I passed by them and stepped around the curtain to Tip. Tip had no family in his room; I was alone with him. He was laying in bed, his right leg suspended in the air, two IV tubes inserted into his right arm. His face was covered with cuts, and his left eye was purple and swollen. As I neared his bedside, his eyes were closed. I stood there for a minute, fighting the urge to run out of the room, but then I grabbed a nearby uncomfortable chair and sat by the foot of the bed.

After a minute, I started flipping through the *Sports Illustrated*, and became absorbed. At some point, I happened to look up, and Tip was eyeing me quizzically.

I blurted out, "Tip! How are you doing?"

"JM. It is you. I thought I was dreaming when I saw you there. They've got me on so much pain medicine I am in a constant fog."

I stood and walked to his bedside, "So, how are you?"

"Look at me, asshole. What do you think?"

"Yeah. Not good."

"Oh, man. I want to get out of here."

"I'll bet." I handed him the card, and the *Sports Illustrated*. "This is for you."

He grabbed the card and *Sports Illustrated* with his left hand, set the magazine on his lap, and then opened the card. He read the card slowly, then looked up.

"Thanks, man. You're too sentimental."

"I can't help it. You know that."

"Ah, JM, we've been through a lot, haven't we?"

"Yeah. Do you remember anything about that night?"

"No. I keep trying to grab a memory, but I'm just a blank. I remember being in Tucker's Geometry class that day—God I hate that fucking class—and that is it until I woke up in here. My dad told me I got nailed by a car on my way home from the game. You told him that, right?"

"Yeah, I told him that."

"Were we together?"

"Sort of. Do you remember drinking beer that night?"

"JM, I don't drink during athletic season. You should know that."

"Tip, you were blasted." I then told him what had occurred that night.

"I wasn't drinking that night. I'm sure of it."

"Tip, you can believe what you want. But you ask Nolan. He was there, he saw. He'll tell you that you were drunk."

"Hey, how did we do against Central?"

"We lost. They popped us pretty good."

"Shit. We should have pounded those guys. We'll get them next year on varsity."

He pointed at his suspended right leg: "This isn't going to stop me; I'll be back. You wait and see."

But of course, he never came back. He lingered in the hospital for a month, enduring two surgeries on his leg and hip. When he finally came home, he was laid up for another month, and didn't finally return to school until January. He was in and out of rehab for nearly a year, but he never fully recovered, and ended up with a right leg that was shorter than his left leg by an inch and a quarter, and walking with a pronounced limp.

When he first got out of the hospital, he put a good face on his plight, still carrying the old Tip swagger. He would often tell me and other guys at CC that he had found a way to avoid the draft and going to Vietnam, and we would be envying him when the Viet Cong were firing their AK-47s at us in a couple of years.

But as the months of rehab continued, and his leg failed him, he became increasingly bitter, and by our high school graduation, ended up without hope. It was painful to observe, and there was little I could do to comfort him, or pick him up. He was inconsolable; his self-image was as badly fractured as his leg and hip had been.

He never attended another CC sporting event, even our sectional basketball championship game in March of our senior year. That was another pain he could not endure. I would sit with him at his house after each game, and relay a description of the game. He would listen, nod, make a comment, insult an opposing player even, but his affection for sports was gone.

He started hanging out with kids who had graduated from

high school and were living in make-shift dumpy houses, charitably characterized as communes, on the Northside of Binghamton. He stumbled through junior year and by the end of senior year, he had checked out, and was mostly mute and non-responsive in class, and teachers knew it, and after vainly trying for a while, ignored him. Somehow, he graduated, but college was out of the question, not that he was interested in it.

Shortly after graduation, he drove cross country with some of his new head friends. They smoked pot in Pittsburgh, Columbus, Bloomington, Iowa City, Fargo (Fargo!!!), Billings, Boise, Eugene, and then landed their craft in San Francisco. I knew the locations because he was kind enough to send me a postcard from each city, with a brief remark about the quality of the pot, and ending with a warm "Fuck You." The postcard from San Francisco was the last one I received while they were on the road. I bumped into his father in late August of 1972, and he informed me disgustedly that they had decided to plant roots in San Francisco.

I had heard nothing from Tip until he showed up at our door on a bleak Friday, December 22, 1972; I was on Christmas break from SUNY-Binghamton. I hardly recognized him, his once-short hair was now past his shoulders, and he had a full but unkempt beard. He was wearing a long grey coat, and a fedora that had been in style decades before.

"Hi, JM," he croaked as I opened the front door. "Miss me?"

I exclaimed in genuine surprise, "What the hell are you doing here, man?"

"You gonna let me in, man, it's freezing out here. I've been in California, and my blood has thinned out."

I threw the door open, and clapped him on the shoulder. "It's great to see you, Tip!"

He limped in and shivered. Mary Kate came out of the kitchen to see who it was. She arched her back and pronounced, "Hello, Thomas, welcome home."

"Hi, Mrs. Moron—Moran. Sorry about that. Merry Christmas."

Mary Kate backed up, saying, "Merry Christmas to you. Please tell your family Merry Christmas from us."

"I will do that." Then, turning to me, "So, college boy, how's JEWNY-Binghamton, you flunked out yet?"

I pointed up the stairs, "C'mon, up to the room."

Once in my room, he dropped his coat and hat on my floor, and fell on my un-made bed.

Trailing him into the room, I said, "Make yourself at home, asshole."

He put a pillow under his right leg, and eyed me. "Asshole? That's a nice way to greet your Christmas present."

"Oh, you're my Christmas present, are you?"

"Why else do you think I came to fucking Binghamton? For my health and well-being?"

"Yeah, right … So, when did you get in?"

"Last night. I just woke up a few minutes ago. I needed sleep. I don't think the old man is too happy with me. Of course, he hasn't been too happy with me for a long time."

"I'm not too happy with you either. How about a postcard or letter every now and then?"

He protested, "I sent you postcards!"

"Yeah, like three months ago."

"I was busy."

"Busy smoking weed."

He smiled broadly. "I did do a lot of weed. You can't believe the pot from Mexico that I smoked in Frisco. It was intense."

"So, why did you come back?"

"It's Christmas, man. You need snow and ice and freezing your ass off, or it wouldn't really be Christmas, now would it?"

"I could do without snow and ice. You just come back for your Christmas present?"

He chuckled, "Yeah. Christmas present all right. My mom has cancer."

I stepped back, "What?"

"Yeah, she was diagnosed a few weeks ago."

"What's the story? Is she gonna be OK?"

"No, JM, she is not going to be OK. The cancer is in her lymph nodes and spreading. Her doctor gives her six months."

She actually lasted a little over four months. Tip lived at home and was a primary caregiver for her during that time, until she got so bad that she had to go into Lourdes Hospital for her final days. I saw him infrequently, and he always put on a good show of being tough, saying little about her condition. I knew nothing I could do or say would make it any easier for him.

After her death, he only lasted three months living with his father. He found refuge from his pain in his twin demons of alcohol and grass. After constant battles over his dissolute lifestyle with his father, he moved to his uncle's garage apartment off Beethoven Street on the Westside of Binghamton, not far from The Pine Lounge. Within a year, Tip's father had remarried, to a widow from Johnson City. Tip didn't attend the wedding, he was too angry with his father for remarrying too soon after his mother's death. He thought it was just insulting to her memory, especially to marry Cruella Deville (as he affectionately referred to his new stepmother).

After he moved out, Tip and I rebuilt our friendship. Perhaps it was because we were still in Binghamton while most of our CC friends had left for college. While he still led a dissipated life, he became more interested in the world of ideas. He began to read voraciously, as if making up for his youth. At first he was fond of Hemingway and Salinger, but later became fervent about Vonnegut and Heller, often quoting from *Catch-22*. In the summer of 1975, he discovered Carlos Casteneda, and was soon fascinated with the spiritual journey described in Casteneda's books, or maybe it was the liberal use of psychotropic plants described in the books that appealed to him.

Often on Friday nights we would often go see the latest films together, including several remarkable films of the period: *The Godfather Part 2, The Exorcist, American Graffiti, Jaws, Chinatown, Serpico, Shampoo, Lenny*, etcetera. After seeing a film, we would retreat to The Pine Lounge to discuss the film over a few Rocks, debating the plot and characters. Sometimes, we would come to 59 Vine Street and hang out in my room, listening to my rock albums, and do the same. Those are happy memories of an engaged, thoughtful, and often passionate Tip.

Oh, he still got high and drunk far too often. While he would hang with me on most Friday nights, on Saturday nights he would disappear with his drug crowd. That annoyed and confused me, but it seemed that he was returning slowly to life, perhaps to leave the dark places behind at some point.

I recall how energized he was by Watergate. Tip hated Nixon, Agnew, Mitchell, Ehrlichmann, Haldeman. All of them. So did I. Tip was in San Francisco when Nixon was reelected. For my first presidential vote, I voted for George McGovern. I couldn't believe that he was beaten that convincingly. It was shocking. Before the election, someone had written on the bathroom wall in the Men's Room of The Pine Lounge with a black magic marker, "Why change Dicks in the middle of a screw-Vote For Nixon in '72!" I fully expected Nixon to screw the country even more after he was elected.

But not long after Nixon's reelection, the Watergate scandal broke, and a ray of sunshine broke through the clouds. Tip and I followed the Watergate saga fervently. Since Tip was working his furniture delivery job by then, and I was going to SUNY-B, I had more free time, so I would often watch the hearings during the day when I could and later call him to report the latest news. We were seated at the bar in The Pine Lounge on August 8, 1974, when Nixon announced his resignation. The packed bar erupted in cheers, with Tip's being the loudest and most vehement. Mack gave everybody in the bar a free drink that night. *That* was a good night.

CHAPTER 9

If

If I were a good man,
I'd talk with you
More often than I do
—Roger Waters

Binghamton, New York, October, 1975

THE SECOND FULL WEEK OF OCTOBER 1975 was a long and dispiriting one. I had a test in my Medieval History class on Thursday, October 16, 1975, and I didn't think I had done as well as I knew I should have done. A steady rain had fallen all that week, adding to my gloom. My thoughts (and fantasies) were filled with ML; her image and voice were playing on the screen in my head over and over. Concentration was difficult; avoiding her in my head was impossible.

When I arrived at The Captain's home on Friday, October 17, 1975, I was tired and down. A steady rain was pounding the Galaxie 500 as I parked in front of The Captain's house under the arms of that huge maple tree, and dashed to The Captain's covered porch. Even though it took only several seconds to reach the porch, I still was soaked. I shook myself, shedding water like a dog after a bath. I turned and looked at the rain sweeping across Oliver Street. After a moment, I turned, opened the front door, and entered The Captain's house to find him seated in his leather recliner, reading the Binghamton Press, watching me with a bemused expression. A half-filled glass of port sat on the table next to him.

"You look like a drowned rat, Johnny boy. Don't you have an umbrella?"

"It's in the trunk along with my backpack. They were wet from school, so I was letting them dry off."

"Well, hang that jacket up in the laundry room. Oh, and I got a pizza from Cortese's. It's on the kitchen table; I ate already."

"Thanks, Grandpa. I'll just toss the jacket out on the porch." I opened the front door, stepped out, laid my drenched jacket over the closest chair, and then stepped back inside, closing the door behind me. The Captain had returned to reading his newspaper. He flipped a page, and said, "Oh, you've also got a letter from a girl. I put that on the kitchen table too."

My heart fluttering, I muttered, "OK, thanks," and quickly walked to the kitchen. A pizza box from Cortese's sat on the table; next to it was a long blue envelope. I grabbed the envelope and studied it. It was from Mary Lou; her return address was in the left corner. She had addressed the letter to "Mr. John Moran" at The Captain's address. I chuckled at that formality. I turned the letter over, and written in large capital letters across the edge was "MISS YOU!" I felt my face get flushed.

Carrying the letter, I walked out of the kitchen and headed to the stairs. The Captain lowered his paper from across the room, and eyed me, "You didn't eat anything."

I stopped at the base of the stairs, "I'm going to put on some dry things first."

"OK," he looked at the letter in my hand. "Good news?"

I looked down at the letter, "Oh, I haven't read it yet."

"Is that the girl you went to the wedding with?"

"Yeah."

"Hmmm. I saw that she misses you."

"Yeah."

"Not going to say much, are you?"

"I guess not."

"I understand. I was young once. A long time ago unfortunately." He lifted the paper up as if to read. "OK. I'll see you later. Be sure to eat that pizza. I got it for you."

I started to walk up the creaking stairs. "I will."

I walked into my bedroom, and quietly shut the door. I sat down on the un-made bed, tossed the envelope by the pillow, took off my black Converse sneakers, and lay down on my back, with my head on the pillow. I grabbed the envelope, studied it for another moment, and then sniffed it. I thought I could catch the hint of her perfume lingering on the envelope. I carefully opened the envelope, making sure not to rip the "MISS YOU" in any way.

Inside the envelope, were two white pages, obviously ripped from a notebook. I quickly looked at the two pages (there was writing only on one side of each page); she had handwritten a letter in her beautiful cursive, a testament to the Palmer Method that had been so carefully taught to her by the nuns of her youth. I began to read it:

October 12, 1975

Dear John:

Hi from Boston! You probably didn't think I was going to respond so quickly, but I was really bored and had nothing else to do. Just kidding! I am really psyched about your visit on November 7. YOU ARE STILL COMING? RIGHT? RIGHT?

I've been finding out what is going on here that week-end, and there's some fun stuff. It will be a blast. I'm getting excited already.

What time do you think you can get here on Friday? We (me and my roommate) are going to celebrate surviving two tests that week, one of which is on that Friday. I will need a good stiff drink (or more!) to relax from that hellacious week. If you can't make it for happy hour, we'll do something later for sure.

How is everything at SUNY-B? Studying hard? Hardly studying (haha)?

School is going OK. I am busy with classes, projects, papers. It never ends. I am so ready to graduate. Not as ready as I was to get out of CC, but still ready to move on. It's kind of exciting, don't you think? I wonder where we will be a year from now. So many possibilities. And there's so many things I want to do and see. I've been kind of thinking about taking a trip after graduation. I've always wanted to see Paris, and London, and Rome. So, I'm really thinking about back-packing to Europe for a few weeks. I've never done anything like that, and it's a little scary, but it's time for me to "spread my wings." My dad will probably have a cow when I tell him about my plan. What do you think about Europe? Do you want to go sometime?

By the way, thanks again for going with me to the wedding. I hope you had a good time. My family can be overwhelming sometimes, but you seemed to fit in. Having you there with me certainly made it more fun for me.

Other than Ann, I haven't heard from anybody else from CC. I remember when we graduated, I thought our class was so close, that we would keep in touch afterwards, but it hasn't turned out that way.

Have you seen Tip? What is the latest with him? It makes me sad to think about what has happened to him. I hope he can turn his life around.

Oh, well, I've gotta sign off now, I need to leave for class. Write me and confirm that you are coming. I find myself thinking about you during the day, and I miss you. SO BE SURE TO COME TO BOSTON, like the song!

ML

P.S. I've also included directions to our apartment and our phone number on the enclosed sheet!

After finishing the letter, I reread it a second time, and then a third time. After the third reading, I closed my eyes, put my head on the pillow, and inhaled the trace of her perfume on the letter for a few moments and watched her image flicker on the wide screen in my head, first, holding me tightly as we danced at the reception, then as she drunkenly pleaded with me by the Susquehanna river that night in August. I replayed that latter image again and again in my head, alternating between feelings of regret at not taking advantage of that moment, and anticipation for being with her in Boston, when I *knew* that we would become one.

Later, I wrote my response to her letter, agonizing over every sentence, every clause, every word. It had to be perfect, witty without being offensive, direct without being needy, adult without being boring. It took me two hours to finish that first draft, and the paper was littered with edits.

On Saturday night, October 18, 1975, I reviewed the first draft, and rewrote the letter again, as I thought it was too direct in expressing how I felt about her. Although I desperately wanted to write that I was now MADLY IN LOVE WITH HER, I decided it wasn't a good idea to come on too strong, as that might scare her as she would conclude that I was too intense, too quickly.

In the SUNY-B Library on the afternoon of Sunday, October 19, 1975, I was trying to study for the GRE test the following Saturday, but my thoughts were consumed with ML. I pulled the letter from my backpack and scrutinized it again. This time, I decided to prepare an outline for the letter, establishing the information I wanted to relay in a more cohesive manner. Then, I rewrote the letter for the third time, reusing parts of both the first and second letter. I decided to go with a lighter tone, as I decided that was a better approach given our relationship, and I didn't want to be perceived as a jerk. I told her that I would try to be there by five o'clock on the seventh, and that I was looking forward to seeing Boston, but looking forward more to seeing her.

First thing Monday morning, before heading to SUNY-B for classes, I drove to the Binghamton Post Office, parked, walked into the building, and deposited my letter to ML in the outgoing mail slot. I lingered for a moment in the cavernous building, and then walked out into a sunny, clear, fall day. All was good in the world; I was going to rise above it all. That exuberant feeling lasted for a few days, and then the world reached out to slap me again.

On Friday, October 24, 1975, I had headed to The Captain's house earlier than usual after classes ended. After eating dinner with The Captain, I was in my room, cramming for the GRE the next morning, when I heard the phone ring downstairs. After a moment of muffled conversation, The Captain called up to me, "Johnny, phone call for you!" I immediately thought that ML was calling. I leaped out of bed and flew down the stairs, two at a time.

I picked up the phone that was lying on the table in the entryway.

Trying to stay calm, I blurted out, "Hello."

"Hey asshole, it's me." It was Tip, my heart sank back into place, and he continued on, "How's it hanging? What are you doing?"

"Nothing. Studying for the GRE tomorrow. It's gonna be tough."

"Tough, my ass! You should have to work for a living, then you'd know what tough is."

"Thanks for that advice. I'll try it in a few years."

"Hey, stick it where the sun don't shine, JM."

"I'll try that too sometime."

"You're a real funny man today. Dancing Dennis is having a blow-out party tonight. We are gonna party hardy. Be there or be square. You desperately need to go."

"That's nowhere, Tip. Why do I need to go?"

"Because there is going to be powerful narcotics there and chicks, and you NEED to be there, getting down and dirty with the rest of us. You might even get laid, something that will never happen with ML, you big dope."

"OK."

"Party starts blowing out at nine. Same place we went to a couple of weeks ago. You remember?"

"Yeah, I know where it is."

"Great, so what time you going to pick me up?"

"Tip, those people are low rent. What are you doing with them?"

"Low rent? Wow. Listen to mister high and mighty. Who made you God?"

"I'm not God, Tip, but those people are trouble. Listen, I can't go tonight, but come on over tomorrow night. We'll play a game, then we'll hang out at The Pine, have some beers, talk about old times. Let's just hang out."

There was a pause. "I can't do that, JM. To quote Casteneda: 'Nobody knows who I am or what I do. Not even I.' I'm flying a new course now, and forgetting my miserable past."

"Unlike you, Tip, I remember a lot of good times when we were young. The past wasn't completely miserable."

"If it wasn't, I don't remember it."

"You don't remember fishing at Rock Bottom Dam in the summer?"

"No. Are you going to pick me up or not?"

"Tip, I've got the GRE tomorrow. Are you not listening?"

"Fuck you, Moron," he slammed the phone in my ear. I said, "Peace out" to nobody, set the phone back on the receiver, and stood there a moment.

"What was that all about?" The Captain called out from the kitchen. I turned and walked into the kitchen; he was seated at the kitchen table, eating an apple, and reading the Binghamton *Press*. I pulled out a chair and sat down.

"That was my friend Tip. He wants me to go to a party tonight. But that's not going to happen."

"Well, tonight, young man, I'm playing cards with some of the guys I worked with at BPD."

"Have fun. Oh, by the way, I'm going to be gone for the weekend in two weeks."

He arched an eyebrow, and sat back in his chair. "What do you mean gone?"

"I'm going out of town to visit a friend. A road trip."

"Really? Where you going?"

"Out of town."

"I got that part. Where ... out of town?"

"Boston."

"Really ... Visiting that girl?"

"Yeah, just for a couple of days. I leave on Friday, the seventh, and I'll be back late Sunday night."

"Where does she live?"

"In an apartment near Boston College, that's where she goes to school."

"She living with any roommates?"

"Yeah, she lives with another girl."

"Where are you staying?"

"In the apartment, somewhere. Probably on a couch."

"I see. You must like this girl."

"I kinda do."

"Well, since I'm the parent figure, I guess I can only say, don't do anything stupid."

"I'm not planning on it."

He looked at his watch and rose, "I've got to go." He walked by me, stopped, and placed his hand on my shoulder. I turned to look at him. "You're a good kid, Johnny. You've been dealt some bad cards, but you can still make a good hand. You're smart and capable. I'm getting pretty darn old, but I want to help you. Just don't make any big decisions or mistakes while you're young. That's all I ask."

"Don't worry about me, Grampa."

He removed his hand, "But I do worry about you, Johnny. I do worry. I can't help it; it's my nature. Well, I've gotta go. I'll see you later."

"Yeah. See you later."

He headed out of the kitchen, then turned back, and said, "We've got to get ready for Halloween this week. You got some time to help me tomorrow after your big test?"

"Yeah, sure."

He said, "Good," and walked away. I heard him grab his jacket from his recliner, and open the front door. He called out, "Have a good night, Johnny."

I answered, "Will do." I heard the door close, and his steps shuffle across the wooden porch and down the steps.

The GRE exam the next morning at SUNY-B was brutal. I had not slept well the night before worrying about the test, and completing the test was a race for time. Unsurprisingly, I thought I had done better on the Verbal section than the Math section. It was a huge relief to walk out of the packed lecture hall that day.

Later, The Captain and I went out and bought four large pumpkins. The two of us carved the pumpkins, first removing the messy pulp, and then creating a smiley face on the front of the pumpkins. The Captain found some candles and holders in his basement, and we carefully placed them in the pumpkins. Then, we carried the pumpkins to the porch, and lit the candles to make sure that they worked, which they did.

The Captain and I went back to his basement, and after searching for a few minutes, he found a box on a dusty wooden shelf labeled "Halloween." In it he found a smiling scarecrow, dressed in blue overhauls carrying in a broom. Also in the box was a cardboard sign with a smiling ghost saying "BOO!" that could be attached to the door with tape. Finally, there was a large plastic pumpkin dish to hold candy.

The Captain set the scarecrow on a chair on the porch that he moved near the front door, and taped the sign on the front door. Then, he and I went to the A&P grocery store nearby, and bought a few bags of Baby Ruth candy bars. "The best candy bar," The Captain proclaimed to me, as we waited in line.

When we returned to the house, he filled the pumpkin bowl with the Baby Ruth candy bars, while leaving two of them out for us. He grabbed the two bars, and sat down on the sofa on the porch. He motioned me to join him on the sofa, and I did. He handed me a Baby Ruth, and I unwrapped it, and devoured it quickly.

"You're supposed to savor a Baby Ruth, not inhale it," he joked. His Baby Ruth was half-eaten.

"It was too good. I can't remember the last time I had one of those."

"You've always loved candy bars. I remember when your mom would bring you over when you were a little shaver, and I would offer you a candy bar from the leftovers from Halloween, and your eyes would grow big as saucers, and you would ask if you could have two candy bars. Your mother would say no, but I would sneak you another one anyway, without her finding out. Do you remember any of that?"

"No. When was this?"

"Many years ago."

The next few days moved at a glacial pace. I found myself looking at clocks frequently, wishing that time would move faster. It was a struggle to concentrate on lectures, reading assignments, paper research. It took longer to fall asleep at night, as my images of ML danced in my head, preventing slumber.

On Friday, October 31, 1975, it was Halloween. Around five thirty, I carried the bucket full of Baby Ruth's to the porch and set it on the porch near the steps. I grabbed some matches from the kitchen and, fighting the gusty wind that night, lit the candles in our carved pumpkins. When I went back inside, The Captain and I opened a couple of Michelob bottles in the kitchen, tapped them together lightly, and took them out to the porch. We then pulled two chairs over by the overflowing bucket and sat in the chairs, awaiting our first visitors.

As we sat there in silence, I started thinking about my Halloween evenings from many years before. When Tip and I were young boys in elementary school, as the sun would set around five o'clock in the evening, we would put on our costumes. I generally went with the cowboy look, Tip preferred the GI Joe costume. We would patiently wait for our parents to give us the signal when we could burst forth from our houses, usually around five thirty. We would first race around our neighborhood in search of candy. Instead of carrying cheap little plastic orange buckets painted with pumpkins or ghosts, we would strip our pillow case from our pillows and carry the pillow case as more candy could be stuffed into the pillow case than a cheap plastic bucket. Once we had finished going up Vine Street and back down, hitting only the houses with porch lights on, we would run home, and dump our candy into a bowl, and then sprint back outside. Like locusts we would descend on a nearby street, and quickly strip it of candy. We ran with abandon, energized by the search for candy and the freedom to run wildly from house to house, ringing the doorbell, yelling "Trick or Treat," holding out our pillow cases for the candy, watching the candy falling into the bag, and then running to the next house.

Once our bag was full again, we would run home and dump the pillow case into the bowl. As the night went on, our sprinting slowed down to jogging, then to a fast walk, and ending with a slow march back to our houses. Depending upon how much candy we scored, we might have two or three bowls of candy when we finished for the night. It was always a bittersweet moment when I trudged up the front steps with the half full pillow case over my shoulder, and left the then cold night air and walked into our brightly lit, warm house on a Halloween night. After dumping the final candy haul into the candy bowl, I would collapse on the floor, recalling the laughter, excitement, and thrill of the evening.

Although Mary Kate would try to grab the pillow case to wash it, I would not let her. After she insisted that I go to bed, I would drag the pillow case upstairs to my room, and pull it over my pillow. I would get ready for bed, and then climb underneath the warm blankets, and rest my head on the pillow, which carried the sweet perfume of candy, quickly dropping off to a deep, happy sleep.

And soon those innocent days of Halloween ended. When I was in middle school, Halloween night, and the nights leading up to Halloween night, became a time for mischief. Once it was dark, at a predetermined time, Tip would tell his folks that he was coming over to my house to play or watch TV, and I would tell Mary Kate that I was going over to Tip's to do the same. We would meet halfway, and then head out, far away from our neighborhood, and we would engage in offensive acts, like ringing doorbells (and then running away), or soaping the windows of a car or a house using the edge of a bar of Ivory soap, or worse, waxing those same windows with a bar of wax.

We would often be joined by other friends from St. John's, or by other juvenile hooligans we met while out in those far away neighborhoods. It was intoxicatingly liberating to run amuck without care or concern about our acts. And there was danger. Occasionally, police cars would circle the neighborhoods, after being called by concerned homeowners, and we would scatter and hide. Of more concern were the homeowners themselves. A handful of times a homeowner would burst out of his house catching us in the act, and chase us, screaming bloody murder. Without words, we would dash away, and split up, forcing the angry homeowner to pursue just one of us. Fortunately, I was never the one the homeowner went after, probably because I was one of the faster kids. They always seemed to go after Tip. Perhaps it was because he was cocky and laughed at them as they were pursuing him.

After those chases, I would surreptitiously make my way back to our neighborhood, taking a broad circular route home to avoid the neighborhood where the angry homeowner lived. Inevitably, I would end up at 59 Vine Street, sweating inside my jacket, with my legs tired from running. I would silently climb up on our front porch and sit, recovering from evening. Tip would come along in a few minutes and join me, and tell me how he had avoided capture, laughing with glee.

We grew out of such obnoxious behavior late in middle school, and the days before Halloween changed from committing acts of delinquency to preventing such acts on our houses. Nobody in eighth grade soaped windows; that was kids' stuff. Tip and I worked on our plan to attack those creeps that would try to soap our windows or cars. Our best plans involved water as there was no worse feeling than to be soaked with cold water on a brisk late October evening in upstate New York. At first, we filled up balloons with water, and hid on our front porch, until the youthful offenders approached, and then we would launch a furious water balloon attack. While this was somewhat effective and highly enjoyable, we decided we needed to have another plan, as inevitably the offenders would not get that close to us before we had to start winging the balloons, and it was hard to throw very many water-filled balloons as the offenders scrambled away, plus it was hard to be accurate throwing such water balloons.

So, our next idea, which proved to be very successful, was to turn on the water to the garden hose at Tip's house, and wait until our victims showed up. Tip's house was more appealing than ours, as our porch was long and sat completely in front, while his house only had steps and no front porch, and there were two windows about eye height at the front of the house that were attractive for mischief. As the pack of brats would scurry down our street looking for houses to hit, Tip and I would hide in the bushes at the front corner of Tip's house. One of us would be near the water faucet, and the other would hold the water hose and be responsible to run at them at the right moment. As the offenders neared us, it was all we could do to stop laughing from the excitement soon to be unleashed. Just as they got within a few yards of the inviting windows, the one holding the hose would burst forth, cold water shooting and soaking the young punks, who would holler in fear as they ran away. We would laugh uproariously as the soaked delinquents would run around the corner, and that would be the last of that group.

The next year, the delinquents got smarter; they would walk by Tip's house and confirm that Tip and I were hiding near the big bush on the corner. If they saw us, they would move on. So, we changed tactics. We got out the ladder, and pulled the hose up on Tip's roof, and then we waited on the roof. This was even more devastating to the perpetrators because as they approached Tip's front windows, all of a sudden, the heavens would open up on them, and they would take a shower of ice-cold water. Oh, it was a satisfying moment to see those dripping punks run off!

But the word got out, and over time, the delinquents chose other neighborhoods to terrorize. And there was Tip's accident. We never climbed on to his roof after that. Halloween became merely an evening of handing out candy to small children. Boring. Humdrum.

"John, can I have the matches?" The Captain asked breaking my reverie.

I handed the matches to him. He pulled a Tiparillo from

his shirt pocket, put it in his mouth, lit a match, and puffed the Tiparillo to life.

"No pipe? No cigar?" I asked him. I had only seen him smoke cigars or his pipe.

"No, not tonight. I don't smoke the pipe outside, and I only smoke cigars now when I have something to celebrate." He removed the Tiparillo from his mouth, looked at it, and said, "This little beauty is perfect for tonight." He pointed to our left, "Looks like we finally got company."

I looked in the direction he was pointing, and saw three small children dressed as a witch, a ghost, and cowboy, respectively, trot towards our neighbor's house. We would be next.

The Captain puffed on the Tiparillo, and then exclaimed, "Well, get ready. It won't stop for hours now."

It didn't. We had a steady stream of children, in all manner of costumes show up at our porch, and as the evening continued, the children turned into adolescents, and the parade did not stop until almost nine thirty, when three giggling teenage girls showed up, and then it became quiet.

I leaned back on the steps and looked up into the mostly barren branches of the maple tree overhanging the porch. The Captain pulled out another Tiparillo and lit it. We sat in quiet wonder.

After a few moments, The Captain said, "It's been a good night."

I grunted in approval.

He held the Tiparillo out, and flicked away some ashes that blew away in the breeze scattering on the lawn below us. "I wonder if your mother gave out candy tonight."

"I don't know and I don't care."

"John, she is your mother."

"Not anymore."

"Well, sport, you have every reason to feel anger. But I believe in forgiveness, and that people can be redeemed. So, I hold out hope for her. I think I'll try to contact her again."

"You can do whatever you want to, Grampa. But I am done with her."

He inhaled deeply, then blew a perfect "O" smoke ring, which dissipated quickly.

"She's your mother; you can't really be done with her. This is just a speed bump."

"It's no speed bump, it's Mount Everest."

He snorted. "Ahh… Well, we'll see…"

He ground the Tiparillo into the porch until it was out and then he tossed its remains on the lawn. "Ready to head in?"

"Yeah."

I carried the bowl containing only a handful of Baby Ruth bars into the kitchen, and set it on the kitchen table. I grabbed the few remaining candy bars from the bowl and took them to a cabinet in the pantry, and stuck them in a drawer with the other candy bars aging quietly within.

When I walked out of the kitchen, The Captain was sitting in his recliner, feet up.

"That was a good night, Johnny boy. At my age, you never know how many more Halloweens you are going to see."

That was the first time I had heard The Captain mention

his own mortality, and it surprised me. "C'mon, Grampa, you've got a lot of years left."

"We'll see. I hope you are right."

"I'm going to head upstairs and get some reading done for school."

"OK. Say Johnny, I really mean it, don't give up on your mother. Please. If I have learned one thing in my years on this planet, it is that strange things can and do happen. And I think she might just come around."

"I hope you're right." I started up the stairs. "See you in the morning."

"God willing you will. Sleep well."

On Tuesday and Wednesday of that week, I finally finished my other graduate school applications and mailed them.

On Thursday, November 6, 1975, I attended my classes as usual at SUNY-B, studied in the library, and left for The Captain's house at 6:00 p.m. When I got to The Captain's house, I discovered that The Captain had bought a bucket of Kentucky Fried Chicken and two sides: mashed potatoes with gravy, and cole slaw. After dumping my backpack in my room, I ravenously attacked the KFC food on a tray table in the living room while watching the CBS Evening News with Walter Cronkite with The Captain.

At seven forty, the phone rang, and I said, "I'll get it." I hurried to the phone in the entryway and answered. I was shocked to hear the voice of Tip's dad.

"John, is that you?"

"Yes. Hi, Mr. O'Neill. Were you calling for my grandfather?"

"No, John, I was calling for you."

My stomach began to churn. "Oh. What's up?"

He sighed deeply, and then said, "Do you know where Tip is?"

"Tip? No, I don't. Why? What's going on?"

"His employer called me tonight and said he hasn't showed up for work all week, and they sent someone over to his apartment, and he didn't answer the door. So, I thought you might know where he is."

"Wow, Mr. O'Neill, I'm kinda stunned here. But I really don't know."

"John, this is very important. You and Tip have been friends a long time. I don't want you to protect him now. We need to find him."

"I'll do anything to help you."

"When was the last time you saw Tip?"

"Uh, it's been a few weeks. But I talked to him on the phone last Friday."

"Where was he?"

"I don't know."

"Did he say anything that would be helpful to finding him?"

And I paused, because I could now see where this was going. And I knew right away that this could end badly. If I told him about the party and the house, Tip would be pissed at me. But I couldn't hide that information, especially if Tip was in trouble or needed help. So, I dove in the deep end. "Well, he did invite me to go to a party with him that night but I declined."

"Where was this party?" The sudden anxiety in his

voice revealed his interest in this information. I gave him the address of the house in Conklin, and told him general directions to get there.

"Thanks, John. That could be extremely helpful. Could you put your grandfather on the phone for a moment?"

"Uh, sure, hold on."

I called out, "Grampa, can you come to the phone?"

I heard The Captain get up, walk to the TV, and turn the sound down. He appeared a moment later, a puzzled look on his face, and silently mouthed, "Who is that?"

I covered up the mouthpiece, and whispered, "It's my friend Tip O'Neill's dad. He's looking for Tip." I thrust the phone to him and he took it.

"Patrick Moran here. Who is this?"

What followed was The Captain saying "Yes" and "I see" and "Hummmm." After a few minutes of explanation from Tip's dad, The Captain said, "I'll call Jim Greene tomorrow and see if anything can be done … I understand … You're welcome … Your number is in the book, right? … Good, I'll call you if I hear anything … Yes … Good night."

As he hung up the phone, I asked, "What did he want?"

The Captain placed the phone gently back in its receiver, and said, "Help."

"What kind of help?"

The Captain looked at me. "He wants to find his son — your friend."

He went by me, and walked back into the living room, and returned to his easy chair, as I followed him into the room, asking, "Who's Jim Greene?"

"He's a captain on the force. He and I used to work

together years ago. I told O'Neill that I would call Jim and see if they could do anything to find your friend. I'm going to need the address of that house in Conklin. Write it down for me before you go to bed and leave it by the phone. I'll call Jim early in the morning."

I stepped backwards, until I sat down on the couch, opposite from him.

"Why do you need that address?"

"Well, you told O'Neill that his son went to a party there, right? That's a good place to start looking."

"I don't know. I'm kinda uncomfortable about that."

"What are you talking about?"

"Well, that was almost a week ago. He's not there anymore. They should be looking elsewhere."

"John, in any investigation, you start with what you know. You already told us that your friend was going to a party there. We know that."

"Yeah. I just don't like sending the cops there. No offense, Grampa."

"Why the hell not?"

"I'm kinda afraid that the cops might actually find him there."

But I did write the Conklin house address on a slip of paper and left it by the phone before I went to bed.

I barely slept that night, consumed with the thought of seeing ML the next night, and fantasizing about how I would kiss her, touch her, possess her, and seal our relationship for good. In between my lurid fantasies, as I tossed and turned, I also thought about Tip, and where he might be, and desperately hoping he was not at the Conklin house.

After falling asleep late in the night, I awoke a few hours later, dragging from lack of sleep. When I came downstairs about eight thirty after showering, shaving, and dressing, The Captain was seated at the kitchen table, drinking his coffee and reading the *Sun-Bulletin* newspaper. He glanced up as heard me coming.

"Good morning, sport."

"Morning."

"What time is your class?"

"Nine thirty. I've got to get going. I'm just going to grab a couple of donuts and go."

He shook his head. "I don't know how you can eat in the car like that… By the way, I spoke with Jim Greene this morning. He's going to have a couple of the boys go by that house in Conklin."

I grabbed two glazed donuts from a Dunkin Donuts bag that The Captain had bought the day before. "OK. I hope they don't find him." I looked at my watch. "I really gotta go," and headed to the front door to pick up my backpack. "See you later. I'll be back about noon."

He called out from the kitchen, "I might not be here when you get back. I'm having lunch with some friends."

I called back, "Don't forget I'm gone this weekend."

"I didn't forget. Have fun, but don't do anything I wouldn't do."

I shook my head, and exhaled. "Right. See ya." I opened the front door and left.

After enduring a boring Medieval History class for seventy-five minutes, where my attention span was nearly non-existent, I vaulted from my desk, and swiftly walked to my car and drove back to The Captain's house, my stomach in knots. He was indeed gone when I got home. I flew up the stairs into my bedroom, and packed my clothes for the weekend into a green duffel bag, considering each item carefully so that I would not wear something that might embarrass ML. So, I left the SUNY-B sweatshirts out, and packed the Cornell sweatshirt that I had bought a few years prior when I had been in nearby Ithaca.

After packing my clothes, I went into the bathroom, and put my toothbrush, Crest toothpaste, Gillette electric razor, Right Guard deodorant, Head and Shoulders shampoo, and Brut 33 cologne (a 1974 Christmas present from Lizzie) in the duffel bag, and then leaped down the stairs. I dropped the duffel bag by the front door, and walked into the kitchen. I found three slices of cold Cortese's pizza in the refrigerator, and ate them quickly while downing a big glass of milk.

After eating I headed towards the front door, thinking about what I must have left behind. As I stood there contemplating, the phone rang, startling me. I briefly considered ignoring the phone, but then moved to it and picked it up. It was Tip.

"Hey, JM, I need your help."

I could hear noise in the background and people talking. It sounded like he was in a bar. "You need my help? What do you need, a few bucks for some more drinks?"

"Hey, asshole, cut with the crap. This is serious. I'm in jail, and this is my one phone call."

My heart sank. "Jail? What happened?"

"I've been arrested by the fuzz for possession of pot. Look, I really need your help. It seems that Judge Gorman is out of town, so I'm not going to make bail until Monday at the earliest. I need you to go over and feed my cat this weekend."

"You gotta be kidding me. You called to ask me to feed your cat?"

"That's right, asshole. I need help and you owe me."

"Why don't you get your dad to do it?"

"Fuck him. I don't want anybody going in that apartment that I don't trust. *Capisce?* Look, I hid a key underneath the first step in the stairs. I taped it there. Just go in the apartment one time this weekend that's all I'm asking. I've got some milk in the fridge, and there's some cat food cans in a cabinet. Whatever you do, don't let anybody else in there. And ignore anything else you see in the apartment. Oh, and it's a bit of a mess at the moment, so don't expect it to be neat."

"Tip, I'd like to help you out, you know I would, but I really can't. I'm actually on my way out the door. I'm driving to Boston; I'm going to be gone all weekend. I'm actually kind of late already."

"What? You dumb ass. You're going to going to visit ML?"

"Yeah, I'm going to visit ML. She invited me."

"What a dumb fuckin' schmuck. You think you're ever gonna get a piece of that action? Dream on! I've warned you since we were freshmen in high school to watch out for her. But you never listened to me, JM. Listen to me now: give her up; you're only going to get burned, big time."

"Are you done? The problem with you, Tip, is that you don't ever try to shoot for the moon. You just want to stay stuck in your lifestyle and not try to achieve anything better. Well, I want to achieve more in life."

"You're fuckin' hopeless. Are you going to help me or not?"

"Hey, Tip, you're the one in jail, speaking of hopeless."

"That's your fuckin' comeback, Moron? You're not only a schmuck, you're a putz too."

I was boiling now. "Hey, Tip, your stupid cat will be OK for a weekend. And I think I've had enough of this conversation. I'm sorry you're in jail. But I am leaving right now, so either wait until I get back or find another schmuck or putz to take care of your stupid fuckin' cat. Bye!"

I slammed the phone into the receiver as I heard Tip swearing at me, and stood there for a moment, shaking in anger and frustration with him. I stood for a moment, seething, feelings of anger at myself for helping to get Tip arrested and anger at him for just being an asshole, allowing himself to deteriorate to this, and also trying to lay the cat feeding on me at the last minute before I left. I briefly considered dashing over to Tip's apartment to take care of the cat, but I looked at my watch. It was nearly twelve forty-five. I knew that going to Tip's apartment and taking care of that damn cat would cost me probably an hour, at least, and I was behind schedule. Plus, I knew that it was going to take me about six or seven hours to get to Boston as it was. I wasn't too excited about searching for ML's apartment late at night in unfamiliar Boston. I shouted to myself, "Fuck it!" I grabbed my duffel bag, opened The Captain's front door, and stormed out.

CHAPTER 10
Serenade

Is it the end of another affair
An open engagement with gloom
Or will you be smiling
When the sun conjures up
A broken spell au clair de lune?

—Bryan Ferry

I THREW THE DUFFEL BAG into the Galaxie 500 and drove away. I stopped for gas at a nearby Esso station, filled up, and hopped on to Interstate 81 heading north. Today, if you want to drive to Boston from Binghamton, you would get on Interstate 88 and head northeast until it connects with Interstate 87 around Albany. Back then, Interstate 88 was not completed, so I had to drive Interstate 81 north to Syracuse, and then jump on Interstate 87, heading east.

It had been a sunny day, but as I drove north to Syracuse, clouds were forming to the west, and when I reached Syracuse an hour and fifteen minutes later, the sky was cloudy. Of course, it's always cloudy in Syracuse. How people live there with that climate remains a mystery. It could be the only city with worse weather than Binghamton.

At Syracuse, I turned east, got on Interstate 87, heading to Albany. I emerged from the Syracuse clouds near Utica, and the late afternoon sunshine in my rearview mirror made it impossible to use that mirror, and I had to use my driver's side mirror to watch the trucks race by me. I was constantly searching for a radio station to listen to music, but it seemed just as I would find one, it would soon disappear in a crackling cacophony of static.

I drove by Schenectady, and then Albany, and then in a few miles, just past the New York state line, I entered I-90 heading east. Soon I was in Massachusetts, and my anxiety grew. I started thinking about Tip's acerbic comments about ML, and then I was overcome with negative thoughts which, up until that point, I had ignored. What if Tip was right, and this was not just a stupid idea, but a spectacularly stupid idea? I kneaded that idea into shape over the next fifty miles or so, growing increasingly anxious.

A few miles before the Springfield exit, I glanced at the clock, and I saw that it was nearly five, and I realized that I was starving. I started paying closer attention to the road signs, and saw that there was an exit coming up at Ludlow just past Springfield with a rest stop. As a basketball player and fan, if it had been any other trip, I would have made plans to stop in Springfield and visit the Basketball Hall of Fame. Not this trip.

I soon veered off the road onto the exit ramp that led to the Ludlow rest stop parking lot. I parked and locked the car as the last sunlight fought to shine, and headed into the rest stop. It was a nondescript one-story bunker that housed a cafeteria style restaurant, a small store, and restrooms. After peeing, I went into the cafeteria, ordered a cheeseburger, fries, and a Coke from a sullen server who took my order and flung my number at me. After a short wait, my order was ready and I carried it to an empty table in the back, surrounded by heavy-set truckers who all sounded like they were from Georgia and eyeing me suspiciously as I walked to an empty table.

I quickly ate the cardboard tasting cheeseburger, about half of the greasy fries, along with most of the flat Coke, and then left, carrying the plastic cup of Coke to finish in the car. The truckers paid no attention as I left. As I walked out of the rest stop, it had become nearly dark. All of the cars now had their lights on. I didn't relish the idea of driving in the dark in Boston.

I eased the car out of its parking spot, and drove slowly through the parking lot, reaching the exit road leading to I-90, and I was soon back on the highway, heading east. I drove mile after monotonous mile, as the darkness descended. My doubt grew with each mile, wondering what I was doing on this crazy trip. And then every few miles, I would shake those self-doubts away, focusing on ML's amazing face, and that would be a shot of courage. But the self-doubts always returned.

An hour and a half later, the traffic on I-90 was noticeably heavier, and I began to see signs for Boston. I turned on the overhead light and checked ML's directions she had earlier sent me. I got off I-90 at exit 17 for Newton, then a right on Centre Street, left on Commonwealth, then another right on Chestnut Hill Avenue, a left on Sutherland, and finally a right on Orkney. I was looking for 44 Orkney, an apartment building on the right side of the street. As I turned onto Orkney, I scanned the building numbers, and I quickly

stopped in front of 44 Orkney. It was an older three-story
stone apartment building with a set of short steps leading up
to the entrance. I knew that ML was on the third floor, and
I looked up and saw the lights on behind a set of curtains in
windows on the third floor. I couldn't believe I was there; I
had actually done it. She was only minutes away.

And then a loud car horn blew behind me, and a car
passed by, and the young male driver gave me the finger,
and blew his horn again at me for sitting like a boulder on
Orkney. I looked around and could see absolutely no parking places. So, I drove down Orkney, searching for a parking
place. No luck.

At Strathmore Road, I took a right, went up to the
next block, turned right, and then circled back to Orkney
Avenue, but again there was no parking near her building. I
went further down Orkney, but every parking spot was filled.
I circled back again and started to panic. The third time I
turned onto Orkney I finally had a break: a car pulled away
from the curb near Strathmore, and I eased into a tiny parking space that sat between two driveways.

I turned the Galaxie 500 off, got out, and inspected the
parking spot. The Galaxy 500 was just long enough to block
a fraction of two driveways, but both were clearly passable. I
felt immense relief. I returned to the Galaxy 500 to retrieve
my duffle bag. The side door was locked. I was overcome
with a sickening feeling; I raced to the driver's side door, and
pulled the handle. Locked!

I had locked it unconsciously but had left the keys inside.
I could see them dangling from the ignition. I cursed loudly,
"Son of a Bitch!" I frantically considered what I could do to

avoid embarrassment, but no solution emerged other than calling AAA to break into the Galaxie 500, and I needed a phone to make that call. Luckily, my AAA membership was current through January, courtesy of Mary Kate.

I quickly walked to ML's apartment building. Reaching her building, I bounded up the small steps, opened the glass door, noted the mailboxes that sat next to a wooden staircase leading to the upstairs, and then ran up the stairs. I quickly located #300 at the west end of the third floor and knocked on the door.

After a moment, ML opened the door a crack, and then recognizing me, shouted, "Oh, my God, look who's here!" She threw the door open and rushed to me, throwing her arms around me, "John's here!" She was wearing a light pink sweater and a pair of jeans that hugged her in a pleasing way. Her perfume drifted up to me as she held me for a moment. Oh, that perfume!

I mumbled a "Hi" as she let me go. She opened the door more and said, "Ann, look who's here!" Upon hearing "Ann" my heart sank like a rock thrown in a pond. And there she was. Ann rose from a couch and walked to me, a "shit-eating" grin on her face. I stared at her as if she was ghost, and said, "Hi, Ann." She wrapped me in a bear hug, and said, "Bet you didn't expect to see me?"

As we separated, I looked at her, and said, "Wow, yea, this is a surprise."

ML pulled me into her apartment, "C'mon in. This is so great." She closed the door emphatically. "We've already had a couple of screwdrivers, so we're already ahead of you. Want one?"

"Yeah, thanks. I need one. It's been a wild day."

ML steered me to a chair in the small living room. "Oh, I'll bet. That is an awful drive. I hate it. How long did it take?"

I sat down in an older plush chair and sank down. "Man, it seemed like it took forever."

Ann sat on the couch across from me, and lifted her screwdriver from a table next to the couch. "How was the traffic?"

"Not bad, until I hit Boston. It's a little busier than Binghamton."

The girls snickered. ML touched me on my shoulder. "Let me get you that drink. Ann, you ready for another one?"

Ann barked out, "No, I'm good."

ML walked in the direction of the kitchen entrance. "OK, be right back."

Ann sipped her drink. "Oh, that's good. Sometimes a screwdriver just tastes so good."

"Yeah. When did you get here?"

"Last night. I don't actually have any classes on Friday."

"Lucky."

"Oh I know. So, I took the train up last night, and we've just been hanging out."

The full impact of Ann being there was slowly enveloping me, as I realized my dreams of being with ML, of holding her, kissing her, consummating my deep feelings for her, were now dashed. It was a moment of despair.

"I didn't know you were coming. ML didn't say anything."

She snorted and yelled out, "HEY, ML, JOHN DIDN'T KNOW I WAS COMING!"

ML emerged from the kitchen, carrying a screwdriver in a glass. "Didn't I put that in my letter, John?" She handed me the glass.

I said, "Thanks. No, I don't think so."

ML sat on the couch next to Ann, and Ann handed her a half-full screwdriver that had been sitting on the table.

"Hmmm, maybe I didn't. Ann and I worked out that she could come this weekend too, and I am so happy that the two of you could come. This is so great."

She raised her glass, and said, "Here's to good friends and good times." I leaned over and we clinked glasses. I sipped the screwdriver; it didn't lack for vodka, but it tasted surprisingly good for a drink that I never usually drank.

As she sat there, smiling at me and Ann, ML glowed, sending off a golden light, bathing me in its warmth. I was at her mercy.

Ann slammed the screwdriver, and then setting her glass down on the table, said, "So, where's your stuff, Johnny? Or, are you wearing those clothes for the whole weekend?"

The brief reverie was broken; Ann brought me crashing back to earth. "My stuff is in my car. And actually, I've got a little problem."

ML frowned, and asked, "What's the problem?"

I chuckled, and rubbing my chin, said, "Well, you see, I kinda made a little mistake, and locked my keys in the car. So, I think I need to call AAA to get some help."

Before I finished, a tall blond girl, wearing jeans and a Boston College sweater, entered the living room. ML noticed her immediately, and interrupted me, "Oh, Meg, I want you to meet John. John Moran. You remember? John, this is my roommate, Meg Brown."

Meg strode to me, saying, "Aha, this is the John Moran I've been hearing about."

I rose, "I hope it was good things you heard."

I put my glass in left hand, wiped my right hand on my jeans, and shook hands with Meg. She laughed, and said, "My lips are sealed." She held my hand firmly.

I said, "Sorry if my hand is a little cold from the glass."

"No problem." Meg released my hand and looked at us, "So, you guys are drinking screwdrivers?"

ML said, "Indeed. Go make yourself one."

Meg looked in the direction of the kitchen. "Good idea. I just finished my reading." Then, looking back at us, she said, "So, it's time to party. Refill anyone?" Ann grabbed her empty glass and held it out to Meg, "I'll take another pop." Meg took her glass and marched off to the kitchen.

As she walked away, I turned back to Ann and ML. That Face! "ML, do you have a phonebook, so I can look up the AAA?"

Ann said, "Are you a member of AAA?"

"Yeah, luckily."

Reaching over Ann, ML put her drink on the table, and stood. "Yeah, we have a phonebook. Let me look around." She looked around the living room, walked to a small book case, moved some books and magazines around, searching for the phonebook. After looking for a few moments, she said, "Let me look in my room," and she walked out of the living room, leaving Ann and I alone.

Ann snickered, "How do you lock the keys in your car?"

"I got out to check my parking spot, and I just, you know, was on autopilot, and just pushed the lock down. It's been a long day, give me a break." I took a slug of the screwdriver.

Ann shook her head, and looked at me with disdain. "Typical."

"What do you mean by that?"

"Feel the burn! You know, Moron."

ML reemerged, "I can't find it in my room. Maybe Meg knows."

At that moment, Meg reemerged from the kitchen, carrying the two screwdrivers. "What would I know?"

"Do you know where the phonebook is? I couldn't find it anywhere."

Meg handed one screwdriver to Ann, who said, "thanks," and then gracefully sat on the floor, without splashing a drop of her screwdriver. "Yeah, it's in my bedroom, next to my bed. I was looking up the phone number for Pino's pizza. I was going to order one later. What do you need the phonebook for?"

"John needs to call AAA. His keys are locked in his car."

Meg said, "You're kidding?"

I said, "Sadly, I am not joshing."

Meg set her screwdriver on the coffee table, and asked, "What kind of car is it?"

I said, "1965 Galaxie 500. Baby blue convertible. A work of art."

They laughed, fueled by the alcohol.

Meg continued, "You know, my dad taught me a trick with older cars on how to break in, if you are locked out. You want me to try? I'm pretty sure I can get in."

Sitting up, I set my drink on the table. "How do you do it?"

She said, "You use a hanger. I'll be right back." She walked quickly out of the living room, and said over her shoulder, "Get your coats. Mar, bring your flashlight too."

Ann said, "Well, Johnny, looks like you may be saved."

Five minutes later, after the girls had peed and grabbed their coats, we left the apartment. Meg was carrying a metal hanger with her. ML carried a flashlight and Ann had refueled her screwdriver and carried it with her, proclaiming that she was going to need it for the walk.

As we left the building, it seemed the temperature had dropped ten degrees since I had entered a few minutes ago, and the wind was blowing, tossing leaves and trash around the street. Meg and I walked side by side, with a giggling ML and Ann behind. A few minutes later, we neared the Galaxie 500.

"That's it," I said, pointing at the Galaxie 500 ahead.

The four of us stepped off the curb and approached the driver's side door.

I said, "I have got to see how this works."

Setting the hangar on the roof, Meg examined the door and the window. "Mar, flash the light on the window here." ML turned the flashlight on and shined it where Meg was pointing.

ML sighed, "John, I do love this car. That baby blue is my color."

Meg agreed, "Yeah, this is a nice car. I want to get a convertible so bad."

Ann snorted, "Yeah, it's a real chick car, right, John?"

I flashed her a dagger, but she was looking away from me, sipping from her glass.

Meg turned to me, "I think it will work." The she pointed to the top of the window. "See, these older cars have this flexible plastic, along the top of the window. You can fit a hanger in there and reach down and pull up the lock on the door. I've done it on our older car at home."

I said to her, "Wow. Great. Give it a shot."

Meg grabbed the hanger and handed it to me, "Here, I now need some muscles; twist the hanger so that the question mark remains, but the rest of the hanger is one straight line."

I struggled with the hanger for a few minutes, with Meg coaching me how to untwist the hanger, while ML shone the light on my struggle, and Ann leaned against the car, sipping from her cup.

After a few minutes I managed to untwist the hanger, and handed it to Meg. "How's that?"

Meg took it from me, and looked it over, "That's good. It should work. OK, Mar, hold that light up at the top here." She stood near the door, and gingerly started forcing the hanger question mark through the top of the window.

"I expect cops to show up any minute now," Ann joked.

I fired back, "You better hope not. Isn't the drinking age twenty-one in Massachusetts?"

"I got a fake ID."

"I should have known."

Meg exclaimed, "Hey, this is working." She pushed the hanger slowly through the top of the window, and we could see the tip of the question mark now inside the car, and slowly heading to the lock at the bottom of the window. Seeing the progress, the rest of us moved to her.

ML said, "Meg, you are amazing. Keep going."

Ann said, "Hey, John, you're a guy, how come you don't know this car trick?"

That pissed me off some more, but I was trying to act cool, despite her provocation. "I've never locked my keys in my car before."

Meg kept wedging the hanger lower and lower, getting nearer the lock, tantalizingly close, and then the tip of the hanger reached the lock.

I cried out, "That's it!"

Meg stopped for a moment, and looked around, "See, I told you. Now watch this." She wiggled the hanger around the lock for a moment, as I watched intently. She circled the lock trying to grab it for a few moments, then she did surround it, jerked the hanger up, and the lock popped up, and she cried out, "Aha." She pulled the door open, "There you go."

I said, "Wowzers!" I stepped forward, reached into the car, and grabbed my keys, and backed out to see ML and Ann congratulating Meg.

I moved to her, saying, "Wow, I can't thank you enough. Can I give you a hug at least?"

Meg smiled, and hugged me, "I never turn down a hug."

We parted, and I said to ML and Ann, "I think I love this girl."

ML laughed, but Ann said, "Don't get your hopes up, Johnny, she's got a stud boyfriend who's a hockey player and would kick your ass."

I stepped back and threw my hands up in mock fear. "Hey, I don't need to get my ass kicked in Boston."

Laughing, Meg said, "He's out of town tonight, so you're safe."

I turned to the car, "Let me grab my duffle bag, and then we can really celebrate."

I grabbed the duffle bag, shut the doors, and locked the car (from the outside this time!), and then we walked back to ML's apartment.

When we reached the apartment, we took off our coats, and Meg and Ann grabbed the glasses and went to the kitchen to refill. I asked ML, pointing to the duffle bag, "Where should I put this?"

She pointed to the wall next to the couch, "Just put it over there, next to the couch. I'm sorry we don't have a bed for you. You OK with the couch?"

I dropped the duffle bag next to the couch, "No problem," and then I retreated to the chair, "I can sleep anywhere."

ML sat on the couch. "Not me. I need a nice comfy bed."

I leaned forward, "It's good to be here, ML."

"I know. It's so good to have old friends around. I love BC and my friends here, of course, but I miss my friends from home. Reminds me of the poem my mother used to say when I was a child. Make new friends but keep the old, one is silver, and the other's gold."

"So, I'm golden?"

Those eyes…burning a hole in my soul…

"You are in my book."

"That isn't a work of fiction, is it?"

She laughed. "Good one."

Carrying two full glasses each, Ann and Meg emerged from the kitchen, and Ann announced, "The nurses are here with the medicine." Ann handed one glass to ML, and sat next to her on the couch, as Meg handed me a glass.

I held my glass up, and said, "Here's a toast to my new best friend Meg for saving my weekend and my wallet." ML and Ann laughed, and took a hit of screwdriver, as did I.

Meg laughed, "I'll drink to that," and chugged almost

the entire glass. "Wow that burns smooth. And I needed that."

So, we continued drinking screwdrivers for a while, refilling our glasses twice, and I listened to the girls talk about school, music, celebrities, movies, etcetera. I sat there listening, and chiming in with a clever remark from time to time, and mostly sneaking glances at ML. Oh…*that face…* it could launch my thousand ships.

A half hour later, I interjected, "Are you guys hungry at all? I haven't eaten much today, so I need to get some food."

ML said, "Oh my God, we are at BC so you have to go to 'Maryann's.' It's kind of obligatory."

Meg said, "We also call it 'Scary Ann's.' Don't get anything but the pizza."

I said, "Thanks for the warning."

ML waved her hand, "Don't listen to her. It's a fun place."

I said, "It can't be any more of a dive than The Pine Lounge."

Meg said that she was going to stay in and just order a pizza. I told her that her meal was on me, and after some gentle coaxing she agreed. The girls of course had to prepare to leave by hitting the bathroom to pee, to touch-up makeup, comb hair, and whatever the hell else girls do in the bathroom.

We finally headed out about ten. It had started to spit rain intermittently, and the wind had picked up. Maryann's was not far away so we hurried there, laughing with the encouragement of the screwdrivers.

Upon reaching Maryann's, I opened the door, and the girls entered. Maryann's bar was in an old one-story stone building. A long u-shaped bar dominated the dark interior that smelled of pizza and beer. Wooden booths sat up against the brick walls. On this night, Maryann's was packed and hopping, no surprise on a Friday night. It was deafening inside; a mix of Top 40 music in combat with the voices of the youthful crowd yelling to each other.

We circled the first floor looking for a booth, but none were available. We gave our name to an unfriendly hostess, and she told us it would be about fifteen minutes. We took up position near a window by the bar, and I volunteered to buy drinks and bring them back. Not surprisingly, they decided to continue with screwdrivers. I elbowed my way to the bar, and finally got the attention of a young beefy bartender, whose face was as crimson as a red rose. I ordered the three screwdrivers and then a Michelob for me (Rolling Rock was not on their menu). Almost everyone sitting at the bar was smoking, and a haze of grey smoke hung over the bar like a New England coastal fog bank.

After paying for the drinks, and leaving a tip on the bar for beefy boy, I carried two of the screwdrivers back to them, handing one to ML and Meg. Ann feigned anger, "Hey, what about me?"

Over my shoulder, I yelled back, "It's coming. Quit your bitchin'."

I returned with Ann's screwdriver and my Michelob bottle. I handed the screwdriver to Ann, saying, "Here. Give me a break."

She took the drink, snorting out, "About time. I could have got them five minutes ago."

ML came to my defense, "Hey, Ann, it's not like you bought these."

I pointed at ML, "Yeah. Let her have it."

Ten minutes later, the unsmiling hostess found us and brought us to a booth. I slid in first, and Ann sat down across from me. To my dismay, ML sat down next to Ann, and Meg settled in next to me. We debated what to order for a few minutes, decided on a large pizza, half cheese, and half sausage and mushroom. A waitress appeared and the pizza order was submitted, and another round of drinks was ordered as well.

After the waitress left, I yelled to ML, "So, what are we going to do tomorrow?"

She leaned over and raised her voice. "I thought we would do the tourist thing around Boston. Go to Faneuil Hall, the Old State House, Boston Common. It'll be a gas. There's so much to see here."

Ignoring her, I continued, "I'd also like to go to Harvard. I'd like to see where the really smart assholes are."

Ann chortled. "You would."

ML laughed, and said, "Sure. We can do it all."

After the next round was delivered, Meg and ML then proceeded to explain to us the history of Boston, the neighborhoods, how much fun it was to live there. For once, Ann sat quietly, sucking on her screwdriver and listening. I pretended to pay rapt attention, but was focused solely on ML and the halo that surrounded her. That was a halo, I'm sure. She was magnificent.

When the pizza was delivered, all conversation stopped as we attacked it. I was so hungry that my first two pieces disappeared quickly. It was excellent pizza, or at least the booze convinced me that it was excellent. As I sat there, a warm glow descended over me. It was swell to be with ML anywhere, but here I was in Boston, away from Tip, away from Mary Kate, away from Godforsaken Binghamton. Sure, Ann was there, but as annoying as hell as it was to have her there, it was a small price to be with my ML.

The glow didn't last long. Within ten minutes two preppy guys walked by our table, and Meg reached out and grabbed one of them. It turned out they were BC seniors too, and knew ML and Meg. They pulled up chairs to our table, and sat their beers down on it. Introductions were made. Rick (or was it Mick?) was from Groton, about six foot two and muscular, with blond hair, slightly longer over his collar. He was a pitcher on the BC baseball team. Terry (or was it Harry?) was a forward on the BC hockey team, had shorter black hair and a thick mustache, and he was from a small town in Quebec.

After introductions were made, Rick/Mick asked me, "Where do you go to school, John?"

ML intervened, "SUNY-Binghamton."

Rick/Mick asked, "Where the hell is that?"

I said, "Binghamton, New York. That's upstate New York."

Terry/Harry then asked, "Is that near Buffalo? I know where Buffalo is. The Sabres, you know, eh."

ML said, "Binghamton is hours away from Buffalo. It's in the middle of the state, an hour south of Syracuse. It's where I grew up. John and Ann went to high school with me."

Rick/Mick said, "Cool," and then looked at Ann, "So, Ann, where you going to school?"

Ann said, "Columbia. It's in New York. I'm sure you know where that is?"

Laughs all around on that one.

Rick/Mick said, "Yeah, I've been there."

Then the preppy boys, ML, and Meg began talking among themselves about BC specific matters. With the music blaring overhead, and sitting on the inside, it was hard to hear the conversation, and to follow it with any interest. After a few minutes, I tuned out, but maintained a dumb smile looking in their direction, of course, mostly looking at ML, as she laughed at the stories and memories that were being shared among them.

I felt a tap on my beer glass. It was Ann. She looked at me, "Not much point, huh?"

"I guess not."

"So, how's everything in Bingo-town?"

"Always the same. Grey, dreary, and depressing."

"You have my sympathy for staying around. You know there's a whole world beyond Broome County."

"As soon as I graduate, I am so out of there."

"Good for you. I thought you might be a lifer like all those robotic IBMers living there."

"You couldn't pay me enough money to work at IBM. I have no interest in a white collar prison."

"How's Tip?"

"Uh, not so good."

"What's wrong with him?"

I explained what happened to Tip over the past two months, including his recent arrest. She grew wide-eyed when I told her that Tip had been arrested. "You are fucking kidding me." She aggressively elbowed ML, and when ML turned to her, she blurted out, "Tip got arrested. Listen to this story. Tell her."

I told Tip's story again with less details this time, and ML stared at me with those big beautiful blue eyes boring into me.

When I finished, ML said, "Wow. That is so sad. What can we do for him?"

"I don't know. I just don't know. I get so frustrated when I see him; he is wasting his life. He is such a capable guy."

ML said, "Maybe at Christmastime when we are all there, we can get together with him and pull him together."

When I heard Christmas, I got excited at the thought of ML being home for a month around the holidays.

Ann said, "But if the idiot doesn't want any help, what can you do?"

I said, "You seem to be able to convince him to do things, Ann, based on this summer."

She grew red in the face. "Oh, you had to go there, didn't you? That was a low blow."

ML leaped in, "Aw, Ann, John was just teasing you. Weren't you, John?" Her eyes were not smiling now.

I retreated. "That's right. Ann, I was just joshing. Shit happens." Turning to ML, I said, "I know that better than anyone."

At that point, Meg, who had been still talking with the preppy guys, leaned over and interjected, "You guys want another one? The guys are buying." The waitress had appeared and the preppy guys were chatting her up.

I said, "Is the Pope Catholic? Hell, yes. Ann?"

She laughed and said, "If they're buying, order two for me."

ML said, "Ann!"

A half-hour later, the preppy guys left, but not before inviting us to a party the following evening. Well, mostly inviting Meg and ML, but by way of courtesy, Ann and I.

We left Maryann's not long after the preppy guys. It was cold outside now, but the wind had died down. We hurried home along the wet streets glistening from the streetlights above, until we dashed up the steps of ML's apartment building. Laughing and shivering, we urged Meg to hurry, as she struggled to find her key to open their apartment door.

Once inside the apartment, the girls announced that they were exhausted and going to bed, and Meg headed off to the back. Ann sarcastically said, "Good-night, John-boy."

ML and I groaned, and then I said, "You know how much I hate The Waltons?"

Ann laughed and, as she walked away, said, "I know. I couldn't resist. Catch you on the flip side."

ML stayed with me. "You sure you're going to be OK on the couch?"

"Yeah, I'll be fine. I'll sleep like a baby."

"Let me get you a couple of blankets and a pillow." She walked into her bedroom. I sat on the couch and leaned back against the cushions and relaxed. ML returned after a few moments. She had two blankets and a pillow. One of the blankets was maroon and had BC written all over it. She handed that one to me first. "Got that freshman year. It kept me warm that whole first year here." Then she handed me the other blanket and the pillow. "That's it."

I set them on the couch next to me. "I'm good."

She asked, "Do you want to use the bathroom first?"

"No, you guys go ahead. Just let me know when it's open."

After she left, I stood up and opened the duffle bag, removed sweatpants and a white T-shirt, along with my Dopp kit containing my toothbrush and toothpaste. I looked around to make sure nobody was in view, and quickly took off my jeans and shirt and slipped on the sweats and white T-shirt. I could hear Ann and ML talking in her room, and Meg getting ready for bed in the bathroom. I put my pants and shirt next to the couch, on top of the duffle bag.

Then I sat on the couch and grabbed a *Boston Globe* from earlier in the week that lay on the coffee table and pretended to read it, while not paying any attention to it.

Twenty minutes later, ML came out to the couch. She had washed her makeup off, and if anything her face was lovelier. She was wearing a pair of running shorts, and a white T-shirt with a large BC Eagle on it. Immediately, I noticed without trying to stare that she was not wearing a bra and her nipples were proudly butting up against the T-shirt. Desire arose within me.

"We're all done. The bathroom is yours."

Looking up at her, I fought the urge to view the outline of her breast and the pressing nipples. "Great. I'm in."

She surprised me by leaning down and planting a kiss on my cheek. My face grew red, and she pulled back.

I asked, "What was that for?"

"That's for coming to see me."

"I guess I should come see you more often then."

There was an awkward pause for a moment, and then Ann walked out of ML's bedroom and came to the couch. She was wearing sweats and a Columbia sweatshirt. "So, John, how's it feel to be the only guy at our girls' slumber party?"

"I'm just one of the girls."

They laughed. Ann said, "Wait until I tell your buddies in Binghamton that news."

I protested. "Please don't. That's our little secret."

ML said, "Alrighty then, with that, it's bedtime, girl." She linked her arm with Ann's arm, and they headed to ML's room, laughing the whole way.

I waited a few moments, then headed to the bathroom, shutting the door behind me. I quickly brushed my teeth. Then I peed—sitting down—I was too embarrassed to make a splashing sound standing up. After flushing, I turned the light off and returned to the couch. I spread the blankets out on the couch, and placed the pillow on the end near the coffee table. Leaving the lamp on the coffee table still on, I turned the other lights in the living room and kitchen off, and returned to the couch. I lay down on the couch, and started to read the *Boston Globe* again. After a few minutes, I felt sleep near, so I tossed the paper aside and reached up to the lamp and turned the light off.

I lay there in the dark, thinking about ML. Being so close to her after all this time was so intoxicating but yet being banished to this lonely couch instead of the warm embraces that I knew could await me only a few feet away was frustratingly painful. I began to fantasize, conceiving that ML might slip out in the night, and join me on the couch. I could taste the sweet kisses that we would share. I heard a giggle from ML's room. Were they laughing at me and my fantasy?

Then I started thinking about Ann being here, and got miffed that ML had not at least told me. Would I have come if I had known Ann was going to be coming as well? I reflected on that question awhile, but ultimately I accepted that I would have made the trip. Any chance to be with ML was sublime, it was worth having Ann there just for an opportunity to be with ML. Maybe. Definitely. Maybe she'll leave early. What am I doing here? I am such a loser. Obsessed with a girl that I have no chance with. Tip was right. God, I should get in the car right now, accept defeat, and go home. Well, maybe in the morning. I was too tired now. Too tired.

The next thing I knew, a hand was rubbing my shoulder, and an angel was talking to me, "John, wake up. John, it's time to get up."

I swam to the surface, and opened my eyes, to the most beautiful face I knew, smiling at me. ML said, "C'mon sleepyhead, time to get up." Her hair was pulled back into a ponytail. She was still wearing the shorts and T-shirt from the prior night.

I stammered, "What time is it?"

"Eleven."

"AM?"

She laughed. "Now that's funny. Of course."

I rubbed my sleepy eyes. "You been up for a while?"

"We've been up for about forty minutes. Ann is in the shower."

From behind me, I heard Meg say, "Morning, John. You snore."

I turned, and she was seated at the table behind me wearing her BC sweatpants and a Patriots sweatshirt, holding a coffee cup, glancing at the *Boston Globe* that I had been reading the night before.

I asked her, "How long have you been there?"

She sipped and then said, "About a half an hour."

"I really snored?"

"Not like my dad. But loud enough."

ML jumped in. "Don't listen to Meg. She has extra sensitive ears. She thinks I sing off-key."

"You do."

"See?"

I sat up. "Wow. I was really out." I rubbed my eyes again.

ML asked, "You ready for some breakfast?"

"That sounds great."

"Eggs and bacon sound good?"

"Yeah."

Meg leaped in, "Sounds good to me too, Mar."

ML walked towards the kitchen, saying to Meg, "What? I've got to cook for you too?"

"Thanks, honey."

ML went into the kitchen, and I heard the refrigerator open, and items being removed. I stood up, stretched and walked to the window and looked through the blinds. It was raining.

Meg said, "Crummy day, huh?"

I responded, "Yeah. Looks like a Syracuse day." I turned away, and walked to the kitchen table. "Actually, this is a good day in Syracuse."

"Is it really that bad there?"

"Well, that's the joke in Binghamton. Because no matter how bad the weather is in Binghamton, it will always be worse in Syracuse."

She asked, "Want some coffee?"

I said, "Sure."

ML called out from the kitchen, "Hey, I want some too!"

Meg pointed to the kitchen. "There's some cups in the cabinet above the sink. Better grab three of them. The coffee pot is on the stove."

I strode into the kitchen. ML was putting a beat up frying pan on the stove. I asked her, "Do you want anything in your coffee?"

She turned on the gas burner. "Yeah, cream and sugar. Cream is in the fridge, and the sugar is …"

"Out here," Meg called out.

I walked to the white porcelain sink that was filled with glasses from the prior night and opened the cabinet over the sink. I grabbed two white coffee cups from the cabinet and set them on the counter next to the sink, and then grabbed a third cup and set it down as well. ML had moved away from the stove and was stirring eggs and cheese in a small bowl. I went to the stove, my eyes focused on her rear moving suggestively against her shorts as she stirred away.

At the stove I grabbed the coffee pot and filled two of the cups with coffee. Then I went to the refrigerator, opened it, did a quick survey of its contents, found the cream container, and carried it back to the counter. I asked ML, "How much cream do you want, ML?"

"A couple of splashes, please." I followed her direction, and then dropped some cream into my cup as well. She moved to the stove and poured the egg mixture into the hot pan, and it began to sizzle. She stirred the eggs around.

"Do you want your coffee now?"

"No, just put it on the table. These will be done in a couple of minutes."

I carried the three cups back into the dining area, and set one cup down on the table at the head of the table and put the second cup in front of Meg. She said, "thanks," but didn't look away from the newspaper. I sipped my coffee. Strong. I set my cup on the table across from Meg, and went back into the kitchen. ML was managing the pile of eggs in the frying pan.

I asked, "Where are your plates and silverware?"

"Oh, aren't you sweet? The plates are in the cabinet next to the sink, and the silverware is in the drawer right above it."

Ann walked into the kitchen, her hair still wet, wearing jeans and her Columbia sweatshirt, and cheerily announced, "Something smells good. I am starving. Morning, Moron."

I felt my face flush as I pulled out four dishes, and I snapped, "And a good morning to you, Ann."

Ann responded: "Oh, it's going to be that kind of a day, is it?"

As I set the plates on the counter, ML jumped in, "Hey, c'mon, you two, it's gonna be a great day, even if the weather is crappy. We're going to have so much fun exploring Boston. And these eggs are ready."

I said, "Now that is music to my ears. Let's eat. Whatdya say, Ann?"

She replied, "Right on."

We quickly scarfed the entire pan of eggs, and made our plan for the day. Meg was heading to the BC Library to work on a paper, so we would see her later at the apartment. ML, Ann, and I were going to take the T and explore the tourist attractions of Boston.

After breakfast, ML jumped in the shower while Ann and I cleaned up. We were very cordial to one another. She told me about her plan after she graduated: she was planning to backpack in Europe for six weeks with friends from Columbia, and then get her master's in English at NYU. She asked about my plans and I informed her that I was also planning on going for a master's degree in English but I had made no decision on a school. For once she seemed thoughtful and spoke matter of factly without being sardonic, and it was a welcome moment. It reminded me of how close Ann and I had once been at CC when we had dated for seven crazy months, and the many profound conversations we had as we held each other close. I felt a brief pang of regret how distant we had become.

ML emerged from her room a few minutes later, and then I grabbed some clothes from my duffel bag and hit the shower.

Forty-five minutes later, ML, Ann, and I left the apartment and emerged into Boston rain. They shared an umbrella and I carried a small umbrella ML dug up in her room.

We sloshed our way a couple of blocks to the T stop near the BC campus, huddled together with other wet BC students for a few minutes, and then leaped aboard the T as the doors opened. The girls found a seat, and I stood above them, holding a rail, the water dripping off me, and the closed umbrella, to the floor.

Despite the ominous weather when we left, it turned out to be a marvelous day. When we surfaced from the T at Park Street Station, the rain had stopped, and we crossed through Boston Common on the broad walkways that crisscrossed the park. There was hardly anybody there due to the weather, so we had it almost to ourselves. We stopped at the lake where

ML pointed out the Swan Boats tied up that could be taken out in better weather. She then guided us to Brewer Fountain proudly standing in the middle of Boston Common, and from there we could view the impressive Massachusetts State House that towered over Boston Common. We walked up the hill to the Massachusetts State House, and ML explained its history and construction. Ann told ML that she should consider being a tour guide when she graduated, and we laughed. ML said that she had given these tours so many times to her family, that she had become well educated about Boston and its history. Plus, as she admitted, she loved living in a city filled with so much history and personality. I was envious of her. I had never felt any affection for the city in which I had lived my whole life. I was in many ways an alien living in Binghamton, and my break with Mary Kate had only contributed to my feelings of alienation.

As we walked from the Massachusetts State House to The Granary Burying Ground, I thought how wonderful it would be to be in Boston with ML, sharing her beloved city. Despite the chilly day, this intoxicating idea warmed me, as we walked into and around the cemetery. ML pointed out the graves of Paul Revere, Sam Adams, and John Hancock, and we each placed an obligatory penny on the memorial stone of the five victims of the Boston Massacre.

The sun was fighting through the clouds and occasionally winning as we left the The Granary Burying Ground and slowly walked to the Old State House. After walking through the museum inside the Old State House, we left and walked to the rear of the Old State House. ML pointed out a spot in the middle of the intersection of busy State

Street and Congress Street behind the Old State House where she said the Boston Massacre had taken place. Ann and I agreed that the busy intersection surrounded by commercial buildings was a less than impressive setting for such a famous historical event.

When ML asked we wanted to do next, I said I wanted to see Harvard. So we entered the State Street T station underneath the Old State House, got on the train for Harvard, and in twenty minutes, we emerged from the T into Cambridge arising into Harvard Square. With the rain now over, the streets were filled with pedestrians, mostly college students. We made our way to Harvard, and slowly walked through the campus. I was surprised how plain the campus looked after all I had read about it; it was not a striking campus for the reputation it held. I thought a school populated with the rich elites would be more attractive. BC's campus was much more attractive, sitting on its hill above Boston.

After walking around the Harvard campus, we walked to Cambridge Street, and wandered the busy street, stopping at a few stores selling Harvard memorabilia. Ann bought a sweatshirt, and the girls convinced me to buy a Harvard T-shirt. Later, we stopped at the Harvard Book Store on Massachusetts Avenue, and strolled by book cases filled with both recent best sellers and obscure academic tomes. After a few minutes, I ended up at the magazine rack, near the entrance, where I skimmed the latest *Sports Illustrated* issue. Later, ML sidled up to me, "What are you reading?"

I held up the *SI.*

She chuckled, "I thought it was a *Playboy.*"

"C'mon! But if you want to buy me one?"

"Fat chance of that. You buy your own."

Ann joined us, and we left. We worked our way back to the T station, but, at ML's urging, we stopped at Grendel's Den, and ordered three pints of Guinness. In those days it was rare to get Guinness in a bar in upstate New York, just as it was almost impossible to get Coors, so this was a treat. The brown frothy beer was served cool and tasted delicious, at least to me. Ann and ML were less enthused, but soldiered on. All the walking had made me thirsty so I quickly drank my Guinness. The waitress asked if I wanted another, but I declined, as ML and Ann were slowly working their beers. After they finished, we left the payment on the table, and walked back to the T, hopped on it, and rode it back downtown.

On the train, ML insisted that we had to visit Durgin Park to eat. I was getting hungry as we had only had the beer since breakfast, so that sounded good to me.

We exited the train at the State Street T stop, and climbed the stairs, emerging near the Boston Massacre site again. We waited for the light at State and Congress, and quickly crossed when the light permitted and happily goose-stepped to Faneuil Hall, me in the middle, my arms interlocked with theirs.

After exploring Faneuil Hall for a few minutes we walked to Durgin Park, and were soon seated in the busy dining room. Almost every table was filled but it was early so we got in quickly. An older, heavy-set, bespectacled wait-ress appeared at our table, and impatiently took our orders. "Whatdya have?" Ann and ML ordered ham sandwiches, I went for the hand-carved turkey sandwich, and we ordered three Cokes too. Mrs. Friendly wrote the order on her small pad of paper and left.

ML said, "I love this restaurant; it's my favorite in Boston. It has the feel of what old Boston must have been like."

I responded, "Our waitress gives me the feel of what old Boston was like. She's older than Grandma Moses."

They laughed. It made me feel good to make ML laugh so I could see those blue eyes sparkle as she laughed, and those glimmering white teeth revealed to their fullest, as she carelessly threw that mane of golden-white hair behind her.

After Grandma Moses tossed the Cokes onto the table, ML said, "My dad brought me here when we first visited BC, and we've come here ever since. Supposedly it has the worst service in Boston but the food is outstanding, and people here just accept the service as a rite of passage one must go through."

After gulping her Coke, Ann said, "I wish there was some rum in this." Setting it down, she said, "So, what are the plans for tonight?"

Twirling her fingers around her Coke glass, ML replied, "Remember those two guys from last night? Rick and Terry?"

I replied, "Yeah."

"They invited us to a party tonight. It should be fun. They'll have some kegs, food, and music. You can see how we party at BC."

Ann said, "Sounds good to me. How about you, Moron? You came to party at BC with two good-looking guys right?"

"Actually, I came to party with two good-looking girls. ML and Meg."

Ann snorted, "Asshole."

ML hit me softly on the arm and scolded me with mock disappointment, "John, that wasn't very nice."

I held up my hands, "I'm kidding. It was a joke. C'mon, you guys know that." I held my glass to Ann, "C'mon. You know."

She tapped her glass on mine. "It was a good line, Moron. Especially for you."

I tapped ML on her arm. "There, see. Ann and I are on the same wavelength. We can kid each other at will, and it's no harm, no foul."

ML sighed, "You guys are something. But you do make me smile, and I can't thank you enough for coming to visit. It's been a rough semester, so seeing old friends is going to get me through the next couple of weeks until I come home for Thanksgiving, and then a few weeks later, Christmas break."

I interrupted, "Let's hear it for Christmas break." We tapped our glasses together. "It can't some soon enough."

After we finished our sandwiches, upon ML's exuberant recommendation, we ordered apple pie and vanilla ice cream. And the pie was delicious, filled with chunks of tart apples swimming in a compost of sugar and cinnamon.

We emerged into early November darkness, and the cold wind pushed us back to the Old State House, and then down the stairs to the T stop. We grabbed the next train and headed back to ML's apartment.

Upon entering ML's apartment, I walked right over to the couch, and dropped on it. I could have fallen asleep. ML and Ann headed back to ML's room, and I heard them talking and laughing back there. It felt good to be inside, and the aroma of ML's perfume lingered over the apartment as if she had sprayed it randomly. I lay there and contemplated our day, and how the time I spent with ML always raced by too fast, and how she could raise my spirits at even their lowest points. I considered that perhaps that is what love is really about: being with someone who can make you feel better about yourself and your life, despite all the hurdles in your way. I so much wanted to break her away from Ann and tell her my feelings. It was difficult to keep my façade of being cool together; I was a moth to her flame, I didn't just need her light to thrive, I needed her light to live.

I suddenly awoke to Ann shaking me, "Hey, lightweight, wake up and give me some room."

I sat up. "Wow, I fell asleep."

"Yeah. No shit, Sherlock. C'mon, move over."

I moved down the couch, and Ann sat down.

I asked, "Where's ML?"

"Taking a shower."

"Again?"

"She's just trying to look beautiful for you."

My face reddened. "What?"

"You heard me."

"Where's Meg?"

"Not here."

I took off my jacket, as the room seemed warmer now. I dropped it on the floor near my duffle bag, and when I turned back Ann was studying me as if I was a bug under a microscope. "What are you looking at?"

"You."

"And?"

"I'm just wondering if you are as dumb as you appear to be."

"What the hell is that supposed to mean?"

"What are you doing here, John?"

I held my hands up. "The same thing you are. Visiting ML."

"Bullshit."

"So?"

"Do you really think ML would ever have a thing with you? Honestly? She could have any guy she wants."

Oh how it burned to hear that.

She continued stabbing. "Oh, it's not that she doesn't like you, John, she does. But only as a friend. You're like a brother that she never had. A girl needs a brother in her life, either a real one, or one she sets out to acquire. I have two you know."

I wanted to run out the door right then, but I was power-less to move from her withering assault.

"You caught her at a vulnerable time, breaking up with her boyfriend. She latched on to you because you were familiar and not threatening. If you try to go for more, she's going to pull back, and you'll lose her. Kinda sucks for you, but you should have known better."

I spat out, "She tell you all this?"

"No. But I know her. And I know you. And it isn't happening."

"Well, Ann, that's pretty cold."

"Cold? Hah! Just honest."

"So, why tell me this? What do you care?"

"I guess I care just enough to clue you in. It would be cruel to see you carry on until you get burned badly. It's our Catholic upbringing, Johnny. Do unto others as you would have them do unto you. Or something like that."

"So, what do you recommend from your lofty perch? What should I do? Go out with you instead? Like in high school."

That remark frosted her. "You would think that. We were over then and forever."

"Tip's still available."

"That was a one shot thing. Horniness combined with alcohol combined with curiosity. But there's nothing there. You and I are not going down the same path. I'm going to live in New York after I graduate, and, despite what you say, you're going to stay in Binghamton, complaining the whole time, but you'll never split."

"What are you, Kreskin now? How do you know what I'm going to do?"

"I can tell. You, Tip, and all those other guys from CC that never left Binghamton. You all had a chance, but you didn't take it, and so there you'll be until you die. When I come home in twenty years to visit my family, you'll be hanging out at The Pine Lounge, watching the Yankees on the TV over the bar, sucking on a Rolling Rock, and complaining about how bad winter is in Binghamton."

ML walked into the living room, newly changed into a pair of denim jeans and tie-dyed T-shirt, and asked, "Complaining about winter weather in Binghamton? What's that about?"

I said, "Ann is giving me advice and also forecasting how miserable my life is going to be if I don't follow her advice, right, Ann?"

ML sat in the recliner. "Really? Ann?"

Ann turned to ML. "He needs to get out of Binghamton. Or he'll get sucked down by the crushing oppression of living there. You know that, John."

"I've told both of you that I'm going to grad school when I graduate. I'm waiting to hear from several schools. But I am definitely leaving. Have no worries."

ML said, "That is so great to hear you say that. I just don't think you can appreciate how depressing Binghamton is until you are away for a while. After I was here as a freshman for a couple of weeks, I suddenly realized that this whole negative energy was missing and that there were places where the burdens of the past are far behind, and you can start fresh. That was such a revelation. I guess that's why I so seldom go home. As much as I love my family, I don't feel comfortable there; it's a place looking for a me that doesn't exist anymore. God, that sounds pathetic."

We laughed, and Ann said, "Yeah, it's getting thick in here. How about our first screwdriver of the day?"

And so the screwdrivers were made. As we started to drink our first set, ML turned the stereo on in the living room, and played the album, *One of These Nights*, by the Eagles. Don Henley wailed:

One of these nights
In between the dark and the light
Coming right behind you
Swear I'm gonna find you
Get 'ya baby one of these nights
One of these nights
One of these nights
I can feel it

I can feel it
One of these nights
Coming right behind you
Swear I'm gonna find you now
One of these nights...

Those lyrics hit me hard. That WAS me. I so badly wanted to get ML one of these nights.

What if Ann was right? That I was way out of my league? But ML and I had that spark together. *I KNEW it*; it was real. And then there was that hot August night in my car. Hadn't that been real? It seemed like a long time ago now, but the memory of her eyes filled with desire as she gazed at me would never leave me.

Later, after being suitably lubricated with alcohol, and bundling up for the cold night, we left ML's apartment, and walked several blocks to an older two-story brick house nearby. As we neared the house, we could hear The Who's "Baba O'Reilly" rocking the house, and saw group of people entering the house. We walked into a dimly lit first floor filled with partygoers, all holding red plastic cups filled with beer or some dubious looking punch. The house reeked of alcohol, cigarettes, and pot, and the temperature seemed like it was fifty degrees higher than the outside. Over the shouting conversations, the electric violin solo at the end of "Baba O'Reilly" screeched its urgency, driving us impulsively forward until reaching its climax as we squeezed into the kitchen. We took our coats off as we looked around the kitchen as partygoers walked into and out of the room.

There were three kegs sitting on the linoleum kitchen floor, already wet with spilled beer. Stacks of red plastic cups lay on the kitchen table next to a metal half-filled punch bowl. In the background, Roger Daltrey wailed, *"Nobody knows what it's like to be the bad man, to be the sad man."* ML and Ann tasted the punch, approved it, and ladled some into their cups. I waved off the punch, grabbed a cup, and went over to the kegs. There was a short line of guys waiting.

The guy in front of me yelled to his buddy at the keg, "What are we drinking, Mikey?"

"Molson Golden."

"Fuckin' sweet." He turned to me. He was three sheets to the wind already. "I fuckin' love Molson Golden. That's good shit. FUCKIN' PRIMO!"

I said, "Damn straight."

After my new friend poured too much beer into his cup, and the head overflowed,

he licked the sides of the cup as if it were an ice cream cone, and stumbled away. I moved forward and tilting my glass, I filled it with beer. I then stepped away from the keg, and to the side, and tasted the beer. It did go down smooth.

I looked around the kitchen. ML and Ann were gone. I headed out in search of them.

I walked into what must have been the dining room off the kitchen. The opening chords of "Won't Get Fooled Again" burst forth from the next room. There was an old Brunswick pool table sitting incongruously there, and the room was filled with guys either playing team eight-ball, or guys that had deposited one of several quarters sitting on the table and awaiting their turn. I moved through that room and walked into living room from where the music was blasting. Stacked Advent speakers lined the opposite wall. Pete Townsend sang, *"There'll be fighting in the streets."* And my body could almost feel the sound waves fighting it as the music burst forth into the room. Groups of guys and girls were standing there, throwing their fists in the air, and some guys were playing air guitar in the corner, their arms wind milling around the invisible guitars.

I forced my way through the pulsating crowd, and stepped out onto the crowded porch, where the cold night air felt refreshing after the sauna inside the house. I scanned the porch, looking for Ann and ML, but they were not there. I retreated back into the house. I inched my way to the stairs leading to the second floor, and passed by a few glassy eyed guys sitting on the steps.

When I reached the landing, I looked in one room. In that room, there was a bed littered with coats, and on top of the coats, a couple were making out, vigorously. I stepped back, and looked into the other bedroom, and in that room, there were a group of guys and girls seated in a circle doing whippets. As I looked in, they looked up at me, with vacant eyes and fixed smiles. An empty-eyed girl asked me, "Want some?"

I replied, "Uh ... no thanks."

I retreated and went back down the stairs, getting frustrated that I had not found ML and Ann. As I neared the bottom of the stairs, Roger Daltrey's chilling scream at the end of "Won't Get Fooled Again" roared from the stacked Advents in the living room, and everybody near me also screamed as loudly as they could in concert with the song. It was deafening, and a little chilling, a primal scream of release.

I fought my way towards the kitchen, but as I walked through a hallway leading to the kitchen, a door opened up and a guy exited, shutting the door behind him. I waited a moment, and then went to the door and opened it. Steps were leading down. I could hear music, and lights were flashing. I headed down the stairs. As I came to the bottom of the stairs, I could see that there was large basement filled with more partygoers dancing to "Get Down Tonight" by KC and the Sunshine Band. It hit me as I listened to it that it was the same song that ML and I had danced to at The Bank back in August. A spinning metallic globe hung from the ceiling, casting shards of bright reflected light on the dancers. It was a phantasmagorical scene, with the pulsating music inspiring the dancers to dance around each other or into each other, with many voices echoing the lyrics:

Do a little dance, make a little love,
Get down tonight.
Get down tonight.
Do a little dance, make a little love,
Get down tonight.(Woo)
Get down tonight. Baby.

Off to the side there was a bar, cluttered with bottles of alcohol, and a keg sat next to the bar. I headed to the keg, and refilled my half-empty cup, and scanned the crowd.

And I saw ML dancing with Terry; they were dancing the bump and laughing. Ann was next to her dancing with a guy I did not recognize. My face became flushed, and I tried, without much success, to contain my jealousy. I leaned back against the bar, and pretended to look around the floor, while actually focusing the corner of my eye on ML and this bozo.

It seemed like the song went on forever. I knew this Terry guy was a phony and coming on to her. His smile was a little too cheesy, his hair a little too perfect, his pants a lot too tight. I had come all this way, and now this torture was my reward. It was not fair, and Ann's bitter words seared into me again. I considered escaping from this place where I knew so few and flee home, forgetting my humiliation. But I couldn't leave; I was frozen to the spot.

ML looked over at me and waved. Seeing her respond, the phony looked back and icily looked me over before recognizing and acknowledging me.

When that song ended, it was immediately followed by another KC and the Sunshine Band hit, "That's the Way (I Like It)," and ML came rushing over to me. She grabbed me, shouting, "C'mon, John! Your turn!" and started pulling me to the crowded floor. I first set my cup on the bar, and we passed by the phony heading off the floor. We began dancing around each other; she was singing the lyrics, while I was watching her. Then, she grabbed my side, and forced me to bump with her, dropping to the floor and then slowly rising as our hips touched at each point as we rose and fell. I was drawn back to the evening in August when we had danced in Binghamton. My head was spinning with the alcohol, the throbbing music, the dancers gyrating around me, the look in those blue eyes (… *those eyes*), the flashing beams of light reflecting off her long blond hair.

We continued to dance through the next few songs. I saw Ann dancing with a guy in the back. She was oblivious to us. That was fine with me.

After that song ended, ML grabbed my hand, and yelled in my ear, "Let's get a drink, I'm dying in here."

We left the dance floor, and walked to the bar where she grabbed my beer and took a long drink, draining it, and then held it out to me, yelling, "Don't hate me."

I laughed, and shouted back, "Thanks for leaving me dry."

"Sorry."

She and I moved to the keg, and I refilled my cup. The music was deafening. She squeezed me, and leaned in to my ear, "Let's get some fresh air. It's hot as hell down here."

I followed her up the stairs, and she opened the door and moved out into the pack that filled the first floor. I shut the door behind me, and she grabbed my hand and led me through the crowd, until we emerged through the front door to the porch where the crisp air was a relief from the smoke and the burning heat inside.

The porch was now empty, we were alone. She exhaled, "Oh, my God, that air feels good."

She released my hand and walked to the wooden railing in the middle of the porch, as I watched and admired her derriere, her hourglass figure, and that blond hair bouncing as she walked. She turned and sat on the railing and patted the railing next to her. I quickly walked over and sat next to her. She grabbed my beer and drank from it, then handed it back to me, and I took a swig.

"Ahh, John. What a night." She placed her head on my shoulder. "Are you having fun?"

"I always have fun with you."

"I know I've said it before, but I'm so glad you came this

weekend. This has been such a tough semester, you can't believe how much I needed this."

"I needed this too. I need you in my life."

She turned and looked at me, quizzically.

I took a breath. It was now or never; this was my chance. I jumped out of the plane without a parachute, "Mary Lou, I can't tell you how hard this is for me, but I think I've fallen for you in a big way. I wake up in the morning, and I go to bed at night, thinking about you. I know it's crazy, but we're good together. I think it was destiny that brought us first together in ninth grade and then back together now. I just want to be with you, to see you smile and laugh, to make you happy. God, I'm babbling like an idiot. C'mon, you can't be surprised by this."

She grabbed my beer again, and drank, while looking down at the porch, then handed it back to me.

"John, John, John." She looked away.

I put my arm around her shoulder, "Whatever happened in the past with Dino, it doesn't matter now. I can make you happy."

She turned back and smiled, "You have made me happy, John. I was so down when Dino broke up with me and you rescued me. I really like you, but, I know this is gonna come out wrong, I'm just not ready for a relationship right now."

The knots in my stomach started doing back flips.

She continued, "After being with Dino for such a long time, I'm enjoying being single again, the freedom to do what I want when I want to do it. We're graduating in like seven months, and now is the time I need to focus on my life and what comes next."

I removed my arm from her shoulder and drank from my beer, while I sifted through the remains of her words.

She put her hand on my cheek. "C'mon, that doesn't mean we can't be friends still and do things together."

I looked at her face, she was smiling, her dancing blue eyes appeared almost black in the dim light. I leaned forward to kiss her. She didn't move, so I kissed her delicately on her lips, and held my lips lightly embraced with her lips. As I was about to move forward, she pulled back, "That's a good kiss for friends."

"Oh, man, Mary Lou. I want so much more. What can I do to make you want me as much as I want you?"

"John, there's nothing you can do. There's nothing wrong with you. I'm not ready to be with anyone."

Shaking my head, I said, "Tip was right. I should have listened to him."

"Tip? What did he say?"

"He said that you could never be interested in me. That I was not in your league. And I was wasting my time."

"Tip has always thought I was stuck up so I'm not surprised. It has little to do with you. I just want to be free. Free to do what I want. I'm not trying to hurt you, I just want you to know where I'm at."

"ML, I don't know how I can go back to Binghamton like this. I have nothing good in my life. You are it."

"I'm still in your life, John. And I will be in your life. Don't forget Thanksgiving is coming up, and then Christmas. I'll be in town for both of those breaks, and we'll get together, and have amazing fun. And I promise at the New Year's Eve party this year, you'll be the only guy I am with, and the only guy I kiss."

"Am I the only guy you'll be with between now and then?"

"I can't promise that, John."

I sipped on my beer, and then said, "That's what is going to drive me crazy."

"If you want to be my friend, you have to accept me, not as I was in high school, but as I am now. Can you see that?"

"Yeah."

She shivered. "It's getting cold out here, and I want to dance some more."

She jumped off the railing and held her hand out to me. I sat there, holding my beer.

"You coming with me?"

"I think I'll hang here for a few minutes. The night air will help my clear my head."

She put her hand on my shoulder. "I'm sorry, John. I don't want to make you sad.

Please stay with me."

"Yeah. I'll see you downstairs in a few minutes."

She hesitated for a moment, then said, "OK, but don't stay out here too long." She turned and headed to the front door, where she turned back and smiled at me, and then she was gone inside, squeezing by two guys leaving, who did a double take at her as they were leaving the party.

I sat on the railing and let my bitterness envelop me. I replayed the entire conversation in my mind over and over, seeking a ray of hope desperately, but there was none. No matter how I tried to position her words, her true feeling was clear, and shattering. I finished the beer, and angrily threw the cup over the side.

I was starting to shiver as the cold night air hugged me close. I felt like an absolute fool. Tip and Ann had been right; I was the sap. I had let my guard down, and being under her spell, flew too close to the sun. I thought again about leaving the party, walking to the Galaxie 500, driving back to my Binghamton prison, escaping my ignominy, and sealing the shame of this evening.

But after contemplating that move for a few minutes, I realized that my keys were in my duffle bag, and I had no way to get into ML's apartment. I was stuck. That depressed me even further.

And then Ann came out the front door and walked over to me, saying, "ML said you were out here. What are you doing? It's freezing."

"It's too hot in there; I'm just cooling off for a minute."

"Sure you are. I warned you, John, but you went right ahead and were a dumbass."

"It didn't take long for her to tell you."

"I'm her best friend, of course she's going to tell me."

"So are you out here to gloat? To make fun of me? To tell me again what a pathetic loser I am?"

"Get real! I'm just here to commiserate. I know what it's like to want someone so badly that you can hardly sleep at night. I know what it's like to have your heart race like a speeding car every time you are with that person. I feel for you, John. I hate to see this happen. If we had never shown up at The Pine Lounge that night, none of this would have happened. So, I kinda wish I could go back in time and change that. But I can't. You just need to accept the way it is and move on. You and ML will never be together, John. It's never going to happen. You have to accept your fate."

"And are you my fate, Ann?"

"You should be so lucky. I told you earlier we are not happening. But I'm sure there's a nice girl in Binghamton that you will meet, and marry her in a big Catholic wedding, with Tip as your best man, and everybody will get drunk, and you'll honeymoon in Florida, and then she'll start popping out kids, and the two of you will live on the Southside of Binghamton for the rest of your lives, in lower middle class heaven. It'll be a wonderful life."

"Jimmy Stewart."

"Good culture reference."

"Fuck you."

"Whoa. That's classy."

I hopped off the railing. "I'm going to get a beer. See you later."

As I strode to the front door, Ann trailed me, and said, "That's it. Have a few beers. Life goes on."

As I entered the crowded entryway, I gave her the finger over my shoulder, and pressed through the crowd to the kitchen, where I poured a beer, downed it quickly, and poured a second one. I watched the pool play for a while, and then went back down the stairs, now sticky with beer, to the basement. ML was in the middle of the crowd dancing wildly to the thumping music. I chugged my beer, and then poured another beer from the keg next to the bar.

I started to feel a little tipsy, and asked a girl at the bar if she wanted to dance. She assented, and we walked to the crowd, and began to dance. She paid little attention to me as she bounced around, but I didn't care. I was surprised to find emotional release in the beat of the music, the dancing, the crowded floor, the shining disco ball. I pretended to ignore ML but could not keep the corner of my eye off her as she danced, laughing and singing with abandon.

And so the night continued, as I sought out any girl I didn't know that was available and got them to dance with me. An hour later, I was alone at the bar, drinking my beer, the sweat glistening on my face from the heat of the room, and ML came dashing over to me, grabbed my hand and dragged me out to the floor, and whirled around me like a dervish, flashing her eyes at me suggestively, and smiling broadly. When the song ended, she scooted away and found another guy, and led him by the hand to the dance floor. I stood on the floor for a moment, and then closed my eyes and just started to dance by myself; dancing away the heartbreak and the suffering.

Around two thirty, ML, Ann, and I left the party, and we stumbled back through the cold night to ML's apartment. My ears were ringing from the music. We spoke little as we hurried across the streets.

When we got to ML's apartment, I fell into the couch; I was exhausted. ML and

Ann went to ML's bedroom. I lay on the couch for a several minutes, staring into space, and thinking about the evening, and its disappointments.

ML came out later, wearing sweatpants and a T-shirt, and told me I could use the bathroom.

"Cool," I said.

"You OK?"

"Yeah. Just tired. And bitter."

"John, don't be bitter. We are friends and I'll be there for you. I just want you to be happy."

"You could make me very happy. The happiest guy in Boston right now. Kiss me like I'm the one. You know how to do that."

"John, don't be ridiculous." She started to walk away, "We'll talk in the morning."

After she left the room, I waited a few more minutes, and headed into the bathroom, where I deliberately made more noise than necessary acting out my frustration. I brushed my teeth, and looked into the mirror over the sink, and didn't like what I saw. My hair was too long and unruly. I had a couple of pimples on my chin that hadn't seemed to be there on Friday when I left. My nose seemed more bulbous than ever. My hazel eyes were as unremarkable as they were bloodshot. I spat out the toothpaste with extra vigor, rinsed with water, dried my hands, turned out the light, and headed back to the living room, pausing to say, "Good Night" at ML's door. I heard no response.

I turned out the light next to the couch, and pulled the blankets over my head, with the echo of the music still ringing in my ears.

I woke up with a start early the next morning. I had been dreaming that ML and I were on a beach and I had gone into the water alone. As I was swimming along the shore, suddenly the waves became larger and more fierce, and a riptide was pulling me out to open water. I was swimming desperately for shore, but ML was baking on her towel, and not hearing my cries over the crashing waves. As a mammoth wave crested over me and roared at me, I awoke. It was unsettling. It took me a moment to get my bearings, and to realize that I was in ML's apartment.

It was quiet in the apartment and outside. I looked at my watch. It was six fifteen in the morning. I sighed and closed my eyes. I recalled the prior evening, and I began to dread facing ML and Ann. I was overcome with anxiety, and began to sweat uncomfortably. I suddenly knew that I had to get out of there right away.

I arose and quickly dressed, then stuffed my gear into my duffle bag. I briefly considered leaving a note, but had no idea what to say, so I didn't.

I grabbed my jacket off the chair, put it on, picked up the duffle bag, walked to the front door, slowly and quietly opened it, and walked out, pulling the door firmly shut behind me. I trotted down the stairs, opened the door at the entrance, and walked out into the cold Sunday morning air. I hurried to the Galaxie 500.

As I arrived at my car, I noticed that there was a parking ticket stuck underneath my windshield wiper. After unlocking the car, I threw the duffle bag in the back seat. I then pulled the parking ticket from the wiper, threw it on the passenger seat, and got in. That ticket was never going to be paid; I knew I would never come back to Boston again.

The Galaxie 500 came to life as I turned the key and I drove away. I turned the radio on, found the first rock station I could, and raised the volume as loud as I could stand, to shut out my grim thoughts.

Soon I was rolling on the mostly empty I-90 heading

west with the rising sun in my rearview mirror. Even with the heater on high, I could not get rid of the chill I felt in my bones. I pulled off at the Framingham Plaza, not far outside of Boston, found a Dunkin Donuts, and bought two glazed donuts and a cup of coffee. I finished one of the donuts in the DD, and brought the remaining donut and coffee to the Galaxie 500.

I ate that donut and sipped on the coffee over the next hour as I headed west. I tried to not think of my disastrous weekend in Boston, although the images and sounds of my failure kept fighting to enter my consciousness. As the sun continued to rise, the interior of the Galaxie 500 warmed up, and I finally thawed out.

Shortly before noon, I stopped just past Albany, and bought a hamburger, fries, and vanilla shake at a McDonald's just off the New York State Thruway. After using the anti-septic bathroom, I drove to a Sunoco station, filled up, and then I was back on the Thruway, reaching Syracuse two hours later, exiting onto I-81 heading south, and seventy-five minutes later I exited I-81 at the Front Street exit, and drove through the decaying Binghamton surface streets to The Captain's house.

I heard the sounds of the New York Giants football game on TV when I walked in. The Captain called out from the living room, "Hey, young man, you're earlier than I expected. How was your weekend?" I dropped the duffle bag at the bottom of the stairs and walked into the living room. He was seated in his chair, wearing a suit and tie. He had obviously been to church earlier.

I sat on the couch across from him. "It was OK."

"OK? That's not very convincing. What happened with this girl?"

"It didn't go as well as I had hoped."

"That's too bad. Women? You just never know how it's going to go. You'll learn that."

"I think I just did. What's the score?"

"Giants are losing to the Eagles again. I wish we could bring back YA Tittle. Now there was a quarterback. By God, he was a tough piece of work."

I watched the dismal Giants performance for a few minutes, then stood, and said, "Well, I've got some school work to do, so I'm gonna head up to my room."

"Did you go to Mass today?"

I snickered, "No, Grampa, I didn't."

"There's a five thirty at St. Mary's."

"Uh, I'm not going to make it today."

The Captain looked at his watch, "OK. We'll hit it next Sunday."

"Yeah. Next Sunday."

"If you're not going to Mass, you want to go the Little Venice about six?"

"Yeah, that'd be great, Grampa."

"OK, I'll see you down here then at six."

I said, "OK," as I walked to the stairs, grabbed my duffle bag, and slowly climbed the creaking stairs. I walked into my room, closed the door, dropped the duffle bag on the floor, lay down on the bed, and closed my eyes. I soon fell asleep.

My bad mood continued that night and into the next day. The Captain realized this, of course, and he smartly didn't probe me with questions. At SUNY-B, I meandered to my classes and paid little attention to the droning professors, spending my time doodling in my notebook, but ML was never far from my thoughts. Her rejection was incredibly painful to recall. I could not understand how she could not envision a happy future together like I could, two streams combining into one river, making our way together through life. And always such thoughts inevitably ended in self-pity, and once the self-pity party started, it was like a fire igniting a grove of eucalyptus trees: nothing was to going to stop it.

After fidgeting in the library for hours on Monday, November 10, 1975, dwelling on God's sadistic punishment of me for my unknown sins, I headed to The Captain's house.

No lights were on at The Captain's house when I arrived, and his car was gone. I dropped my backpack by the stairs and went into the kitchen. I checked the refrigerator, saw that there was a slice of Cortese's pizza, and I wolfed it down. As I was checking the pantry to see if there were any sodas left, the phone rang.

After I said "Hello," Tip's angry voice yelled in my ear, "You fucking bastard, Moron." He was drunk.

"Nice to speak with you too."

"You fuckin bastard, Moron."

"You're blasted, Tip."

"You're goddamn right, I'm blasted. I've got every reason to be blasted. I got out of jail today and I come home and my cat is dead. You hear that, Moron, he's dead! And that's all because of you, you shithead. I asked you to look after him, but no, you had to run off to Boston in search of pussy that you'll never have. You dumb mother fucker. After all I've done for you, you couldn't do this one thing for me? You asshole. I hope you can sleep at night."

"How did your cat die?"

"How the hell should I know? I came home and he was dead. He wasn't given any food because my friend didn't give him any. Or should I say someone who I thought was my friend, but couldn't take five minutes out of his busy schedule to feed him. Thanks for nothing, Moron. Don't think I'm going to forget this. You bastard! You bastard! You bastard!"

I hung up. The phone rang again. I didn't pick up the receiver. I walked upstairs to my room, closed the door, lay down on my bed, and felt the walls closing in on me. I shut my eyes, and thought about how everything had ended up in the shits. God's lonely man. I buried my head in the pillow.

Over the years, I had contemplated suicide, of course, like most hopeless romantics. After much consideration, I had determined that jumping off the Washington Street Bridge into the swirling brown waters of the Susquehanna would be the best method, as it was the last bridge in Binghamton, so nobody would see a body for miles, if ever. No blood to clean up, very little pain, an exuberant high of flying, if ever so briefly, and hopefully my body being washed out to sea after a long voyage. Oh, and no suicide note. A suicide note troubles and confuses those left behind. I spent the next hour that Monday evening thinking about committing such a final act and its impact on Tip and ML, most importantly ML. I wanted her to have some pain in her life, just as she had caused me so much pain.

Of course, those desperate thoughts were just thoughts. I didn't really have the guts to end it all.

The next night, Tuesday, November 11, 1975, I was lethargically reading in my room, when I heard the phone rang downstairs. I heard The Captain's muffled voice, and then he called up from the bottom of the stairs, "Hey, Johnny, phone call."

I walked downstairs to the table holding the phone, picked it up, and said, "Hello?" into the receiver. It was Tip.

"Why, hello there, Moron." He was out of it again.

"What's up, Tip?"

"What's up? I'm not up, Moron. In fact, I'm pretty down."

"Tip, I told you I was sorry about the cat, man. What do you want me to say?"

"Nothing you can say will bring him back."

"Yeah?"

"You know what else, Moron. I got fired from my job today. When I didn't show up for a few days, the boss fired me. So, I don't have a job, I'm out on bail, facing certain jail time, my cat is dead, and I've got a traitor as a friend."

"That's bogus. What is that supposed to mean?"

"You damn well know what that means. My worthless father told me that your cop grandfather let the Bingo fuzz know where I was and that's why we got raided. He thought I would appreciate the steps he had taken. Stupid dick! After what he did to me and my mother. He doesn't get it and neither do you, Moron. How did your grandfather know where I was? Hmmm, let's see. Who could have told him where I was? Oh, that's right, my GOOD FRIEND,

Johnny Moron, is not only his grandson, not only living with Grampa cop, but Johnny Moron has been to the house where I got picked up. Hey, I don't go to college like you, Moron, but I think even a dumb ass like me can figure out that one plus fucking one equals two. You think I'm a dumb ass now, Johnny Moron?"

"You done ranting?"

"No, I'm just getting started. Because of you, I got nothing to live for. My cat is dead. I lost my job. I'm going to jail to get it up the butt. I got a bad leg. And all of that is because of you, Moron."

"Um, why am I responsible for your bad leg?"

"If it hadn't been for you, I never would have been hurt. If you had stayed with me and we fought those guys, I never would have run across Court Street. But you were too chicken shit to fight. You've never fought for anything. You've always run away from everything. Especially your friends. How's it feel to be a rat, Moron? You traitor, you sold me down the river. Now I'll end up in jail for possession because you sold me out. You're a fucking Judas. And to think I saved your ass all those times when we were kids. You putz. You mother fucking putz. If I had a good leg, and I don't because of you, I'd come over that right now, and kick your ass. Aren't you going to say anything, Moron? Too afraid to fight back? Pussy!"

"Are you done now, Tip?"

"You know that gun I have, Moron?"

Now I started to get a bad feeling in my stomach. "Yeah, Tip, I know."

"If I had a car, I would drive over to you right now, and

I'd stick it in your sorry ass and pull the trigger. I am so FUCKING MAD at you."

"Tip, I'm sorry you're in trouble. "

"Sorry? You bet you're sorry. One sorry asshole. You wait. Pretty soon you're going to be real, real sorry, my former friend. My man Casteneda says: 'The average man is hooked to his fellow men, while the warrior is hooked only to infinity.' I am that warrior, Moron. You know tonight I just might put this shotgun I'm holding right now in my mouth, and pull the trigger. Boom! And you know who I'm going to be blaming as I pull that trigger? You! Your ugly face would be the last thing I see in my head."

"Tip, get some help. I can't do anything for you."

"Yeah, you've done enough. You think about it, Moron. You're responsible!

"YOU'RE RESPONSIBLE!!!"

I hung the phone up, and disconnected the set from the phone line to prevent him calling back.

"What the heck was that all about?" called out The Captain from the living room.

He was seated in his chair, reading the evening newspaper, as I shuffled to the couch and lay down. "Tip is really upset with me. He's blaming me because he got arrested."

"Johnny, you didn't cause him to be arrested. That's all his own fault. He chose to do drugs."

"Yeah, but if I hadn't told you where he was, he wouldn't have been arrested."

"It would have happened sooner or later. He's on a downward spiral, and needs a wake-up call. Maybe this will help him turn his life around."

"Maybe, Grampa, but I've lost him as a friend. Even if he somehow avoids jail—"

" He won't."

"Oh, don't say that."

"I know the DA, Johnny, he's gonna throw the book at that crowd. Your friend was in the wrong place at the wrong time. He's collateral."

"Oh, man. I really wished I hadn't said anything."

"You did the right thing, Johnny. That boy is crying out for help, and this might end up being the best thing for him."

"So, I can expect him to thank me later?"

"Maybe."

"I don't think so. Not based on that call."

"Pretty rough, was he?"

"Yeah."

"Your conscience should be clean, young man."

"You keep saying that. And maybe if you keep saying that I'll believe you, but right now, I don't."

"Well, Johnny, you live long enough, you'll be surprised at what happens. I won't be around to confirm that wisdom in thirty years or so, but you just wait."

"I hope you are right, Grampa, God knows I hope you are right."

He wasn't right after all. But neither of us could know how wrong he was. When I arrived at The Captain's house late in the afternoon of the next day, Wednesday, November 12, 1975, he was in the kitchen, having a cup of coffee. "Hey, there young man. How'd it go today?" A stack of mail sat on the kitchen table, but he was holding the new Reader's Digest.

"Fine. Fine."

He pointed to the mail. "Letter came for you from that girl. Got a lot of perfume on it."

I sorted through the mail, until I found the light blue envelope with ML's writing on it. I stuck the envelope in my back pocket and grabbed half of a ham and cheese sandwich sitting in the refrigerator, and then turned to head upstairs.

"Where you going?"

"To my room."

"You can read your letter here, you know."

"Thanks, but I need a little privacy."

He laughed. "I may be old, but I'm not dead yet. See you later. I hope it's good news."

"Yeah. Me too."

I walked out of the kitchen, and took a bite of the sandwich. I lifted my backpack, and skipped up the stairs.

I shut the door behind me, threw the backpack on the floor, and lay down on the bed. I reached behind me and pulled the letter from my back pocket. I sniffed it, Grampa was right, the envelope carried ML's perfume with it, almost as if she had dipped it into her perfume before sending it. Once again I admired her elegantly flowing cursive writing. I tore the envelope open, and extracted the letter. I unfolded it, and began to read it.

November 9, 1975

Dear John:

You're probably surprised to get this letter from me. I know you're hurt by what I said to you, and I didn't really appreciate how you really felt until you were gone. That was pretty shocking and made me think about things between us.

I guess I was a little blind to not see how you were feeling, or maybe I was too self-absorbed. When you opened up to me on the porch, I was taken aback; I think I was mostly scared, as I guess I have been fearing commitment since I broke up with Dino. To get involved means to get hurt, but you know that.

After you left, Ann and I discussed you and this situation. Ann thinks you were an ass, and I should ignore you now, and let you drift away. Maybe that is the right thing to do. We are so different and I have baggage, but you have baggage too.

But as I have thought about you a lot today (BTW, thanks for making me not do homework today!) I have suddenly realized that you are the one guy that I have known over the last eight years that I am the most comfortable with. I have always had fun with you, and we share a lot of the same views and sense of humor (nothing wrong with a little sarcasm, right?).

I wish you were here now, so I could give you a big hug, and we could lie on my bed and talk things out. I guess having Ann here was a bad idea; I was probably using her as another form of protection against involvement.

This is reading badly to me. God, I'm twenty-one years old, and this seems kinda young. When do we get to be adults, anyway?

We need to get together over Thanksgiving, and I know we can make it work between us. I now know I want to be with you, and whatever the future brings, it brings. I hope you still feel the same way. I think you do.

I will see you in a few weeks, and we'll have fun together, and put this behind us. How does that grab you?So, study hard, get lots of sleep, drink lots of beer, and think of me from time to time.

Love,

ML

I was stunned. I reread the letter again to verify that I was not dreaming. And luckily, I wasn't. I had to read it a third time, poring over each and every word, especially the "Love." She had never written or spoken that word to me before. I was filled with joy, and overwhelming energy. I had to get up and pace around my room to relax; I dropped to the floor and did fifty sit-ups, and then thirty pushups.

Now breathing heavily, I ripped sheets of paper from a notebook in my backpack, sat on my bed, and feverishly wrote a response to ML, telling her how happy her letter had made me, and that I was incredibly excited for Thanksgiving. I didn't mention Tip's vitriolic phone calls. I worked on that letter for two hours, carefully crafting each word, and then positioning phrases and sentences for optimum effect. It was thrilling.

Later, I decided to sleep on it, and finish it after school the next day, hoping that a little distance would improve the final result. As it turned out, I never did finish or send that letter.

CHAPTER 11
The Great Gig in the Sky

Binghamton, New York, November, 1975

THURSDAY, NOVEMBER 13, 1975, was a sparkling, sunny day, and the temperature actually got into the high 60s. It was a last taste of warm weather before the brutal upstate New York winter weather would begin. I remember being so happy that day. I floated through my classes. Maybe it was due to the delightful weather, but it seemed that the other SUNY-B students were in a good mood that day as well; the campus was filled with laughter and good cheer. Or, maybe I just noticed it more, since I was so filled with good cheer.

Later, when I came home from school, I was surprised to see The Captain, ashen faced, sitting outside on the porch, holding a glass filled with Jameson's over ice.

"Hey, Grampa, what's going on?"

He blankly looked at me, "You haven't heard, boy?"

"Heard what?"

His hand shaking, he pointed to the empty chair next to him. "Sit down, John. I've got some bad news for you."

My stomach rushed to my throat. I don't know why but I immediately thought of

Mary Kate; it was a premonition. I dropped my backpack on the porch, and sat down next to The Captain. "What is it, Grampa?"

"This is going to be a mighty bitter pill to swallow, John, but your friend Tip killed himself."

The world went dark, and I felt suddenly nauseous, as The Captain continued, "He shot himself to death. The boys think it was Tuesday night."

I went numb, and blood rushed to my head. The porch started spinning. The Captain continued, "His uncle found him this morning. He hadn't seen him in a couple of days, so he broke into the apartment, and found him there."

I needed to lie down. I stumbled to my feet, walked into The Captain's house, and lurched to the couch in the living room. I dropped on it.

The Captain trailed behind me, "Johnny, I am so sorry. Who knew it would turn out like this?" I lay on the couch, suddenly chilled to the bone, every muscle on high alert. "But I want you to know, it wasn't your fault."

I looked up at The Captain, "It wasn't my fault? Of course, it was my fault!"

"No, no, it wasn't your fault! He was a mess and you just happened to be his friend at the wrong time."

"God, Grampa, can you just stop? I don't want to hear it now. Maybe later, but right now I'm just numb, and shaking.

Just look at me. I think I just want to grab a beer and go to my room, and be alone."

"Sure, Johnny. Go ahead. But just promise me that no matter how bleak it seems to you, that you would never do anything like this."

I bitterly spat out, "What would it matter, Grampa? Would anybody care? Would Mary Kate care? The world would forget me quickly, just like it will forget Tip."

"I would care, boy. Your sister would care. That girl in Boston would care."

With his words, ML's face swam to the surface of my brain, and I wanted to be with her more than ever.

"Ah, don't worry, Grampa. I'm not gonna kill myself."

"I know you wouldn't, but I'm responsible, so I've got to say it."

I stood up, and walked past him, as he stared at me with hollow eyes. I marched into the kitchen, threw open the refrigerator, grabbed a Michelob bottle, and then, after a moment, grabbed a second Michelob bottle. One beer for me, and one beer for Tip, I thought. I climbed the stairs laboriously as if carrying a two-hundred-pound backpack.

I shut my door and set the two beers down on the floor next my bed, and then sat on the bed. I propped up the pillow on the bed and sat against it, with the wall behind. I reached over, grabbed one of the Michelob's, opened it with a violent twist, and drank from it, the cold beer cooling the heat I felt burning me up from the inside. I held the Michelob bottle against my forehead dripping with sweat. All I could think about was Tip and I didn't think about much else.

A few hours later, as I sat in my pitch-black room, with the two empty Michelob bottles lying next to me, The Captain knocked on my door. "Johnny, you hungry?"

"I'm OK."

"I brought you a ham sandwich with cheese and mustard."

I got up, went to the door, and opened it a crack. The hallway light was almost blindingly painful. The Captain stood there, holding a plate with the sandwich on it. He also was holding another Michelob bottle. "You sitting in there with the lights off?"

"Yeah."

"You want to talk about it?"

"No."

"OK, well, here you go. I brought you a beer. I figured you needed another one. I've had a couple of glasses of Jameson's on ice myself."

I flicked on the overhead light, opened the door wider, and took the plate and the

Michelob. "Thanks."

"You're welcome. I'm downstairs if you want to talk." He turned to go.

"Okay, thanks. See you later." I closed the door with my foot, set the plate on the bed, and the Michelob on the floor by the bed. I put the two empty Michelob bottles on the floor by the door. I sat down on the bed, and suddenly ravenous, quickly ate the sandwich, while washing it down with the beer. The sandwich tasted like cardboard, and I took no pleasure from the beer.

The night moved slowly; I was unable to capture more

than a few minutes of sleep as I replayed Tip tapes in my head over and over, looking for a clue to explain it away, and finding none.

Somehow, the next morning, Friday, November 14, 1975, I was able to rise and get ready for school as if it was any other day. The Captain and I shared toast, coffee, and the morning paper and said little to one another. I sat through my Postwar British Literature class, looking out the window at the hills in the distance mostly stripped of color, except for the deep green of pine trees, and I thought about how Tip and I as kids pretended we were Daniel Boone, and would hunt for squirrels and birds with our BB guns on Ross Mountain, quietly creeping through the lush summer forest, waiting for the right moment to shoot, and even occasionally hitting, a squirrel, but rarely killing one.

After class, I drove to The Pine Lounge, and sat on a stool at the bar. It was quiet inside, a couple of older regulars slouched at the end of the bar, nursing their beers. Mack was bartending. Did he ever go home? He waddled to me, with a surprised look on his face.

"A little early for you, isn't it?"

"Yeah, it is. But it's not a normal day."

"Every day in here is a normal day."

"Tip's dead."

His jaw was on the floor, but he managed to stammer, "What?"

"He shot himself. I had to come because we had so many good times here."

"You are shitting me!"

"I wish I was."

"Wow. Jesus H. Fucking Christ."

"I'm going to have a Rolling Rock in his honor."

"Yeah. Yeah. Let me set you up." He walked away, speaking to the deadbeats at the end of the bar, "Jesus Christ, Fucking Tip O'Neil killed himself. Do you believe that?" The two deadbeats looked at Mack with dead eyes; they had no idea who Fucking Tip O'Neil was, but they drank from their beer anyway.

I looked around the bar. How tawdry and depressing it looked in the daytime. I recalled the last time Tip and I had been together at The Pine Lounge; it was the beginning of the end for Tip, that pathetic party in Conklin that evening was the nail in the coffin that doomed him. If only I had been smart enough to see where that evening would take him. My eyes began to fill with tears, and I fought them off by looking up to the ceiling.

Mack returned with two Rolling Rock bottles, and he set them down on the bar in front of me. He reached behind and grabbed a bottle of Jameson's, turned and set that in front of me as well. He retrieved two shot glasses from under the bar, and slammed them down on the bar. Opening the Jameson's, he filled the two shot glasses full of the whiskey, and handed one to me, and then lifted the other one up. We clinked glasses, and Mack said, "Here's to you, Tip O'Neill, you sad son of a bitch."

"I'll drink to that."

We both slammed down the whiskey. It burned as it raced down my throat. "Whew," I said as I set the shot glass on the bar.

Mack grabbed the shot glass, and set it and his empty

shot glass in the sink under the bar. He opened both of the Rolling Rocks, and took a swig of his. "These drinks are on the house."

I took a draw of the Rolling Rock, and the amber liquid washed away the burning whiskey. I pointed the Rolling Rock at Mack, "Thanks. You're OK, Mack."

Mack replied, "Yeah, well don't let that get out. It'll ruin my reputation with the ladies."

One of the deadbeats spoke up, "Hey, Mack, what about us? We feel bad about the kid dying too."

Mack sipped again, and looking at the two deadbeats, he responded, "Nice try, asshole. You didn't know the kid, you don't know this kid here. They was best friends. I never saw one of them in here without the other one. When either one of you lushes keels over, I'll give the other one a shot and a beer too. Until then, nothing, or in other words, GO FUCK YOURSELF!"

After I finished the beer, I shook hands with Mack, and got off my stool. The two deadbeats told me how sorry they were about my friend. I thanked them too, and walked out the door into the cold November air.

The Captain and I ate a pizza from Cortese's that night in awkward silence. He wasn't pushing conversation; he knew I wasn't open to it. Later, we started watching TV.

Around nine that night the phone rang, and we looked at each other, neither moving at first. Then I said, "I got it," rose up, and went to the phone.

After I said, "Hello," I heard Tip's dad ask, "John?"

I grew queasy again. "Uh, yes."

"Hi, John, this is Tip's dad."

"Hi, Mister O'Neill."

"You know about Tip, right?"

"Yeah. I'm sorry, Mister O'Neil. About everything. I don't know what to say."

"You don't need to say anything, Johnny. There's only two people to blame for what happened. One is Tip, and the other is me. There's nobody else." He started to sniffle. "I'm the one to blame really. I was the adult and I let my boy down." I heard the sound of crying, and I just stood there, unable to comfort him. Finally, he regained control, and said, "Ah, I'm losing it, Johnny. Excuse me." He sighed loudly, and then pressed on. "I'm back now. The reason I'm calling is I would like you to be a pallbearer for Tip. You were his best friend, and I'd really be a whole lot happier if you could carry him to his final resting place. I think he'd like it too, wherever he is."

I blurted out, "Sure, Mister O'Neill, I can do that for you."

"No, it's for him, Johnny. Not for me. It's for him."

He then filled me in about the details. There would be a viewing of the body at McCormack's funeral home on Monday, November 17 from 6–9 PM, and then a Mass on Tuesday, November 18, at nine in the morning at St. John's, followed by burial at Calvary Cemetery. I had to be at McCormack's at eight on that Tuesday morning, and I needed to wear a suit and tie.

"You got all that, Johnny?"

"Yeah. I'll be there and I'll see you Monday night too."

"Thanks, Johnny. I always liked you, you were dealt a rough hand, but I know you're going to overcome it. When you get old like me, remember the good parts of Tip. Oh, I'm just a rambling fool now. I'll see you Monday then. Good night."

I heard a click, and he was gone. I set the receiver in its cradle and returned to the living room.

The Captain asked, "Tip's dad wants you to be a pall-bearer, huh?"

"Yeah."

"You said yes, so I guess you're OK with that."

"Not really. But what was I going to say? No? I couldn't do that to him. Besides, I kinda owe one to Tip."

"Johnny, you don't owe him anything. He made his own bed, and, rest his soul, he's now sleeping in it."

"Someday, I hope I believe you."

On Saturday, November 15, 1975, in the afternoon, as I lay on the bed in my room at The Captain's house, I was staring at a textbook, trying to read assigned pages, without interest or success. I heard the phone ring downstairs, and Grampa's muffled conversation, and then he shouted up from the bottom of the stairs, "Hey, Johnny, phone call for you!"

I rose, shuffled out of my room, and walked down-stairs. He was standing, near the phone, holding the phone receiver with his hand over the mouthpiece.

As I reached the bottom of the steps, I asked, "Who is it?"

He spoke in a soft voice, "It's some girl. It could be that one from Boston."

My face immediately reddened, and I hurried to the phone; he handed me the receiver and left the room.

I took a moment to compose myself, and then said, "Hello?"

"Hi, John, this is Mary Lou."

"Hi."

"I heard about Tip. My dad saw the obituary in the paper and called me. I'm in shock. What happened?"

"He killed himself. He put a shotgun in his mouth and pulled the trigger."

"Oh my God. Oh my God. I'm so sorry, John."

"Yeah."

"Why did he do it?"

"He just gave up, ML. He couldn't deal with it anymore."

"Wow. I just cannot believe it. When is the funeral?"

"On Tuesday. I'm a pallbearer."

"Really? That will be kinda rough, won't it?"

"Yeah, it isn't going to be a day at the beach."

"Oh, John, I am so, so sorry. Is there anything I can do?"

I wanted to blurt out, "LOVE ME!" but I restrained myself. "I guess not."

"I sent you a letter."

It suddenly hit me that I had not responded to her letter as I intended. Tip's death had intervened.

"I got it."

"It's not important right now, but we do need to talk when I'm home."

"Yeah, we do. In your letter you wrote that you hoped that I feel the same way. I do, ML, I really, truly, madly do feel the same way."

There was an awkward moment of silence, and then she haltingly spoke, "That is so sweet ... I don't know what to say."

"You don't need to say anything right now. But please tell me at Thanksgiving."

"I'll get there. Just bear with me. This is hard for me."

"I'll be there for you the whole way."

"I know you will be. I've gotta go; I'm calling from a pay phone, and my time is running out. But I'll see you in a couple of weeks. I get home on the Tuesday before Thanksgiving. Meet me at The Pine Lounge at nine that Tuesday. OK?"

"I'll be there waiting for you."

"Be strong, John. You're not Tip, you are strong."

"Don't hang up, ML."

"I have to, John. I really have to. Good-bye. I'll see you soon."

She hung up as I said "I love you," and she probably didn't hear it.

CHAPTER 12
Funeral for a Friend

The roses in the window box
Have tilted to one side
Everything about this house
Was born to grow and die

—Bernie Taupin

Binghamton, New York, November, 1975

LATE IN THE AFTERNOON ON THE FOLLOWING MONDAY, November 17, 1975, I slowly dressed for Tip's viewing. I put on my white button-down Arrow shirt, foulard tie, navy blue pinstriped suit, and black shoes. It was the same outfit I had worn to the wedding only a few weeks before. After dressing, I headed down to the kitchen, where I ate two ham and cheese sandwiches. The Captain was out, but he had told me earlier in the day that he wasn't going to go as he felt that he did not really know the family that well, although he did send a bouquet of flowers to the funeral home.

I drove through a light rain to McCormack's funeral home on East Main Street in Binghamton. It was a large colonial style building, with bright white paint and green shutters. It looked far too much like a home for the living than a place to revere the dead. I found an empty spot in the parking lot, and jogged through to the entrance that was covered by a green awning flapping in the breeze. As I entered McCormack's, I heard muffled voices and organ music. A tall gaunt white-haired older man in a black pin-stripe suit greeted me as I moved into the funeral home, "Who are you here for?"

"Tommy O'Neill."

He introduced himself as Bill McCormack and pointed to his left. "The family is down the hallway there."

I shuffled in the direction he pointed, my stomach start-ing to seethe with dread. I could see an open doorway and a room beyond, filled with portable metal chairs. As I reached the doorway, I cautiously peered in. To my right, and at the front of the room, sat a brown shiny coffin, with its top open, and large bouquets of flowers on both sides. Next to the flowers nearest me was a stand with a signature book sitting on it. An elderly woman dressed in black was slowly writing in the book.

In front of the coffin was a kneeler. Across from me against the wall, after the bouquets of flowers, on the far side of Tip's coffin stood Tip's family: his father, stepmother, and two younger brothers. They looked in shock. A few mourners sat in the chairs facing the coffin. One was a girl that we had gone to high school with; she was crying, and holding a tissue to her nose. The organ music was noticeably louder in this room.

I made my way to the stand. As I did, I saw the older woman in front of me limped to the coffin and slowly descended onto the kneeler in front of it. At the stand I signed my name quickly, and then turned to the coffin. The elderly woman had her eyes closed, and then after a few moments she rose with difficulty and limped to the family. I stepped forward, but it was as if I was walking in deep mud. As I finally reached the kneeler, I knelt down, and crossed my hands as if in prayer. I then looked at what remained of Tip.

He was lying on his back, with only his top half revealed by the open coffin. He was dressed in in an ill-fitting suit, a starched white shirt and blue tie. I should have said a prayer, but instead I examined my friend. His skin was pasty white, and his eyes were closed. His hands were clasped over his chest and held rosary beads. I looked at his face, it was unmarked. Of course, he had put the shotgun in his mouth, and blew off the back of his head, so we couldn't see that damage. I stared at his closed eyes for a moment, half expecting a quick wink.

Oh, if only Tip could see himself now, I thought. *He would have one hell of a laugh.* Maybe he was laughing at me, looking right down and laughing at me. I could almost hear him, "Hey, JM, what do you think of me now?"

Eventually, it struck me that I had been there a while, and I became aware of a man standing behind me, so I crossed myself, stood up, took one more look at Tip, and moved away.

Tip's two younger brothers were in a line ahead of me, followed by Tip's Dad and his wife. They were all ashen faced, and there would be no smiles today.

I shook hands with the two brothers, and they nodded to me, but no words were exchanged. When I reached Tip's dad, his tears started flowing again, silently making their way down familiar paths. "Oh, Johnny. God love you, boy," Tip's dad cried out as he gave me a big hug. "Tip loved you like one of his brothers."

His body wracked with convulsions as he held me close. I blurted out, "I'm sorry for your loss, Mr. O'Neill," just like The Captain had told me to. My voice was weak and not very convincing.

He released me and looked at me. "Bless you, Johnny. Thanks for being there for Tip."

I stupidly shook my head in affirmation, and then moved to Tip's stepmother, standing next to his father. I shook hands with her, and neither of us said anything. She was not crying, and I sensed she was going through the motions.

I stepped away from the family, and found an empty row of chairs, walked to the middle, and sat down.

And there I sat for the next two hours, occasionally joined by an old high school classmate or two, and we would talk about our shock at Tip's death. He was the first member of our class to die. They knew I was his best friend in high school, but nobody pushed me for my feelings. I appreciated the discretion.

At seven thirty, Father Quinn, the elderly white-haired parish priest from St. John's, walked into the room. He strode to Tip's family, and exchanged words with them, and then after a few minutes of conversation, he retreated to stand next to Tip's coffin. Bill McCormack then announced to the remaining mourners that Father Quinn would say a few prayers.

Father Quinn then gravely began by repeating a few "Hail Marys" and then a couple of "Our Fathers" for good measure. When he stopped his recitation of the obligatory prayers, Bill McCormack announced that services would be at 9:00 AM the next morning at St. John's and that the O'Neill family thanked us for coming that evening, and hoped we would see them the next day.

At eight the next morning, I returned to McCormack's, ready for my last day with Tip. As I entered McCormack's, I went directly to the viewing room where Tip's corpse lay. Unlike the previous evening, the room was empty, and the awful organ music was silent. There was no family yet, and no sign of any McCormack's employees. The coffin was still open.

I walked over to the coffin, and stared down at my friend. I silently apologized to him for everything, and told him I wished he was back with me, so we could laugh again, go fishing again, ring doorbells again, watch *Star Trek* again, listen to Pink Floyd again, have a Rolling Rock at The Pine Lounge again, shoot baskets again, play Stratego again. Do it all again.

On a sudden urge, I removed my class ring from CC that I had not taken off in nearly four years, and, after looking around the room and seeing nobody else there, I slipped it on his stiff right ring finger, and then tried to position the hands as they were when I came in the room.

I stepped away and then sat down in the front row of chairs. A few minutes later, Tip's family arrived, spectral figures walking in a nightmare. I nodded to them as they entered, and Mr. O'Neill gave me a small wave. One by one they knelt at Tip's coffin and said their good-byes. Some other family members arrived and also spent their time at the coffin.

Shortly thereafter, Bill McCormack entered the room, and spoke with Mr. O'Neill, then moved in front of the coffin, and informed us that we would say a prayer first, and then the coffin would be loaded in the hearse and taken to St. John's for Mass, followed by internment at Calvary Cemetery. He then said a Hail Mary and an Our Father, with most assembled, me excluded, repeating the prayers.

When Bill McCormack finished, he requested that everyone, other than the pallbearers, get in their cars, wait for the hearse to depart, and then follow the hearse to St. John's. He then asked the pallbearers to come with him into the next room. I stood and followed Tip's two brothers and three cousins. As I left the room, I turned back and saw Mr. O'Neill standing at the coffin, looking down at Tip, tears streaming down his face. It was too painful to bear. I turned away, and hurried out of the viewing room, and caught up to the group walking into an office next door.

When we were inside the small office, Bill McCormack explained our role and timing in the upcoming ceremony, and then asked us to sign a document signifying that we were the pallbearers for one Thomas O'Neill. One of the cousins offered a mint to all; I declined. Bill McCormack told us that we would have to remove the casket in a few minutes and then he left to complete the preparations. We stood awkwardly and silently in the room. What could we say to each other?

A few minutes later, Bill McCormack returned and directed us to accompany the casket, now closed, as he rolled the casket rack with rollers to the rear of McCormack's. When we reached the rear, another McCormack employee, the driver of the McCormack hearse, was propping open double doors leading to the parking lot behind. We could see the long black hearse backed up to the double doors. At the short stairs that led to the double doors, Bill McCormack stopped rolling the casket holder, and then asked us to move to our positions, and to grab a handle, and we did so. Then, he asked us to lift the casket off the casket rack, and each of us grabbed a handle and lifted the casket. He then told us to slowly carry the casket down the stairs to the hearse, and we complied, although the casket was surprisingly heavy. As we carried the casket outside, a few drops of cold rain fell and pooled on the casket. At the hearse, the McCormack's driver helped us to lift and guide the casket onto the hearse, and then we collectively pushed it in, and slid it into the hearse.

The pallbearers split up, and walked to their cars. Tip's youngest brother, Robby, came with me. We got into the Galaxie 500, and I pulled around so that it was third in line behind the hearse, which had now moved to the entrance to McCormack's parking lot. We waited in silence for the motorcade to begin. Robby was looking out the window at the sullen grey skies. He had always looked up to Tip as his oldest brother, and I knew that of the two brothers, he was taking it the worst, but I didn't know what to say to him. And there was really nothing to say to him.

After a few moments, the motorcade began. Bill McCormack was standing in Main Street stopping traffic, and the hearse slowly turned right onto Main Street, followed by the other cars. It was raining softly, and I turned the windshield wipers on. The drumbeat of the wipers was the only sound in the car.

At Beethoven Avenue, the hearse turned right, and passed by the older homes that lined the first part of the street, and we drove by Tip's uncle's house, and I glanced at the grim apartment in the back where Tip had left us. Robby only looked straight ahead.

In a few moments, we passed by a deserted Rec Park, and then the hearse turned left onto Seminary Avenue, and we went up the slight hill, and drove by CC, ablaze with lights, its parking lot filled with cars on that school day. I sadly recalled how Tip's life had reached its apex at CC in his fateful sophomore year, and then spiraled out of control leading to this day.

The hearse then turned right onto Chestnut Street, finally taking a left on Riverside Drive, and we drove by the aging mansions inhabited so many years ago by Binghamton's rich, and now slowly decaying with the fortunes of the city.

Soon we were on the Veteran's Memorial Bridge, crossing the Chenango River. And then a quick right onto the Washington Street Bridge, crossing over the Susquehanna River, straight onto South Washington Street on the Southside, and then we turned left onto Vestal Avenue, and the hearse led us up Vine Street. We drove by Tip's old house, and as the falling rain fell from the roof, it looked like the house was crying. Then, past my old house; I looked over, but it was dark and without light. We drove around the old neighborhood until the hearse made its way back to Vestal Avenue.

We continued down Vestal Avenue, and then the hearse turned into the entrance in front of St. John's Church. The hearse stopped at the steps leading to the entrance to the church, as two older women, bundled up against the cold, ascended the steps to the church. I drove the Galaxie 500 into the parking lot next to the church; it was half-filled with cars.

Robbie and I emerged into drizzle and walked to the hearse. When all the pallbearers were there, the McCormack's driver told us to wait in the vestibule, until it was time to carry the casket in. The six of us climbed the steps and entered the church. We could see the altar in the distance swathed in bright light. A young altar boy from St. John's school was placing items on the altar. Ten years earlier that could have been me. There were people sitting in the pews awaiting the beginning of services. The church was not full, perhaps twenty percent occupied. The organ that sat upstairs in the loft was being played by an unseen organist, and the sad notes danced around the church.

We moved away from the church entrance, and huddled off to the side. Little was said. Robbie had tears in his eyes. He dabbed at them with a handkerchief. I put an arm around him, but Robbie unhappily shook me off.

After a few uncomfortable minutes, Bill McCormack came to us and told us it was time. We went back to the church entrance and saw an older couple putting their fingers in the holy water font. The casket rack now sat inside the vestibule. We walked out of the church into the cold drizzle and walked to the hearse.

The rear door of the hearse was open. We took up our positions as before, pulled the casket out, grabbing the handle and lifting the casket as it emerged. Then, we turned and carried the casket back up the church steps. Bill McCormack had propped the large wooden church doors open, and we carried and placed the casket inside and upon a count of three we lowered the casket onto the casket rack.

As Bill McCormack had earlier instructed us, we slowly walked down the aisle to the accompaniment of the organist playing a slow dirge, and Bill McCormack pushed the roller bearing the casket behind us. As we kept walking, Father Quinn emerged from the sacristy and walked to the front of the altar facing us, accompanied by two young altar boys, one holding a vessel with incense, and a light smoke from the incense vessel lifted into the air. As we neared the altar, I could smell the sweet odor of the incense.

We stopped at the second pew; Tip's Father and step-mother were seated on the right side. Tip's two brothers left the casket and joined their father and stepmother. The three cousins and I entered the second pew on the left side, across from the family, separated by the casket. Within moments the Mass began.

Father Quinn led us through the ancient rituals and we stood, sat, knelt, and responded with words memorized as young children through years of instruction. I looked around the church as discretely as I could and saw neighbors from Vine Street, classmates from St. John's elementary school, classmates from CC, other faces I recognized but could not identify.

After the gospel, Father Quinn began his homily with Genesis 3:19: "In the sweat of thy face shalt thou eat bread, till thou return unto the ground; for out of it waste thou taken: for dust thou art, and unto dust shalt thou return." He then told us that while our lives were temporary, God's love was eternal, and that if we would only follow God's instructions for us that we can sit with him and his son in heaven. He then proceeded to tell us about Tip, his life, his accomplishments, his impact on his family. I looked around the church, and there weren't many dry eyes. Mr. O'Neill held a handkerchief to his eyes and dried them as best he could while fighting the tears that flowed like water from a spring.

Father Quinn then told us that if we were feeling guilt over Tip's death, that we were wrong. His death was not our fault, nothing we did or could have done caused his actions. Tip ended up a troubled young man, and there were many reasons behind his actions, but we were not responsible in any way. Even though I knew he was addressing his words to the family, I was moved deeply at that moment, more than at any time since I had heard about Tip's death. Tears fought to stream from my eyes but I stared at the ceiling to stop them.

Father Quinn finished by reciting 1 Corinthians 15:51–58: "Behold, I tell you a mystery. We shall all indeed rise again: but we shall not all be changed. In a moment, in the twinkling of an eye, at the last trumpet: for the trumpet shall sound and the dead shall rise again incorruptible. And we shall be changed. For this corruptible must put on incorruption: and this mortal must put on immortality. And when this mortal hath put on immortality, then shall come to pass the saying that is written: Death is swallowed up in victory. O death, where is thy victory? O death, where is thy sting? Now the sting of death is sin: and the power of sin is the law. But thanks be to God, who hath given us the victory through our Lord Jesus Christ. Therefore, my beloved brethren, be ye steadfast and unmovable: always abounding in the work of the Lord, knowing that your labor is not in vain in the Lord."

As he left the lectern and moved back to the altar, I regained control, and the urge to cry ceased. Despite Father Quinn's words, I still felt responsible, and as I sat there, I could not relieve myself of that yawning guilt. I knew I could have done something; I should have done something. But I was powerless to tell anyone in that church about my guilt as I feared blame and, worse yet, their hate. Only Mr. O'Neill knew about my involvement with Tip's last days, and he had forgiven me for my role, although it gave me no comfort.

After the Mass concluded, Father Quinn left the altar and walked to Tip's casket, and standing at the foot of the casket, he granted Tip absolution. After proclaiming other prayers he passed twice around the casket, sprinkling it with holy water and waving the smoking incense vessel over it. He then asked that the holy angels to bear the departed to paradise, and then he motioned us pallbearers out from our seats.

We took up our positions alongside Tip's casket, and Bill McCormack rolled the casket rack to the rear of the church as we walked alongside, with the melancholy organ music rising overhead. We rolled the casket by pews of mourners, some crying, others somberly staring at the casket.

At the rear of the church, the doors were already opened. As we neared the open doors I could see that it had stopped drizzling outside, although it was still cloudy and grey. Bill McCormack stopped rolling the casket at the entrance, and then asked us to lift our casket handles and carry the casket to the back of the hearse, and we complied. After we rolled the casket into the hearse, Robby and I walked to my car, as the mourners drifted out of the church.

I started up the Galaxie 500, and then drove it around the parking lot so it was positioned to follow the hearse to Calvary Cemetery in nearby Johnson City. After a few minutes, the hearse began its inexorable journey, taking a different route this time, heading west on Vestal Avenue, a quick right on Livingston Street, and then a left onto Conklin Avenue, which turned into Vestal Parkway west.

As we drove west on the Vestal Parkway, it paralleled the Susquehanna River for a while, and seeing the brown water of the Susquehanna flashed images in my brain of fishing with Tip on its banks in those warm summer days of our youth.

Turning off the Vestal Parkway, we crossed back over the Susquehanna River, entered Johnson City, and continued to Calvary Cemetery.

Calvary Cemetery was the cemetery for Catholics in Broome County, and the tombstones of the cemetery filled out a large flat open space, scattered with maple trees, and climbing hillsides newly stripped of trees. As we drove into the cemetery, we passed by a small stone chapel with bright red wooden doors, the only sign of bright color in the cemetery on this cool November day. We slowly crawled on a narrow lane leading to the western part of the cemetery. We passed the part of the cemetery containing my father's grave, and I looked for it, but could not see it clearly.

When I had been younger, Mary Kate, Lizzie, and I would bring flowers to my father's grave on every Memorial Day, and carefully plant them in the soil near his marker. As I drove by on this day, I realized that I couldn't remember the last time I had visited his grave.

As the hearse and the cars in front of me stopped on the side of the lane ahead, I parked the Galaxie 500 behind the car in front, and Robby and I walked to the back of the hearse. To my right I saw a large green awning, blowing in the breeze, set up near a tombstone twenty yards from the lane where we were parked. There were a few chairs underneath the awning, and the bouquets of flowers that had sat in the viewing room at McCormack's now sat under the awning, next to the open grave.

Far less mourners were at the cemetery than at St. John's; mostly it was Tip's family. We pallbearers repeated our efforts at the church, although this time we had to carry the heavy casket from the hearse across the wet grass to the grave site. We struggled to keep the casket from slipping as our feet sank into the wet ground. As we reached the awning, Bill McCormack directed us to set the casket on a green plastic cover near the open grave, and we eased the casket onto the cover. Tip's dad and stepmother were already seated in the chairs facing the grave, and his brothers walked to the remaining two chairs and sat down.

Still wearing his black cassock, white surplice and violet stole, Father Quinn began the burial service by announcing that Catholics who commit suicide are denied the benefit of a Catholic burial unless the individual was of unsound mind, and that after consultation with the O'Neill family, he had determined that Tip was of unsound mind, and entitled to a Catholic burial. I successfully fought the urge to burst into laughter.

Then, Father Quinn tossed holy water in the grave and over the casket, while rushing through some prayers. He asked his God that Tip's soul rest in peace, and issued another prayer for mercy on Tip. He finished the service by making the Cross, and saying, "Eternal rest grant unto him, O Lord. And let perpetual light shine upon him. May he rest in peace. Amen. May his soul, and the souls of all the faithful departed, through the mercy of God, rest in peace. Amen."

And with that, Father Quinn walked to the seated O'Neill family and shook hands with each of them, while the small crowd dissipated. I approached the casket lying alone on the cover, next to the open grave, touched it lightly with my cold right hand, and silently said good-bye one last time. I hurried away, passing by the O'Neill family, still seated and staring blankly at the grave in front of them and the casket next to it.

At that time, after a Catholic funeral, the bereaved family would invite the mourners to the family's house for a wake, where generous portions of food and drink would be consumed, and as time went on, in a cathartic exercise, tears would flow in equal proportion to the alcohol drunk. However, Tip's father had vetoed a wake. He didn't think it was right to have such a wake given the tragedy of his son's death.

I strode through the wet grass, past silent tombstones, and headed for the Galaxie 500 on the nearby lane. As I reached the Galaxie 500, I almost opened the door, but remembered that I should really view my father's grave. I turned from the Galaxie 500, and headed back along the gravel lane away from Tip's grave. After about fifty yards, I recognized the area where my father's grave rested; it was by a large maple tree near the road that cast its shadow over my father's grave. I headed to the familiar row of graves and made my way to the Moran tombstone only a few yards in.

I stood in front of the large marble Moran tombstone. On it was carved Jesus and his disciples at the Last Supper. On the right of the tombstone, "Elizabeth Moran" was carved into the marble with "1890–1968" carved below. The left side of the tombstone was empty, waiting for The Captain's information. On the upper right side of the tombstone in small letters was carved "Jack Moran" with "1920–1957" below.

I turned away from the Moran tombstone and looked for my father's marker. The wet grass was thick, and my father's small rectangular marker which sat in front of the Moran tombstone was easy to miss. But I knew he lay at his mother's feet, so looking in that direction I cleared the grass, and found the small marker with the name "Jack Moran" on it.

As I crouched there, by a forgotten marker for a forgotten man, in a forgotten section of a cemetery on a cold November morning, with the sun peeking through puffy grey clouds overhead, I was hit with a wave of profound sadness. The tears really started to flow now, and this time I did not fight them off. I was crying for my father, for Tip, for me, for the grim world outside the cemetery gates.

After a few moments, I recovered, and wiped my eyes with my cold fingers. I stood and looked around the cemetery. I could see Tip's gravesite with the green awning lightly blowing in the wind, and his family still sitting underneath it, rigid as statutes. Otherwise, the cemetery was quiet, even the birds were silent that morning.

I slowly stumbled away from my father's grave, climbed the short bank to the gravel lane, and walked back to the Galaxie 500. I drove away from Calvary Cemetery and, after a while, drifted back to The Captain's house.

CHAPTER 13
I Thought

I thought I would be your streetcar named desire
Your man — the one you seek
I thought I would take you deep within myself
Subtitles when we speak

—Bryan Ferry

Binghamton, New York, November, 1975

LATER IN THE WEEK, I received a condolences card from ML, but there was only the following:

"I am so sorry about Tip. I wish I could have been there for you and him. See you soon. Miss you a lot. Love, ML."

I tried to call her on the following Saturday, November 22, 1975, when The Captain had left to go play cards with his retired cop buddies, but there was no answer the two times I called, so I gave up.

On that Saturday, I also was surprised to receive a condolence card from Ann, in which she wrote:

"Wow, I was totally shocked to hear about Tip. I don't know what to say. I liked him a lot. I think beneath his tough shell, there was a good person fighting to get out, but that good person could never break through. I am so sorry, I can't imagine being in Binghamton without him there. My thoughts go out to you. I'll see you over the holidays and we'll work through this tragedy together. I don't know how I am going to study now, but I guess we just go on, and do our best. Ann."

The next few days went by too slowly. The weather turned for the worse on the next Monday, November 24, 1975, as a nasty sleet storm rolled into Broome County. It prevented me from going to SUNY-B, so I stayed in bed that day, bundled up in the covers, trying to focus on my upcoming school projects and tests, but burdened with guilt about Tip and as a counterpart, filled with renewed desire for ML.

On that fateful Tuesday, November 25, 1975, I sat in a stool at the end of the bar in The Pine Lounge as nine o'clock neared. Funny how you remember more details surrounding incidents in your life that you would like to forget. The Pine Lounge was crowded with college students returning for the Thanksgiving holiday, and it was noisy. Someone kept putting quarters in the jukebox; I remember "Bohemian Rhapsody" by Queen being played more than once, and random people in the crowd would burst into parts of the song as the moment hit them.

I had drunk two Rolling Rocks waiting for ML; despite his earlier proclamation, Mack had given me the first one on the house. He asked me how I was doing; I told him I was getting by. He snorted, and said that was the story of his life.

The two Rocks had dulled my nerves, and I was starting to feel no pain; the first time I had relaxed since Tip's death.

The third Rock sat on the bar in front of me. It felt good to be in a crowd of happy, smiling people again, drinking a Rolling Rock, and not thinking about Tip, or Mary Kate, or anything really but my first love, soon to glide through the front door and join me.

I felt a tap on my shoulder, and turned to give my biggest smile, and even bigger hug, to ML. But it was Ann; I scanned the bar quickly. No ML.

"She's not coming."

Oh, man, did that hurt. I slumped back on the stool.

"What do you mean? Where is she?"

"Order me a beer first. I'm going to need it."

I turned, held up my hand, and got Mack's attention. After he wandered over, I ordered a Rolling Rock for Ann. My face was flushed now, I was feeling hot, and The Pine Lounge seemed suddenly very small and crowded. I turned back to Ann. "Are you going to give me really bad news? After what happened to Tip, I don't need any more bad news."

"Sorry, John. I wish I could have been here for the funeral."

"Believe me, you don't. It was horrible."

Mack delivered the Rolling Rock, and I threw two dollars on the bar, which he effortlessly snapped up. I handed the beer to Ann, and she took a long swig, and then took a deep breath. "OK, you ready?"

"No, but tell me the bad news. What's up with ML?"

"She's not coming home for Thanksgiving."

My heart sank further, if such a thing was possible. "What happened?"

"Dino came back to Boston this last weekend. She's with him now."

Shocked. Stunned. "What?"

"I spoke to her on Monday. We had been making plans to go shopping tomorrow.

Apparently, he showed up at her apartment last Friday night, and they went to Maryann's, you know, where we went, and they talked for hours. He told her how much he missed her, and loved her, and wanted to get back together. He was back in Boston to stay and make it work with her. She never really got over him, so she was happy to get back together. She's with him in Boston now. Her parents aren't too happy about it, but she thinks it's more important to make it work with Dino than come home."

I grabbed my half full Rolling Rock and chugged it dry, and then slammed it down on the bar, getting the attention of patrons seated nearby. "Son of a bitch."

"Sorry, John. I tried to warn you."

"I can't believe this."

"You fell hard, didn't you?"

"What do you care?"

"In case you really are that stupid, I do care about the two of you. I want you both to be happy. She is now very happy. Believe me."

"Well, I'm not."

She put her hand on my arm. "I can make you happy, John. I did once, I can again."

"You have got to be kidding, Ann."

Surprisingly, she was not offended by that crack. She started lightly massaging my arm. "No, I'm quite serious,

John. Things happen for some fucked up reason. Tip is gone. Mary Lou is back with her boyfriend. And you and I are left alone here. With all the shit that has happened, maybe we should be together, even if it's only tonight."

My head was spinning and disoriented. "Ann, you are nuts. I mean, I am so crazy about ML, and then you show up, and break my heart, and you can actually think I might be interested in you. Are you serious?"

She laughed, removed her hand, and drank from her Rock. Then, she spoke, "Strike while the iron is hot. That's what my dad always said."

"I'm sorry. It's not funny."

"Oh, c'mon, John. There's no point in moping around, pining for Mary Lou. If she comes back, she comes back. I know she's not coming back, but if you want to believe that, fine. In the meantime, let's have some fun. If you and I have learned anything from Tip's death, it's that we have to grab today and not hold on to the past, or worry about the future. You see that?"

"I'm not seeing anything at the moment."

"C'mon, let's go to The Bank, and just dance the night away. It'll be fun. You'll forget about ML, and we'll both forget about Tip, at least for tonight. Is that so bad?"

I hopped off my stool, zipped up my jacket, and looked at Ann, examining her clearly. She was looking up at me, with a slight, knowing smile, her eyes imploring me to join her.

"This is wrong, Ann. It's very wrong. I can't let go of ML that easily. I'm going."

"Where you going?"

"I don't know. Anywhere but here."

"Can I come?"

"No. That's not a good idea."

"John, when you change your mind, call me. I'll be around until Sunday."

And I stepped right by her, and left her at the bar in The Pine Lounge. I fought through the teeming crowd, opened the front door, and stepped out into the frigid air. I walked directly to the Galaxie 500, got in, and drove to The Captain's house.

CHAPTER 14
A Waste Land

When love's gone
A tear on
A waste land
Your pillow

— Bryan Ferry

Binghamton, New York, December, 1975

FOR THE NEXT FEW WEEKS, I fell into a deep depression, and only left The Captain's house to go to SUNY-B, or out with him for meals, or his required Sunday Mass. I knew he was worried and he kept asking me what was wrong, but I told him I didn't want to talk about it, and he respected my privacy. It was a bleak December month at The Captain's house. Oh, The Captain and I put up a Christmas tree, and decorated it with his old ornaments, and he played Christmas music on his aging stereo system, and he placed his red electric candles in the windows, but I was morose and dispirited. We watched a lot of sports, mostly in silence, him sipping Jameson's and me drinking beer.

I lost my focus on school, and it was all I could do to sit through my classes, research and write final papers, and prepare for final exams before Christmas break.

After deliberating for many nights, and writing and rewriting drafts of my message in a notebook, I decided against sending ML a Christmas card, as my anger at her for returning to her boyfriend ultimately overcame my fervent desire to communicate with her. Perhaps my choice was the correct one, for I did not receive a Christmas card from ML that year (or any year thereafter). Of course, I did receive one from Ann, in which she wished me a Merry Christmas, and hoped she would see me over the holidays.

It snowed two days before Christmas, so we at least had a white Christmas. On Christmas Day, The Captain and I opened our presents to each other late in the morning, after I woke up. He gave me a $50 check, a Yankees cap, and a new basketball. I gave him a gift certificate to The Little Venice, and a bottle of Jameson's.

Later in the afternoon, Lizzie appeared at the front door. I was surprised to see her and happy too. She was delivering our Christmas presents in a large Drazen's shopping bag. As we sat in the living room with the Christmas lights from the tree shining on her, Lizzie reached into the bag and handed me a letter-sized white envelope with my name written on it in Mary Kate's hen scratching writing. I turned it over but there was no message there. Inside was a short letter and a check for $25 attached to the card with a paper clip, both signed by Mary Kate. I read the letter aloud: "Merry Christmas, John. I hope you have a good holiday season with your grandfather. I pray for your soul frequently, and my deepest wish is that you will repent your ways and look to the light of the Lord for your salvation. With all the love of the Baby Jesus, Mom." Lizzie and I laughed derisively at Mary Kate's sudden religious fervor.

Lizzie then pulled out two wrapped presents and handed them to The Captain, one from Lizzie, and the other from Mary Kate. He ripped the wrapping paper off the package from Lizzie, opened a white gift box inside, and held up a dark green sweater vest that buttoned up the middle. "Wow, you know, I could use one of these. I just had to throw out an old sweater because there were too many rips in it." He set the box on the floor, stood up, and put the sweater on. It fit him well. "Look at this, huh. Johnny boy, what do you think?"

"Looks good, Grampa. Lizzie did well."

Then, he gingerly handled the carefully wrapped package from Mary Kate, and turned it over. He held it up to his ear, "Well, it's not ticking."

Lizzie and I laughed.

He tore the wrapping paper off the package, and opened the gift box, to pull out a brand new Bible.

The Captain dropped the gift box on the floor, and examined the Bible. "Ha! A Bible. I've already got one somewhere, but you can use always use another one."

Lizzie and I looked at each other and laughed.

The Captain asked, "What's so funny?"

I said, "That's a ridiculous Christmas gift, Grampa. Who gives a Bible as a gift?"

"I can't say I ever got one before, but there's always a first time for everything."

I said, "Grampa, if going to Sunday Mass every week of your life doesn't qualify you for automatic entry into heaven, reading a few words in the Bible isn't going to do it."

As he set the Bible on the coffee table by the couch, he replied, "Yeah, but it was the things I did on the days other than Sunday that has me worried, boy."

He sat back in his easy chair, "Lizzie, please extend my thanks to your mother. I'll also send her a note as well, but do say thanks."

She assured him she would. I held Mary Kate's card out to The Captain. "Oh, take a look at this, Grampa. Should I thank my mother too?"

He took a hold of Mary Kate's card, and silently read it. I could see him read it twice.

I asked him, "What do you think of that?"

"Well, young man, I think you should thank her for her generous $25 check. That will be good beer money for you."

"Not the check, the card. What she wrote on it."

After he issued a sigh, he looked at both of us, and said, "I told John this before, but you two have to forgive your mother. She's not a perfect woman, and she's had a rough life. But she is your mother, and you only have one of those. I can see in that card that she still loves you, John."

I snorted, "Was there invisible ink?"

"Come on. Read that card again. It's a mother's cry for her child."

Lizzie interrupted him and told him that she had seen Mary Kate wandering around the house in the night and chanting in prayer, and other strange behavior.

The Captain shook his head, "Yes, that does sound odd, I am not going to deny it. But you two are her family, all that she really has. I don't believe in quitting on people, and you two shouldn't quit on her. I urge you to reach out to her, and try to help her."

I said, "How do you reach out to someone who doesn't want to be reached out to? Grampa, you've tried contacting her, and she's ignored you."

"Johnny, I hear you. It's not going to be easy, and maybe it's going to take a long time, but you and I can't stop trying." The Captain looked at his watch, and then said, "It's getting late. I need to go pick up Christmas dinner from The Spot. Lizzie, can you stay for dinner? I can pick up another serving."

She told us that she had to get back as she had promised Mary Kate that she would help her make Christmas dinner, and that if she didn't help her, there wouldn't be any Christmas dinner at 59 Vine Street that year.

After grabbing her presents, and saying good-bye to The Captain, Lizzie walked out to her car, and I accompanied her. We hugged for a moment, and she gripped me tight. We promised each other we would keep in touch (but we didn't).Then she stepped back, opened the rear door of her car, set her presents on the back seat, shut that door, opened the driver's side door, looked back at me and smiled, and got in the car. She shut the door, started her car, waved, and pulled away. I waved at the back of the car in the cold air as her car got smaller in the distance.

After Christmas Day, I tried to keep busy and not think about ML, or Tip, or Mary Kate, and sometimes I was even successful. But not very often. There were always reminders of each of them in my life, so I was never far from a place that roused a painful memory. One day I was driving on Riverside Drive heading to a pickup basketball game at CC, but I drove by ML's house first. I slowed down, and looked over at the house, as my mind flashed memories of ML and me from only a few months ago, which now seemed like ancient history. I could see me walking her to my car on the day of her cousin's wedding, I could almost still smell her perfume that lingered in my car for days after. I could see her gazing at me with *that LOOK* by the Susquehanna on that hot August night not long ago. It was all I could do to grip the steering wheel and focus on driving as I continued on my way.

Almost every day on my way to or from The Captain's house, I would drive by the exact spot on Court Street where Tips' life changed forever, and I could rarely pass that spot, particularly at night, without seeing him bounce off that car into the air, and slam down on the pavement with a sickening thud.

My one real contact with the outside world was my old basketball teammate Mark Nolan. He made sure I was informed about and invited to pickup basketball games or poker parties over the holidays. At one of those poker games, he announced that he was having a New Years' Eve party at his parents' house. I asked what girls were coming, hoping against hope that ML might somehow be in town. But he didn't mention her. He did say that he had called Ann and invited her, and she said she might come.

New Years' Eve 1975 was a cold and clear day. Luckily,

no snow was forecast for that night, at least in any significant amount. I arrived at Nolan's party about nine thirty that night, and the house was rocking already. There were three Budweiser kegs on the back porch, and a large punch bowl on the kitchen table, containing a red punch liberally dosed with vodka. Sheets of pizza, bowls of chips, and open bags of pretzels all sat on the dining room table.

I walked through the house, exchanging perfunctory greetings and catching up with the few CC classmates I recognized there. I was surprised to see how many people younger than me were there, although since Mark Nolan had two younger siblings, I shouldn't have been that surprised. As I lingered at the party, I started to feel a little old and a lot out of place, and considered where were all the rest of my classmates from the CC Class of '72 were on this bitter cold night. When I caught up to Mark Nolan at one point, I asked him where Ann was, and he said that she had called the day before, and said she was going to a party in New York City with her college friends.

I wandered from room to room, squeezing by crowded, intoxicated partiers, with the music blasting from speakers in the living room. At one point I stumbled into the kitchen, and I looked at the clock in the kitchen; it read eleven fifteen. I suddenly knew I didn't want to be there. It struck me that being there at midnight would be the worst place in the world to be. I would be hopelessly alone and unwanted. I had to get out of there.

I escaped through the back door into the cold night. There were three guys standing outside sharing a joint. They looked at me and offered me a hit. I declined, and walked away. As I walked down the driveway to the street, the muffled music, laughter, and voices escorted me to the Galaxie 500.

I got in the Galaxie 500, started it up, watched my breath turn into vapor for a few moments as the car heated up. I thought about where I was going, didn't reach a conclusion, and pulled away.

I drove aimlessly around the familiar bleak streets of Binghamton, not caring where I was going, but enjoying the silence and the loneliness. At one point I found myself on Riverside Drive, and I slowed down as I came to ML's house. It was ablaze with light, and large cars filled the driveway and the street in front of her home. I was tempted to park and march into her home and see if she was there. The thought of that scene filled me with the first joy I had experienced in some time.

But that didn't happen, of course. I drove by, and didn't look back. I crossed the Veteran's Memorial Bridge over the roiling Chenango River, and then crossed over the Washington Street Bridge, and drove into my neighborhood. I turned off Vestal Avenue onto Vine Street, and slowly drove up the hill until I reached my old house.

There were no lights on in the house. Fifty-nine Vine Street was dark and forbidding. I had a sudden vision of Mary Kate sitting in that living room in the dark, staring out at me, with her cold unforgiving eyes. I shivered at that thought, said "Good-bye" to the house, and drove away.

I drove to the Park Diner and parked on Clinton Street. I got out of the Galaxie 500, locked it, and walked over to a path next to the Park Diner that I knew led down to the

Susquehanna River. I slowly walked down the muddy path past barren maple trees, with the winter wind whistling through the tree limbs, shaking them in a dark dance.

As I emerged from the path, the coal-black Susquehanna River lay before me, rushing to its fatal meeting with the Delaware River far in the distance. Across from me, the lights of downtown Binghamton shined on the river. A few yards upstream from me was Rock Bottom Dam. I gingerly made my way to the dam. As I reached the dam, I heard firecrackers and M80s being blown up in the distance. It was too dark to see my watch, but I knew that it was midnight. And I was alone. Desperately alone.

The Susquehanna was higher than normal, as recent winter rains had melted the snow upstream, and the river was angrily flowing over Rock Bottom Dam, yelling into the night as the tumbling water fell over the dam. I made out a large block of ice racing to the dam, and then toppling over, to be crushed into the maelstrom below.

I sat down on a large rock near the edge of the dam and gazed at the river. I thought about the last few months, and all that had happened.

I thought of how I wanted to punish both Mary Kate and ML for not loving me as I had wanted to be so loved. Especially ML. The anger inside me was palpable, and I was finding it harder and harder to contain it. At times it overpowered me.

And in my mind that was all due to ML. I had loved her so much and she was tossing me away like a piece of garbage. Who does that to a person that you care about, or even to another human? How could she treat me that way? Oh, how that hurt. As I sat there I thought of what steps I could take. Drive to Boston and cause a scene right there at her apartment? Bombard her with letters and phone calls until she spoke with me? I needed her to speak to me, and force her to explain what had happened to her, to us.

And then my thoughts grew as dark as the Susquehanna that bleak night. There was nothing I could do or say. She was gone and not coming back. It was just the way it was. And with that acceptance, my despair reached new depths. I thought how easy it would be to just become one with the Susquehanna, accompanying it on its long journey to the Atlantic. I thought about how ML would react to that news. I could see her face in shock and tears flowing from those blue eyes. *THOSE EYES*. And that made me smile for a moment.

I could end my pain that night so very easily, and so few would mourn or care. I could soon be forgotten, just another statistic, another death certificate to be filled out by a nameless, faceless bureaucrat.

A chill passed through me and I shivered in the cold night air as the black Susquehanna swiftly flowed over Rock Bottom Dam on its way to meet the Delaware River, and eventually, the Atlantic Ocean. As with every other romantic suicide fantasy, I didn't have the guts or stupidity to do it. As I sat there, I suddenly thought, "Where's the fucking deus ex machine?" And that made me laugh.

When I pulled up in front of The Captain's house an hour later, I was shocked to see him sitting in a chair on the porch wearing his winter coat, rocking slowly back and forth, and smoking a cigar.

As I climbed the steps, I asked, "Grampa, what are you doing out here so late?"

"Hi there, Johnny Boy, I watched the Guy Lombardo special on TV, and decided that it's my one night of the year I can stay up. So, here I am. Grab yourself a cold one and sit out here with me."

I could tell he was a little lit, surprising for The Captain. He usually held his liquor very well.

"Sure, I'll be right back."

I went inside the warm house, walked to the kitchen, grabbed a Genesee Cream Ale from the refrigerator, opened it, and headed out to the porch. As I exited the house, he looked over to me, and said, "Have a seat here."

He patted the chair next to him. I crossed in front of him, and sat down next to him.

"Johnny boy, as I was sitting there tonight watching the show, I started thinking about the many New Year's Eves I've spent in my lifetime. And that is a quite a few." He inhaled from his cigar, and then blew smoke out his mouth. "When I was your age ... twenty-one, right?"

"Twenty-one."

"Twenty-one? What I wouldn't give to be twenty-one again. So much to look forward to. When I was twenty-one, your grandmother and I and a few other couples went to Monaco's restaurant in Binghamton for New Years' Eve. It was 1919, right after the War. Monaco's was a real classy joint that closed about fifteen years ago. God, Elizabeth was beautiful that night. That might have been the night that I realized that I was madly in love with her. I proposed to her on Valentine's Day of 1919. Did you know that?"

"No."

"I bought her a red corsage that night. She was wearing a white dress that hugged her so well. Oh, she had a figure back then. That red corsage on that white dress. I can see it so clearly in my mind, and both of us laughing with not a care in the world. It was a magical night."

"I hope I have a night like that someday, Grampa."

"Oh, you young people today, so worried about yourselves and the future. It will be OK. It all works out somehow. As long as you don't give up, Johnny. You just can't give up. Like your friend Tip. He gave up too soon. Things would have turned for him."

"It's nice to think so."

"Listen to you, 'It's nice to think so.' Such pessimism! Honestly! But maybe my beliefs are slipping away, and when I finally depart this veil of tears, my beliefs will be buried with me."

"Well, that won't be for a long time, Grampa."

"I am not hoping it comes any sooner, boy, that's for sure."

He took the cigar out of his mouth, looked at it, and flung it to the snow outside the front porch, reached into his coat, and pulled another cigar out. He put it delicately in his mouth, and then lit it with his lighter. After lighting the cigar, he inhaled deeply again, then blew three smoke rings into the air.

After admiring them for a moment, he asked me, "You want one?"

"No thanks. No offense, Grampa, but I don't really like cigars."

"Good. Terrible habit. But I love my Cubans. I've only got a handful left. You know you can't buy them anymore. Goddamn Castro. He ruined my cigar habit. I have to smoke Cuban imitators. I only smoke these Cubans now when I've got something to celebrate."

"What are you celebrating tonight?"

He pulled the cigar out of his mouth, looked at it, flicked the ash at the end off, turned to me and said, "I'm celebrating life, Johnny boy. Overall, I think it's a pretty good deal."

I drank from my Genny. We sat for a while longer until he finished that cigar and then we both got so cold that we had to go inside.

CHAPTER 15
Wish You Were Here

How I wish, how I wish you were here.

—Pink Floyd

Binghamton, New York, January, 1976

AS MY LAST SEMESTER BEGAN AT SUNY-B in January of 1976, I thought many times about writing ML, and even drafted a few letters, but I could never find the right tone. My letters would be either too angry or too needy. Frustrated, I gave up writing them.

I drifted through my last semester in those early months of 1976 barely existing. I bathed in my guilt about Tip and my bitterness towards ML. That bitterness grew in intensity and swelled, reaching an apex when, for the first time since I had met her in freshman year of high school, I did not get a birthday card from her on my birthday, March 21. My grades slipped badly that last semester, none better than a B-. I retreated into hermit status, rarely coming out of my room. The Captain was worried, and tried to break through my shell, but I gave him the silent treatment. After a while he gave up.

I did not see or hear from Ann either. My view of all women turned sour and suspicious.

During this period, I often thought about a *Star Trek* episode that Tip and I had watched many times where, after Captain Kirk's lover dies, Spock employs the Vulcan Mind Meld on Captain Kirk, and says "Forget," and the good captain did. I had no Spock; there was no Vulcan Mind Meld, and I could not forget any of it.

In April, I received an acceptance letter from Boston College for its master's program in English. The day it came, I ripped it up, and threw the pieces in the trash can in the kitchen. I was also accepted at Syracuse and NYU (but rejected by Cornell again), but I decided that I was done with school, and that I needed a radical change. After spending far too much time contemplating my next steps, I decided that I would move to Los Angeles right after graduation. Why Los Angeles? Well, I wanted to be as far away as possible; I was tired of the ugly East Coast weather, and LA carried a romantic impression from movies. Maybe it was the LA that Tip and I had seen in Chinatown, one of our recent favorite movies that swayed me to move there.

In order to fund my trip west, I decided to sell the Galaxie 500 after I graduated, and try to catch a ride west. In April, I had posted a 3x5 card on SUNY-B's ride sharing wall with The Captain's phone number, asking to share a ride and expenses to California in June. A week later, Adam Levine called and said he was driving to Los Angeles to attend UCLA, starting in the summer. After a few minutes of forced conversation, I had my ride west.

I graduated from SUNY-B in late May of 1976. I didn't attend the ceremony at the Broome County Veterans Memorial Arena in downtown Binghamton. The Captain strongly encouraged me to attend, but I didn't give a shit at that point. I only wanted to get out; it was time to move on.

I sold the Galaxie 500 for $500 shortly after graduation to a used car dealer on upper Court Street who was excited to get a convertible on his lot. It wasn't until I handed him the keys that I it hit me that I would never ride in that car again, and neither would Tip, or ML, or The Captain, or Mary Kate, or anyone else I knew. I walked over to the Galaxie 500 sitting alone on the lot and looked in the windows one last time. Of course, the memory that hit me was that hot humid night almost a year earlier when ML had sat next to me by the Susquehanna when she had begged me to make love to her, and I had so stupidly rejected her advances.

I stepped away from the Galaxie 500, admired her clean lines one last time, turned, and walked away, leaving her alone in the parking lot of a used car lot on Court Street filled with aging, salt-rusted cars.

On my last night in Binghamton, The Captain took me out to dinner at the Little Venice. It was crowded as usual, but we were lucky and were led to a booth, even though we didn't have a reservation. Perhaps, we weren't really lucky and he had slipped the owner a fiver for the booth. That would have been like him.

After his glass of Jameson's and my Rock was delivered, he held up his glass to me. "Cheers, Johnny boy." I tapped his glass with my Rock.

"Thanks, Grampa."

"I'm not going to lie, young man, I'm going to miss you. If you're alone, you don't realize you miss companionship until you get it. So, these last few months together as room-mates has been good for me. Maybe not so good for you, but it's been good for me."

"You did a lot for me, Grampa. I can't thank you enough for taking me in. I don't know what I would have done when Mary Kate threw my ass out."

"That's about all I can do at my age, Johnny, is to help my family. I'm too old to do much of anything else."

"C'mon, you are still in good shape, Grampa. You'll live to be a hundred."

"No, I won't. And I don't want to, really. Because I'd be some old fossil stuck in a nursing home wearing a diaper and not recognizing anything or anyone. That's not me. I want to go out while I'm still capable of thinking."

"No chance of that. I'm serious—you'll live to be a hundred."

He laughed. "I'm glad you think so. Not much chance of that. I would like to live long enough to see the Yankees win another World Series. I was spoiled with Ruth, DiMaggio, and Mantle." He looked heavenwards. "Just one more World Series win, that's all I ask, Lord."

The waitress dropped off our salads liberally drizzled with Italian salad dressing, which we attacked.

"Well, I hope you come back here when you've seen enough of California. I'm sure it's a fun place to visit, but not to raise a family."

"Who says I want to raise a family? After my family, I'm thinking that being alone is a better way."

"Ah, you're young. Lots of you young guys feel that way. But then you get a little older, a little settled. And you realize marriage is right."

"Well, Grampa, as the old joke goes, marriage is an institution, and who the hell wants to be in an institution."

That shut him up.

After dinner, I drove his 1972 white Cadillac Fleetwood Brougham D'Elegance through the decaying Binghamton streets, filled with potholes from the winter salt, awaiting summer repairs. After I parked the Caddy in his driveway, we got out and walked to the front door, as the last light of the June day fought its demise. He opened the door, and started to go in. I stood on the porch for a moment.

"You coming in, Johnny?"

"No, it's a nice night out, I think I'll just hang out here for a few minutes."

"OK." He walked into house, and turned on a light in the entryway; I saw the light from the living room go on, and then flickering lights from the TV started.

I sat on the lounge chair that we had moved out to the porch over Memorial Day, and got comfortable. It was turning into a beautiful evening. The leaves of the big maple tree in front of the porch were brilliantly green in the last rays of the sun, and birds were flying into the tree to get into their nests for the night.

It struck me finally that this was my last night in Binghamton, and that I was really moving on in the morning.

I thought I should consecrate the moment somehow, but couldn't come up with the right method.

I was bombarded with memories in a kaleidoscopic swirl, some fond, many painful. Living in any one place for twenty-two years can result in a collage of memories, and I embraced the memories, even the painful ones, as they had shaped me and made me now stronger.

Although the bitterness of ML's rejection was so painful to live with and accept, I knew that I was stronger because of it, and that I would never let anyone get inside my soul that way again. I would always have a last wall up, one impervious to emotion.

As the sun's rays disappeared behind the hills to the west, the streetlights flashed on. In the small corn patch in the backyard of the house across the street, I saw fireflies flash their yellow signals as they flew around the young corn stalks.

I suddenly realized that I should have gone to Calvary Cemetery to say good-bye to Tip and my father. But it was too late now.

In the morning I would be reborn. Good-bye ML. Screw you and your boyfriend. Good-bye Ann. Screw you and your big hooters. Good-bye, Mary Kate, thanks for abandoning me and never showing me what love was. Screw your madness. Good-bye Tip, you stupid son of a bitch. Just screw you too.

I hardly slept that night, as my mind raced feverishly, filled with equal parts anticipation and sadness. Early the next morning, I stumbled out of bed bleary-eyed and carried my packed duffel bag and backpack downstairs and dropped them by the front door. The Captain made me cheesy eggs with bacon for breakfast and we laughed as we recalled the last nine months together. At eight thirty the doorbell rang; Adam Levine was at the door. He was driving a new blue Pontiac Firebird, a graduation present from his parents. I introduced him to The Captain, and they exchanged pleasantries while I carried my stuff to the car, and jammed it into the open trunk filled with his gear. I shut the trunk with finality and walked back to the steps leading up to the front porch. Adam and The Captain came down the steps, and Adam kept walking to the car.

I said to The Captain, "This is it, Grampa, you don't have to babysit me anymore. You're free again."

He snorted, "Free! Ha! With family, you're never free. You'll see."

I stuck my hand out, "Well, thanks for everything, Grampa."

He waved the handshake off, "Handshake! Come here, you never get too old or too big for a hug."

We hugged, and he squeezed me more than I anticipated. As we pulled away, I laughed and said, "You better not rent my room out because you never know when I might be back."

I saw that he was fighting off a tear. "It'll be there for you when you come back, Johnny."

"If I come back, if I come back."

"You'll be back."

I turned to go, walked away, but looked back, "Only if the Yankees win the World Series."

He called out, "That's cruel."

I kept on walking. Reaching the Firebird, I got in the passenger seat, and Adam asked, "You got everything?"

"Yeah, let's go."

He started the car, and we pulled away. I looked over at The Captain, He was standing at the porch steps waving, and I waved back. As we picked up speed, I turned in my seat and watched him and his house recede in the distance. At the corner of Court Street, we turned left and I saw The Captain, tiny in the distance, still standing there.

We soon got onto Highway 81 heading south to Pennsylvania. We quickly were away from Binghamton, and I could see the city buildings receding in the side mirror. I felt energized and vibrantly alive; and laughed to myself as I realized that it wasn't only the rearview mirror that was the best place to see Binghamton, the side view mirror was pretty damn good too.

CHAPTER 16
Can't Let Go

They said go west young man, that's best
It's there you'll feel no pain
Bel-Air's okay if you dig the grave
But I want to live again
Can't let go
There's a madness in my soul tonight
Can't let go
Must ride like the storm
Can't let go
Will I run out of control tonight
Can't let go
Until every trace is gone

—Bryan Ferry

Los Angeles, California, 1976-1979

IT TOOK A WEEK FOR ADAM AND ME to get to Los Angeles. After leaving Binghamton, we drove straight to Harrisburg, then connected to Highway 80 west, and drove for twelve hours until we arrived in South Bend, Indiana, where he had a buddy going to Notre Dame. We crashed there for the night, and then spent the next day with his friend. The following day we got up early and drove straight to Boulder, Colorado, where he had another friend at the University of Colorado. We spend two days in Boulder, including one day hiking in the nearby Rockies. It was the first time I had seen real mountains and I was amazed.

Then we drove to Las Vegas. We rented a room in a dumpy motel near the old downtown, and we hit the casinos. I stuck mostly to blackjack and made a few bucks.

In our last leg we drove from Las Vegas to LA, arriving in the early evening to a huge traffic jam. Adam insisted upon driving to Venice, and, after we parked, we walked out to the Pacific and stuck our feet into the surprisingly cold ocean water. As I stood on the shore, with gentle waves flowing over my feet and ankles, I was struck by the jagged mountains to the north, and lights of the city behind us. After driving through the blazing hot deserts, the cool ocean breeze blowing off the Pacific felt sublime.

We checked into a room with twin beds at a Holiday Inn not too far from UCLA. The next day Adam registered and moved into his graduate housing. He let me sleep on the floor for a couple of nights, and I avoided the resident advisors.

A few days later, I rented a small furnished dumpy apartment carved out of an older house on Kelton Avenue, about a mile from UCLA, across Wilshire Boulevard. There was no bedroom; it was just a one room apartment with a creaky sofa-bed, and a tiny kitchen with a gas oven that was so old I was scared to use it, and rarely did.

A day later, I landed a job with the Record Warehouse in Westwood as a stocking clerk. From a drugstore in Westwood I bought two postcards of the Hollywood sign, and sent one to The Captain and one to Lizzie, informing them of my new address and phone number, and also telling them that I was OK.

At first, I fell in love with Westwood, especially in comparison to grey, deteriorating Binghamton. I would walk to and from work, and I was always amazed at the low humidity and constant smoggy sunshine. In my off hours, I would often explore the shops of Westwood or would walk to UCLA to catch any cultural activities there. A Cineplex was a block away from my apartment, and I would go there to watch movies by myself, and as I sat in the darkened theater I would recall the many fine evenings that Tip and I had shared in film darkness.

Even in the confines of my tawdry little apartment, I felt liberated and free from the chains of my former life. I found myself gradually spending less and less time thinking about ML and Tip.

After working at the Record Warehouse for six weeks, I went out with Sandy. She was another clerk from the Record Warehouse; she was from Modesto and had moved to LA to get away from the boredom of the Central Valley. We soon were having sex on my sofa-bed regularly, and she introduced me to coke, a drug she enjoyed and insisted that we both snort before having sex. I was so anxious to have sex, any sex, that I just dumbly went along.

Over time I learned the bus system in LA and would ride around town, many times being the only white person on a bus. I loved to take a bus early in the morning to Santa Monica, and walk the beach and out on the pier, staring in amazement at the dark blue ocean and its distant horizon, with a fogbank lurking offshore. But I could never get used to the cold Pacific water, and after my first dip at the beach in Santa Monica, I gave up ocean swimming.

Other days I would go to Beverly Hills, and stroll around its high-end shops, looking for celebrities, and spotting a few of them (Richard Dreyfuss, Jacqueline Bissett, Bob Barker). One day I discovered Trader Vic's Tiki Room bar on Wilshire, and I soon began to hang out there with a regular crowd of show-biz wannabees and displaced persons like me. After a while we became a pack, and someone coined the name the "Crap Pack" playing off the "Rat Pack" name. Despite my low economic means, I was welcomed and included in the many debaucheries. It was mostly guys but there were some girls that floated in the Crap Pack for a time, as they slept with a member and then disappeared after the inevitable break up. I brought Sandy to a few gatherings of the Crap Pack, and other than enjoying the prodigious amounts of coke that were there, she didn't care for the group.

On April 2, 1977, the Crap Pack and assorted wannabes drove to Palm Springs for a week of Easter partying. I had to use my first earned week of vacation to go, but I wasn't missing the major party action. It was a nonstop festival of booze, drugs, and women, as we tore up staid Palm Springs, setting new standards for sybaritism. By the time I was dropped off at my dismal apartment late on Easter night, I was baked and fried. I carried my duffle bag into the apartment, dropped it on faded shag carpet, fell on the sofa-bed, and was soon asleep.

I was rudely awoken the next morning by the phone ringing on the wall in the kitchen. I rose groggily, and stumbled to the phone. It was Lizzie. After berating me for not answering my phone for a week, she told me that Mary Kate was dead. I thought I was still asleep and shook my head. I told her I had been out of town for a week. She continued and

told me that Mary Kate had been discovered a week ago, dead
of a cerebral edema; her brain had swelled and exploded. I
should have felt something, even numbness, but I felt nothing. I was beyond feeling or caring; I still had too much party
goods in my system. I briefly asked her if I should come back
for the funeral, but she told me that she had taken care of the
wake and funeral, and Mary Kate had been buried on Good
Friday. She then gave me the highlights of the services, and I
threw in some grunts infrequently, but I wasn't really paying
any attention. At that point, I couldn't care less about Mary
Kate or Binghamton; it was all a bad dream put to rest. After
she finished, I asked her if there was anything she needed
from me; she said there wasn't. She also let me know that she
had hired a real estate agent and was selling 59 Vine Street.
She was going through all the contents and wanted to know if
I wanted anything; I told her that there was nothing I wanted
in that house, she could sell it, keep it, or burn it in the backyard. She let me know that in Mary Kate's will we were still
equal beneficiaries but she was the executor and that she
would send me a check when the estate was settled. I told her
thanks. And then she ripped into me, letting me know how
angry she was with me and how disappointed The Captain
had been that I was not there. I politely mumbled that I was
sorry (but I wasn't). We ended the call by promising to keep
in touch more (but we didn't).

After I hung the phone up, I returned to my gamy sofa
bed, lay back down, and shut my eyes. I felt a black cloud
rise from me and dissipate; I was finally free. It was going to
be a good day.

I threw myself into the my new Crap Pack family with

abandon, getting wasted or high, or both, on a regular basis, as we sailed to Catalina, skied at Mammoth, or pounded Margarita's in Acapulco. It was one long moveable hazy party.

One day in September of 1979, I woke up and realized, despite another pounding hangover, that three years had raced by, and it was time to move on. I was the only clerk left at the Record Warehouse in Westwood from when I had started. Sandy had moved back to Modesto before Christmas in 1978, and we exchanged a couple of letters, and then nothing. I had grown weary of LA: the unending traffic, the brown smog, the shallow, narcissistic people (my friends!), the snooty rich, the frat brothers at UCLA. I was sick of it all.

Although I had thought about places to move to over the prior years, it had not been with specific intent. I now grew focused. I thought about the hip college towns that were reasonably low key and low cost: Eugene, Boulder, Madison. Eventually, I became interested in Athens, Georgia, because of the active music scene there. Plus, it was warm, and the University of Georgia had a good football team (Herschel!).

With some of my inheritance money that I had not yet blown on partying, I bought a beater 1970 Chevy Impala for peanuts, and had a mechanic neighbor give it a good once-over and make necessary repairs. I just needed it to get me to where I was going, and then I would dump it.

I gave thirty days' notice on September 30, 1979, to my surly elderly landlord, who took my notice, and just shut the door on me, without a word. So LA.

I gave two weeks' notice on October 1 to the Record Warehouse. The manager was sorry to see me go and thanked me for being a good employee. He was a decent guy; that praise felt surprisingly good. On October 13, some of the Record Warehouse crew met at a Mexican restaurant nearby and they toasted my departure, and we got trashed. It was a long night, I don't know how I got home, but I did.

I cleaned out the money remaining in my Wells Fargo bank account on October 14, gassed up the Chevy Impala, crawled onto the 405 Freeway and headed east, driving through a confusing number of freeways, until I hit I-10 east, and kept going. After a while, I was out of the LA sprawl and into the dry interior counties, and then reaching the desert. I passed by Palm Springs, and kept driving into Arizona, and then into New Mexico. Exhausted, I stopped for the night in Las Cruces. I knew New Mexico State was there, so I thought I would look around.

I was unimpressed with the city and the campus. I did find a Pizza Hut, and ate a large pepperoni pizza and finished a pitcher of Coors. I pulled the Impala into a shopping center parking lot, got in the backseat, locked the doors, then lay down with a blanket I had thrown in the backseat and was soon asleep.

When I awoke early the next morning, the sun was low in the sky. I drove to a McDonald's that I had seen the night before, and went inside. I ordered two Egg McMuffins and an orange juice. After I devoured breakfast, I went into the men's bathroom and cleaned up, including shaving with a razor I had carried in my pocket into the McDonald's.

I drove back onto I-10 and continued east. Within a

couple of hours, I crossed into the deserts of west Texas. And I kept going. I drove for hours across those stunningly flat, barren plains of west Texas. After being in LA for three years where you were surrounded by mountains (when you could see them), it was odd and even unsettling to see the horizon in every direction that you looked.

Late in the day, I reached San Antonio, and I briefly considered stopping there, but I had decided in LA that my second stop would be in Austin because of the University of Texas and the fact that the Longhorns were ranked number one in college football polls at the time.

A little over an hour later I drove into Austin, and was pleasantly surprised at how green the city was, and that there were actual hills to the west to admire. I parked near the Capitol and walked to it, and then walked the few blocks to reach UT. I explored the campus, and was pleased by the limestone buildings. I stopped in the Student Union and ordered a hamburger and a Coke. As I sat there, a number of beautiful coeds walked by, many in jeans so tight I could not imagine how they slipped into them.

I walked along Guadalupe Street, window shopping the small shops carrying mostly UT gear. At one store, I bought a postcard to send to The Captain, and asked the clerk what I should do in Austin if I was here for one day. He suggested that I head out to Lake Travis, and then catch live music on Sixth Street in the evening. I thanked him and walked back to my car.

I drove away from Austin on FM2222 and drove its winding path out to Lake Travis, and I was struck by the hills and Colorado River snaking its way below. This was not the flat, dusty, dry Texas I had imagined from all the Duke's movies of my youth. When I reached Lake Travis, I saw a massive brilliantly blue lake stretching to the west, filled with sailboats gliding along the surface under the late October sun.

I returned to the city after the sun had set and headed to Sixth Street. I couldn't find a parking place, so I parked on Fifth Street and walked back over to Sixth Street. Even though it was early in the evening, the street was filled with partying people. I didn't go very far, when I came to a bar named Maggie Mae's. It carried an Irish flag proudly flying overhead. I stepped inside, to a long thin bar with an open seating area beyond, and a small stage at the back. I sat down at an open stool at the bar, and was pleased to see that Guinness and Harp were on tap. I ordered a Guinness, and was quickly served. I sipped the beer and it pleased my throat as it tumbled down.

Irish music was emanating from the speakers, and a game of darts was underway in front of me. As I looked around, I was struck that the crowd was young, sun-bleached, and happy. It was such a difference from LA, where it was gauche to smile at any time.

After my second Guinness, I ordered a corned beef sandwich, and when delivered, I was pleased to find that it was real corned beef, and ate it quickly.

As the night went on, Maggie Mae's got more crowded and some fine looking women were there. About nine o'clock, two guys began playing folk music on acoustic guitars, and they were both skilled pickers. As I sat there, drinking my Guinness, looking around at the crowd, and listening to the music, I knew that this was the place for me. Right there in Maggie Mae's I changed my mind, and decided to stay in Austin, and not continue on to Athens.

That night, I stopped at a cheap hotel on South Congress Avenue, with the Capitol brightly lit in the distance, and paid for a room.

The next day I went in search of employment. My second stop was a Record Warehouse store on North Lamar Street. With my experience at the Westwood store, the manager was impressed, and he hired me to start the next day.

Within a couple of days, I rented a small apartment not far from the UT campus, and began my life as a Texan. I explored the astounding music scene, Willie Nelson at the Austin Opry House, the Fabulous Thunderbirds at the Shoal Creek Saloon, B.B. King and Dr. Bobby Blue Bland at Antone's. I ate chicken fried steak and the best barbecue in the world at the Salt Lick. I drank gallons of Shiner Bock by the bottle and Margarita's at Fonda San Miguel. I explored Central Texas: the LBJ Library on the UT campus and the LBJ Ranch in Johnson City. The Riverwalk and the Alamo in San Antonio. The sparse beauty of the Texas Hill Country and the shimmering lakes that sat above and fed into Lake Travis: Buchanan, LBJ, Marble Falls.

Even though my fellow workers at the Record Warehouse accused me of contributing to the Californication of Austin merely by my presence, I was grateful to be accepted by the group so openly as both an ex-Californian and a frostback. They invited me to parties and concerts, and I soon felt part of something special living in Austin.

CHAPTER 17
Prairie Rose

Though I'm not sure
I can explain
Your strange allure
Texas Prairie rose

—Bryan Ferry & Phil Manzanera

Austin, Texas, 1980 & Beyond

MAY 12, 1980, WAS ONE OF THE FIRST hot days of that year in Austin. It was my day off, so I rode my bicycle to Barton Springs Park in South Austin to go for a swim. I laid out my towel on the grassy hill above the large spring-fed swimming pool, and relaxed in the hot Texas sun, a small cooler filled with Lone Star beer bottles next to me.

After the sun baked me for a while, I walked down to the pool, and jumped in, and the year round sixty-eight degree water froze my body instantaneously. I swam several long languid laps, and it felt good to be swimming through the icy-cold water with the hot sun on my back.

After a few laps, I headed to the metal stairs, climbed out, and quickly walked up the hill to my towel. Two attractive women were now seated on towels next to mine: one was a thin, tall woman, with long flowing blond hair, the other a shorter redhead with a prominent bosom. I smiled at them as I lay down on my towel and let the sun warm me again. I could hear their conversation, in strong Texas accents, about a club on Sixth Street and the people they had met there the previous evening.

A few minutes later, I sat up, and reached into my cooler, and pulled a Lone Star out, opened it, and drank deeply.

"You got any more of those?" asked the blond woman.

"Yeah. You want one?"

"I could sure use a Lone Star right now."

I asked the redhead, "You too?"

"No thanks, I'm still recovering from last night."

I reached into the cooler, grabbed a Lone Star bottle, opened it with an opener inside the cooler, and handed the cold bottle to the blond woman. "Here you go."

She took it from me with her left hand, and extended her right hand. "Thanks, I'm Rose. Rose Collins from Corpus Christi." We shook hands; she had a nice firm grip. "This is Suzanne. She's from godawful Amarillo."

"Hi, Rose. Hi, Suzanne. I'm John; I'm from New York. I've been in Austin six months and this is only my second time to Barton Springs. You guys look like veterans."

Rose spoke, "We both went to UT so we've been here a few times. Now we work for *Texas Monthly*. But we have today off. Which is why we are here."

"*Texas Monthly*? Wow, that's a great magazine. I've been reading it since I moved here. Trying to find out more about Austin and Texas."

"What are you doing in Austin?"

"Like most people, I'm trying to find myself."

"How is that going?"

"I'm making progress. In another thirty years, I should be done."

"Well, here's to the search." She held her bottle out to me, and we tapped our bottles, and drank. Then, Rose put her bottle down, looked at Suzanne, and said, "Are you finally ready to go in?"

"Rose, that water is going to be so cold. I don't know if I can do it."

"C'mon, you wussy. It'll shake them cobwebs out of you. Let's go. Countdown 3...2...1..."

Suzanne stood. "Rose, you are a demanding friend."

Rose stood up, looked over to me. "Hah, I got her going. Can you watch our stuff, Juan?"

"Yeah, got you covered."

"Here we go."

Rose and Suzanne walked down the gentle slope to the pool, and I admired Rose's long lanky frame with every graceful step she took. I was suddenly very interested in this astonishing looking woman, and when she finally emerged from the pool, and trotted up the hill, water dripping off her lightly tanned firm body, with her perky breasts fighting against her bikini top, I was hooked.

Over the course of the afternoon, I shared another Lone Star with Rose, and she asked a lot about me. She had amazing hazel eyes that studied you with open fascination, and I could feel her trying to figure me out. She was fascinated to hear about my experiences growing up in upstate New York and later in LA. She had never lived anywhere but Texas.

Later, as they were leaving, I asked her if we could get together sometime, and she gave me her phone number. For the first time since I had been with ML, I felt an overpowering attraction. Even though I was nervous as a freshman at a high school dance when I called Rose that night to ask her out, she agreed, and we made plans to meet at Liberty Lunch on West Second Street to see a band on Friday night. When I got off the phone, I shouted "YES!" as loud as I could, and I could barely sleep that evening, as I kept thinking about Rose.

On the following Friday night, May 16, 1980, I arrived fifteen minutes early at the Liberty Lunch Club on West Second Street and waited anxiously on a bar stool at the crowded bar inside the long shed that housed Liberty Lunch. I ordered a Shiner Bock, and it tasted good. A little after nine, I saw Rose enter, and walk around. She was wearing a white fitted blouse, jeans that were so tight they looked like they were ironed on, and stiletto heels that added two inches to her height. Her long blond hair was tightly pulled into a ponytail that bounced assertively as she strode through the patio. My stomach was churning feverishly.

I waved to her and she smiled and walked over, her smile melting me. "Hi there."

I stood. "Hi."

"You been waiting long?"

"A few minutes. Have a seat."

Rose said, "Thanks," as she sat on the stool while I hovered next to her. She continued, "I see you're drinking a Shiner."

"Yeah. I kinda like them. You want one?"

"Yeah. I feel like beer tonight."

I ordered her a Shiner, and threw a five on the bar.

She said, "You're getting to be a real Texan. Drinking Shiner, hanging out at Barton Creek, jamming at Liberty Lunch. Now you need some Tony Lema boots and a cowboy hat. And a taste for country music. I think I'll get you out two-stepping."

"I can't see myself in a cowboy hat. And country music is not my cup of tea."

"We'll just see. It'll grow on you. Just like Texas. You wait. A year from now, you'll never leave."

When her Shiner Bock arrived, we tapped bottles and drank. She impressively sucked down about a third of her bottle, and then smiled at me, throwing her ponytail back with her other hand.

We didn't stay long at Liberty Lunch as the music was too loud when it started, and we couldn't carry on a conversation. We walked a couple of blocks to Hut's Hamburgers, serving the biggest hamburgers in town. Over our giant burgers and cold Shiner Bocks, she told me about herself.

Rose grew up in Corpus Christi, her father owned a small oil development company, and her mother had been a teacher when first married, but then became a housewife when Rose was born. She had a younger sister, Colleen, who was a senior at SMU. Her mother and father were devout Catholics. That was unusual; most native white Texans were Protestant. Both sides of her family had been in Texas since shortly after Texas became a Republic. Her father still owned a family ranch near Wimberley in the Texas Hill Country where the family would spend time in the summer.

Rose had been a cheerleader in high school and editor of the school newspaper. At UT she had majored in journalism, and had interned for two summers at Texas Monthly, prior to being hired full-time after she graduated in 1978. She was a devout Longhorn fan and insisted that I had to go to a football game. As we sat in the Hut that warm October evening so many years ago, she taught me the Hook 'Em Horns hand gesture, and told me several Aggie jokes about Texas A&M.

While at UT, she told me that she had dated, and then became girlfriend of a petroleum engineering student from Houston who also graduated in 1978. While Rose stayed in Austin after graduating, working at the *Texas Monthly*, the boyfriend had joined an oil company in Houston. They had discussed marriage, and it seemed they were headed in that direction, but then his company asked him to go to Saudi Arabia on assignment. Rose refused to go, and they ultimately drifted apart. I asked her if she had ever dated a frostback before.

"Good God, no."

"So, does that mean I'm out of luck? Because I really think I like you, Rose."

"That's sweet, but how can I tell my family I'm dating a guy from north of the Red River?"

"Don't tell them."

"I like that. Besides, you might not make the cut."

"What do I have to do to make the cut, Rose?"

"I think I have low requirements. Just don't be a flaming asshole."

We were inseparable from that night. I was smitten bad, and for some reason she liked me. We went out for nine months, and then I moved into her old house on Austin's Westside that her father had bought for her in college. While she continued to work at *Texas Monthly*, I got an entry-level job in the admissions office at the University of Texas. I was blissfully happy.

On June 20, 1982, Rose and I were married in the small but ornate Corpus Christi Cathedral. Colleen was the maid of honor. Tip should have been my best man, but my old high school buddy Mark Nolan took his place that day, flying down from Binghamton. Although we invited 175 guests, only about twenty-five were mine, and most of them were friends from Austin. My only family that attended were my sister and her husband. The Captain had been in poor health recently and had to decline attending the wedding, much to my disappointment.

As I stood at the altar on that hot June day, watching Rose and her father walk down the aisle, I was in a daze; I felt I was in a dream watching myself from on high. Rose never looked lovelier than she did on that June day. She glowed like a sun, and I was so overcome with the light beaming from her eyes, and my happiness, that I bumbled my way through the ceremony. When we finally kissed at the end, her lips were as sweet as honey, and a soft as a pillow.

We spent our honeymoon at the Hyatt on Maui. Most days we just sat by the pool, baking in the sun, and silently holding hands. One afternoon we drove the Road to Hana, stopping at every waterfall to take a picture. We also got up before dawn one morning to drive to Haleakala to watch the sun rise over the mountain and chase the clouds out of the yawning canyon at the top. We ate too much shaved ice in

Lahaina, and drank too many Mai Tai's at the bar at the Hyatt. We told each other what our future would be like, and then reworked our story each day. Each story always ended up with us together in old age, holding hands on a porch, rocking in our chairs, as we watched the sun set over our lives. And every night, we made tender impassioned love in our room, falling into a deep sleep holding one another close.

In September of 1982, The Captain died alone in his house of a heart attack. I found out on Monday, September 13, 1982, when Lizzie called and told me that an old BPD buddy had come to 26 Oliver Street to check up on him and saw his body lying lifeless by the front door.

Rose and I quickly arranged flights back to Binghamton, arriving late in the evening of Wednesday, September 15. We picked up our rental car and drove to the Holiday Inn Arena in Binghamton, where I had attended that wedding ceremony with ML in 1975. After checking in, Rose and I met Lizzie and her husband in their room. Lizzie informed me that The Captain's daughter, Margaret, as his sole heir, was running the funeral services. There was to be a wake on the next day, Thursday the sixteenth, followed by burial on that Friday. Margaret wanted me to be a pallbearer for The Captain.

The Captain's viewing was held at McCormack's, of course. As I entered McCormack's, I felt uneasy returning to the place of Tip's funeral. Rose seemed to notice and grabbed my arm tighter as we walked into The Captain's viewing room.

We both knelt down by The Captain's open casket, and I said good-bye. His once ruddy complexion was washed out by the liberal white makeup applied to his cheeks. The empty shell of a man lying there seemed smaller than the great bear of a man I remembered from my youth. As I knelt there, it hit me that The Captain at least had seen his beloved Yankees win two more World Series victories before he died. That was small comfort.

After an appropriate time, we arose, and greeted my Aunt Margaret standing to the side of the casket, with her husband and children. Then we walked to the front row of chairs and sat next to Lizzie and her husband.

Over the next few hours, a steady stream of mourners arrived, stayed for a while and then left. A few members of my high school class stopped by and I spoke with each of them for a few minutes before they drifted away.

After the viewing ended, Margaret invited us back to 26 Oliver Street for pizza and drinks. She and her family were staying there.

I showed Rose around The Captain's house, which had not changed since I had left on that June day in 1976. It was like a time capsule. The Captain's pipe and a half-empty bottle of Jameson's sat on the table next his recliner. I led Rose upstairs to my former bedroom. I sat down on the bed that had housed me so many lonely nights and I was overcome with emotion. As I thought about the bitter young man that had lived in this room, and I thought about The Captain, who had taken that young man into his house, in a time of need, and helped to carry him through those grim times, the tears started to flow. Rose joined me on the bed, and I turned to her and embraced her firmly, astonished more than ever that this beautiful woman had joined her life with mine.

The Captain's funeral service was at St. Paul's the next morning. The church was full of mourners; a large contingent of BPD officers attended. After the service, there was a brief service at The Captain's grave next to his wife, and near Jack and Michael, his two sons. Buried next to Jack was Mary Kate, and only a small marker indicated that her remains were underneath.

After the service at The Captain's open grave, I took Rose's hand and we walked over to Tip's grave. His tombstone carried only his name, date of birth, and date of death. The grass was thick over his grave, and there were no flowers near the tombstone. I was hit with a memory, and I told Rose that my CC class ring was buried forever in Tip's grave. She appreciated the gesture.

The next morning, I got up early and drove to the Binghamton Public Library while Rose lounged at the hotel. For the last few years, I had a desire to find out more about my father, and knew that I needed to research the Binghamton *Press* archives to find out more about him.

I found articles about his football success and promotions at the BPD. But I also discovered the truth about my father's death in the Binghamton *Press* microfiche repository that morning. He had been drunk the night he wrapped his car around the tree that killed him, coming home from a party with his fellow officers after his shift. I was shocked and somehow angry to find this out, angry at him for dying that way, but angry again at Mary Kate for never telling us the truth.

After leaving the library, I picked up Rose and drove her around Binghamton, showing her the key sites of my youth, the house on 59 Vine Street, McArthur Park, St.

John's, CC, SUNY-B. We even stopped near the Park Diner and climbed down the now dusty trail to the Susquehanna, and walked to Rock Bottom Dam. The flow in the brown Susquehanna was less than what I remembered, but there was still one fisherman standing below it, casting his line into the swirling pools.

That night I bought pasta to-go from the Little Venice and brought it over for dinner with my remaining family at The Captain's house. Over wine and pasta, Margaret told us about growing up in that house, and about my father Jack, and about her long dead brother Michael, and about The Captain and Elizabeth. She only broke down crying once.

Back at the hotel, I informed Lizzie what I had found about our father that morning, and she was even more surprised than I because she could remember when he died. We said good-bye that night, and promised to do a better job of keeping in touch, and Rose and I flew back to Austin on Sunday, September 19, 1982.

Our son, James, arrived on June 24, 1984, the first day of summer, and the longest day of the year, a fact we endlessly reminded him of. His sister, Katie, joined us on March 15, 1987. We had hopes that she would be born on St. Patrick's Day, but she didn't quite make it.

After James arrived, Rose stopped working at *Texas Monthly*, and became a housewife. I continued to work in the Admissions Office at the University of Texas, finally rising to the position of Associate Director that I currently have. It has been a surprisingly satisfying career. I have found that I enjoy helping potential students and their parents learn about the University and its vast opportunities. I know that I have reached my career peak as I can never become Provost for the Admissions Office without a graduate degree, but that is OK. It has been a good ride, and life has rewarded me as I never thought it would back on the shores of the Susquehanna on that frozen New Years' Eve in 1975.

After The Captain's death, I never returned to Binghamton. There was nothing for me there. Although I was invited to class reunions, I never went. Although I wanted to show off Rose to my former classmates, as if to say, "Fuck You, Look What I Got!", I dreaded seeing ML or Ann, and dredging up the feelings that had been safely buried under the years that had passed. Two years ago, one of our CC classmates had created a Facebook site for the CC Class of 1972, and it contained photos from prior class reunions. It was odd to see ML in those photos, sometimes with Dino, whom she did end up marrying, sometimes alone. I could see her age from thirty-three (fifteen-year reunion) to forty-three (twenty-five-year reunion) to forty-eight (thirty-year reunion) to the last reunion (thirty-five years), that beautiful face adding lines and a little paunch with the passage of time, and that blond hair changing in length and color, becoming noticeably colored in the later photos, losing its once magnificent luster. I never sent a Facebook friend request to her, and she never sent one to me. Would I have rejected her friend request? I wonder. Probably not. Even today I am not that strong.

Ann attended a few of the reunions as well, and the passage of time was not as kind to her, as she put on more weight, becoming almost unrecognizable at the last reunion. One of our classmates sent me a friend request to Ann, but I never followed through, and she never sent one to me directly.

CHAPTER 18
The Heart of the Matter

I've been tryin' to get down to the Heart of the Matter
But my will gets weak
And my thoughts seem to scatter
But I think it's about forgiveness
Forgiveness

—Don Henley

Austin, Texas, The Present

LYING IN THE LOUNGE CHAIR on our deck in the hot August night, I felt a profound sadness reliving the events of so many years ago. The katydids continued to call out to each other, and I heard a bat fly overhead, a common occurrence in the hills west of Austin. So many players on my stage gone, and in a few years, I would join them, and then the past would be wiped clean, and all the ephemeral pain of my youth would be gone, and nobody would know what happened, or what is was like to be in ML's arms, holding her tight, that smell of lemons in her hair, the taste of her soft supple lips, her inquisitive tongue in my mouth. Or, what is was like to hang with Tip in his basement as we read *Mad* magazine, bursting into laughter, or playing Stratego for hours in middle school, or fishing with Tip in Silver Creek in Pennsylvania, where I caught my first brook trout at age eleven, Tip more excited than me. Or, what is was like to suffer through Mary Kate's increasingly bizarre behavior, and crippling psychological decline. I shivered and shook my head trying to kill those images.

And yet as I sat there struggling with those late night demons that have haunted me, I knew with cold clarity again a realization that has percolated over the years and from which there was no escape: I was the one responsible for it all. It wasn't them. I could have done something about each of them. And if I had, events would have been different.

I could have stopped Tip from being in the car accident that sent him on his downward spiral. I was right there; I could have done something, yelled at him so that even though he was drunk, he would have listened to me. I was his best friend; I had an obligation to look out for him. He had looked out for me when I needed him. After the accident I could have and should have done more; I hadn't gone the extra mile for him. I had let him live his squalid, empty life while I was going to SUNY-B. I had let him get involved with that druggie bunch on Conklin Avenue that led to his arrest. I could have stepped in and stopped him, or at least tried more actively. And then, when he cried out for my help at the end, I wasn't there for him, and didn't want to be bothered by him. Where I should have been selfless, I was selfish. And I've paid a price in guilt for that selfishness ever since.

As for Mary Kate, she was my mother, she had raised me in incredibly trying circumstances, alone with two small children, and limited resources. She had tried to do her best, and meant well. What I saw as stifling oppressiveness may have really been motherly concern that manifested itself in ways that annoyed a boy struggling with his identity. The circumstances of my father's death that I discovered in 1982 finally explained for me her constant and unrelenting anger about my drinking, and gave me a chilling insight into the night she tossed me out of my home.

And I had not appreciated the strain of her failed relationship with Owen, and how devastating that must have been for her. After experiencing menopause with Rose in the last few years, I believe that Mary Kate had undoubtedly been suffering from that condition during my last years with her: the mood swings, the red face, the feeling of being constantly hot. I hadn't been aware, and it's easy to say that I was twenty-one and couldn't have been aware, and I have tried to convince myself over a lifetime of that excuse. If I had been less self-absorbed and critical, I could have been more understanding and solicitous of her health. But I wasn't. And after she threw me out, I didn't really reach out to her again, as I blamed her for it all. How lonely she must have been in our home on 59 Vine Street, sitting in that cold living room in the dark, staring out her living room window for the son who would never return.

And then there was ML. Who really is to blame but me for this lifetime of regret? Ann was right; ML was out of my league from the very beginning, and only an idiot would be blind to see that truth. Sure, ML could have and should have handled me differently, and communicated with me after her boyfriend returned. That would have been the right gesture, but looking back now, I can see that she was so overwhelmed to have him back in her life, that all else was cast aside. When I had fallen head over heels for Rose, my thoughts about other people were absent due to my desire for her. I can see that now, and appreciate ML's motivations.

As I sit on my deck alone in the hot, humid Texas night, with the far-off twinkling stars overhead, it strikes me that this regret has hung on to me these many years, because there had been no resolution with ML. It had just ended. It would have been far better if we had ended in a screaming match with each other, both of us walking away, because there would have been an actual end. Or, if she had only written me a "Dear John" letter when her boyfriend returned. That at least would have provided some form of closure. I think that even if I had written her a letter, when I found out about the returning boyfriend, expressing my anger, there would have been closure of a kind.

Nor was there consummation. If we had actually made love only one time, just one time, even if it was that one drunken time in the Galaxie 500, I would have that memory of our passion that would be the defining memory of her. Instead, the regret lies below the surface, just waiting for the right moment, either awake or asleep, to rise up and reawaken. With ML, my aging memories remain imprisoned in limbo.

A true romantic always remembers, always forgives, but never forgets. I've worked hard at the university, making a difference in some students' lives; been a good and monogamous husband, ever grateful for Rose who rescued me from deep despair; tried to be a loving and nurturing parent, careful to treat my children differently than Mary Kate. I like to think I have led a decent life. But what I lost in the fall of 1975 is a wound that while healed can easily be reopened, with just a little reminiscing. It all still hurts.

I arose from the lounge chair, and felt the sweat on my skin. It had taken many years to get used to the oppressive central Texas heat, but I could not imagine living anywhere else now.

I strode to the sliding door to the house, opened it, and entered. I was hit with a blast of cool air-conditioned air that enveloped me and raised goose bumps on my skin.

I continued into my office and sat down at my desk. I was exhausted, but I knew I could not sleep. I picked up the obituary notice lying on the desk, and examined it again. In that photo, she looked full of life, and had a twinkle in her eye as she always does in my memory. I wondered what kind of a wife, mother, or friend she had been. When was the last time that she had thought about me? Was it with regret? Anger? I wonder if she had ever dreamed about me as I had sometimes dreamed about her?

Or maybe she had dreamed about Tip. Or thought about him over the years. I did wonder about Ann Dunn as I looked at that photo of her.

Then I thought about Ann's breasts, for it was her large breasts that had made the guys in my high school lust after her, including me. And now she was dead from those very same breasts. It was God's cruel joke on Ann, infecting her breasts with the cancer that killed her.

I got my checkbook out of the desk and wrote a check out to the Susan Komen foundation for $100 in Ann's honor, filled out an envelope, and placed a stamp on the envelope. I would mail it in the morning.

I opened up my laptop, waited far too long for it to boot up, signed in, and opened up my rarely viewed Facebook page. I went to the Facebook page of my CC class. A class member had posted the news of Ann's death, and a link to her obituary at the Binghamton *Press & Sun-Bulletin* website. There were several comments under the posting from other classmates, recalling Ann and expressing their sorrow at her passing.

ML had posted a comment, and her genuine grief was evident. Near the end of her comment, she had typed, "I look back fondly on the fun times that Ann and I had at CC." I clicked on her photo, and it brought me to her Profile page which just showed her photo as she did not permit creepers to view her profile. In the photo, she was standing next to two younger women, as striking in appearance as she had been when younger. They must have been her two daughters. I suspected they also had left a trail of broken hearts behind, like their mother.

I considered sending her a Facebook invite for a few moments. But I finally realized that there would be no point. The ML that I had so feverishly desired was alive in my youth a long time ago, and nothing would bring that young woman alive again.

Nonetheless, I sat there staring at her Facebook photo late into the Texas night, with the sound of the ceiling fan circling overhead being the only sound in the house, and I thought what a short burst of time our past really was, just a couple of years, in a long life. And yet those painful memories haunt me, and it is a rare day that goes by that I don't recall some incident from the fall of 1975. And if I don't think about them during the day, they arise in my dreams, and I see Ann, Tip, ML, Mary Kate, and The Captain in my dreams. He who lives in the past is condemned to suffer the past over and over again. They live again in me as they were when I was young. I know that on the day I take my last breath, they will finally rest in me. Perhaps as I age, and the ravages of time or disease inevitably eat away at my brain, I will no longer see them as they were. It's nice to think so.

THE END

www.ingramcontent.com/pod-product-compliance
Lightning Source LLC
Chambersburg PA
CBHW060153260626
47160CB00001B/247